A Piece of Ground

Charles McRaven

**A Wings ePress, Inc.
Historical Fiction Novel**

Wings ePress, Inc.

Edited by: Jeanne Smith
Copy Edited by: April Bennett
Executive Editor: Jeanne Smith
Cover Artist: Trisha FitzGerald-Jung

All rights reserved

Wings ePress Books
www.wingsepress.com

Published In the United States Of America

Wings ePress Inc.
3000 N. Rock Road
Newton, KS 67114

Dedication

For Linda, my modern-day pioneer woman,
inspiration and other self.

One

Stephen Davis shouldered his rifle, turned from the ragged, dispersing regiment and walked away. His boots—the boots of a dead British infantryman—were good still, and the cloak he'd found at Yorktown would warm him on the way. It was October, and the nights were chill.

The men had not been formally dismissed, but the captain had said meaningfully that there wouldn't be roll call the next morning, or any other morning. There was a deal of confusion now, and promised to be for days. "Go home, men," he'd told them.

Ned Drake fell in beside his messmate.

"Goin', huh? Not staying for the speeches?"

"Guess not. Been too long already. Goochland's a far walk. And one speech sounds a lot like the next."

Stephen was tall, still young, and unscathed after his years of fighting the British. And while not overly introverted, there was a certain reserve about him, possibly from his specialty in the army, one he did not like talking about. No one ever shortened his name to "Steve." He was almost withdrawn, preferring absorption in a book, whenever he could find one, to the company of the other enlisted men.

"There's talk of land grants and such." Ned twisted a rope of tobacco, bit off a chew.

"Be like everything else in this war, I'm afraid. Late and little and leave you empty." Stephen's pace was steady, and the shorter man had to hurry a little to keep up.

"Well, I can see you're in one of your moods, so I'll just tag along and keep quiet."

Stephen grunted, strode on.

The October air was amber, and turning leaves carpeted the dirt road. A wagon creaked toward them, its mule team rhythmic in slow, stepped-off miles. Harness leather smell, the barn smell of the animals, the nodding, dozing driver, old, unhurried as the mules.

It was over. Finally over. The French had cut off Cornwallis, and it was all over. Stephen had one regret left.

"Damn shame we couldn't have gotten to Tarleton before all the ceremony and niceties. Like to have put a rifle ball in that one. Don't care about the rest."

"Devil, all right. Had 'im guarded too good. Folks'd have torn him to shreds, otherwise."

"Probably die of old age back in England, after all he did. No justice."

"No. But th' war's over, Stephen. No use grudgin' about one Redcoat. Hell, maybe his ship'll sink." Ned grinned, his freckles making him look like a ten-year-old. He was Stephen's age, twenty-four, and had killed his share of the enemy, with only a minor wound. Ned had a knack for fitting in, whether with backwoodsmen or the gentry, adjusting his speech to fit any group. Lately, he seemed to favor the country talk of the woodsmen.

"Maybe so. I'm just tired of it all, Ned. Want to go on home, get started on a life again. Guess Tarleton can sink or swim, for all of me."

"Sink, I hope. Reckon that girl's waited for you?"

"Maybe. About forgotten what she looks like. No letter for months."

"You write her?"

"Hell, no. And you haven't written your folks either, have you?"

"Naw. War's gone sour on me, too. Made me an unlettered rustic, 'stead of an impoverished but genteel planter's son. How far's Richmond?"

"I forget. Be there late, looks like. Or tomorrow. Don't plan to stop, myself. Stay at it all night, I could be near home another day or two."

"Well, I'm gonna stay. Been too long since I had me a good bed an' a good woman. Figure t'squander what's left of my pay, make me some memories." Again the grin. "Reckon you'll save yours."

"Maybe. Not much there, anyway. Like to buy a good horse, maybe travel some. Haven't thought on it much."

"We've done a sight of travelin' already, Stephen. Y'oughta marry that girl an' stick."

"We'll see. I'll just have to let it happen."

Late in the day Ned bade his friend goodbye, and followed the widening road toward the capital, while Stephen turned off to pass it. He reflected that Ned was as close a friend as he'd ever had. When things settled down more, he'd have to go look him up at his parents' plantation. He'd certainly livened things up in the camps with his good humor and outrageous adventures. Memory of some of these made Stephen smile.

He spotted windfall apples just over a rail fence. The deer hadn't found them yet. Two of those, a crust of bread and a bit of cheese he had would keep him, he figured, at least till morning.

He tried to picture home as he'd left it on his last leave, two years earlier, and then before. Yes, when he'd first left, over the protests of his miller father, but the image was dim. George Davis was a working man, but as a transplanted Englishman, had seen to it that his children, even the girls, had attended the subscription school, and acquired whatever learning the region offered.

"A miller need not be an ignoramus," was his oft-repeated maxim. And Stephen's plan to enlist in the Continental Army did not fit at all with his ambitions for his only son.

"The mill's too important, boy, for you to go off soldiering. Why, where's General Washington to get flour and meal for all those troops, you young fellows all gone? I'm aging, and I can't run the thing by myself."

"Get help, Pa, though I know you wouldn't have a slave on the place. I've sat out this war too long. I'm not about to be another Banks Mabry."

"Nothing wrong with Mabry, now. If a man can hire himself a substitute, he ought to do it. Stay safe."

"Safe? And all the boys I grew with off getting shot up? And how safe will it be when the lobsterbacks come through here?"

"Oh, they'll not come here. What's here they'd want? Why—"

And on and on. Till he'd just picked up his rifle and a pack and walked off. Maybe a dumb thing to do, but he'd done it. When a man was grown, he had to do what seemed right. And what if he had stayed, been a slacker like that Mabry?

Well, I'd probably have married Betsy, that's for sure. Had a couple young ones by now. Been the miller, sure enough, the way Pa was set on my taking it over. Now, what would that've been like? Hearing about all the boys I knew getting shot up, killed off, and there I'd be, holed up safe on that creek, getting babies. And how'd I handle it, now they'd be coming back—the ones who made it back?

No, may not have been the right thing to do, but I did it, and I suppose there wasn't any right thing, really. Wonder about Betsy. Be...twenty, now? Older. Still young. Still got time, if that's what's right for me—us. Have to see, is all. She was still waiting last winter. Good girl, I guess. Well—

But this damn war. Got me all mean inside. Don't know if I'd be fit company for a woman. Maybe running the mill will settle me a little. Been so long, I've this crazy notion I might just keep on going...

No. Go on home, see everybody. Help with the harvest, the grinding. See what's supposed to happen. Winter coming soon. Man'd be a fool to set out in winter. Had some cold ones, we did, and not a whole coat to the bunch of us, nor a pair of boots. War's a scary thing, all right. Eats at a man. Glad it's over.

He strode on into dusk, re-living battles, troop movements, camps in the rain, in the snow. Youthful wartime escapades with Ned Drake, who'd always seemed to find something exciting to do, besides getting shot at. Now he met travelers on the road: riders, wagons, men on foot like himself. War surely shuffles folks around. But this close to Richmond, a lot of people were out, anyway.

He spoke to these people seldom, preferring the cloak of his own thoughts and memories. A nod in passing, automatic, the faces not registering. Dogs barked, and once a big cur ran at him, snarling. He held it off with the rifle barrel, backing until the brute turned away. Sudden devil. *Somebody'll shoot you next time, teach you manners.*

Around midnight his feet began to burn, and an ache started in each calf. A piece of a moon was almost down, but shone through ragged clouds. He looked for a stream. When he reached one, it was small and bore a swamp smell. But he sat, removed the boots, and eased his feet into the icy water. The chill moved up his legs, numbing them, but the burning in his feet eased. It felt good just to sit. Maybe he should find a place to sleep, after all. There'd be a haystack, one of these farms, soon.

But the leaves here would do, too. He rubbed his feet dry on the legs of his trousers and put the boots back on. Off the narrow road were big oaks and a carpet of leaves. He raked a pile of them together with a dead branch, wrapped the cloak around him and slept.

And he awakened in a sweat only once, groaning, seeing faces before him, British faces, contorted in death. Each lifeless form had a hole in it from his long rifle, and exactly in the spot he'd aimed for.

Morning light was gray, and Stephen thought it must be still early. But heavy clouds veiled the sun, and there was the smell of rain coming. Well, no help for that, he shrugged. October, so maybe only a shower, and if I'm in luck, I might find some breakfast, and shelter, too.

The first yard he turned into led to an empty house. Smoke wisped from the brick chimney, but it looked as if the family were out in the fields. He walked on.

A short lane led to a newish cabin of hewn logs, with a muscular woman gathering clothes off a line. Her hair was graying, her movements quick.

"Hello," he called. "Rain coming."

"Looks it. An' these just dry. You a soldier?"

"I am that. On my way home. Would you suppose I could trouble you for a bite?"

"I'd say so. Sent m'boys out daylight, but there's ham, an' some biscuits."

"I'd appreciate it. Here, let me help you, there. Smelled the rain a bit back, but it's held off."

"Oh, it'll bust loose. An' I daren't start somethin' else, er it'll ketch me. Thankee. I'm Thelma Doane. What's yer name?"

"Stephen Davis. We have the mill up above Rock Castle, off the river."

"Don't know it. I've heered of Rock Castle—Th' Flemin's, ain't it?"

"That's them. We're up, off the James a ways. Out of Goochland."

"Wal, we ain't been here long. Left out of North Caroliny when th' British was there, an' shore 'nuff, they come through here too, right after. Hadn't hardly got th' crops in."

"Cornwallis. Yes, he reasoned Governor Jefferson had sent all the troops up to New York, or down with Greene, and he could waltz right across us, cut the country in two. Almost did it, too." Stephen was aware of his speech, different from that of this country woman, although their social status, if any, was not that far apart.

"What they say. Woulda got th' guv'nor, an' some others, too, but a boy from up Cuckoo, name of Jouett, rode all night, got th' word out. That'uz Tarleton, made that raid. Oughta hung him."

"That's the way I feel. But it's over, finally. Your boys fight?"

"Naw. Too young. M'man did, though, early on. Died up in godawful Saratoga."

"Sorry to hear that. I missed that one. Got in on Valley Forge in '77. We almost froze, then. This's mighty good ham, ma'am. Hope you could spare it."

"Glad y'like it. Oh, we done all right in Caroliny till them Brits come. Tarleton agin. Burned a lotta folks out. Raided us till I wasn't about to take it no more. Planter wanted to buy us out since on back, so I sold." She looked out an open shutter. "Rain's here." A pause, listening to the drops on the shake roof.

"Yes. Good ground here, appears to be."

"Is that. Not wore out. Flatter'n I like, but it's close in t'th' capital, so there's trade. Y'goin' to go back t'millin'?"

"For awhile. Have to see what's there for me. Lot of us got sort of nervous, sour, with the war, and can't seem to stay still. I got a little of that."

"I reckon. Got y'self a girl?" The eyes crinkled, but their look was shrewd.

"I did. No word for a while. Thought about marrying instead of going off, but 'twouldn't do. Not for me."

"Way my man felt. Just glad m'boys were too young. Too many got shot up."

"How many do you have, ma'am?"

"Got four. Sixteen on down t'ten. An' they're a workin' bunch. Be in outta this, at least to th' barn. Hope it's just a shower."

"Ought to be. October's dry here, mostly. You get much planted?"

"Right much. Corn, mostly. Let th' hogs run, keep 'nuff corn out so they come in. First cold spell, we'll butcher."

"They'll fatten on these acorns. We let ours run, too. Cold weather, we get together with neighbors, divide up. Always been plenty." He remembered the community hog-scaldings, the big cast-iron pots steaming, the shouts, laughter, the children everywhere, the hurrying, before a warm spell could return. He hadn't thought of a hog-scald in years.

"You missin' home, aint'cha?" She could read his thoughts.

"I am that. Know 'twon't be the same, though. It wasn't, last time I got leave."

"How long ago?"

"Two years. Pa'd found help for the mill, fellow from Ireland. My girl was still waiting. But it seemed like I was ready to go on back, before time. Didn't make sense." He found he enjoyed talking with this plain, direct woman, and reflected that it had been a long time since he'd discussed home.

"I guess not. An' yer right, 'twon't be th' same...Oh, here's m'boys."

The four trooped in, soaked, looking like young colts. The eldest stood as tall as Stephen, over six feet, and the others stair-stepped down. They eyed him matter-of-factly.

"Howdy, name's Roark," the tall one extended a hardened hand.

"Stephen Davis. Heading home from the war. Sorry the rain got you."

"We'll dry. This's Ed, Stuart, Billy. You from close by?"

"On up the river. Goochland. Folks have a mill there."

"Miller. Lotta millers, gunsmiths, too. Y'make that rifle?"

"My pa did. I turned the stock, but he did the iron work. I never got that good."

"Looks sound. Y'git fed?"

"I did, an' thanks to you all. Slacking any?" He peered out.

"Not yet, but 'twill. We drove fer th' corn crib 'fore it come on, but not soon 'nuff. Reckoned we'd stay f'dinner."

"Is it that late? I slept in the woods, and got off slow."

"Don't rush off, now," the boys' mother said. "Y'll make Goochland by t'morrow dark, easy."

The boys dried themselves before the fire, and asked about the war. He could tell it had probably taken their mother's firm hand to keep Roark home, and maybe Ed, too. He remembered how romantic and exciting it had all sounded, before grim reality had forced its way in.

"Reckon y'got a few Redcoats," that one observed.

"A few. But they got a lot of us, too."

"Shame nobody got that Tarleton."

"It really was. I was hoping, myself."

"Mean, that'n. Burn you out, shoot you after y'd surrender, way we heard it."

"True. He did that at Waxhaws. Supposed to have cut a drummer boy of ours with his saber when he wouldn't shine the Brit's boots. Little fellow, Andrew Jackson."

"Never heered that'n. Y'goin' back to millin'?"

"Maybe. Depends on what I find. It's been two years since I've seen the place. Pa's got help, now."

"Mm. Wal, yer shore welcome t'stay with us, ain't he, Ma? We c'n make room."

Stephen glanced around the tiny cabin, just the one room with a loft above, and the rough pit-sawn lean-to kitchen with back-to-back fireplaces. He knew all four boys would share the loft.

"Thanks, but I'll get on. You all built this house, did you, Roark?"

"Did. Land come off a big place, a'ready had a barn here, so we put up th' cabin early this year, me'n th' boys."

"Yes, an' y'split th' shakes wrong sign, too," his mother interrupted. "They're curlin', like I said they would." She opened the kitchen door and threw a dishpan of water out into the slackening rain. "Cain't tell these boys a thing. You know 'bout th' signs bein' right, I'll wager, don't you, Mr. Davis?"

"Always heard it had to be right, but I couldn't say, myself. Pa always had us watch for the signs."

"See, I told you, son. Won't last th' winter."

"Aw, Ma, ain't nothin to that old idee. Wood's wood, way I see it."

"Jest like yer pa, God rest him. Cain't tell you a thing."

"Well, it's slacked off, it appears." Stephen rose, took his rifle. "Here's some coin, ma'am, and I thank you."

"We 'preciate it, son, but y'got t'take this along, too. Be hungry 'fore y'git home." She pressed more biscuits and two sweet potatoes on him, wrapped in a bit of worn cloth. He shook hands with each of the sturdy sons and bade the family goodbye.

On the road again, he reflected on how well these settlers seemed to be managing, even without the father. A piece of ground was really all a man needed—that and a rifle and a few tools. Two people and a piece of ground: where had he heard that? Well, maybe Betsy was the other person, all right…

He'd seen that the logs in the Doane cabin hadn't fully seasoned, so the initial chinking would loosen with the shrinkage. But no matter, in a year they could replace it, with clay or lime-and-sand mortar. You often had to do that, with new timber. They'd bought or fired brick for the foundation and chimney. No need for that around Goochland, where there was river bank stone for the taking.

Well, I'll have time to plan a place all out, I guess. If I—we—move West, we won't need much, but if I can't homestead, I couldn't buy land. I mostly donated my time in the war, no more than we got paid, and no more often. Five years out of my life, but we whipped the Redcoats, that's a fact. Now, just what we'll make out of this new country nobody knows. A man can go where he pleases, though, without England hindering him.

The miles slipped past as Stephen remembered home, surprised at how seldom of late he'd thought of it. Growing away from it, seemed like, he realized. *Well, I'll spend the winter, anyway. See what Betsy says.*

Two

"Lot's changed, son, since you were home," Stephen's father announced, after his mother and sisters had greeted him. George Davis had offered his hand, about as demonstrative as he'd ever been, his son remembered. Sheila and Susanna and their mother had made much of his homecoming, and chattered on. Stephen sensed the small talk was a little forced, though, and caught each of his family turning eyes away quickly when he looked. *Something's on, here. Well, it'll out; just let it happen.*

"How changed, Pa?" It was quieter, now, nearing bedtime.

"Well, you know I've had Eames working the mill with me. Had to have help, after you left us..."

"I know that. Nothing new there." He eyed his father keenly.

"Somewhat new, yes. The fellow wants to buy me out. He's been courting Sheila, and wants to set up properly. Now, I haven't promised anything. 'Twouldn't be right, even though you did leave me short. Blood's definitely thick, I say..."

Well. So the hired hand wanted into the family. And he wanted the mill, too. So where's that leave me? I had two choices: stay and take over, try to build up a life again, or move on. Now I'm pushed.

"Pa, I don't know just what I'll do yet. I'd say it'll depend on Betsy Simmons. She was still waiting, the last time I heard. Ought to see where we stand, and I guess that'll tell me what's right to do."

Mention of the girl's name brought a chill to the room, it seemed. Both sisters stopped what they were doing for a beat, his mother set a plate down with a noise, and his father raised his brows. Stephen looked from one to another.

"All right, what is it I need to know about Betsy?"

"Well, son..." His father looked at his wife for support. No one spoke.

"She's either dead or found another man, I'll wager. Which is it? You don't need to sugar it: I'm a big boy, now."

It was his mother who came to him, misery in her eyes. Sarah Davis was a sensitive woman, and had always been close to her only son. More so since she'd lost two boys as babies. She crossed from the kitchen door, nervously wiping her hands.

"She's...well, Stevie, she's...promised." A pause, while she looked to the others, as if for help. "To Banks Mabry."

"Banks! The slacker?" Disbelief flooded him. "Why, she practically called him a coward when I went off, and he wouldn't."

"Times change, son," his father said. "He's got his pa's place now, and built himself a fine house. Plans to be a major figure, about. And I suppose Betsy just got tired of...waiting." He spread his hands. That subject was closed, for him.

"Well...Well, that's news. Does make it somewhat simpler though, it seems." He hadn't quite been able to envision settling with Betsy, these months past, and now, well, now he needn't. The quick flash of anger that had come with the name of her intended faded. Hell, let him have her. Nobody said this life was fair. Mabry got out of the war, got his pa's place, and now he had Stephen's woman. Wonder what he'd have done if he'd had to face grapeshot. Probably peed his pants. Well, enough about him.

"As I said, it depends. Unless you've made up your mind, Pa. I'll look things over a mite."

"And as I said, there's blood. But of course Sheila's ours, too."

His sister crimsoned, and Stephen sensed this might just be already a fact. Patrick Eames, it seemed, was to be ranked with him, the heir. Well.

Next day he spent some time at the mill, noting the repairs, the increased business, the larger set of millstones his father and Eames had installed. They'd also raised the dam on the creek, enlarging the forebay so the mill could run longer on the drawdown. The work was sound, and it seemed mostly to be Eames' influence, or his outright work. Well.

The man himself was nervous, with the rightful heir inspecting everything he'd done. Stephen said little, noting with an appreciative eye the improvements.

"Well, Patrick, I'm told you and Sheila plan to marry, and that you fancy buying the mill."

"I do that, Mr. Davis. That is, if yourself is past wantin' it." The man had an earnest red face that reddened more. He looked at his shoes in confusion.

"Seems you've done a fair lot of work here on it. Can't say I'd have done that. I'd probably have been satisfied with things as they were."

"Yes, sir. I mean...whatever y'd have thought was right..."

"Oh, dammit, Patrick Eames. You're a good man, and the one to have this mill. I'll be moving West, anyway, since there's but little for me here. Oh," and he shook the young man by the hand, "and welcome to the family."

The settlement Stephen made with his father was for a middling riding horse, and a small set of millstones if and when he should ever need them. He stayed around for the few days of harvest, gathering corn, shocking the fodder, all the getting-in of the season. And he spent some time with his father in his workshop, refurbishing his rifle.

But he'd become anxious to be on his way. His time at his parents' was getting over with, and he'd not stay till spring. It was on into November, but not really cold yet. Time to move on.

He'd avoided Betsy Simmons on purpose, and was feeling he'd escaped seeing Banks Mabry, too. Then one day when he'd made a rare trip into Goochland, he met the man on the street.

"Well, if 'tisn't the soldier boy, come home from savin' the world," Mabry called out, as if anxious for a face-off. He came toward Stephen, a riding crop in his hand.

"It is, Banks. Done your fighting for you, it seems." Stephen was in no mood to be overly civil.

Mabry colored. He was in a powdered wig and there was lace at his cuffs. Stephen had never liked a man who wore lace. And he'd never liked this man, even before he became a shirker.

"I hired a substitute, all legal, Davis, and you know it."

"Aye, and I know the poor devil got shot in the head at Cowpens. Aren't you glad 'twasn't you?"

"See here, are you trying to pick a quarrel with me? Because if you are, I'll have you horsewhipped." Mabry was losing his temper, and Stephen didn't care.

"Have me horsewhipped? Yes, you would do that, not being man enough to do the job yourself." He turned coolly away down the plank walkway, nodding to two farmers he knew, seated on a bench before the cobbler's shop.

Mabry fumed for an instant, then launched himself after his sometime rival. Stephen turned, too late, and took the riding crop across his shoulder. His hand shot out, gripping the other's wrist, clamping hard. The whip fell.

"Mistake, Mabry. Now, you men saw this coward jump me from behind, did you not?"

"Aye," they chorused, "an' we saw him pick the quarrel too, Stephen."

Mabry's eyes were hot as he struggled. He lashed out with a foot, but the soldier twisted, deflecting the blow. Deliberately, he pulled Mabry toward him, then, releasing his wrist, slammed his fist into the man's face. Hard. Blood spurted, and he crumpled. Stephen bent down and wiped his hand on the lace cuffs. Mabry did not stir.

"Serves him right, Stephen," one of the farmers cackled. "He laid out of th' war an' sent young Eldridge off to get kilt. High time somebody busted his face."

"If he doesn't come around soon, Silas, you might pour well water on him. Be doing him a favor." And Stephen mounted and rode away.

~ * ~

"Well, where to, horse?" he asked aloud. "There's a whole world out there. Maybe Kentucky. Few men from there I met. George Clark's boys. Indians bad, though, I hear. Don't fancy losing my scalp just yet. Well, waiting to see has freed me from home; maybe it'll find me a place to settle." The horse flicked his ears, plodded on.

He traveled up the James River to Columbia, then on impulse turned up the Rivanna. The land was pleasant, but settled. Jefferson's burned-out Elk Hill plantation told of how recently the British had desecrated here. After capturing Charlottesville in June, the cavalry and mounted infantry under Tarleton had retreated from a Patriot ambush at the Blue Ridge. On their way back to Richmond and then Yorktown, they'd burned and pillaged a path of destruction.

Next day, he came to the village of Charlottesville itself, a dozen houses, Jouett's Swan tavern and the courthouse. The hills were a little steeper here, and the Blue Ridge loomed beyond. The pike led west toward Rockfish Gap, but he followed the river up a few miles to where a sizeable creek came in from the west. A pyramidal mountain off to itself intrigued him, and the stream seemed to come from beyond it.

"Buck Mountain," a farmer told him. "This's Buck Mountain Creek, runs by it. Comes down outta th' Blue Ridge on up."

"What's the land like, up near the mountains?" Stephen queried.

"Good land, but all taken up. Big places, with some little holdin's between. You a farmer?"

"Miller. Or I was, before the war. This's a good creek for a mill."

"Is. But th' Squire—Hezekiah Thomas, he is—he's got one on up, an' he owns purt-near all th' land 'long th' creek."

"Well, just looking. Thomas, his name is? Don't suppose he'd need help at his mill?"

"No tellin'. I grind on up th' river at Adams', m'self. Don't keer fer th' squire none."

"Hard to deal with, is he?"

"No worsen' any, I reckon. Just figger he don't need my business, 'long with ever'body else's."

~ * ~

At the same time Stephen was traveling west, another man was making a similar journey, with a wagon train of slaves, equipment, and some construction workers from the Tidewater region.They traveled a more northerly route from Caroline County, where they'd made a lengthy stop, striking out west from Richmond over Swift Run Gap and down into the Shenandoah Valley. There, German settlers from Pennsylvania and Maryland had taken the best land, and the leader of this band was headed further west, over the first high range of the Appalachian Mountains.

He'd already taken land there, established himself in temporary quarters during the War of Independence, far from most of the fighting. True, General George Rogers Clark and his army had fought the British in the region and had prevented any western uniting of the enemy with forces under Cornwallis. Now, shortly after the cessation of hostilities, this adventurer was returning to his extensive property armed with everything necessary to establish a great plantation. He had paid generously for much of the equipment, and some of the rest he'd acquired by means certainly not legal.

Legalities weren't high on this explorer/settler's priorities. He was a man of business, and his business was acquiring land and possessions, by whatever means proved most productive. When necessary, he spent large sums of money, but he was by nature not a spendthrift.

~ * ~

The creek did wind around the lone peak, and Stephen rode up it, noting the broadening fields. In time he reached a major plantation, with barns, shops, and an impressive two-story plantation house atop a hill. The creek came from the west, and the house faced it from the north, down a tailored lawn and a still-green meadow. He hadn't reached the mill yet, but he turned into the long drive. The outbuildings were off to the right, and they were extensive. He imagined this Thomas was very much the successful planter, a bit rare in hills like these.

He stopped at the smithy. A stooped, white-haired man in a leather apron answered his greeting.

"This Squire Thomas' place?"

"Is that. I'm Ike Collins. You lookin' fer work?"

"Could be. Name's Davis. Stephen Davis. Heard he had a mill on this creek. Now, I did a sight of milling before the war, and thought maybe..."

"You c'n dress stones, then? Shorely can, if y'done much 'round a mill."

"Can. Don't have the tools, but if your owner has them, I can set a buhr to rights."

"Don't have 'em. Last feller he hired left with ever' mill pick th' squire had. Most travelin' dressers got 'em, so he ain't got more."

"You don't say? You don't forge them here?"

"Can, but never could git 'em hard 'nuff fer them French stones. No good steel 'round, an' I ain't good at case-hardenin'. You?"

"I know how, but I don't call myself a smith. You have to heat the iron a lot of times to get much carbon in. Do you think the squire would hire me? You and I could forge the tools between us."

"Mebbe so. He won't be to th' house. Gone upcreek t'look at land. Allus buyin' more land."

"What's the ground like, on up?"

"No big bottom land, only a strip 'long th' creek. Oh, they's little places, but th' good land's on over th' Ridge, in th' Valley, what little th' Germans ain't settled. Y'aimin' to git y'self a place?"

"Like to, but don't have much money. Maybe work a place off, if I could get a man to sell me some."

"Might happen some'ers. But seems like th' squire wants to own all that joins him." The smith let that old saying sink in, grinning expectantly.

It was at this point in the exchange that a striking young woman rode up on a spirited black mare. She rode astride, and wore a divided suede skirt. Stephen had never seen a woman ride that way other than farm girls, and never seen a girl that pretty. She had auburn hair, and eyes the color of...well, molasses came to mind. Not an inspired simile, he realized. She rode with a lean grace.

"Shoe's loose, Ike. I wanted to ride up Pig Mountain, but you'd better fix it, first." She ran her eyes over the soldier as the smith helped her down.

"Shore, Miss Abby. This here's Stephen Davis. He's jist out'n th' army. Miss Abby's th' squire's daughter, Stephen."

"Ma'am." He swept off his tricorner and bowed. She nodded, smiled, then turned back to the horse. *Now, how'd the smith know I was a soldier?*

"This one, Ike. But you'd best see to them all. I don't fancy laming Shelly up on the mountain."

The two immediately forgot Stephen existed as they examined the loose shoe. He let his eyes run over the girl and realized he'd hardly even noticed a young woman other than his sisters, for months. This was certainly a fine-looking one. About twenty, he guessed, and still, in November, with the brown of the sun on her. A horsewoman for sure, and yes, a rich man's daughter. Well, he'd never rate more than that glance from such as her, he was certain.

So it was a surprise when she turned the horse over to the smith and called to him.

"Mr. Davis, was it? What is your business, sir?"

He'd been gazing out from the open smithy at the lush meadow toward the creek.

"Why, ma'am, I am—or was—a miller. Heard your father might have need of help at his mill."

"Well, then. The fact is, as Ike probably told you, we have a miller who seems competent at milling, but not necessarily at maintaining the equipment. Can you dress stones?"

"I can, but your smith tells me you have no tools here."

"True. They departed with the last dresser, not an honest man. So we have one miller who can't dress, and another who can, but no tools with which to perform the task. We may have to wait for a traveling millwright, then."

"Not necessarily, ma'am. I was telling Mr. Collins, there, that I can harden and temper mill picks. Would you happen to know what size buhr you have?"

"I do, sir. Thirty-six inch. French stones."

"One set?"

"And a spare, imported through Philadelphia. My father may well want to speak with you, Mr. Davis, as we are getting little done as it is, with much grain waiting."

"I'd be obliged, Miss Thomas."

"In fact, why don't you ride up to the mill yourself, now, even though Father is absent? Abner Cocke is the miller. You may tell him I sent you."

He bowed again, replaced his hat, and mounted.

"Under whom did you fight, Mr. Davis, in the war?"

"Under Generals Greene and Dan Morgan, until Yorktown. We did a lot of playing tag with Cornwallis."

"General Morgan is one of my father's heroes. Were you at Cowpens, by chance?"

"I was. You probably know then, that the militia there wanted to bolt in the face of the British advance, but Morgan told them to hold, then run, and decoy the enemy into our reserves."

"Brilliant strategy. You look like a soldier, sir."

"I'll take that as positive, ma'am." He touched his hat, turned the horse and rode. So old Ike could spot it in me, too. Too much drilling, he guessed. But he didn't intend to go around all starch-stiff. Forget the war.

Fine-looking girl, he could not help noting, and he let his mind dwell on her: *Make a man want to stay around. Friendly, after she got started. Knows the mill, along with horses. Shame I'm such a backwoodsman. Still, as Ned said once, a uniform levels men out. But then, I'm not in uniform anymore. Well, have to be a land baron to bridge the social gap with such as her. Money attracts money. Always has.*

But thought of the girl wouldn't leave him as he rode upcreek. With the new country and its opportunities, a man might make something of himself, if he went about it right. Not milling, though. Richest miller alive wouldn't rate such a woman. No, land was the thing to have. And necessary, if he were to aspire to socializing with the Misses Abby Thomas of the world.

The mill was not elaborate, with its one operating buhr. Rough-hewn timbers framed the structure, and there was a twelve-foot overshot wheel. The creek was dammed at a bend well upstream, which sent the millrace straight on to the wheel, overflow going on around the curve in the stream-bed. The forebay was generous, which would allow long runs. Buck Mountain Creek was not large here, so closing the sluice gates to impound water would be a necessity, except maybe in springtime.

The miller Cocke was young like Stephen, probably not long off an apprenticeship. His not being able to dress the hard French granite stones was no condemnation; some millers never learned. But there were other evidences of less-than-adept millwrighting: in the shafting, bearing blocks, leather belting and general gear. Millwrights were the world's most exacting woodworkers, with the gears, pulleys, hoppers, spouts and a host of other mechanical contrivances—all made of wood. Stephen loved working with wood, and prided himself on the parts of his father's mill he'd built.

"Can you grind flour at all?" he asked the miller.

"Not with the stones like they are. Been doin' meal only, last few days." It was standard practice, using worn stones for meal until they could be sharpened. The stone ridges turned against each other, much like scissors, to cut the grain, and the sharper the dressed edges and truer the flat "lands," the finer the possible grind.

He looked over the spare stones. Not totally worn, but very much in need of dressing. With good, hard mill picks, he could do the job in four days. Then switch stones, and another four for the other set. Say ten to twelve days, with forging the tools.

Then he could be off again. Unless...No, idle to imagine he could settle here, mount a suit for Abby Thomas. Still, this country was good. If he could get a start, there was mountain land he could get, surely. timber there, and little spring creek bottoms were fine land, small though they were.

He returned from inspecting the dam and sluice to see an older man talking with Abner Cocke. The man was richly dressed, but Stephen was relieved to see he wore no lace. His riding boots shone, and there was the air about him, of a ranking officer, or a judge. Squire Hezekiah Thomas's handshake was firm.

"Abner tells me you dress stones. Can I see your metal?"

"You could, sir, but I've been five years at war, and the metal's all worn off." Both men meant the tiny chips of hardened steel from the mill picks that embedded themselves in a stonedresser's hands and forearms.

"Ah. Where are you from, Mr. Davis?" The voice was brusque, but not condescending.

"Goochland. My father has the mill off the James above Rock Castle, sir. I grew there, till the war."

"Yes, the war. You weren't by any chance with Morgan, were you?" The man's interest was in his eyes.

"I was. Your daughter, back at your place, mentioned you admired him. So do I. Greatly."

"Morgan could have won the war if he'd had the men. Whatever do you imagine General Washington meant, laying siege to New York that way? The fight was south."

"He felt he must have New York, sir. And he may have been right, if your militia here hadn't turned Tarleton and Cornwallis, and the French hadn't cut them off at Yorktown."

"Perhaps. Perhaps. Never know what's in a commander's mind. Or what he's found out that he won't share. Well. So you've met Abby, my one child still at home. She could run the place. But, to business: You've no tools, but Abner says you can work with my smith. That correct?"

"Yes, sir. 'Twon't be quick, though, with no good steel. Takes time to case-harden."

"I see. Well, from what you've seen, how long would it take you?"

"Should do it in less than two weeks. That will leave your man here with a good set of tools for next time."

"Only I cain't dress stones, Mr. Thomas. Don't seem to work right fer me."

"That's right. So I'd have another set of tools I couldn't use, is that right, Davis? Not a good bargain."

"That depends. If you should ever get another miller, say Mr. Cocke here moves on, you'd be provided for."

"Or, if not, a traveling dresser, at least an honest one, would have his own picks and such."

"Sorry, I can't help with that one. Maybe you'd be best served just to wait for or find a dresser now."

"Haven't been able to get one. Man out of Charlottesville died, a month back. Say we did strike a trade, what'd be your fee?"

"Well, sir, you've just sparked an idea. I'd rather trade than be paid in coin. What I'd like to do is find a bit of land I could work off. Now, I don't know if you yourself would be disposed, but let's say you might be. I could certainly keep your stones in order, and," looking around at the rough mill, "maybe set some other things to rights, too."

"Are you a millwright, too?"

"Not really, but I work wood, and begging your pardon, sir, this mill needs a few touches."

"No offense taken. But I'll tell you, and anyone, I aim to keep all the land I have, and am looking at more."

"Just the way I hear it. Well, only an idea. All I'd need would be a few acres. Hill slope would do, though. I'd need at least a small stream."

"So you could set up in competition with me? Not likely, young man."

"Oh, no sir. I'd not need a stream the likes of this. But I've done some gunsmithing, made some furniture. As I mentioned, I've the desire to work wood, Mr. Thomas, not grind. I've done that all my life."

"Ah. Well, I like a trade too, Davis. Now, just supposing I did agree to part with a bit, say up a hollow somewhere. You'd be handy to aid here, and maybe also at the smithy? We might talk some more along those lines."

"Glad to, sir. I'd thought to go on west, maybe Kentucky, but it's right pleasant here, I find."

"Yes, and you've seen my daughter. But don't get your hopes up there, lad."

"Oh, not at all, sir. It's just that, if I travel to Kentucky, I'll want to keep on traveling, I fear. I'm finding war does that to some."

"That it does. So that's why you didn't stay in Goochland?"

"Nothing for me there, sir. Sister's husband buying the mill and the place just won't hold me anymore."

"So you've ambition, then. Woodworking. Not much of that available this side of Williamsburg. Might be a future in that. Tell you what, Davis, you come on back to the place. Work up some tools with Ike. We'll see how good you are..."

"Beg pardon, sir, but I'll need a bargain struck before I make the tools."

"Ah, a shrewd one. All right, let's talk prices, as if we weren't to trade." The man almost rubbed his hands together.

Terms were soon agreed on. Stephen would sleep in the loft over the smithy, and begin the next day on mill picks, calipers, gauges and the millstone land leveling device. He would take meals at the plantation kitchen, a separate building where the white employees ate. The slaves had their cabins on up the slope along a tiny branch.

Well now, maybe I'm onto something here. Thomas talked of maybe a piece of rough land or two. Don't want too rough. Close trader. Probably how he's gained so much. Watch him, or I'll be afoot. Keep on his good side, maybe, with my war stories. And be close to Miss Abby, for what that might be worth.

Three

The forging took little time, as Ike Collins proved a competent smith. Then Stephen pounded charcoal, bone, and brittle, dried-up leather into a powder. As soon as Ike had a mill pick shaped of wrought iron, he heated it to high red and plunged it into the powder. It smoked and stank, but some of the carbon was absorbed into the soft surface iron. Over and over he repeated the process, each time adding more carbon to the tool, maybe as much thickness as a coat of paint. It would take perhaps fifty heatings to make steel of the working surface of these tools.

"Why do they call it case-hardenin'?"Ike asked. "I've heered moren' one story, but never knew."

"The way I hear it, some smiths make up a box, or case, of clay. They put this powder in, and the iron. Then they seal it up, and leave it in the forge, keep it hot two, three days running. The stuff's trapped in there, and all the carbon goes into the iron. Gets in the way of what else you're doing, though. I do it this way. Don't know which is better."

"Y'got enny way o' knowin' how much steel y'got built up? Either way?"

"No. All I know is to try and overdo it—get as much as I can. Then I watch the tempering closely. Too much carbon in, and you have to draw the temper more to keep it from breaking. Not enough and it'll never harden."

"That's been my trouble: not 'nuff. I git tired heatin' an' powderin'. Don't build up fast, does it?"

"No. But you know the old saying, Ike, 'You don't do anything in a hurry in the forge but burn yourself'."

Abby Thomas came into the smithy once to watch the process. The smoke and smell soon sent her away, but not before she'd passed the time of day with Stephen. He liked having her talk to him, even if he did know it wouldn't lead anywhere. He couldn't get over how pretty she was. And she wasn't silly, the way a lot of the nice-looking ones were.

Well, I have this job to do, but I don't suppose it hurts to think about her a little, while my hands are busy. Let's see, he'd need a set of thickness gauges—hammer and file them even. The leveler would be some trouble, but wagon tire iron would do for it. Upset the legs a bit, give them a little thickness, sit better…

The smith and he worked together, one heating in the forge while the other hammered out the tools, then they'd switch off. Stephen found he liked the old man, who lived over a ridge to the south. Neither man said much, but each knew what to do, and the work went smoothly.

So much so that when the squire came to check on progress, the collection of tools impressed him.

"Now, no miller I've seen had that fine a set, Stephen. You should stay with smithing." He handled the calipers, gauges, the partially-hardened mill picks.

"Thanks, sir, but making the same pieces over and over never took my fancy. Forging chain, now. Some men can do it day after day. When I've made the chain I need, I'm ready to go use it, instead of making more."

"I see. When will you be able to start dressing? Abner's going on about those dull stones."

"Tomorrow, for certain. I'm not steeling these picks too deeply, on account of the time it takes. Ike has it down now, and he can harden them again when they wear."

"Tomorrow it is, then. I'll want to watch your work there. Shouldn't wonder Abby will, too. Uncommonly curious about the workings of things, that girl is. None of the others cared much."

"That is unusual. My sisters never wanted to know what we did in the mill."

"Just so. Ike, I'll need you to sharpen plows starting tomorrow, then. We'll need to turn the fields under."

The next day dawned gray: typical November. That would make for poor light, Stephen observed, but the fine dressing could come later, on a bright day. Let it rain; he was in the dry. Been out in it most times for five years.

He was conscious of taking care with his manners when around the Thomases. Wouldn't hurt, he speculated, to get back to reading, either. He'd done as much of that as he could, growing up. A doctor in Goochland had loaned him books, and he'd been drawn to them any time he could spare, unlike the other boys at the subscription school.

He and Abner Cocke pried the two spare stones over nearer the door where the light was better. The upper had been turned in the lifting tongs with their jack-screw, so it was face up, too. He set himself a block of wood to sit on, then began the rhythmic, two-handed chipping of the stone. The procedure was to use the straight chisel edge a few strokes, then switch to the cross-edge on the opposite face of the same mill pick. The weight of the pick was critical: too light and the pick would bounce, or wear the user out forcing it down. Too heavy, and it'd chip too much, and wear the user out lifting it, hour after hour. Stephen had learned to strike, then lift slowly, resisting the common urge to hurry the upstroke. He'd seen millers with lamed arms from inflamed tendons from just that hurrying.

This French stone was harder than the American granite. It apparently occurred in small pieces, which the craftsmen of that country shaped and fitted exactly, then bound together with two iron bands, heated to expand, then shrunk onto the pieced, circular stones. The chips were hard, too, and he kept his hands between the impact point and his eyes as he worked.

"Slow going," the squire remarked, standing back from the steady blows. "Why do you let the pick die on the stone?"

Stephen told him, and the man nodded in understanding. He'd had millers rush a dressing job, then have it to do all over in a few weeks as the stones wore. He wanted it done right. He'd see what this fellow could do, then. He stepped away and conferred with his miller. Stephen knew they were assessing his work, which bothered him not at all. Only one right way to do this: his way, and to hell with the time it took.

Too many millers chipped back the leading edge of the grooves only, leaving the lands level. That would grind the grain, but it meant slower production. Stephen carefully sloped the lands, working his way around. This would move the ground grain out toward the edges as the stone turned, so that it fell into the spout trough properly.

In two days he'd rough-dressed the stones. Then he set the leveler to measure the finished height and get it even. Its feet held the straight bar above the face of the stone, and he used the thickness gauges to dress for the exact height. A few bright days gave him light for this task.

Then the stones were finished, and he and Abner Cocke swung the crane, set the tongs in the rim sockets of the working stones, and turned the screw lift to raise the dull top stone. They pivoted it in the tongs, and laid it aside, face up. The bedstone followed, then they set the two dressed spare millstones in place. Stephen checked the top stone for balance, chipping here and there to achieve perfection. Millstones must never actually touch, so this setting was crucial. Then the clearance setting, with the screw-threaded crank at the end of a long beam that carried the vertical shaft balancing and driving the top stone "runner" on its T-shaped end. This stone rested on a mortised-in crossed bar of iron, driven by a slot in the shaft.

Finally satisfied, Stephen nodded to Abner, and the miller filled the hopper with corn, pulled a rope that attached to a pivoting pole that raised the sluice gate outside. Water rushed, the wheel began to turn, and the wooden gears transferred the power to the top-runner stone. It ran true.

Stephen watched the stream of meal flow from the buhr spout, rubbed some between his fingers. He showed it to Abner, who smiled.

"Now, let's put some wheat in…see how fine we can make it."

Abner ran the hopper full of corn out, bagged the meal in jute-fiber sacks, and poured wheat grains in. He set the stone to get the first grind he wanted, then caught it in a portable screened shaker. Carrying it outside, he shook the coarse grind in the breeze to blow the chaff and hulls away.

Then he poured the wheat meal back into the hopper and set the stones for flour. He sifted, and re-ground finer. What came out was fine whole wheat flour, and he smiled again at the volume and quality.

"Quite good," came from Squire Hezekiah Thomas, who'd been watching from behind the men. He took a pinch, tested it between his teeth. "Yes, quite good. Now, will you dress the other set? I think we can discuss that piece of ground, if you still want a trade."

"I will, and I do. Wrong time to go over into Kentucky anyway, and I've come to like it hereabouts."

"Well, then. I've a little hollow I can show you tomorrow, downcreek a bit. Small stream, but I'm certain you could dam it for short runs of a wheel to power a lathe. And I believe you could just get at least a rough cabin up before cold weather, and still work some for us, along."

"Obliged, sir. Oh, and I've a kindness to ask of you."

"Certainly, if I can."

"Well, I'm missing reading, sir. Could you consider loaning me a book or two?"

"Ah, a man who reads. What did you have in mind?"

"Perhaps Shakespeare, if you have it, and I'd say you would. Bacon, Johnson: Ben or Sam. Anything, really."

"Done. Have you read Tristram Shandy?"

"I have, sir, and must say I did not care for it."

"Really? Well, then, we disagree. Perhaps we could discuss that work anyway, sometime. Yes, I'd be glad to loan you books. You must come to the house after we return tomorrow, and select a few volumes. I've Pliny, of course, and Virgil."

"I'm afraid I know little Latin, Mr. Thomas. My schooling was scant."

"Nonetheless, you've an inquiring mind. You're welcome to share my library."

So Stephen Davis rode with his employer next day down Buck Mountain Creek to a spot on the north bank where a small stream entered. It had no name, but created a small, rich flat just there, still in yellow pine, chestnut, poplar and oak, with some tall white pine on up. The hollow narrowed after a few hundred feet, then split into two streambeds. The one to the east was smaller, and ended soon in a spring. The other wound a half mile, fed by several small springs. Great trees stood thick over the hollow, and here and there granite outcroppings showed. Except for the potential small field at the larger creek, it was not good farmland. But, a stand of corn, mast for hogs, a vegetable patch near a cabin—it could do nicely.

"Now, Stephen, how much land had you in mind? Or, seeing this, what would be good boundaries?"

"I'd thought of a hundred sixty acres, sir, but this doesn't lay right for even a small farm. I'd say, up that west ridge to the head of the branch, then over in a rough rectangle, back to take in the smaller one. To Buck Mountain Creek. More like eighty or eighty-five acres, wouldn't you estimate?" A quarter mile by a half mile was 80 acres.

"Close to that. Now, I should tell you the main creek floods this flat place, but not often. No good for your water wheel, anyway; creek runs almost level. Why don't we set corners now, and you can record it any way you want?"

They set stone piles at the corners, and blazed trees near each. The agreement was for Stephen to work off a mortgage or, failing that in a stated time, to purchase the remainder for an agreed-on price per acre. If he failed at that too, he would simply lose it. The arrangement: take it or leave it. The squire owned a big part of this original 6,000-acre king's grant, and would hardly miss 80 acres or so, with no good field land and minimally valuable trees, given their poor marketability. This trade would be good business. For both parties.

Stephen was well aware of the shrewdness of the planter's offer, but also that he'd edged his way into the other's good graces with his work and the war stories and the reading. Well, it was all honest, so why not? Not as if he were lying to the man. But he also knew, no matter how he managed to ingratiate himself with the squire, that gentleman would never see him as an equal, never allow his daughter...No, no point in going after that idea. Still, two people and a piece of ground...

He borrowed a collection of 17th-century English poets, and plays by Ben Jonson, to read. Jonson was no match for Shakespeare in his opinion, but in truth he wasn't ready for the bard's plays again, yet. The planter's library was small, but good.

While at the house, he met Mrs. Thomas, a hearty, somewhat direct lady, who frankly sized him up. Abigail was also present, and Stephen was uncomfortably aware of his plain clothes and the worn British boots. The women were polite to him without being condescending, but, feeling every bit the hired man, he took his leave as soon as he could courteously do so.

"Take the rest of the day, Stephen," Thomas offered. "Get to know that piece of land. I'm not sure yet how I let you talk me out of it. Anyway, now we'll be neighbors, and I'm glad for it."

What you're glad for is having me useful at hand, Stephen thought, through his parting smile. *But you'll get just what we agreed on. I'm not about to be your man, beyond getting that little hollow.* But, mustn't be uncharitable. A few days ago he'd nothing but a few Continental coins, and now he had land, such as it was. An improvement, by any measure.

~ * ~

Now there's an intriguing young man, Gertrude Thomas observed. In no way a gentleman, or at least in the conventional sense, but he's intelligent, speaks well, and is apparently a master craftsman. And he's managed to do Hezekiah out of a piece of land, a minor miracle. *I'll want to watch this one, see what he makes of himself.*

And of course it's possible—barely—that Abby might take a fancy to him. Certainly far different from the prideful planters' sons of our acquaintance. The war's hardened this young man, clearly. There's something…haunting him, I'd say. Seen too much death, surely.

Well, I suppose there's to be a new order now, with independence from England. The old ways, values, customs will probably erode over time, and who knows? Perhaps young ambitious men like this Stephen will rise to positions of influence and even power, given the probable shift in the makeup of society.

Pleasant chap, if a little in awe of us. I daresay he's already smitten with Abby, as all of them are. But somehow I don't think this one will be slavish, which is something she can't stand.

Yes, our Mr. Davis may be an example of what the future holds for this new nation. At least here in the back country. In Boston or Williamsburg he might not stand out, but this is a small pond, and likely to be for some time in the future. He might just become a significant, even oversize frog, here.

The plantation mistress' musings were interrupted by her husband's return from seeing Stephen off, but not before she noted her daughter's watching him ride away, a small smile on her face. *Go easy on this one, my dear; he'll not be just an amusement for you.*

~ * ~

Stephen rode again to his holding after leaving the books in the smithy loft. No likely spot for a cabin had caught his eye earlier, so now he considered: above flooding from the main creek, certainly. Say, above a likely spot for his dam, which would mean near where the two small branches came together, for more flow.

But he didn't like anything he saw there, so went up the longer branch farther. Up above was a sort of miniature bench before the ground dropped off steeply to a deep hole in the stream, below where the water had cascaded over granite. The sound of the water was pleasant here, and there was a flatter place a little higher up that could become a garden. There'd be a steep path to the mill, but he liked the idea of a cabin up above the stream.

He noted some smaller poplar trees among the big timber, and a few chestnuts of manageable size. These latter were the wood of choice, along with the old-growth yellow pine, for construction. He'd hew out cabin logs and raise them alone or with little help, so he must cut trees he could handle.

Stephen had found time during the forging of the mill tools to shape an axe for himself. Now he'd need a broadaxe for hewing logs, a froe for riving shakes, a hammer, forged nails. Reflecting, he decided it would be better to set up a forge of his own than to chip away time from his trade with Thomas by using his. Let's see, some leather for a bellows, iron for the firebox, and any slab of metal I can fasten onto a block of wood for an anvil, will do it. Clay-lay stones to build up the sides of the forge...this would take precious time.

So he resolved finally, to trade out work for the few absolute necessities, then make the rest himself as he could find time to set up here. Figuring a month or more of his free time to put up the cabin, he'd be into cold weather. And there was the little detail of food through the winter, for him and his horse. But he could live on squirrels if he had to. Trade for grain. Could sell the horse, but he didn't like the idea of being afoot. And he'd be right handy to skid logs with. Work something out, he guessed.

But I have to get moving here, if I'm to be any better off than in the war, sleeping on the ground. Have to figure on cutting a couple of trees a day, steady. Hack out a log a day—no, that'll run me too long. Well, get started; see how it goes. Won't have to put in steady time at the squire's. And I'm certain he'll give me some slack, as long as I don't go after his daughter.

Four

A log cabin can be raised quickly, if the builder doesn't care what it looks like or whether it's weather-tight. He can cobble together some round poles and fashion a roof in a hurry. But Stephen Davis was a careful crafts-man, and would not throw up a shack on his land. His house would be built like a piece of mill machinery, precise and neat, no matter how long it took. And that would mean working steadily from first light into dark, every day he could manage.

He laid heavy corner stones, leveled and squared to each other, for the 16x20-foot structure. Then he hewed chestnut timbers for the sills, and dragged them into position with the horse, using harness borrowed from Ike Collins. He levered these sills onto the foundation stones, prying, blocking up, prying again.

As he split logs for the puncheon floor, Stephen reflected on how a man takes for granted the ordinary tools and supplies a farmer or miller acquires over time. Here he had no wedges, no chain, no saw, no seasoned boards, no scraps of iron or drawn wire or rope. Have to borrow, create, or do without—no way around it. He'd much prefer a floor of carefully tongue-in-grooved heart pine boards, done painstakingly with pitsaw, smoothing and shaping planes, but there was no time or money for that. His puncheons would rest off the ground on the sills, split side up, adzed smooth. They would shrink, and he must move them tight together several times, adding another half log when needed.

It was with some exultation that he stood on his own poplar floor midway through December. But that wouldn't keep the rain off. He needed his logs up quickly, and a roof overhead before serious snow.

He felt sure Squire Thomas would have traded him slave help if he'd asked. But he'd never worked slaves, and didn't want his house slave-built. So he hewed the logs, and set the first few himself, inching them up skids with a pry-pole, dovetail-notching as he went.

Then his friend Ike brought his sixteen-year-old grandson Web over for a day of work, and the three men, using the horse, cross-hauled the remaining dozen logs into place.

"Now all y'need is a roof an' a place t'build a fire," young Web observed. He was a strong boy, a hunter, with an easy grin.

"Might wanta door, too," Ike observed wryly. "'Less he plans to hole up in thar all winter, boy." He gave his grandson a friendly shove.

"Git hisself a woman, he mightn't wanta come out, wouldja, Stephen?" the lad laughed, winking.

"Not considering a woman for yet awhile, Web. Last one threw me over, hard."

"Oh, sorry to hear that. What you think of Miss Abby?" The grin, again.

"Don't think about her at all. Don't imagine it'd do me much good. No, I plan on living like a hermit here for quite a spell, maybe get a dog for company."

"Oh, there's other sweet young things around," Ike said, gathering his tools. "You jist ain't noticed."

"Guess not. War sort of got me soured on women. Well, I'm obliged to the two of you. You let me know when I can help you in turn, Ike, Web."

"Oh, don't think on it, Stephen. Glad to help. Boy there, is hankerin' fer a good huntin' knife, though, y'get th' chancet."

"Glad to. You want a whittler, or a wood splitter, Web?"

"'Bout in between, if I could. An' one will hold 'n edge. Tired of sharpenin' soft iron. Granpa says you c'n git a hard edge."

"That I can. Just you let me get my roof on and chimney in, and you've got yourself a knife."

It was a lopsided trade, a fine knife being worth more than a day's work, but Stephen knew the boy would be over to help more. In a few years, he'd probably be building a cabin up some hollow for himself, with maybe a new bride. Help one another, that's how it's always gone, and a good thing.

Horizontal roof purlins instead of gable-end poles went up in a day, to span the triangular gables. Then the business of riving chestnut shakes began, and here Stephen needed help, too. The big blocks should be sawn for easier splitting. He borrowed a crosscut saw from the Thomases, and worked a big trunk he'd felled into three-foot sections. He used wedges to reduce these into smaller pieces, then used the froe and mallet to split the shakes. Being straight-grained and all heart, chestnut was ideal for this use, and the tannic acid the wood contained kept it from rotting for many years.

While he had the saw, he cut out the openings for door, window, and fireplace. He split and smoothed buck boards for the log ends at these openings and pegged them in place. His auger had been a quick hour's forging, and another for filing and hardening. He'd used it also for holes to pin the purlins and top log plates. Now he shaped boards for the door and window shutter, having no glass for a sash. Then he sharpened the saw and returned it.

"I've a good mason I can trade you labor for your chimney, Stephen," the planter offered. "He'd only waste my provender otherwise, this weather. But then you'll know stone, being a miller."

"Well, yes, sir. But thanks just the same. I'm gambling the bad weather will hold off till I've the fireplace in." Typically, heavy snow would come around mid-January here, and that was upon them already.

"No need to rush. The smithy loft would go empty without you. Have you had the chance to read Donne?"

"Little, except for that rain we had. He's a deep one."

"A fine mind, that man. Few churchmen have the time, or take it, to write more than tracts. He did mankind more than one service."

"He did, sir. Let's hope for writers like him among us. How's Abner getting on at the mill?"

"Steady. The rush is off grinding now. He'll set up the whipsaw soon. We could use your help, then."

"Of course. I've only a few more days for my hardware and the chimney, and I can be there any days."

"Fine. I must ride over to see your creation. For a one-man job, you've been prompt."

"Oh, Ike and his boy Web helped, and it's only a cabin. I'm much obliged to you for the use of the saw."

What the squire evidently was not aware of was that his daughter had ridden several times to visit Stephen at his work. She was off on horseback every day, and her father rarely knew where. Her presence at the rising cabin was pleasant for Stephen, but he did not let her interrupt his work. He was polite, but could work while he talked, and did so. For her part, she was both friendly and reserved, never suggesting that the planter/craftsman barrier might be breached. She stayed only a short time each visit, but he found he looked forward to seeing her.

From her he'd learned of the other families in the area, and earlier of upcoming Christmas celebrations and other community events. When she'd suggested he might enjoy some local society, he'd graciously declined.

"Perhaps in the spring, Miss Abby. I've yet to finish building my nest, here. I'm not good at half-measures, and I want to be well set for my sojourn here."

"Sojourn? Do you plan to leave us? So soon?"

"I was referring to my life's sojourn, ma'am. None of us knows how long that may be."

"Ah. But you've survived five years of evidently poor British marksmanship. I'd say you'll last."

"Their aim was frequently good, I'm afraid. Either luck or a providential God protected me. For some reason."

"Oh, you don't feel you're a vital part of humanity, Mr. Davis?" She was teasing. "You don't believe you were spared for a good purpose?"

"Possibly. But that purpose remains obscure, at present. Unless, of course, there is some celestial plan involving my riving of these shakes."

"Oh, I sense you will go on to far greater things than riving shakes. Or dressing millstones, for that matter. Father says you're reading Donne, and Marvel."

"I am, but there live many better scholars."

"But not here. And not just now. One lives in the present, and in his immediate environment, don't you agree?"

Stephen was having a little trouble following the girl's line of reasoning, if it could be called that. *She's just passing idle time with me—that's obvious. Well...*

"And in the present, I'm splitting shakes. In this environment."

"So you are. Let me know if you feel any man's death diminishing you, will you, please?" Her eyes were merry as she quoted Donne, then rode away.

"Actually, I'm feeling a bit diminished, just now," he called after her. Her laughter floated back from the trail down to the forks of the stream. *Now let her take that any way she chooses. As for me, I've a cabin to finish. Should have enough nails if I use just one in each shake. Pa would frown on that, but I know it works.*

Devilishly pretty girl. Knows it, too. Seems set on adding me to her list of admirers. All right, I'm on the list. Inactively, and that's to be the way of it. And that makes me wonder about what other girls there are hereabouts, as Web said. Maybe I'll look about, when I've this place done.

He'd have preferred lime-and-sand mortar for his chimney, but hadn't the money for the lime. He used the red clay from his land, trusting in dry days to finish outside. The roof had more overhang at this gable to shelter the chimney, but a soaking rain of any duration would wash some of the fill away. He was able to find squares of ledge granite scattered about in the woods for his chimney, saving stone-cutting and shaping time. He fashioned a low sled for moving the stones with the horse, and the work went steadily, if not quickly. Faint trails appeared between the trees where the sled's runners had passed, from wherever he'd found the stones.

Stephen had learned not to let the slow pace of stonework intimidate him; he looked often back at what he'd accomplished instead of ahead to what still remained. By using only the best stones, laid horizontally, he could use a minimum of clay, and the chimney would suffer little if that washed out.

Finally, that was done. It was February, and except for a few days, the really cold weather had held off. That was unusual here, and he wondered if that providential God had smiled on his efforts.

Then the hearth was finished, with its andirons and cooking crane. The cabin door was hung and the window shuttered. When he could, he'd buy glass, and perhaps add a second window, and maybe one in the loft, too. And also when he could, he'd lay a floor up there, with a ladder to reach it, and sleep there instead of before the fire. Some of his mother's insistence on a proper parlor must have rubbed off in him, he reflected. Not that he'd have many visitors, but he didn't want his bed right near the door, either.

Sleep, now. That was still a problem, with the images from the war still coming to trouble him. Even the exhausted sleep from his labors failed to obliterate them. But they were coming less frequently, at least. The phantom eyes still haunted, but they were growing dim.

Two light snows had fallen during the weeks of building, but hadn't lasted long. Now, late, the weather came. It snowed all one day and that night, and the branch froze in the still places. He'd bought meal and potatoes, and other staples, with what little remained of his money. Now it was time to go hunting.

He'd seen the game trails along the stream and followed one now, tracked in the deep snow by deer and rabbits. Beaver, raccoon and opossum tracks joined the trail too, and branched off here and there. Up near the head of the stream he leaned against a tree and waited, rifle ready.

It had been a busy time, this building and working for the squire. He couldn't recall a time in his life when he'd compressed more work into so short a time. It was only deep winter, and he'd a cabin just about complete, on land he was working off, with more work assured. Not a bad few weeks. Seemed the more a man had to do, the more he was able to get done. Well.

It would be time by the end of March to plant the little patch he'd cleared on up from the cabin, getting his logs. That would mean crooking the rows around remaining stumps, but they'd rot eventually. Meantime, he'd work steadily at the mill. Then, when the water was low, in summer, he could dam his own stream, get started on his little woodworking shop. In a year then, he could be pretty well set up...

The movement against white snow was cautious, but upwind. Turkeys. They emerged from dense cedar cover where granite had kept larger trees from growing, peered around, began scratching through the snow. Slowly, very slowly, he inched the rifle up, shifting position by mere degrees. They were sixty yards away, coming a step at a time toward him. The slight breeze held, making his eyes water in the cold. He muffled the sound of the flintlock in his cloak as he cocked it. It seemed to take an hour for him to get a bird in his sights, but finally he did. Their darting heads as they scratched and pecked made their bodies jerk.

He squeezed the trigger, and the roar of the rifle sent the flock into the trees, tearing branches, scattering loads of snow, crashing the forest. The one bird flopped in the snow as the others vanished, and the blue smoke drifted.

He reloaded stiffly, feeling the cold that had settled with the long wait. His legs were stiff too, as he walked among boulders to the fallen bird. Shot its head off, neat. He smiled grimly, remembering other clean shots, in the war. The bird was heavy; perhaps he wouldn't hunt any more today, then. Thought of his new hearth cheered him.

Prickly feeling returned to his feet on the tramp downcreek toward his cabin, and he realized just how cold it was. No need to stay out in this; good day to read, roast this bird.

He smelled his own woodsmoke first, then the horses. He'd left his own with the squire's animals where there was hay. He recognized Abby's mare Shelly and her father's roan, even though the muffled riders were indistinct, now riding away.

"Hallo, there!" he called after them. They turned, rode back.

"Well, and we thought we'd missed you," the squire greeted. "Should have guessed you'd be out hunting."

"Alight, sir, Miss Abigail, and come in. No need to turn away…my house is yours. Always." He helped Abby down.

"Thank you. Quite snug, it appears. Fine bird."

"Yes, thanks." He tied the horses, swung the door open. They stamped snow from their boots. "I've some cider that should still be hot, here." He moved to a pot hung well back from the coals on the fireplace crane, slid it closer, put logs on.

"Ah, now. Abby, warm your toes here," her father moved aside.

"Here's a chair and a bench. Let me just get a ladle and some mugs." Stephen moved the rough furniture up, helped them out of coats, then took heavy pewter from a sparsely-laden shelf. Abby was looking around her.

"Well, Mr. Davis, I see you've quite the cozy bear's den here on the edge of the precipice." Not unkindly, and with no hint of her previous visits. Well, he could play that game.

"I'm afraid I've practiced the old farmer's rule of building on that piece of ground that won't grow anything, Miss Abigail. But I like the sound of the water from below."

"Let's hope you don't sleepwalk, Stephen," the planter chuckled, accepting cider.

"Oh, Mama sent some cakes," Abby remembered, and retrieved a packet from her coat pocket. "Have you a plate?"

"One, yes," and he handed it down from the shelf, with a knife. She cut the shortbread into squares, and the three settled back before the blaze.

"Ah," Hezekiah Thomas repeated contentedly. "We were both going crazy, shut up in the house, Stephen. Cold as the devil, but I'd been putting off this visit, and Abby was game, so here we are. You've done a lot in a few weeks."

"Thanks, sir. Just did get inside in time. I'll be at your place on through now, to help with the sawing."

"Let's let this cold spell break, first. Wheel will ice up, this weather—but of course you know that."

"Well, I can do some of the woodwork in the mill. It appears to have been built in somewhat of a hurry."

"Was. Former owner sort of threw it up. Only ground meal. I brought in the French stones. Yes, let's set it to rights. I'm afraid to climb those steps to the hopper, myself." He looked around. "And let's get you some boards sawed for your loft. I know you don't fancy setting your bed afire from sparks down here."

Stephen had built a one-poster, a bed with two rails set into logs in a corner of his cabin, their other ends mortised into the one post out in the room. Hemp rope crisscrossed between the rails. He had a cornshuck mattress and a bearskin on it. And yes, he did worry about stray sparks from his fire setting him ablaze at night. So he banked the coals and let the room go frigid, which made for cold feet in the mornings.

"I'd appreciate that, sir. You've been most kind, helping me get settled here."

The planter waved a hand in dismissal, savoring the heat of the fire and the steaming cider. Just now Stephen knew he was feeling generous. But for her part, Abby obviously hadn't let her father know she'd visited on her own, and that intrigued him. Just where did he stand in her estimation? Probably just a way to pass time, as he'd reflected before. If the girl just weren't so damn pretty...The firelight caught red highlights in her hair and made her eyes dance.

"And you really should get yourself a window too, Mr. Davis," she observed. "These bitter days, you could get in a lot of reading, but not in the dark."

"Oh, I've managed a few bayberry candles, Miss Abigail, though my den, as you called it, is somewhat Stygian. And I look forward to the Bacon volume, sir, now that I've a bit of leisure, thank you."

"Ah, yes. Learned man. Bit dry, some say, but I haven't found him so. I'll be interested to hear your views."

The talk went on easily, and Stephen lost some of the nervousness he'd felt at hosting the worldly squire and his daughter in his hovel. Indeed, these two had a way of making him feel almost an equal, within limits. It was a good feeling.

They eventually took their leave, both complimenting him on the soundness of his cabin's workmanship. He watched them off down the trail to the larger creek, the warmth of their visit lingering.

Then he retrieved the turkey, set water to boil in his one large pot, cleaned the bird, plucked its larger feathers. He'd have to scald it to get the pinfeathers free. Then, roasted on a spit between his andirons, it would make a feast.

~ * ~

The rest of the winter passed with Stephen systematically clearing the garden space above his cabin, where he'd cut most of his logs. The best of the trees he saved for his shop building, and the rest he cut for firewood. The sound of his axe echoed among the great trees day after day. He searched out standing and fallen dead trees for the fuel he needed now, and stacked the rest to season.

He had spent time at the Thomas mill, helping young Abner Cocke with setting up the whipsaw. There was periodic grinding to do also, but the miller had that well in hand. It was the complexities of the gearing and levers of the up-and-down saw blade that perplexed him, and this was the part Stephen enjoyed. Once set up, a water-powered saw could be left to work its way through a log unattended.

The method was to hew the log square so it would sit solidly, then saw it into planks. That left the two at the outside with one sawn surface and one hewn, each. A ratcheting device advanced the log as the cut was made. Most of the machinery was hand-forged or wooden, but the saw blade was from the roller mills at Fort Pitt in Pennsylvania. The squire had traveled extensively and brought equipment here to this remote spot for many years.

~ * ~

Just a few more days, and it'll be warm enough I can run. Master's so stingy, I can't even hide me a knife, but I've got to go, no matter what. Move fast and far, and maybe I can get away with it. Slave catchers be after me first day, though.

I'll go north first, like that's my route. Then, maybe second day, cut east to lose any trail. If I wade every shallow stream up or down a ways, dogs won't be able to trail me. Should strike some road soon, make travelin' easier.

But that'll be dangerous; have to be ready to hide every minute. Travel only at night; get lost easy. Black man anywhere's fair game in this country's supposed to be free, now. Get stolen again, some mean master maybe cut me so I can't run again.

But I can't stay here, out in these mountains away from everything I've ever known. Hackin' brush on these steep hillsides, overseer beatin' us, master not carin' if we drop dead. Get back to Caroline County, Mistis take care of me.

The man named Tom watched and waited as the days grew warmer in the mountains west and south of the Virginia settlements. The master was driving his hands hard to establish his plantation in these high hills, though the only good land was along the creeks and river.

To Tom, who'd served a wise master, it was obvious the man couldn't make this place pay, and he wondered at his spending so much money trying to develop it. *Well, he's stole some of us, but that won't let him make a living, here. Man surely don't know what he's doin'. Word is, he's got money from others, claimin' land for them. Fool's errand, all of this.*

But that was no concern of his. The immediate plan was to flee, to survive somehow till he could reach home and safety. With no weapons but

40

perhaps a sharp rock, that was going to be nearly impossible. Maybe noodle a fish now'n then, or hit a rabbit with a rock, but no way to cook anything. Well, folks way on back had survived, and he'd have to, now.

Work harder meantime, get th' overseer's eyes off me. Prob'ly best to go in a storm, make it harder to follow me. Know the way at first, an' then it'll be stay off in the woods, travel by th' stars. Long way, an' th' Lord's gonna have to be my guide. White man's God, but maybe He don't care I'm black.

Five

Stephen planted corn, beans, pumpkins and squash around the stumps in his cleared ground and set a rail fence around it. He'd need a dog to keep varmints out of his garden, and made a trade with Abner Cocke for a pup of uncertain lineage.

"Don't know how he'll turn out, but his sire's a good tree dog," the miller told him. The pup was mostly black, with one ear that stood up like a question mark.

"He'll do. What I want is mostly something to chase 'coons out of my corn. Deer smell him, they'll stay away, too." He named the creature Raphael, for a reason he soon forgot.

And whatever the dog's shortcomings, he soon developed a closeness with his master that worked well. Once he learned he was to stay with the place and guard it, he did so with zeal. No approaching squirrel, grouse or fox got close, let alone bear or deer, without Rafe's sounding the alarm, often blasting his master from sleep.

"Well, it's what I feed you for," Stephen would mutter, rolling over to doze off again. He soon learned to distinguish between the routine warnings to smaller intruders and the more frantic cries a bear or mountain lion might inspire.

So it was one early pre-dawn in April, with spring a greening reality, that the dog's insistent growling and snarling jolted Stephen awake and sent him for his rifle. The half-grown dog's hair was on end, and he couldn't seem to make up his mind to run into the woods after whatever had alarmed him, or under the house for safety.

A chill ran up Stephen's spine as he strained to see in the shadows. Nothing. Well, whatever it was, it could wait for daylight. Horse was safe at the plantation, and the dog could get under the house. Could be a panther, but not likely. Wait, then.

Unless it was a man. At that thought, he ducked back inside. Could be a stray Indian, but not likely. Or robbers, off the main road. Sure scaring my dog. Something's not right, here.

Can't see a thing. Should get a glass window in this place, maybe two. Well. Rafe's still at it. Something's out there, and it's not going off. Light coming up. Just wait a bit; see what's what.

He ate some cold cornbread and ham, and drank water. The dog would pause, then sniff the air and start barking again, from just by the door. That told Stephen something: All right then, it's a man. Or men, or it'd have gone off by now. And off down the trail, the way Rafe's barking. So he, or they're waiting for me to come out, and they can see I have only the one door.

But I've got a window, and on the back side. He slid the catch quietly and opened the shutter a crack. Almost full light out; the woods empty. He swung the shutter wide and leaned out. Nothing moved. The dog still barked near the door at something beyond sight.

He went through feet first, then pulled the rifle after him. Then he moved off on the soft ground, keeping the cabin between him and where he reckoned the watcher to be. Circling wide, he cut the trail far below the cabin and looked for tracks. There they were: one set of bare feet, up from the creek road. Bare feet? In this chill? He followed cautiously, gun ready. Full-size tracks; not some boy.

The cabin came in sight, with the prancing pup near the door. This didn't make any sense at all...

Then he saw him. A motionless shape lying in bushes along the path, one bare foot extended, a ragged trouser leg, a bare, black arm.

Runaway slave: has to be. One of Thomas'? No, too close. Now, what the hell?

And what am I going to do with him? He's out, completely. Doesn't even hear the dog. Well.

"All right, vicious dog, calm down, there. You, Rafe!" The man did not stir at the sound of his voice. *Damn then, he's completely gone.* Stephen reached down, turned him over. The eyes opened, rolled, tried to focus, closed again. It was clear he'd collapsed from exhaustion. Stephen had seen it in the war: too much marching, no food, no sleep, till it finally hit a man.

This man was youngish, maybe thirty. Didn't look as if he'd eaten lately. Probably traveled at night, hid out at dawn. Headed somewhere. *Or not. Maybe just away. Not anywhere a runaway could go, in the middle of Virginia. Nothing on him. No knife, no knapsack, no flint and steel. Must have been a rough place, wherever he was, to make him run with nothing.*

Well, what the hell. He could get him to the squire's, he supposed. He'd be able to find who owned him, sooner or later. Maybe Thomas would buy him; give him a better place. Didn't know, though. From what he'd heard and seen, the otherwise enlightened planter didn't think blacks were quite human.

Really not my business. Don't need to get into this at all. I can just...

No. Hell no, I can't, either. He's here on my place, and he's worn clear out, and he's hurting. And I've seen too much hurting these last few years. So let's see, feller, what we can do, here.

He looked at the face again, and saw that the eyes were watching him now, not fearfully, but with a certain resignation, a certain darkness.

"How're you doing, man? About worn out, I'd say."

A perceptible nod. Stephen could sense the man was astonished at his own weakness. It was something new to him.

"Thing to do is get something inside of you, the way I see it. Then we can talk, figure out what's to do next. You lie here and I'll bring a bite. Get some strength back in you."

At the cabin, Stephen cut small bits of the ham, crushed cornbread into it, added hot water. It made a sort of broth. No use worrying what to do with the runaway just yet. Nobody would find him for awhile, at least till he was stronger. Cross that bridge later...

He got the man propped against a tree trunk and supported his head while he spooned the broth into his mouth.

"Weak...weak's a cat," he mumbled. "Been trav'lin'...long...time."

"Appears so. And doesn't look like you've had any way to get any victuals, either. This'll put some strength in you, though."

An hour later the man could stand, and move unsteadily. Stephen got him to the cabin and onto the porch. The pup nosed him curiously.

"My name's Stephen Davis. What do they call you?"

"Tom Logan. An' I thankee kindly for helpin' me, Mist' Davis."

"Well, you needed a hand. Looks as if you're running."

"Pretty much, only it's not that simple."

"No, from what little you've said, you don't sound like an ordinary field hand."

"That's th' complicated part. You see, I was in th' war..."

"Were you?"

"Was. My master, he was Major Logan, got to be a colonel, took me with him. I'd cook, do up his clothes an' such. From over in Caroline County. Logans been there a long time."

"Don't know them; my people are in Goochland. So what happened?"

"Well, Mass' John, he got hit, right at th' last, at Yorktown. Came through it all, then got hit. I carried him off th' field. Didn' seem bad, but he had a bad feelin' 'bout it. An' he had papers made up, givin' me my freedom. Said never to let 'em go. Was witnesses an' all too, y'know.

"So we got him home to Caroline, an' seemed he was doin' better. I was workin' there, same's before, only now I'se gettin' paid, y'know, account of Mass' John, he tells ever'body I'm free."

"This is back last fall, then?" Right after the war? What in the world went wrong?"

"Comin' to that. Then Mass' John, he took bad, an' he died, sudden. Didn't anybody seem t'know why. Mistis, she all broke up, young, didn't know what to do. Lot of trouble 'bout who goin' to do what, who gettin' what, an' all. Few kinfolks. Mostly a cousin of Mass' John's, doctor, tellin' her what she oughta do. His wife'd died, an' I figured he had it made up to take up with th' mistis.

"Well, there was this man Hayes came through. Some kind of friend of th' doctor's. Was goin' west to claim land out on one of th' rivers, set up a plantation. Was buyin' slaves, wagons, plows an' such. Ever'body short, 'count of th' war, but he was payin' high. He asks 'bout me, an' Mistis, she explains I'm free; Mass' give me papers, set me free. So this Hayes, he goes 'round, buyin', gittin' set to go.

"An, Mist' Davis, th' night they left, this Hayes an' his men, they bust into my cabin, an' they tie me up, an' they find my papers and they burn 'em, right there. An' they drag me off, middle of th' night, and we're on th' way west, an' I can't do a thing about it."

"So you got through the winter, then you ran."

"Did. I figure, if I can just get back to Caroline where I'm known, I can be free again."

"Well, that's probably your best chance, but I wouldn't count on it. Any white man who finds you can claim you, keep you, sell you. That's going to be a strong temptation, even back in Caroline. How'd you get away?"

"It's new country out there. No newspapers and no slave catchers much, yet. Hayes didn't trust us with so much as a knife, so he figured we couldn't run. I saved dried meat and biscuits, much as I could, then set out, dark of the moon, kept to water to fool the dogs. I moved fast, and th' Lord was with me."

"Must've been. Well, that's some story, Tom. But you're in settled country here. Hard to move through here without getting caught. Now, I work for a planter—you'd have passed his place upcreek—at his mill, but not all the time. Not many folks come here. You'll stay here—need to get your strength back first—then we'll see what's to do...

"You'll help me? Well, you already have..."

"Well, hell, I was in the war too, and sounds like you got a raw deal, there...Let's just say we'll see what this looks like. Between us we should be able to figure something out."

Tom Logan raised his eyes to Stephen's, held them in wordless gratitude. It was clear he'd been ready to take whatever fate awaited him at this cabin with the barking dog, where he'd sunk to the ground, unable at last to put one foot in front of the other.

~ * ~

"Now, I'm working this place off as I said, blacksmithing and mill-wrighting for Squire Thomas. Cut me off eighty acres because he needed me. Man's a decent sort, but I'd say he'd turn you in as soon as he knew you were here. His daughter rides a lot, and she'll pop in here from time to time. Rides right up." It was after supper the next day.

"So I'd best hide out."

"Been thinking about that. Blacksmith comes by too, and his grandson, hunting and all; we trade out work. Somebody's going to see you, Tom, soon or late. Now, you don't know me from Adam's off ox, but it appears you're going to have to trust me somewhat, here."

"Oh, I trust you, Mist' Davis. You saved m'life."

"Well, it looks like we're going to have to make it up like you're my man while you're here."

"I thought about that, but folks hereabouts bound to know you don't have a slave, don't they?"

"They know I *didn't*, yes. But I've been considering: Suppose I tell them over at the plantation my people back home in Goochland sent you up for me? How'd they know the difference?"

"Maybe. But you said your folks were millers. I don't know a thing 'bout millin'. Mass' John raised me to be his body servant, an' that's all I did till the day that Hayes stole me. 'Fraid anybody come by'd see right through that tall tale sooner'd we could tell it."

"Hmm. And well, the squire might want to borrow you, too. No, t'won't do, then. But wait! I've an old friend...Yes! I'll write him. All right: Here's what we'll do, Tom...oh, this'll be fine!" Stephen's face lit up at the prospect: a letter to his comrade-in-arms Ned Drake, instructing him to fabricate a bill of sale from him for one Negro slave body servant, Tom Logan, to Stephen Davis, for good and valuable considerations. Oh, how Ned would love that!

"And here's where you'll have to trust me, Tom: I'll legally own you if Hayes or anybody else comes to claim you, which I doubt. If anything, Hayes will search around his place, or possibly even around Caroline. He'll figure you died of hunger or a panther got you, most likely.

"Now, I've got a bad feeling about what happened at your old master's place. I doubt the widow had anything to do with it, the way you tell of the family, but I worry about your just showing up there with nothing to protect you. And like I said, it's risky, traveling alone here. I'm going to suggest you stay with me a while, unless you're in a rush to get on. You have a woman there?"

"Thought I did, but she married another man while I was in the war."

"Oh, now. You, too? I know what that's like."

"Mass' John's cousin, Doc Weston, he convince Mistis my Tillie wastin' her time waitin' for me. Oughta marry her off to th' carriage driver, raise some field hands. Carriage driver'd been pushing for her all along, anyway."

"And of course you had nothing to say in that, and neither did she, being slaves."

"You got no idea, Mist' Stephen, what it's like. More like we're cattle than people. Or maybe like one off'cer said: cross b'tween a man an' a mule, closer to th' mule. If Mass' John'd known, he'd likely have had a say in it, but he didn't. Didn't anybody think 'twas important 'nuff to write him."

"And you didn't make your case with him?"

"No, an' that's my fault. I was missin' that woman bad, first off. But as th' war wore on, it got so I couldn't even remember what she looked like. I kind of got sour-like. It's hard to tell now, how it was, lookin' back. Men dyin', marchin', cold. Woman at home seemed like in 'nother life. You ever feel that way?"

"Did. I know exactly how you felt. Didn't care if I ever saw mine again. It got so when it was finally over, it was about even, one way or the other, if she was still waiting or not. Turned out she wasn't." Stephen poked at the dying fire before them. Another life, indeed.

"You said th' planter's daughter rides over here some. I picked up on that. She pretty?"

"Really pretty. Knows it, too. Friendly, but it's clear, father and girl, that she's off-limits to the likes of me. I'm just hired help."

"I see. They use you. So all right: How'd you explain me, say I do stay on?"

"I'm training you. You help me put up my shop, learn woodworking, maybe smithing, millworking. Good trades."

"I guess. Since I been free, which is a joke, way things turned out, it sticks in my craw to go back to bein' a house servant. Reckon I could learn?"

"I'd say so. Common sense, mostly. Patience. Guess you were grubbing stumps and cutting brush out west, mostly. And plowing."

"Oh, yes. Got to know the hind end of a mule real well. Plowin' roots is mean work, now. Yes, I'd welcome learnin' a craft, I really would."

"Well, let's do it then, Tom. Won't anybody challenge my owning you, and Ned will send that bill of sale, if we do need it to back this up. You help me and I'll take care of you till we can prove you're a free man. And in it all, you'll learn a trade or two. Bargain?"

"Bargain. And Mist' Stephen?"

"Yes, Tom?"

"I do trust you. I do."

~ * ~

Abigail Thomas rode her mare through the woods east of the plantation. The land rose over the flank of Greene Mountain, then fell again at the springs that fed Stephen Davis' little creek. There was a glade there with giant trees, a quiet retreat she'd found some years earlier and claimed for her own. Here she was completely alone, and could dream away hours with nothing but birds and small animals for company.

Now she remained still, her dozing horse tethered, and watched chipmunks scurry along the stream bank, inquisitive, busy, bright-eyed. Overhead a jay scolded, and other tiny birds flitted among the shaded branches. Her thoughts this day were full of Stephen Davis.

A workingman, ex-soldier, of whom Papa would never approve for me. But he's alive, not a dressed-up dandy, arrogantly sure of a family's money and position. He has no position, and doesn't give a hang for that. Not a farmer, nor aspires to be a landowner. Craftsman, and happy to remain one. Not a prospect for a planter's daughter, not at all.

I've watched him from hiding, and sense he is a very private person. He and his Tom can work side by side for hours and never say a word. But he's well-read, can carry his end of a conversation well. Of course I'm not shopping for a husband, but spending time with him is pleasant. Not at all like the prideful sons of the gentry in Charlottesville, or the scions of old money in *Richmond and Williamsburg.*

I'd say Stephen is hiding a lot of pain inside, from the war. Or perhaps a broken heart. Did he ride away from love to join the fight? Possibly. He's not exactly handsome, but so sure of himself, so...positive. He's been in charge, made decisions that mattered greatly. Yes, and had to live with the consequences.

I'm twenty-one, and should be appraising the young men of the region, I suppose. Yes, prepare to place my little feet under a wealthy man's table, bear his children, become a marble mistress of an estate, a pillar of next generation's society.

What a dreary prospect.

Or perhaps the helpmeet of a craftsman with no pretensions? My own woman, equal to my husband, half a team taking on the world on our own terms? An adventure, that would be. Scandalize my parents, no matter that they like Stephen.

I wonder how this new nation will bend society to its purpose. Perhaps the old mores will fade, and such men will rise to positions of power. Governor Jefferson writes that free men, common men, equal to any and all others, can and should guide the nation. Men like Stephen, who won't be content to stay hidden off the creek in his little cabin.

A frontiersman, that's what he is. But not like Papa, who took land and tamed it with his money to mirror the established places east. No, a man with an axe and a rifle and a will...Am I fantasizing, here? And why not? I'm not a child any longer, content to ride and play and fill my days with nonsense. I'll soon need to chart some course, and naturally it'll have a man in it—the right man. Not, or I hope not, that aging Rawlins Butler, who's had his eye on me.

Papa would see him as a suitable match: prosperous widower, planter, with two children for me to raise. Be a dutiful stepmother, trying to treat them as I would my own babies. No, I believe I'll choose my own man, when that time comes.

And no, I doubt that it'll be our rough-hewn Stephen Davis, he of the skilled hands. Still...And the imagined feel of those strong hands on her body sent a most unladylike thrill along Abigail Thomas' frame, culminating in her nether regions.

~ * ~

It was a simple matter to explain to the squire, the smith and the miller that Stephen had acquired a helper in settlement of an old debt from a fellow soldier. And the lie did not bother him at all, given the facts.

"Must've been a substantial debt," the perceptive planter observed.

"No, the boy doesn't know much. I'll have to train him."

"Ah, field hand."

"Not even that: body servant. But I believe he can learn to use his hands."

"Well, Stephen, I knew you were on your way up in the world. Find him a wench, and you'll soon have the makings of a work force." Stephen winced inside at the planter's perception of Tom's worth. *But I shouldn't be surprised at that, now, that's going to be the universal thinking, I'm afraid.*

"I'll have to study on that, sir: see how it goes. I intend to focus on getting my shop set up, first."

"Well, good luck. Oh, Ike needs help tempering scythe blades when you're through here. Yes sir, going to be the master, you are." And the planter went away chuckling.

Stephen had set Tom to hewing timbers for the shop building, while he caught up with work at the plantation, cautioning him to go slow.

"It's just a workshop, Tom but I want it done right. Best to do each piece slow and get it right than hurry it and have to do it over. Now, you put your eye on that chalked line you want to hit, and you'll hit it, most times. Go easy at first. Keep your feet out of the way; bring the broadaxe down just so. Let the weight of it do most of the work."

"Looks easy when you do it."

"Been at it since I was big enough to lift an axe. Try it again."

"Don't wanta do right for me. Just don't wanta...There! That was right, now. Do that again. All right, now..."

"You'll get it. Take a rest when you need to. Gets your back, but you're strong. We'll get this thing up and covered, then when the branch is down, we'll put in the dam and water wheel."

Stephen was gratified to find a respectable number of timbers hewn to size at the end of each day as Tom mastered the chore. Although the finished beams weren't quite up to his standards, he praised the work. Tom kept at it despite blisters and sore muscles, and his skill improved. The upright posts and principal rafters were much neater than the long-lasting chestnut sill beams he'd begun with.

"That's why they're under the floor," Stephen told him. "You won't have to look at your mistakes. And we'll adze them smooth before we put in the floorboards."

Abigail Thomas rode up to the shop site as the men were mortising the sills for the posts. The bents were already pegged together, ready for the raising. The bright wood lay clean in a sea of chips along the branch below where the two forks met. She reined in, dismounted, and Tom took her horse naturally, bowing, as he had doubtless done a thousand times in Caroline County. She smiled, thanked him.

"This would be our man Tom I believe, Mr. Davis."

"It would, Miss Abigail. Welcome to what will become our woodworking establishment. I fear we are not equipped properly to receive guests, but please be seated on a beam. It is my understanding that beams were created before chairs, anyway." He bowed. "And Tom, if you would fetch tea from the house, please." Tom was already on his way.

"Why, thank you. I shall. And you can tell me the mysteries of construction." She settled herself, crossing ankles neatly.

"Pretty straightforward, really. We've scoured the woods for smaller trees we can handle, hewed these beams for the bents you see. We'll pull them up using block and tackle and my horse, then brace them with the knee braces. You've probably seen barn construction, and this is similar. Roof purlins and wall plates will be mortised in, then shakes on top.

"The real fun is in the machinery, which is a lot like the mill. We'll have the lathes and saws, of course, and I'll want a trip-hammer for working iron. I've wanted to do serious gunsmithing, too."

"Isn't the stream too small? I know Papa reasoned you'd never be competition for his mill when he sold the place to you."

"Oh, I'll never need sustained power. I'll draw down for an hour or so at a time, then close the gate again. I've no desire to keep up a big dam or a big mill, believe me."

Tom returned with tea and cakes he'd baked the day before. He'd learned to cook tending his master in the war, and Stephen was surprised at his inventiveness at the Dutch oven and hearth. Now he laid out a pleasant repast along a beam.

"My, what a dainty tea party we have here, Stephen. I do believe Tom here will domesticate you. Why, you'll have no need of a woman's touch at all in your little domain."

"Oh, we manage. My friend Ned grew quite dependent on Tom's ingenuity in creating good things to eat during the war."

"Oh? Your friend was a gentleman, then?"

"Not at all. A notorious scoundrel, in fact. But my best friend."

"And what happened to this...scoundrel?"

"Out wandering the frontier somewhere. Settled his debts and went to seek his fortune."

"You'd think he'd want to settle down, after the war." She didn't want to leave it alone, and he knew he'd have to be careful here.

"Well, war does different things to different men. I'm driven to work, build, put things together. Others to roam, others to dig in. I expect many will want to get into the politics of this new country."

"A different kind of fighting."

"As I understand it, yes."

After Abby had ridden away, Stephen apologized to Tom.

"Didn't like to treat you like a servant there, Tom. I very nearly had you join us, but I knew that'd queer the thing right off."

"Oh, no offense, Mist' Stephen. I know I got to bow an' scrape, same's I always did, till I can be my own man, an' prob'ly even then, too. Like I said, folks won't wanta believe a black man's quite human, even if he's free, for a long time, I'm 'fraid."

"Well, you're right, I fear. What'd you think of Abby?"

"Oh, she's beautiful, all right. But y'didn't need me to tell you that. An' she's either set her cap for you, or teasin' you bad."

"Afraid it's teasin' me. I've done a good job of weaseling my way in here, with her pa and all. Loans me books to read, sold me this place when he didn't intend to. But I don't fool myself. He'll want her to pair off with money, and I'll wager she'll want that, too, like all of 'em."

"I notice you're right gallant around her."

"Caught me at it. No shame."

"You do it good. I been tryin' to work on my language too, all th' years I was with Mass' John."

"You're good, too. Say, do you read? Been meaning to ask you."

"Naw. Never had th' chance to learn. Like to."

"Well, now. Maybe we'll take that job on too, now."

With that, a seed—two seeds—were planted in Stephen's mind, and they began to germinate over the next few weeks into summer, with reading lessons. These proceeded with the somewhat difficult literature from the squire's library. The second seed sprouted full when he received Ned Drake's letter.

I don't know what you're up to, Stephen, you old outlaw, but it sounds like a lot of fun. Herewith find enclosed a duly notarized bill of sale for one Tom Logan, slave (I assume he's a he), issue of one Mattie and Joshua, property of Ned Drake, county of Sussex, State of Virginia. None of this is true of course, but why spoil a good adventure with the facts? And of course you've got yourself a good runaway, or stolen him—or rescued him, more likely—and I say good for you. You always did have that penchant for snatching the underdog from the jaws of disaster. Anyway, good luck.

I'm entangled with a red-headed woman here, who, for some perverted reason, wants my body and my name (my fortune is a joke). She's determined to reform me; a mission I've informed her is futile and foolish. I'll let you know the outcome, now that you have an address. I've always thought it prudent for a man to have a place to be. But just where the hell is Nixville? Never mind: If I ever flee this woman, I'll just go up the rivers, asking for a miller who's working his arse off and saving the world. Come see me.

Ned

Good old Ned, Stephen said to himself gratefully. *If he and that woman get together, their offspring will have a million freckles each. He and I should probably have set off together for the West, really. I know his folks' plantation is about worn out. No, you have to play out the cards the way you get them, I suppose. So stay and see if there's anything behind Miss Abby's smile. And no, I wouldn't have run onto Tom, otherwise. He's a bright one, now. Getting reading right along, in spite of my not being much of a teacher.*

"Reading, Tom, the way I see it, is opening up a whole new world. A man can put all he's learned his whole life down in a book, and you can learn all of it in a few hours or days if you can read. Get your mind around new ideas, ways of doing things you never could know otherwise. I guess it's really the difference, when you get down to it, between a man's just…surviving, like the rest of the animals, and breaking through to really understanding what's actually going on in the world. At least as far as we know the world. Some things nobody's figured out yet, and probably won't for a long time. If ever. I imagine God'll keep a lot to Himself."

"Prob'ly. But I'm havin' trouble makin' out words now, let alone ideas."

"And you will, for a while. But keep at it like you've been doing. I'd say by the end of the year you'll be reading anything you want. They start children on easy material, and I don't have anything easy here. But I'm going into the village soon, so I'll see what's there.

Six

Far to the east, the horseman took the heavy box from the man whose name he still didn't know, cradled it on his saddle and rode west. The box was heavier than last time, he noted; pickings had been good. The box was locked, and the horseman knew better than to try to open it. If any of the counted gold should be missing, they'd know where to come looking.

Granted, he'd considered more than once, the possibility of heading West with one of these shipments, to disappear into Kentucky or even further. But the men he worked for would never stop searching, he knew; he'd never dare rest.

Besides, he was paid well enough. A simple courier job once every few months. Stops at taverns rendered safe with regular payments on the way west and south from New York and Philadelphia, where he and his employers were known and protected. And he didn't have to get his hands into the real work: the dangerous stuff, the mercantile stealing, the petty and not-so-petty extortion, the outright robbery…

Virginia was a long ride, but his horse, a big bay, was superb. The two pistols he carried were also of fine workmanship. After the initial run, back before the war, his nerves had settled, and the risk had become routine.

Days later he would ride down the long double row of boxwoods to the plantation house in Caroline County, simply deliver the box, and be paid.

It was a good life.

~ * ~

Stephen rode the fifteen miles to Charlottesville on market day for a multiple purpose. He was able to find a newspaper from Richmond, first of all, only a week old, and a discarded political pamphlet. These were not ideal, but they would have to do as reading material for his friend. There was no bookshop. At the one lawyer's office, he found, he produced his bill of sale for Tom Logan.

"I'd like to free this man," he told George Henley, Esquire.

"That's unusual. May I ask why?"

"You may. He was of great service to both his former owner and me in the war. Mr. Drake settled a debt with me with the man, and now I want to grant him his freedom. I'll continue to employ him, see that he's not a burden to the community."

"I see. Well, that's certainly your right, as legal owner. I should warn you, though, sir, that there have been unscrupulous thefts of freed blacks. But you seem aware of what you're doing. And if the papers of manumission are duly recorded, there will be proof of his status. I must draw up the papers specifically, as this is a rare request."

"How soon can this be done?"

"Oh, by midweek. Where are you located, Mr...ah, Davis?"

"Beyond Nixville five miles. I'll come back Wednesday if that's convenient. Shall I leave the fee in advance?"

"That won't be necessary. You know, my mentor, Governor Jefferson, has wanted to free the slaves for many years, Mr. Davis. I'm not sure it is wise, just yet, and neither is the majority of the populace. But on his behalf, I commend you on your principle."

Outside again, Stephen counted his money. He'd made and sold several fine hunting knives over the last of the winter, and estimated he could buy a change of clothes for himself and Tom. He found a shop, the only one selling clothing, and fingered trousers and shirts. Tom was not as tall as he, but heavier. They'd fashioned moccasins, and at any rate, boots, of which there were none available here in this village anyway, would be too expensive.

He left with his purchases, spun and woven cotton shirts and trousers for them both, needles and thread, and some brown cloth for patching their old clothes. Lately they'd begun to look like scarecrows.

As he rode, he felt a rising satisfaction at what he'd just accomplished, setting Tom free. By damn, it was ridiculously easy! And even if that Hayes did show up by some miracle, he couldn't prove Tom had ever been his. It was ironic, but most whites said they couldn't tell one black man from another, he'd observed.

It had occurred to him that Tom might have been lying to him about the whole thing, but that just hadn't stood to reason, these weeks. A slave wouldn't risk everything, traveling through hostile country to try to get to people who could prove who he was if he wasn't...No, t'wouldn't make sense any other way.

And so he'd ride back next week on some pretense, get the papers, and surprise Tom with his freedom.

It was late afternoon when he rode up the trail past the shop, roofed now, to note several large stones Tom had dragged and tumbled down for the dam. Soon they'd set them, and build the wheel. They'd also scouted the woods for dead and seasoned walnut, maple, cherry, oak, for furniture and gunstock material, and would cut more to lay up in the heat of the shop loft to dry for their projects.

The sight of smoke curling from his chimney gave Stephen a welcoming glow, and his dog Rafe ran to meet him. Good, coming home to his own place like this. Good too, having a friend to share it with.

Tom had fried rabbit and biscuits, and a blackberry cobbler made, and Stephen felt his mouth watering.

"Got us some clothes, m'friend. Hope they fit." And he produced the fruits of his visit to the village.

"Well, lookit that. My shirt's 'bout more hole than shirt, at that. I sure thankee, Mist' Stephen. An' lookit you! Why, you be ready to go courtin', 'fore long."

"Hardly. Old Ike's been after me, though. Says there's a tall girl over on Clinch River he says I should pair up with. I want to see how Miss Abby turns out first, though. I have a feeling she'd buck her pa if I could make a go of this woodworking thing, get set up properly. Crazy notion, probably." He eyed Tom, as if seeking an opinion, but maybe fearing one, too.

"I dunno, Mist' Stephen. Money, it goes to money, way I've always seen it, an' you know that. 'Course there's th' Black Jack Davies of this world stealin' women's hearts, but I doubt those stories end happy."

"I'd wager you're right, there. Well, a pretty woman'll make a fool of many a man, I've heard it said, and I guess I'm no sharper'n the next one there."

But the fact was, Stephen had been missing a woman in his life. Perhaps—no, certainly—he'd taken Betsy Simmons for granted, all those years. Lost her anyway, so forget that.

But a man wasn't meant to go through life alone, like half a pair of scissors, as Ben Franklin used to say. Let's see, Ike said there was to be a dance soon, over on the Norton place, on the Lynch river. Just maybe I ought to go, see some people. Couldn't hurt.

He asked the old man about it Monday, while they were welding shafting. It was a three-man job, and Ike's grandson Web helped, swinging the two-heated, scarfed shaft-ends from their overhead chains onto the anvil, holding them with tongs while Ike and Stephen rained precise hammer blows on the white-hot joint. Sparks flew.

"Oh, it'll be a shin-scraper, Stephen, won't it, Web? Ever'body'll be thar. Come on. Bring that boy Tom ''long. Folks bring thar fiel' han's, shore do." He inspected the weld. "That's purty, now...An', say, that long, tall Annie'll shore be thar, one I been tellin' you ''bout. I like that gal, some. Don't you, Web? Don't you reckon Stephen'll like Annie?" The old man cracked a whiskered grin.

"Oh, Annie's all right, Stephen. Boys look past her, ''count of she's so tall, and educated. Part Indian, I b'lieve, ain't she, Gran'pa? I like ''em short ''n sweet, myself. Little Lucy Green's my gal. No bigger'n a minnit, but sweeter'n maple sugar. Whooee!" And the boy danced a quick jig.

"Lord, boy, you thar already. Let's us git this job done first. Ain't till Saturday night. You comin', Stephen?"

"I might, Ike. Been considering it, some. I just might. Don't suppose the squire's family will be there?"

"Abby, you mean. Naw, I hear there's a big to-do down to Charlottesville that day, reckon they'll be off to. Politicians an' such. They stay over an' go to th' ''Piscopal church there now'n then too, so I don't look fer ''em back, few days."

"Oh. Well, we common folks can kick up our heels, then. You much for church-going, Ike?"

"Wife is. Ain't one close, though. She's Presbyterian, an' been missin' it. You?"

"Not much. My folks Presbyterians too, down in Goochland. Guess Charlottesville's the closest. Seems like the gentry's all Episcopal, and the poor folks who have any religion side with the Scots."

"Guess so. They's some travelin' preachers comes through now'n then ever'body goes to hear, git baptized, married, but we're mostly left to sin on our own."

Tom greeted the plan to attend the dance with some reserve, but soon warmed to the idea. After all, he was safe here with his friend and protector, and yes, he could do with some socializing, too. Even before Saturday both men could talk of little else.

"Be some fine black girls there, Ike tells me, Tom. The squire lets his people go, with the overseer and his wife. Be something now, if you met some sweet thing from right around here, wouldn't it?"

"You teasin' now. What if you like that long, tall Annie I been hearin' ''bout? Or maybe Web's sweet Lucy take a fancy to you, latch onto you, follow you home. Be in trouble then, you know it." The two had developed an easy, joking manner with each other, like any two good friends, in the short months they'd been working and living side by side.

That Wednesday Stephen had ridden away again, and returned in the afternoon with the crucial manumission papers, duly recorded in the Albemarle County courthouse. He presented them to Tom without a word, and watched as his friend slowly made out the words.

"Oh. Does this say...Does this say what I think it says? Does...Did you...?"

"I did. You're a free man, Tom. Again. You have these papers to prove it, and they're recorded in the courthouse, if anything should ever happen to this set. Congratulations." He offered his hand.

Tom took it in both his, having laid the precious papers on the table.

"Oh, thank you, Mist' Stephen. Thank you..." and he gave his friend an impulsive bear-hug.

Now, the two men rode Stephen's and a borrowed horse up and over Greene Mountain, past a hastily-emptied cabin that housed the Morris family, and over another steep rise down to the Norton farm on Lynch River. It was only late afternoon, but they could hear fiddle music already drifting while still high up the ridge. Laughter floated up, and soon they could see and smell woodsmoke and barbecue, then wagons and horses came into view, and people in colorful clothes.

Stephen knew the Thomas hands would travel downcreek in wagons to the road that ran north some distance east of his place, up to the crossroads near here. They'd likely be along later, since the squire worked his people late. He knew of a handful of settlers on up this river and from creek valleys nearby, but had met few of them. *I've been a real homebody so far, or maybe even a hermit. Well, see what they're like. Folks about the same all over, from what I've seen. Some meaner than others.*

He could see a separate barbecue area for the blacks, with some of them already gathered. The squire had sent Ike early with a pig to roast for his people, so it'd be ready. Not an unkind master, Stephen reflected, just not about to see any equality there. He glanced at Tom, riding alongside him. He might be equal back on the place, but here couldn't be, among these folks. *Well. That'll take time, is all.*

Ike and young Web hailed them and took them around to meet some of the neighbors, leaving Tom then with the other blacks. Wagons were driving up, and riders arriving. The fiddlers were seated on wooden chairs under a walnut tree, and women were piling food on a long table made of sawhorses and planks. Blackberry and elderberry wine were in crockery jugs, and tea cooled in covered casks in a spring, the head of a small stream that ran down to the river. Pies were everywhere here, and Stephen remembered being almost constantly hungry in the Continental Army. Seemed like in another life.

Web introduced him to a tiny girl of about fifteen who was his Lucy Green. She was indeed a sunny little thing, resembling nothing as much as a daisy, he thought. Lucy was the kind of girl who'd mature early and look young all her life.

Ike steered him toward new arrivals, among whom was a tall girl he knew must be the oft-spoken-of Annie. She was dark, with two braids hanging, and a sunbonnet framing a face that was neither pretty nor plain. Till she smiled. Then she was very pretty, he saw. Really pretty. But Lordy, she was tall. Nearly as tall as he was.

"This here's th' Compton family, Stephen. Isaac, Stephen's th' millwright been workin' with me. Miss Sadie; Miss Annie, th' tall one thar; Bobby, ain't got his growth yit; Becky, an' little Sam. Stephen's got hisself a little place this side of th' squire's, up th' little branch, over Greene from Morris' cabin."

Stephen bowed to the women, shook Isaac's hand, Bobby's and young Sam's.

"Your place close, Mr. Compton?"

"Up th' river a piece. Branch comes in, spreads out flat. Couple hundred acres." The man towered. It was easy to see where Annie got her height. Isaac was red from the sun; his wife dark with Indian blood. "You farmin' enny?"

"Not really. My place is too hilly. Getting set up for working wood. Furniture, gunstocks and the like. Damming the branch for a little power."

"Don't say. Don't reckon I c'd do that; I'm a farmer. Annie here, she's m'best hand. Bobby comin' on. Single man, aint'cha?"

"I am. Got out of the army after Yorktown. Brother-in-law took over the family mill in Goochland, so I calculated to move on. Liked it here. Squire Thomas sold me a few acres."

"Surprised. Usually buys land."

"Rough piece, but all I'll need for what I want to do."

Stephen watched Annie helping her mother with food and drink. He'd noticed that her speech was not that of her father, but bespoke of education. He wondered at that. The girl moved with an easy grace that reminded him of some wild thing. He could picture her slipping through the forest with a rifle, or a strung bow. Most tall girls he'd known were awkward, tried to look smaller; she took her height matter-of-factly, unapologetically using it as an asset. She'd be a real worker on the farm, he knew.

Just then a number of wagons drove up with the Thomas slaves, accompanied by the overseer Ed Byers, and his sunbonneted wife. And with them, on her lively mare, was Abigail Thomas. A ripple of comment went through the crowd of country people as the striking young woman in her divided suede skirt rode among them, swung off her horse, and gave the reins, laughing, to young Web Collins. The low sun caught her free auburn hair as she shook it back, and Stephen knew he had never seen-—would never see—a woman more beautiful. From that moment on, he had eyes for no other girl at the dance.

Just like her, he reflected, to buck her father about the politicians and gentry at the county seat, to come out where the real fun is. Well, Miss Abby Thomas, I'm going to dance your pretty feet off you this night, or there's no justice at all.

He looked guardedly around, gauging the competition, as it were, as he moved forward. There were single men, to be sure: farmers' sons, mostly young, and two men obviously veterans like himself, one of whom leaned on a cane. Then there was an older man, say forty, who'd ridden up on a spirited sorrel. This man had polished boots and neat clothes and carried a riding crop easily. Out of place here. He alone was not casting his eyes about at the others. His eyes were fixed on Abby, but he wasn't moving.

Stephen was.

"Miss Abigail," he bowed low, took her hand. He was doubly glad he'd bought the new clothes, waxed the worn boots. He felt positively dashing in this company. She dropped a nice curtsy.

"Why, Mr. Davis, how nice to see you out of your den, at last. I do hope you've brought poor Tom, too. I shouldn't want to think of you as a cruel master."

"Oh, Tom's here. And I'll tell him of your kind concern." Just then the fiddles started, and at the same time he caught the smart planter, for that's what he appeared to be, starting toward them. "Could I have the pleasure of the first dance?"

"Why, how gallant: the recluse himself. I'm honored." And they were off, to a tune that seemed a mixture of pieces Stephen had known all his life but couldn't identify. No matter, Abby knew them, or her feet did.

All the dances he'd ever been to were structured: reels, sets, where numbered groups went through measured paces. This was a loose free-for-all of couples doing whatever they wanted, to a driving beat the fiddlers seemed to be making up as they went, with the help of a white-whiskered man thumping an upturned tub. All right then, he could improvise. He'd seen the slaves do their buck-and-wing dancing down on the big places on the James River. He threw in some of that, and Abby followed suit. Web and Lucy, dancing nearby, clapped their hands.

"Whooee!" Ike called, from the sidelines. Abby laughed out, flounced her skirt. This was fun.

As the music finally slowed, Stephen looked down the meadow toward the slaves. Tom was dancing with a coal black girl in a red headband from the Thomas place. Good for Tom.

"Say, I never danced like that before," he almost panted to Abby.

"That's just the warm-up. Now will come the reels and regular dancing." A quick look around. "And, Stephen, I'll want you to rescue me after a bit, if you will..."

"Rescue you?"

"Yes. The older man? Smooth-looking? That's Rawlins Butler. Widower. Thinks he ought to own me. If you could just keep him from monopolizing me tonight, I'd be grateful. I'll introduce you. He's a big planter, and just a little too conceited."

"You don't want me to call him out, do you?"

"Oh, heavens, no! Are you serious? Just...Oh, now what have I done? Here he comes. Forget I said anything, please." She stepped forward, outwardly at least, in control.

Now, this is a helluva thing. Well, if she can be cool, I can be, too.

"Mr. Rawlins Butler, how nice to see you. I'd like you to meet Mr. Stephen Davis. Mr. Davis has a business relationship with my father. Stephen, Mr. Butler's plantation is on Swift Run, a few miles east and north of here."

"A pleasure, Mr. Butler. You obviously raise fine horses. Do you grow wheat?" The man's grip was firm.

"That, and hemp. Tobacco, of course. Some cotton, in the bottoms. A farmer, Mr. Davis?" He was looking Stephen over: the competition.

"Craftsman, sir. Furniture maker, millwright." Then, casually, without asking, Stephen reached, poured glasses of blackberry wine for himself and Abby, and handed her one. It was meant to be a proprietary gesture, and was.

"Ah, then you won't be a shooter. Shame, with all the game here." What was the man insinuating?

"Actually, I am. Quite a lot of practice with red-coated targets, for a good five years."

"Oh, there's dear old Ike," Abby intervened. "I've promised him. Excuse me please, both of you," and Abby was off to whirl the blacksmith into the dance.

Stephen bowed.

"Mr. Butler." He turned and drifted away. So this was to be his rival, then. Probably had the father's blessing, too. Well. *But that about rescuing her…* Well, he couldn't keep the man from dancing with her…*Hmm. Good wine.* Oh, there was Annie Compton, by herself.

"Miss Compton, would you dance the next one with me? I'd be most honored." The music was ending.

Without a word, she allowed him to take her hand and lead her to their places in a set. The hand was hard, firm. She didn't smile, until he did a double step and shook his shoulders as they came together, then her face opened the way it had when Ike had introduced them. Her teeth flashed even and white in that dark skin, the eyes so nearly level with his. At the sashay, he felt her fluid body like coiled steel against his. He found himself looking forward to the next pass. Strong woman.

Afterwards, he appropriated some ham and potato salad and pie that Tom had made, and sat with his back to a tree where he could watch both the white dancers and the black. Abner Cocke and his pregnant young wife Nell joined him soon. Moths fluttered around the candle lanterns and fireflies winked down the meadow, where children ran to catch them.

"Good party," Abner observed.

"It is. How you getting along, Miss Nell?"

"Oh, all right. Got ''nother two months. Wisht I could be dancin, but I daren't. Ab, you go on, now. Ain't nobody astin' Annie, since Stephen."

"I'm too short fer Annie, Nellie."

"Oh, go on. Don't matter. Don't no girl like to be left."

"Y'don't mind?"

"'Course I don't. Me'n Stephen'll talk. G'on, now."

Abner left, and he and the tall Annie waved to the two still eating, and joined the dance. She was a full head taller, but it was obvious both loved to dance. Still not smiling, she put a hand palm down on Abner's head and pushed him down even further, and everyone howled. Nell clapped in glee.

"She's a dandy, Stephen. Y'oughta latch onto that'n, now."

"That's what everybody tells me. I'd say Isaac depends on her a lot. Big gap between her and Bobby, seems like."

"Yes, they lost two in between. She's twenty, I b'lieve. Serious-turned. Smiled more tonight than I ever seen her. But a thoughtful one, that. Reads a lot."

"Does she? Where'd she learn? No school close."

"No. Her ma was raised by some folks in Charlottesville: preacher an' his wife took her in, taught her. She taught Annie, an' the girl took to it serious. Talks nice, like you. Preacher's old now, but wants to start a church out here. Sends books."

"Well, now. I've been borrowing books from the squire, but it's mostly dry stuff. Suppose I could work something out?"

"Oh, I'm shore. I've heered Annie say she might start up a school herself, someday. She figgers she'll need a way to make herself a livin', seein's most fellers shies away f'm her, bein' so serious, tall an' all."

"Looks to be maybe six feet, all right."

"Anyways six."

Stephen saw Tom with yet another partner, caught his eye and waved. Sweat stood on his friend's brow. He waved back. And Abby had, it seemed, danced with every available man so far. Butler had managed two dances, but no more. No chance of his monopolizing her, then.

"Yer stuck on that Abby Thomas, ain'tcha, Stephen?" Nell's voice jerked him back to his place against the tree.

"Oh. Well, I don't know rightly, Nell. She's friendly, but seems she's that with everybody. Now, I've been around enough to know a man'll make allowances for a girl who's prettier than most, when she doesn't deserve it. Right now, I'd say I don't know if she'd have a man like me, or just be teasing me."

"She's a tease, Stephen. Believe me."

"You're probably right. Pretty spoiled, too."

"She's that, too. But she ain't mean, an' that's what's hard to figger. Here she coulda went to town with her ma'n pa, to that social thing, an' she comes here with us reg'lar folks. Now, is that who she really is, or is she jis' puttin' on, an' actin' out agin' her pa? She's a hard one to figger. Oh, look, Ab's dancin' with little Lucy. She's a little doll, ain't she? Web'll marry that'n, now."

"Ought to let her grow some. Web's a good boy." He stood. "I see Butler's back with Abby. Know anything about him?"

"Only he's got a big place he wants her on. Wife died with their least'un five years back or so. Got two others ''bout eight an' ten. S'prised to see Butler here, only he prob'ly figgered Abby to've showed. Jis' like her to do it." Nell eyed him. "Money draws to money, Stephen. I'd lay you that's where Abby'll end up."

"Could be. I know I'm just hired help, Nell. I could buy me a couple thousand acres, big house, still be hired help. Some things don't change."

She eyed him, pursing her lips. Then she let her gaze shift to the dancing Rawlins Butler, the other men at the gathered here.

"No, Stephen Davis. You ain't nobody's hired help."

Seven

Stephen and Tom rode back by the road after the dance, partly fearing they'd lose their way in the woods over the two ridges directly to their place. They passed wagons full of sleepy slaves. Abby had accepted the Nortons' invitation to stay over, to Stephen's disappointment. He'd have liked the ride with her. Well, he'd danced with her three more times, anyway.

"So, Tom, you have fun?"

"Did. Been holed up like a ''possum too long. You?"

"Sure did. You know, we didn't talk about whether to tell folks you're a free man or not, so I didn't. Did you?"

"No. I figured it'd be simpler just to let things lie, for now. Get a feel for how folks'll take it. They may wanta ride me outta th' country on a rail, or string me up, for all I know. Anyway, I need a place to be first, and that trade, way to make a livin'."

"I guess so. Shame though, not to make it known. You been free twice and nobody's ready for that."

"Time enough." He turned an idea around in his mind for several minutes as they rode homeward. "There's places up North I could go, if I could get there. I could get set up, after I learn. No rush..." He let the thought die away and several hoofbeats pass as they made their way homeward. "Was a good time, tonight. Some of those gals can sure dance." He stifled a yawn.

"Can. You see that tall woman I danced with? Moved like a cannonball. And Miss Abby could flatten the grass, too."

"Sure could. Tall one had her eye on you all night."

"Nah, she didn't. No way. I'd have seen her."

"Man, you sure blind 'bout women, for a smart white man. Got that Miss Abby all in your eyes." He chuckled, gave his friend an affectionate push to the shoulder.

"Well, I'll have to own to that, all right. She's surely an eyeful, turns heads wherever she goes, I'll wager. Met my rival, though. The slick planter on the sorrel. Got money. I hear he's got his sights set on her."

"Where there's honey, there's bound to be a bee or two. You knew that. I ''spect she'll prance around a while longer, play independent, then settle down, fit in with the likes of him. 'Bout all of ''em do."

"I suppose so. Man can fancy all he wants. Pa always said too pretty a woman was a road to heartbreak, and I guess he was right. See anything you liked tonight?"

"Liked 'em all. But practically, I'd hafta be in a place to buy a gal free, y'know. Wouldn't work very well, be married to a slave, not have a say in our lives at all. And that'd be a real tall order, just now."

"Oh yes, that. Boy, life gets complicated, doesn't it?"

"Does. But thinkin' on it, it sure looks a lot better to me now than it did six months ago."

~ * ~

The four men gathered in the study of the plantation house in Caroline County. Their host, a middle-aged man of obvious means, instructed his young wife that they were to be left strictly alone: business.

He was a planter, lately of a different profession, and his guests were of varied backgrounds. One was a lawyer, who served as prosecutor in some of the less-settled counties. Another was also a planter, established earlier in Greene County, which had been carved from larger adjoining ones. The fourth defied occupational description: tall, nervous, exhibiting a short temper occasionally. He was one of the breed of westward-moving men who were establishing holdings beyond the mountains, the barriers the British had sought to contain and control their tax-paying colonists before the war liberated them.

These meetings were held two or three times a year for the purpose of deciding where certain monies they held in common would be invested. Each man had profited personally from this income in the past, and lately their eyes had been turned toward other, long-term uses for it.

They were well aware that too much expansion here near their homes, the buying of other plantations, property, showy lifestyles, would arouse questions. What they sought were investments beyond the prying eyes of the authorities, such as they were. And they were quite interested in the latest proposals of the "explorer," who'd sold out his holdings in the Tidewater prior to scouting out the territories west.

The land was mountainous, he explained, but the river valleys were fertile, requiring only clearing and fencing to take advantage of the virgin soil, which was deep and rich. The new government was anxious to settle these wilderness areas, to secure them against future threat from any of the new nation's enemies, be they France again, England again, Spain, or some other country eager for expansion. And with enough capital, these new plantations could be set up quickly, with purchases of slaves and equipment, as he'd already done. Then from their produce, marketed overland or down the rivers, the investors would reap profits early and often. Without the interference of meddlesome legal types.

In all, the prospects were intriguing, more so since this man was already expanding his own extensive place in that same territory and could attest to his early success. The men voted to authorize him to proceed on their behalf.

~ * ~

By fall Stephen and Tom had constructed the dam, built of granite blocks dragged from further back in the woods and set closely together, with a coating of clay between and on the upstream side. The wheel was set and working, its shaft set on greased hardwood bearing blocks on stone piers. The two men had built a lathe and a whipsaw. Not a big one like the squire's—they hadn't the power for that. And Stephen had ridden over to the Shenandoah Valley to buy the blade, a worn one, true, but one a mill there had outgrown. Again his sale of hunting knives had provided cash, and he had orders for scissors, razors, and more knives from the small forge he'd built. He'd taught Tom the basics of smithing, moving on from simple nails and chain, and the man was on the way to becoming a competent mechanic.

Iron was always in short supply, but Stephen traded for it with whatever he could. His millwheel shaft was wooden, with just short lengths of iron set into each end, running in the hardwood blocks, lubricated with frequent applications of pork rind. A millwright used as much wood as he could, hoarding the little iron available. Stephen often hammer-welded up worn horseshoe halves and pieces of old iron wagon tire for reusable metal. He case-hardened steel for his knives and other edge tools.

Gradually, that stock of tools grew. Drawknives, adzes, chisels, slicks, planes, saws, squares, rasps—they shaped them, hardened them, oiled them, put them in place on pegs on the wall. And the big grindstone, patiently cut from sandstone from out past the Valley to the west, sat balanced on its shaft, smoothed and ready.

"That was simple, compared to dressing a granite millstone, Tom. You might want to learn that too, but let's wait on that." He'd managed some extra money that way also, traveling to other nearby mills on the Rivanna River, Swift Run and the Moorman's, to dress stones. So much so that he could possibly have this place paid for by spring, at this rate.

It was a good prospect.

They built a pair of walnut tables first, of standing dead and seasoned wood Stephen had split out and planed the previous winter and kept in his loft. He shaped the edges with the shaping plane he'd made, sanded them with sand and leather, worked the surfaces to a velvet.

"Now we wax ''em, Tom. Rub in that beeswax you got." Tom had the peculiar gift of charming bees, and had robbed wild bee trees without getting stung, supplying them with quantities of honey and wax. This too, they'd traded for leather and iron. Now they rubbed the wax on the smooth wood till it gleamed. "Top and bottom, Tom, or it'll warp. Moisture just from the air can get in, otherwise. Ever notice how a table top'll warp up? Wood'll swell from under, just from whatever's in the air, unless you seal it out. So every time you wax the top, you should wax the underside, too."

"Never knew that. So that's why?"

"This wood, now. It'll move some, forever. Just not much. Good and dry already. But put it next to the fire, it'll warp. All right, let's make something out of that cherry. Hard stuff, but I like cherry. Gets redder the older it is."

They began with a simple writing desk. Then a rocking chair. By November, the anniversary of Stephen's coming to this place, the workshop held several pieces, each precisely made, gleaming, some hanging from overhead beams. The place smelled pleasantly of wax, wood, glue, hickory nut and walnut oil. Looking back, he marveled a little at how much he—they—had accomplished, and was thankful for his new partner.

The squire visited the shop one late autumn day, accompanied by Rawlins Butler and Abby, carrying fine rifles. Tom tied their horses.

"Ah, Stephen, I see you've been busy. Well, fine work, this. You've met Mr. Butler, I believe."

"I have. Welcome, sir, and thanks. Mr. Butler, Miss Thomas." A small bow. "We're just getting started, actually. Had to build everything, of course, and train my man here."

"I see. Mr. Butler's visiting for a few days. Fine hunting this season, and Abby's joined us. Well, look at the grain in this piece, Abby. Is this maple, Stephen?"

"Birdseye maple, Mr. Thomas. Lightning-struck tree from up the branch. All this wood is from dead trees, seasoned. We're drying green wood in the loft for future use."

"Ah. And look here, a portable writing desk. Military design?"

"Yes. Patterned after one General Morgan had that I admired."

"Well, now. You know he's one of my heroes, Rawlins. I'll just have to have that. Cherry, isn't it?"

"It is. It hinges this way, for travel. Paper here. Ink, quills here."

"It's so clever, Papa! It takes hardly any room."

Butler was eyeing furniture, another rocking chair in particular.

"You've a good hand, Davis. Where'd you learn?"

"On my own, sir. Before the war. My father was a miller and gunsmith, but I always liked wood. May I ask who made your rifle?"

"Oh, a smith up in Lancaster, Pennsylvania. Fine craftsmen there. I see yours, there. Tiger maple. Long barrel. Your father made it?"

"All but the stock. I made that. Carried it through the war. I like the long barrel for accuracy. You mentioned shooting when we met last summer. I'd say you were a marksman."

"Oh, Rawlins is the best around," Thomas laughed.

"Really? I'd like to see you shoot, sir."

"Would you?" The man's eyes brightened. "I think we could arrange that. Would you care to...shoot against me, perhaps?" He asked it coolly, but his eyes held the challenge. The man was obviously used to winning.

"I'd like that, I think. I've been too long inside." He glanced out. It was a clear morning, no wind. "What would be your pleasure...fixed target, flying target? What distance?"

"Well, now. Both, shall we? Say, two hundred yards to start, stationary, three shots each? Then a thrown—what do you call these big chips from hewing?"

"Juggles."

"Yes, juggles. A flung juggle at, say a hundred feet? Neutral hand?"

"Sounds fair. Shall we make it interesting?"

"You mean a wager? If you like. I rather fancy that walnut rocking chair there. What's its price?"

"Eight pounds. My furniture's not cheap."

"I should say not. Well, eight pounds it is. Your hayfield, Hezekiah?"

"Done. I'll have to put another eight on Rawlins, against the writing desk, Stephen. I've seen him shoot."

"I'll take it. Tom, bring along a basket of those juggles, will you?"

"Then let's be off," the squire said. "What sport!"

"Just a moment, Papa," his daughter put in, "I think I'd like to put five pounds on Mr. Davis. I think my allowance will stand it."

"You would?"

"What do you know that we don't?" Butler asked.

"Nothing. It just seems he's being ganged up on."

"Well, I never..." her father threw up his hands. "You've seen Rawlins shoot..."

"Call it a woman's intuition, Papa," she said sweetly.

Stephen grinned.

What Butler thought he knew was that Stephen had a worn rifle he'd fired all through the war, and no matter how good a shot he was, he'd never match the planter's fine piece. What he didn't know was that Stephen and his father had re-bored and re-rifled the gun the previous fall to a larger caliber.

And he also didn't know that the special, demanding skill Stephen had honed in the war with England was sharpshooting: taking out the British officers directing the charges, the cannoneers loading the deadly grapeshot, the snipers trying to hit their own Patriot officers. Stephen Davis had a number of abilities, but the one that had carried him unscathed through five years of war was his deadly accuracy, his unerring oneness with his rifle.

They reached the long creekside field. The squire summoned one of a distant woodcutting crew and they stepped off two hundred yards from a sharp rise of ground behind the target area. They set up one of the larger juggles, which was the slab of wood a broadaxe splits off when hewing a log into a beam. This one was of tulip poplar, about a foot square, and still light in color. The squire's field hand stood well back, and Butler took his stance. He knew what he was doing, standing sideways, right elbow high, knees slightly bent.

He fired. The smoke rolled in a plume and the dense wood jostled, but did not split. He reloaded deliberately, steadied, fired again. Then again. The field hand ran, fetched the target. It had a pattern of three holes not four inches apart, around the center of the wood. The squire beamed. Abby showed no emotion.

"Fine shooting, sir," Stephen acknowledged. "If that'd been a buck, there'd be venison on the table."

He looked to his prime. Steadied. Elbow high, the long rifle rock-like, as it had been a thousand times before. More than a thousand times.

Fire. Reload. Fire. Fire.

The pattern: three balls within an inch of each other. Center. A look of disbelief on Butler's face, the squire's. Abby quietly triumphant. Stephen cool. Tom with a small smile.

"That was...that was fine, sir," Butler managed.

"And now the moving target?"

"If you say so. And...yes, since I shot first, you, by all means." Butler gestured him ahead.

Stephen selected three smaller chips, about six inches square, paced off a hundred feet, gave them to the field hand.

"Throw them high. They can spin, but keep ''em flat to us, all right? Don't let them turn edgeways."

A flintlock had a time lapse every shooter learned to calculate for a moving target, leading it and keeping it sighted for slight variations in the powder burn.

Another consideration was the chip itself: no matter how it was thrown, it could turn. Most shooters waited for it to peak, slowing at that point and making an easier target. But the further it went, the higher the chance it would turn and present a thin, edge-on surface. Few shooters tried rifle-shooting thrown targets; most used shotguns for that reason.

The mental and muscular calculations were lightning-fast, at a gut level, and only a few riflemen had them. That Stephen Davis was still alive was proof he had them.

His heart rate was down, his hands steady. The first chip shattered on the way up. The second, near the peak. The third halfway up.

Butler was actually sweating. He waited too long, and the first chip peaked, started down, and turned. Miss. He got the second at the peak, the third at the peak.

"Your match, sir," he bowed stiffly. Abby flashed a broad smile.

"Mr. Butler," Stephen said quietly, "You are as fine a shot as I have ever competed against."

"Not fine enough. Mr. Thomas will convey my cheque to you in payment of my debt, sir. My pride is stung: I seldom lose, but I count it no dishonor, in this case. My compliments. Good day, sir." He turned stiffly away.

"By God, Stephen, what shooting! Hold up, Rawlins, I'm coming. I'll be by tomorrow, Stephen, to settle up. Still want that desk. Come along, Abby. Woman's intuition, eh?"

On the way back to the shop, Tom eyed his friend.

"I got it figured you just made twenty-four pounds, time th' squire buys that writin' desk. An' Miss Abby, she gets five from her pa. Butler don't get squat. Now, won't that about pay this place off?"

"Damn right it will. You and I'll both be free, man!" They pounded each other on the back.

Then they walked in silence for a while, Tom still searching his friend's face.

"But it cost you, learnin' to shoot like that. I've heard you, in th' night: bad dreams. You still see those men you killed, don't you?"

"Every one of ''em, Tom. Every last, bleeding one of them."

~ * ~

It was clear that Rawlins Butler had launched a serious suit for Abigail Thomas. And just because Stephen had bested him in a shooting match didn't alter the planter's standing with her father, and probably not with her either, when it came to marriage. Still, no one seemed to be in a hurry, there.

But Stephen had a more immediate problem: how to market his creations. He couldn't exactly borrow a wagon and fill it with furniture, to drive it to Charlottesville market day and hawk it beside the other vendors. He was learning what fine craftsmen the world over must learn: that much of their effort had to go into getting their work sold, at least at first. Demand would come only later, after word got around.

By midwinter, friends of the squire's, after admiring the little writing desk, had bought a table, two chairs and a china cabinet, but that was all. Butler, stung by his defeat, had not bought the rocking chair, nor recommended Stephen's work to his planter acquaintances. And few were apt to find their way to the little shop in the woods unless urged.

The knives, tools and hardware were another matter, however. Every settler needed good steel, and every few days there would come a request for chisels, axes, saws. Few smiths could forge a good handsaw, and Stephen's were soon coveted. This was advanced smithing, and time-consuming, but he was up to the challenge.

The procedure involved case-hardening a rod of iron, working it into a tapered shaft, then hammering it flat with the aid of the elongated peen face of a hammer, which stretched the metal wider. Then he used a set tool appropriately called a flatter, to thin and smooth it. Stephen took pride in working the saw blank to the degree that a minimum of grinding and sanding was necessary for a smooth surface.

Then the teeth were measured and filed in. Then the setting, which involved bending every second tooth slightly outward one way, and those between, the other. The saw was then hardened and tempered, and sharpened. Then a handle of fine wood was affixed, the crowning touch. He charged a high price for his saws from the beginning, because they were fine saws, and while he sold few, no one seemed to complain. Quite the contrary: they bragged on them.

"Tom," he observed, "I'm no businessman, but I see that if you charge low, folks think less of your work, and less of you. Don't sell anything that's not the best, and get a high price. If they want cheap, they can go someplace else. I do believe it's that simple. Pa makes his rifles that way. Doesn't sell many, but then, he doesn't have to."

"Lesson in economics: start at th' top or you'll never get there?"

"Why not? The only thing we don't have is money, Tom, and we'll have that, in time." He put a hand on his friend's shoulder. "But we've got something far better: we've got skill. Real skill."

Tom had proven to be an apt pupil. More patient even than Stephen, he could shave a spindle to its exact dimension, or sand a board to satin, or hone an edged tool to deadly sharpness, take however long it might. And he developed an uncanny sense of steel's hardness, so that his knives held their keen edges while flexing almost magically. Where Stephen's love was wood, Tom's became steel. He learned to do gun springs and locks, and sets of kitchen knives, and mastered the intricacies of door box locks and keys. Soon he too, was forging the difficult but famed saws.

And Tom read. Stephen rode up the Clinch River to the Compton farm to borrow books, eventually presenting Isaac with a hunting knife and his wife Sadie with a pair of Tom's kitchen knives in appreciation. Annie welcomed him civilly, seemingly neither glad nor sorry to see him. That cool demeanor intrigued him, and he made an effort to draw her out about her idea of a school.

"Oh, it's just something I'd thought about. This place could surely do with one. Not many grown people can read, and almost no children." That had been back in the late summer, and they were alone for a moment, looking at her collection of books. He decided to test her.

"What do you think about teaching blacks?"

She stopped, not looking at him.

"Are you teaching your Tom? Are these books for him?"

"What if they are? Would it make a difference?"

Then she turned to him, the dark eyes nearly level with his, that face unsmiling, for a long moment, searching.

"No. Not to me. But you know there's a law against teaching slaves to read."

"And there's a declaration written by our Mr. Jefferson that says all men are created equal."

"And you believe that, don't you." It was a statement, in her low voice. *How could her voice be anything but low?* "It galls you, doesn't it, to own another human being." Another statement.

"You seem to know me."

"I know part of you." Then she turned, selected books, handed them to him. "These will be good. I taught Becky and Sam with these. What have you been using with Tom?"

"The squire's John Donne and Shakespeare, and old newspapers."

"Oh, my goodness!" And, just as he'd hoped, that magnificent smile spread. So much so she put her knuckles to her mouth to keep from bursting into laughter.

"And I'll have something else to say to you, next time I come: a secret, when we can be sure no one else will hear. All right?"

She'd recovered.

"I suppose." Her mother was coming. "You'll enjoy these, Mr. Davis. He's a reader, Mama. I'm trusting our precious books to him for a while."

"Very well, dear. You must stay to supper, Stephen. Isaac's heard of your skill at knife making, and he'll want to work out a trade."

So it had gone. And on a later visit he'd brought the kitchen knives, and returned the books. It was then early winter, a blustery day of fine rain, and the family were all inside before the fire.

"So soon?" Annie asked, taking the books.

"Yes, and thanks. I'm getting the hang of it," with a wink, which the family missed in their excitement over the knives. She raised an eyebrow a fraction. *Girl just doesn't smile enough. Tickle her, she'd probably break my arm.*

He accepted a mug of hot cider and dried out at the fire, steam rising from his woolen cloak. Not a good day to get Annie alone, and stone-faced though she was, he knew she was curious about the promised secret. Well, it'd keep. It was early afternoon, and he'd not stay this time. The pleasant talk went on: hunting, crops...

"I've some works a little harder for you, Mr. Davis, if you'd care to try them," her low voice sounded, near. "Philosophy and economics. A bookseller came through Charlottesville last market day, and I fear I squandered my egg money. You might want to look at them."

He rose, shrugged.

"A little deep for a simple millwright like me, but I guess if you can understand it, I can try. Isaac, you ought to build Miss Anna that schoolhouse."

"May hafta, Stephen, if I c'd spare her outta th' fields."

He followed her into the added-on wing of the house, where were her shelves of books. She went to the far wall, then turned, looked him square-on.

"The secret."

"The...Oh, that. Thought you had books..."

"The secret. Stephen Davis, I don't like playing games. Do you want to be friends with me?"

"Well...yes. Yes, I do."

"All right. No teasing, then. Yes, I have books. But you told me weeks ago you had something to tell me, and you did it to tease me, and I don't like that. I'm not a tease, like a lot of girls you may know, like...Oh!" and her eyes widened as she put her hand to her mouth, realizing she'd said too much.

He covered it quickly, because he thought he saw a trace of angry tears.

"Now, wait a second. I didn't mean to tease. I had and I have, something important to tell you, because I sense you've the kind of mind and understanding to appreciate it. I'm sorry if it upset you to...to set you up ahead of time. All right, here it is, but you've got to swear to keep it to yourself. No, never mind swearing. I don't know you well, Anna, but I know you won't tell." He looked around quickly.

"You mentioned its being against the law to teach slaves. Well, Tom isn't my slave. Or anybody's slave. He's a free man. He was freed by his master for service in the war—papers to prove it. But his master died, and a white man stole him, burned his papers. Took him West. He got away, nearly died, made it to my place. I knew I couldn't protect him unless I owned him legally, so I got that taken care of, never mind how. And I freed him, again. Papers recorded in the courthouse this time, and he has the originals.

"So I'm not teaching a slave. We just figured it'd be best to keep it quiet till he learned a trade, so he could make a living. More so since folks like the good squire Thomas believe black people, as Tom said, are a cross between humans and mules, probably closer to mules.

"Now, you know my secret, and I'm your friend, and I'm sorry I teased you and I won't any more. And now I'm ashamed of myself because you don't smile much, and I've made it so you won't for even longer."

He turned and walked out, holding a book on economics.

"Pretty heavy reading, Miss Anna, but I'll try this one, and much obliged. Rain let up any, Bobby?"

"Seems so. Y'ain't goin' so soon?"

"Guess I ought. Your sister thinks I'm smarter than I am, and I fear she'll find me out. You all come over to see me, now. Gets lonesome, nobody to cuss but Tom and that dog."

He looked at her as he got into his cape. She wasn't smiling, but her eyes were luminous. A friend. Well, maybe. Anyway, it felt better for someone to know.

The book on economics mainly put him to sleep. It dealt with regions, countries, trade in general, not with the individual trying to market his wares. Tom tried it, and improved his reading thereby, but didn't get much out of its pages.

"I get pictures out of Shakespeare," he said. "Scenes, action, like in the war. He makes you believe you're there, once you get past all th' funny English. But not this book."

"Good writing does that. The Bible's that way. We should get us a Bible, Tom. Same English as Shakespeare, since King James had it translated about the same time, but it's powerful language. I'll see if we can find us one."

"What was Miss Anna doin' with a book like this, Stephen?"

"That I can't tell you. Girl's bookish, any way you cut it. She may've thought I'd like it. She's a quiet one, Tom. I can't tell if she likes me or not. Got a good mind; wants to start a school. But in my limited experience I've seen that a lot of girls throw plans out the window when the right man shows."

"She th' right woman?"

"I doubt it. Too glum. Afraid to smile. And I haven't given up on Miss Abigail Thomas. Yet."

Tom just shook his head at that. For a smart white man…

Eight

Eventually, Stephen's marketing plan evolved into making several small pieces over the winter, such as another folding writing desk, a little sewing cabinet, pistol case, chess set, which could be easily transported. These he would take with him as samples on an extended trip in the spring, to Staunton in the Valley, up to Maryland, into Pennsylvania, across and down to Richmond, then home again. He could do simple sketches of larger pieces and take orders, and buyers could come to his shop. He hoped it would work. Individuals probably wouldn't travel far, but storekeepers might order. He'd see.

So he set to work. And Tom hammered away at the orders for the tools that kept coming in. And there were still the millstone-dressing jobs now and then, and specialty work for landowners in the region. It seemed winter would go quickly.

Abigail Thomas still came occasionally, her visits gay interruptions, friendly. She openly admired Stephen's work, and marveled at Tom's fine craftsmanship.

"Why, Stephen, this man's becoming a master."

"He is, Miss Abby. Some people have the gift, and Tom does. I tell him, with all he's learned, thirty years more, and he'll be a smith."

"Oh, don't let him tease you, Tom. My father insists you people can't learn crafts. How narrow. Had you done none of this...before?"

"No ma'am. But Mist' Stephen, he's a fast teacher."

"He must be. Look at these scissors."

"Careful, ma'am. That edge razor sharp."

"Oh, it is. And speaking of razors, these are fine. And these locks! Are these all your work, Tom?"

"Yes'm. All mine."

"Well, now. Stephen, are you aware that there isn't a smith this good in the county?"

"Well aware. But you see, Miss Abby, I don't let Tom do routine work: strap hinges, chain, plows, bolts, wagon tires, horseshoes—all the things most smiths spend their days on. He can concentrate on tools, knives and fine work, and he does. We allow ourselves the luxury of specializing. We don't sell often, but we sell dear. And more often, of late."

"I see. And who will buy this beautiful furniture?"

"Not people around here, I've found. I'll travel soon, and hope to build a following."

"Ah, The House of Davis. And so tell me, Mr. Entrepreneur, where is it all destined to lead?"

"The reward may well be in the journey, Miss Abby, who can tell?"

After she'd left, Tom let out a deep breath.

"I was afraid she was going to offer to buy me there."

"Ouch. That'd have been degrading."

"If you only knew."

"Oh, tell me where to go with my samples, if I get on over toward Caroline County. Or will that get too close to Williamsburg to be able to sell anything?

"Ah, now: Caroline County. I'll have to study on that. You know, I'd been thinking about home for a long time, but now I wonder if I really belong there." His eyes were on the place, remembering.

"It'll be changed, all right."

"Yes. My folks had died before, an' I know Mass' John's widow planned to sell a lot of us off, away."

"Did?"

"Yes, that cousin, Doc Weston, he had his own people, an' I wouldn't doubt but he's married the mistis by now."

"Well, I'd thought to see about marketing my things over that way. Maybe I won't. Long way."

~ * ~

The men received a surprise visit at mid-morning one light snow day from the entire Compton family. Tom was tempering a gun spring and Stephen turning a chair spindle on the lathe when Rafe's barking signaled their wagon's arrival.

"You go on with that; I'll see who ''tis," Stephen told him. He swung a kettle of cider over the coals before going out. They'd built a fireplace here too, to take the chill off, and because Tom liked sleeping here in the loft in his own space.

The snow had let up, and he recognized the team and the muffled figures on the road up through the creekside forest.

"Whoah, thar. Y'd oughta clear this flat, Stephen," Isaac observed. "Good bottomland. Looks t'be th' only decent fields y'll have here. Howdy."

"Oh, I'll get to it, Isaac. Welcome, all. Come inside. Miss Sadie, Miss Anna. Becky, I need a hug, bad. Bobby, Sam, how's my men?" He was fleetingly aware that the natural reserve he'd always had seemed to have left him since coming to this place. Or at least when he was with these people.

The horses tied amid the enthusiastic greetings, they all filed in, greeted Tom, who'd cooled the gun spring.

"Wal, I never," Isaac declared, eyeing the fine gunlock Tom had forged. "You make this, boy? Stephen help you?"

"Didn't help him a bit. Got an eye for steel, Tom has. We haven't got into gun barrels, though. Too busy on other things."

The boys were crowding each other and Isaac, fingering the knives, tools, while Sadie and the girls were running their hands wonderingly over the gleaming surfaces of furniture, eyes wide.

"Now folks, what I'm going to insist on, seeing that you all have fed me to foundering over at your place, is that Tom here, who's one marvel of a cook, go on up to the house and do us up some dinner, while we visit a spell. That all right?" And he included Tom in the question. Tom smiled, nodded, untying his leather apron.

"Wal, we..." Isaac started a mild protest.

"Thought it'd do. And you're welcome. We'll be up after while, Tom. Now ladies, here's a little sewing cabinet I made, but I have to admit, I was just guessing where stuff ought to go. You can tell me how it should be..."

It was a pleasant hour and a half. Despite that former reticence, Stephen played the host well, in this his own space, letting the boys get the feel of the gunlock after he'd put the spring in, setting a rocking chair up for Sadie, showing Becky and her brothers how to hold the chisel while the water-powered lathe turned.

He wondered some at this side of himself; he wasn't outgoing by nature and would never have pictured himself as the affable host. *Maybe it's these unspoiled young ones...never spent much time around such before.*

"Y'don't do reg'lar forge work here atall, do you, Stephen?" Isaac asked, unable to resist fingering the tools.

"No, I've taught Tom steel work, and we both do the close hinges, latches, lockwork we need for the furniture, but steel's our specialty. His, mostly, while I work the wood.

"We do plan to try to sell outside of here if we can. Do finer work; get more for it. Don't know if it'll work or not. Take these pieces: I have so much time and labor in it, the only way I can come out on it is to trade it."

"Ah, you interested in tradin'?" The man's eyes had brightened.

"Always."

"Well, now. Ma there, she's been after me to bring her over t'see what y'had here, an' I tol' her jist whut you said: ''bout havin' too much in th' stuff an' all. But a trade, now. You see ennything y'like, Ma?"

"I like it all, Pa." Her dark eyes were shining.

"Durn. Afraid of that. Lemme start over, then: What you need I might have, Stephen?"

"Now we can talk. I'm in need of another horse, badly. Need to pack some of these small pieces here to travel with, show as samples, take orders around. That's my plan. So far, only the squire and a few of his friends have bought things, and I'll be an old man before I sell much, unless people know I'm here. You got a horse you could part with?"

Isaac fairly rubbed his hands.

"Happens I do. Yer wantin' somethin' you can ride er pack, not work. I've seen that'n of yours. No offense, but he's nothin' special."

"No, he's not. Another one like him or a bit better is what I need. But I have to tell you, that isn't going to trade me out of much."

"Ain't? Hmm. Wal, now...Problem with you is, you don't need much of ennything else I might trade you. Tell you what, though: I've got one fine ridin' hoss worth a lot. Ma oughta be able to pick out a wagon-load fer him. An' truth be told, I don't really need him. Black geldin'. Ride 'im; pack yours. An' say, you git that flat cleared, you could put a couple cows on it. Come spring, put calves on it, have beef by cold weather. How's that sound?"

"Isaac, you're a smooth trader. Miss Sadie, you and Miss Anna see what you like best, and we'll go from there. I'll come over, take a look at that black, Isaac."

Tom had venison from a recent hunt, and a variety of other good things to go with it. The family crowded into the little cabin, now with two glass windows so it was no longer dark. Stephen said an appropriate grace, while Tom insisted on standing and serving, which made everyone a little nervous. Somehow too, he'd managed a curious collection of plates, bowls and pot lids from which to eat, and forks and knives, some of which he'd brought new from the forge. All of this he employed with the solemnity he would accord finest china, his expression matching Anna's usual somber one.

Stephen kept the talk going, hoping for a smile from that lady, who cast Tom an appreciative glance from time to time. He knew she was remembering their secret about his status.

"I tell you, that Tom will civilize me, folks, if I let him."

"No hope," Isaac joked. "You a good cook, Tom. What'd you do before Stephen planted you in front of th' forge?"

"I was a body servant to a planter over t'ward th' Tidewater, Mist' Isaac. Went to th' war with ''im."

"Well. This backwoods life a lot different. Like it better?"

"Sure do. New country."

"How did you like the book on economics, Mr. Davis?" It was about the first words Anna had said all day, he realized. She was skillfully steering the conversation away from Tom.

"Too much for me, to tell the truth. I was hoping for some ideas on marketing my work, but it's geared toward whole economies, nations. If I were a senator, say, I'd need to know that. But I thank you. I'd meant to return it before now."

"I couldn't get into it, either. I was hoping you could. Well, it was cheap, anyway."

"Now, folks, there's apple cobbler too," Tom announced. "Wish we had some cream. Need a cow, Mist' Stephen."

"Cobbler? Well, now. And maybe we'll have us a cow, if Isaac and I make that trade. You think you could hold some apple cobbler in there, Sam?" He poked that young man in the ribs.

The walk back to the shop wasn't long, but Stephen contrived to be beside Anna, behind the others. Tom had insisted on staying at the cabin to wash up. Sadie talked earnestly with Isaac about the furniture.

"You haven't been to see me." A statement. "I had to talk my parents into this visit."

"Wasn't sure I'd be welcome. I didn't treat you well."

"You confided in me. Aren't we friends?"

"I hope so."

"It's hard for Tom. Pretending."

"I know. We'll have to declare soon."

"That'll divide people."

"Will I find who my other friends are, then?" That had become an important issue to Stephen.

"Yes, you will. And you won't like it." She seemed worried at this. He decided to take a gamble.

"Why don't you smile more? You're very pretty when you smile."

"Give me something to smile about." And she stepped out ahead.

They were at the pond. Ice had begun rimming the edges. When it was really cold, water would freeze on the wheel and it couldn't be used. Stephen had a foot-pedal lathe inside also. There, he showed the children how to use it to keep them occupied while the adults talked furniture.

This was a simple contrivance consisting of a bent hickory wythe, with a deerskin strap that came down to encircle the piece of wood to be turned, then was attached to a hinged pedal. Pressure on the pedal pulled the strap down, spinning the wood, which was pinned at each end, for the chisel to shape. The upstroke was powered by the springy hickory, when the chisel wasn't engaged. It proved a fascinating experience for Anna's brothers and sister, who couldn't get enough of shaping scraps.

~ * ~

The gelding proved to be quite an animal. That Isaac would part with him at all made Stephen suspicious, but he could find no fault with the horse. The trade had been made—for a china cabinet, a fine table and set of chairs— the horse. A dry sink brought a heifer and a bull calf, to be picked up when Stephen had pasture.

He'd watched Anna closely as she'd run her hands over the pieces lovingly, but he'd had trouble choosing something he wanted for her. It was to be a gift, just because he wanted to do it. Maybe he'd get a smile. Finally, he'd chosen a small sewing cabinet of burl cherry, one he'd planned to take as a sample. Or, if he were truthful, he'd hoped Abby Thomas would want it, but she hadn't expressed any interest in it.

He'd hidden it near the Compton place when he'd ridden up this time. He liked the gelding, which he was now riding, and felt he'd made a good trade. All right: she was there, helping with supper. He turned the spirited animal past a clump of trees, dismounted and retrieved the gift, wrapped in deerskin. Then he rode back, reining in at the porch. Dismounted.

"Brought a little to boot, Isaac, since you folks have been so good to me." He strode in, past the boys and Becky, and stood before Anna, who turned from the dry sink. Never taking his eyes from her, he pulled the deerskin from the cabinet and held it out, unsmiling.

"Well, I never..." came from Sadie, nearby. Anna's dark eyes lifted from the gleaming cherry wood to Stephen's. Her hands slowly wiped themselves on her apron, then reached to take the gift. Her smile broke like the sun through rain clouds, he thought, and about as big. *Give me something to smile about.* For a long time it held. Then she shook her head.

"I can't accept anything this fine, Mr. Davis, without something in return." She was serious about that. And yes, maybe he had gone a little overboard here. Funny, if it'd been Abby, he'd have felt it was little enough. *Now, that's not fair, not at all.* He felt himself redden.

"No, you've already loaned me books," he protested.

"That's nothing. Oh, you and Tom have got to eat. Will you accept a pair of pigs? That's little enough, but I've raised them. They're acorn-fat."

"Well, all right, if you feel the need. But the cabinet was to have been a gift, pure and simple."

"And I take it as such, and thank you. But it's a treasure. One in my position just doesn't come by such things, and I'd be...well...uneasy, I suppose you'd say." That was clearly how she felt, the eyes troubled.

"Done, then. Tom and I'll be over next butchering day."

After supper, after Stephen had ridden away on the black, leading his old horse, Anna's mother was alone with her in the kitchen.

"There was no need to treat him that way, child, over that gift."

"Oh, Mama..."

"Don't 'Oh, Mama' me. Can't you see he's come courtin'?"

Anna fixed her eyes on her mother.

"No, Mama. Stephen Davis has not come courtin'."

Nine

Stephen wasn't sure what reception he'd get with his wares, but he set out after the worst spring rains were past, with the heavily-waxed samples protected in oilskins. He had a tent for shelter, camping gear, his rifle, a pistol and a knife in his belt. And he'd sleep away from his fire, something he'd learned in the war. He didn't intend to get surprised or robbed.

South a few miles, he struck the Rockfish Pike, and followed it up into the Blue Ridge where he camped. Next day he rode to Staunton, in the Valley. There he showed his pieces to a storekeeper, left a list of prices, and rode north. Wherever he found a village, he'd stop, leave word, show his wares.

"In case some of the planters hereabouts want fine furniture, I'm taking orders. They can come to my shop, fifteen miles northwest of Charlottesville, or ten miles south of the Swift run pike, on Buck Mountain Creek. I'm easy to find."

Stephen traveled light. He hadn't the money for taverns, though he stopped at a few of the better ones to leave word. He had dried venison and meal, dried apples and a few potatoes, and grain for the horses. He'd brought trade knives and tools to sell when the need arose, and he did carry a little money. As always, he planned to see how things went.

Those things weren't encouraging at first. People admired his work, and more than once wanted to buy his samples.

"No," he'd have to tell them. "Need these to show. I can have you anything you want in a few weeks, but not this one. Yes, I know it's a long way, but I'm not that far from the Valley pike—just over the Blue Ridge—and I guarantee you'll see something else you'll like if you come." And yes, his prices were steep. "Good work's always high. You want cheap, I'm not your man, sir."

The Marylanders and Pennsylvanians were more affluent, with fine stone houses and huge barns. But they were thrifty, too. He could soon see he was too far afield. Eventually he dropped down again to cross the Potomac, into the plantations along that river. Here prospects would surely be better, but the distance would still be a factor.

"If I get several orders, I could deliver, yes," he'd promised, but that didn't materialize. It began to look as if he'd have to relocate his operation to some central trading town if he were to have any sales. And he had to admit, perhaps this wasn't to be workable, after all.

Alexandria and Georgetown were such possible places, with the river traffic and the trade from the great plantations nearby. But there were shops established here, he'd found, along with stores already handling wares from England again, just a year and a half after the war.

Well, then: Richmond. There'd be competition there too by then, but it was familiar territory. And at least shipping would be easier, with the main roads and all. And there might be something on the way. Law of averages said he'd sell something, sometime, if he kept at it long enough.

He had the location of the Logan plantation in Caroline County from Tom, and it was not far off his route. Curiosity, more than any hope of sales, led him to ride that way. A substantial dwelling house lay at the head of a long drive bordered in boxwoods. A black, aging butler answered his knock.

"Are you a peddler, sir?" Eyeing the pack horse.

"Oh, no. A friend of Colonel Logan's. From the war: Stephen Davis. Would you tell him I've come to call?"

"Oh. I'm afraid...Just a moment, sir. Please wait." The man disappeared, returning in a moment with a middle-aged man of severe countenance. An attractive younger woman stood beyond him, hand to her throat. *His daughter? Maybe even the widow?*

"Yes? I'm Doctor Weston. What may I do for you, sir?"

"There must be some mistake. I was looking for an old friend I served with in the war: Colonel John Logan. I was told some time ago this was his home. I seem to have been mistaken."

"Oh, no mistake, Mr..."

"Davis. Stephen Davis. He was one of our commanders. I'm a furniture maker by trade, traveling nearby, and thought to call..."

"Do come in, Mr. Davis. Are those your wares?"

"Only small samples, Doctor. But I'm not here to sell. I only meant to call..."

"Well, I regret to inform you, sir, my cousin John died, shortly after the war, of a wound received there at the end. This is his widow, newly my wife, Constance. We all mourned his loss greatly."

"Ah, a shock. A great leader. Unsparing to his men. We thought the wound was not that serious."

"Didn't appear to be, though they carried him from the field, as I'm sure you will recall. Pneumonia set in later, I'm afraid. Most distressing." The doctor was clearly uneasy.

"Do sit, Mr. Davis," Constance Logan invited. "We're honored to meet one of John's comrades, aren't we, Horace? Will you take tea?"

"Why, thank you, Mrs. Weston. Yes, I remember Tom, the colonel's man, carried him off, under fire. Whatever happened to Tom? Still here? We were all fond of him, too."

"Oh. No, Tom was...sold, I'm afraid. Out West somewhere. Don't remember the details. Lot of confusion at the time."

"I see. Well, the war was a confusing time. My, what a handsome breakfront. Is it English?"

"No, Williamsburg, actually. Do you do that caliber work, Mr. Davis?"

"I do, but my workshop is quite small. I build just a few select pieces, for a few clients a year. West of here, in northwest Albemarle County. New planters mostly, furnishing new establishments."

"I see. Were you at New York, then, with John?"

"At the siege, yes," Stephen lied smoothly. "None of us could understand what General Washington was up to there, outnumbered that way. But the march to Yorktown was brilliant, thanks to supporting officers like Colonel Logan."

"What rank did you hold?"

"I was a sharpshooter, Dr. Weston. In my five years I rose only to lieutenant."

"Ah. Dangerous job."

"Yes. Rather like, in medical terms, a surgeon, I'd say."

"Hmm. I suppose." The doctor apparently had run out of things to say.

"Well. Thanks for your hospitality." Stephen rose. "And please accept my condolences, both of you, and my regrets at the colonel's passing. One of the finest men I ever knew."

"Thank you, Mr. Davis. Horace, I'd like to see the furniture samples Mr. Davis has. Will you come, too?"

"Oh, I think not, my dear. You go ahead if you like." He bowed dismissively. "Mr. Davis."

Outside, Constance Weston ran her fingers over several pieces. Something was on her mind.

"Mr. Davis..."

"Yes, Mrs. Weston?"

"Tom. Tom, John's servant. He wasn't sold, sir. He was stolen."

"Really?"

"Yes. You see, John had freed him. There were witnesses, papers..."

"He'd told several of us he planned to do that."

"Yes. And he was as good as his word. Tom saved his life." There was genuine anguish in her eyes at the memory.

"I know. What happened?"

"A man—a friend of Horace's, actually, was going West, buying slaves. Tom disappeared the same night he left. I've no proof, but..."

"I see. And the papers?"

"Gone, of course. Probably destroyed."

"You said there were witnesses. Are any still around?"

Her face paled. She clutched at her throat. Looked nervously over her shoulder.

"One was...was Horace, my husband."

~ * ~

Richmond did indeed prove to be better territory for sales, with storekeepers urging Stephen to bring pieces to leave on consignment.

"No, I won't do that. What I will do, I'll sell you a piece at a discount, so it's yours, not mine, and you can make whatever you want on it. But consignment, no. I'm one craftsman with a few pieces. Can't have something happen to even one."

"Independent cuss, ain't you? But y'build good stuff. All right, bring me a walnut china cabinet, table an' eight chairs, sideboard. Give me yer best price, and by July one."

Stephen calculated, figured in a wagon, travel time and a percentage for—well, unforseen circumstances—and gave his price, which was high. The merchant hesitated, calculating, eyes narrow. Then:

"Done, if you'll throw in a pistol case like this'n in th' deal."

"Done."

"Oh, an' I know yer folks in Goochland. Give m'best t'yer pa," the storekeeper grinned.

Well. Connections never hurt, he realized. *Guess I was just too far from home, most of this trip. Well. Hit a few more merchants, then on to the folks' place. Been a year and a half. Like to see old Ned Drake, too, if I had time. But he's down in Sussex County on that old plantation, too far out of the way, this trip. Have to get home and get busy, anyway.*

The family was glad to see him, and to hear of his fortunes, although he'd written several times. Sheila and Patrick showed off their firstborn, a laughing boy. Susannah was engaged to marry a reportedly industrious veteran with a small farm upriver, a lad Stephen didn't know.

"And have you met a wife, Stevie?" his mother asked him, over her eternal sewing basket.

"Not yet, Ma. There's a planter's daughter so pretty she's got my head turned, but I don't fancy I'll win her, so I've not wasted my time. Other girls about, but I've been seriously busy, what with the cabin, the shop, and the work I've hired out to do, paying for the place and all."

"Ah, but you've got it free and clear, you say," his father approved.

"Such as it is. Only eighty acres, and rough, all but one good bottom. But yes, it's paid for. My partner Tom, helped a lot, but the land's mine, free."

"Partner, eh? He a miller?"

"No, smith. Does the iron—steel, really. We don't do regular work, only knives, razors, tools, the like. Stay busy. That's what's brought in what money we've made, while I've been trying to get furniture built and sold." Stephen saw no reason to tell his family that Tom was black, about as irrelevant a fact as he could imagine.

"This trip's mostly been a waste, till I got to Richmond. Samuel Shepherd's given me a good order, sends his best. I'm hoping to sell some in Scottsville, too. Then maybe some orders will come in from the word I left around. Wait and see."

"Well, don't overlook the girls, Stevie," his mother advised. "You and that Tom'll get tired being bachelors, holed up by yourselves like that."

"Oh, we're already tired of it, Ma. One of us'll commit marriage sooner or later. You'll have more grandbabies like little Pat there than you can count."

~ * ~

Scottsville would have been the seat of Albemarle County if Thomas Jefferson hadn't located his home on that hilltop at Charlottesville. The James River, navigable by bateaux, ran by the town, with tobacco, hemp, furs, grain shipping to Richmond, the Chesapeake and the world beyond. The river plantations were broad and rich, stretching back from the James in deep soil. This soil was being turned, prepared for planting, along with all the other rural industries that fed this agricultural system. It was all abuzz in activity. *Maybe this is where I should've come to settle, instead of the hills.*

There was more interest in his pieces here too, from the merchants and the few planters he encountered in the town.

"Fine work, young man," a rotund planter in a tricorner fingered a chess set of walnut and maple. "How does one find your shop?" Stephen told him. "Bit out of the way, that, but I'm in Charlottesville often. I should like to come by. Would you be near Hezekiah Thomas, by any chance?"

"As a matter of fact, I'm just downcreek…bought my place from him."

"Did you? A first, Hezekiah's selling land. Must be a piece he couldn't use. Never know why he chose those godforsaken hills. Well, Mr. Davis, I'm Milton Cosgrove. A pleasure to encounter one of your skill. I'm building a house for my son and his bride nearby, and we'll want it furnished, of course. Why don't we come see what you have? Let's stop in here at the tavern, and I'll write old Thomas a note, if you'll pass it on to him. We'll come for a visit say, Friday next. Two days will do it nicely, with a stay at Captain Jouett's Swan."

"Easily, Mr. Cosgrove. I shall look forward to seeing you." Stephen rode north with the distinct conviction that he'd arrived at his dreamed-of profession.

~ * ~

Tom had begun clearing the creek bottom at the downstream end in Stephen's absence. The logs were trimmed, brush burned, firewood stacked. There wouldn't be much grass, but they could get seed from neighbors, and buy hay and feed for the animals meantime. Tom had also split a sizeable pile of chestnut rails for fencing, and begun to fence the open area.

Stephen noted the width of the road they'd made through the woods up from the creek ford. To his eye, it seemed wide enough for a carriage. The carriage trade: Finally. Well, I must't count those chicks before they hatch. But a wealthy planter's houseful of furniture!

He found Tom in the shop, making files, concentrating intensely on this demanding job. The heated steel was laid on a lead bar, and the sharp ridges cut carefully with a chisel. Stephen reflected on how far his friend had come in the blacksmith's trade. The dog had run off after some varmint and hadn't seen him coming, so he'd come in the door unannounced.

"Hey, partner. Got back in one piece."

"Well, you did, all right. Didn't hear you. Rafe chased off a minute ago. Good trip?"

"Good enough, finally. Should have started closer, though. I wasted a lot of time too far from home." He told him of his successes.

"Well, now. Work for a year or more, if that Scottsville order comes through. Nothin' in Charlottesville?"

"I could probably take a wagon load down on market day and maybe sell a piece now and then, but I don't want to. Let ''em come to me. Will have to haul some, though. That means a wagon, and time away."

"We're just not in th' right place, I guess."

"Well, can't change that. At least not yet. Anything happen I need to hear of?"

"Not really. Picnic an' dance down at Nixville. Thomas slaves went. I went with old Ike and them. Good time. Then Ike had me over to do some temperin' with him. Th' squire happened by, an' 'bout ran me off."

"No!"

"Wanted to, but Ike showed him what I'd done, an' he cooled down, then. Went off mutterin'."

"Old fool. Told me he wouldn't have a slave smith on th' place."

"Didn't. But of course he didn't know."

"About that: When do you want to let folks know?"

"Not yet awhile. Way I see it, if that makes it too hot to stay here, I'd need to be able to pick up an' go, maybe North, up East, somewhere I could get by. An' I know I don't know enough yet to set up, make a livin' there… strange country, no friends, competition everywhere. End up workin' for some tight-fisted white man, gettin' paid nothin'. No offense."

"Oh, no. But your share of the sales is adding up here, though, I'm sure. I haven't been keeping track."

"Slow, but steady, an' I do appreciate every cent. We could make and sell twice as many knives, we had th' time. Other way I might go, of course, is back t'Caroline County, this time as a sure ''nuff craftsman."

At that, Stephen pulled up a chair, motioned Tom to sit opposite him. A wariness came into the dark eyes as he hesitated. *He's found out somethin'. And no, it's not somethin' good.*

"About that. Bank the forge fire, Tom." He did so, then sat, resigned to whatever bad news was coming. "All right, I did a little snooping on the way. Now, I want you to know I didn't do it because I didn't believe your story of what happened to you—trust me on that. But I've been uneasy all along, knowing you were maybe planning to go back. Hell, I know it's home and all…

"But, to put some…what's the word I want…perspective on it, I've got a friend—well, father's friend—who's close to Governor Jefferson. That man tried to outlaw slavery in Virginia when he was in the House of Burgesses, and when he was governor. When he wrote the Declaration of Independence. Big landowners, slaveowners, wouldn't have it. He lost every time. And the man has slaves of his own all over that hill of his, so it gets complicated, too.

"But anyway, this friend of mine tells me Jefferson, and a lot of other leading citizens, have come to believe completely that freeing a slave in this time and in this place would be the worst thing they could do, because of just what happened to you. Any white man could steal him—you—and you have no protection under the law, when just about everybody wants you to stay slaves."

"I know that dodge, Stephen. And there's bitter truth in it. But what no white man can ever know is, how precious that bein' free is, even if it's full of danger, even if it's only a taste, like I had."

Stephen held up a hand.

"But you don't know how bad the odds are against you. Now the way I understand it, the way you told it, a bastard named...Hayes, wasn't that his name? came through, stole you. All right, so the easy conclusion is, he was maybe just one bad apple in the barrel, like there always is. Tactic is, you just do your best to stay away from the apples that are bad.

"Only in this case, just about all of them were bad, except your late master. Tom, you were *set up and betrayed, sold out* by the family. That Doc Weston, Logan's cousin? He was a witness when your master freed you, right?"

"How'd you know that?"

"John's widow told me. Weston denied any plan your master ever had to free you. Said you were sold West somewhere, along with others. Claimed it was all confusion, with the end of the war, the colonel's death and all. He had to be part of the sell-out. Hayes was his friend, not John's. Miss Constance got me alone, told me. She was never sure of the connection before: your disappearance. But she suspected."

"She knows now?"

"She does. But she won't go against the doctor. He's her husband... wives just don't do that."

"Damn. Weaselin' doctor. And here I was thinkin' I could maybe go back, get it all straightened out..." He envisioned the long-sought homecoming, the grim actuality. "If I ever even tried that..."

"He'd make you disappear again before anybody even knew you were there, Tom. And the hell of it is, nobody in Caroline County would care. Free black man would scare them. They'd say you'd be a threat to their slaves, cause them to get discontented, want to run off."

"Oh, they said that before."

Ten

This part of the forest was always in deep, green shadow. The giant chestnuts and poplars towered high above, but there were hemlocks and white pines here too, where the stream came through big granite boulders with a musical sound. Small birds watered here, twitting in the peaceful air. Stephen had come looking for wood for future furniture projects, and really, to rest from his trip. It was early June, and late laurel still bloomed. The Cosgroves were due soon, and the demands of the work loomed. Just here was peace that let him imagine no other human existed. In this walled-in, green world, he could be really alone. He leaned against a mossy boulder, let his mind drift.

She came on foot quietly, startling him, but somehow fitting the scene. She'd tied her mare down the stream somewhere, and slipped to this place. Did she know he'd be here? Who could tell, with Abby Thomas?

"I used to come here a lot. The sound of the water is different here from anywhere in the word. I'm glad you've found it, too."

"My favorite place. It makes the world go away."

"You've been out in it lately. I've missed you, Stephen."

"Have you? I'm a recluse, even when I'm home."

"But at least I get to see you."

"Pardon me, but I thought our Mr. Butler was keeping you busy."

"Oh, don't be mean to me. Papa thinks I should marry him. But..."

"But?"

"Oh...Stephen, will you be my friend?"

"Not if I can help it."

"What do you mean?"

"My experience is, if a girl wants to be my friend, I can never hope to be anything more than just that."

"Oh. And have you any...desire to be anything...more?"

"Not unless the feeling is mutual. What I do not have is the desire to throw myself at the feet of a woman who'll go off and marry my rival."

"Your...yes, I guess he is your rival. He thinks so. But you've never told me how you really feel. I mean...You're confusing me."

"I doubt that. If I were your friend, what would you tell me?"

"That I...that I don't love Rawlins Butler. And that I don't know if I love anybody yet, or ever will. That I like being just me. That I know the community thinks I'm a flirt and a tease when I'm not. That I want to be your friend, because you know who you are and don't give a hang for the roles of society. That I'm a very lonely person who seems to have everything, but girls resent me and boys are afraid of me and older men want me as an ornament. Those are some of the things I'd say. If you were my friend."

The words had come in such a rush, he hastened to reply, fearing he might lose this new-shown confidence.

"I see. And I'd have to reply that I'd like to be your friend, too, but I know everybody would take it the wrong way, and Butler would probably call me out, and I'm not even sure I could limit the way I feel about you to mere friendship, anyway. I will confess, and probably regret it, that meeting you was most of the reason I did not go on west to Kentucky.

"I'm well aware of the roles of society, as you called the restrictions and castes that exist, though we fought a bloody and haunting war to eliminate that sort of thing. Your father is acutely aware of them, your mother too, and even you, if it were to come, finally, to that. Don't object, now…we seldom are able to analyze ourselves accurately. I like being with you, but you're like fire, Abby. You're like gunpowder.

"Now, I must tell you something: I have killed a lot of men. Deliberately killed men who were trying to kill me and my comrades. I didn't get to be a marksman shooting at targets. It makes you hard inside. It makes you impatient with foolishness, with games, niceties, sparring..."

"With teasing."

"That, too. I've thrown myself into my work here like a machine. Tom says my bad dreams from the war are so loud he moved to the shop. But what I'm really trying to tell you, Abigail Thomas, is something else entirely: that here, in this God-created Eden, this lovely paradise, you are the complete, beautiful pearl, rose, final touch of perfection. It's as if I even dare to breathe, a divine crystal will shatter."

It was a huge effort for him not to take her in his arms. Then her eyes closed, and her lovely lips trembled. It was too much. He was sure he'd crush her to him, but somehow he was gentle, his lips on her yielding, perfect mouth, his arms holding her like fine china. Her fingers were at the back of his neck, caressing. Something hard like metal in his chest seemed to dissolve into warmth and flow outward through his veins.

She finally pulled her face away, looked into his eyes.

"Oh, Stephen. You need a friend so much more than I."

They walked slowly, hand in hand, down the singing stream, silent, each with a tumult of thoughts.

Well, now, what's next? She'd said she didn't know if she loved anybody yet. With a simpler girl, he'd doubt that. So, take it at face value, then. See how it works out. But that kiss: not just friendship, that. And now looks like I've got two girls who want to be my friend. Better keep ''em apart.

That could get lonely.

~ * ~

The visit by the Cosgrove family: father, mother, son and bride, was a success. The girl gushed, and would have bought every piece in the shop, but her mother-in-law wisely planned each room with her, and a large order ensued, as well as several small pieces purchased there, to go back in the carriage.

"Excellent chess set. You play, of course, Mr. Davis." The younger Cosgrove asked, but it wasn't really a question.

"Poorly. I thought I was good till I came upon really fine players among officers in the war."

"I'm dismayed to here that, Stephen," Squire Thomas said. He'd accompanied the Cosgroves to the shop. "I'd begun to believe you were a man who did all things well." He seemed to mean it.

"I'll take that as a compliment, sir, but I've my vast areas of incompetence to keep me humble."

"As do we all. Well, Milton, I believe our young friend here can satisfy your needs. He's certainly been a valuable help to me."

After they left, Tom clapped his friend on the shoulder.

"Now you can just about say you're successful. I been keepin' quiet, holdin' my breath."

"Me, too. Now all I have to do is work my arse off to build the stuff."

"We have enough wood?"

"With the boards we sawed last year, yes. I've depended on the squire for a lot. Without his whipsaw I couldn't have gotten started."

"But you've helped him a lot, too."

"I suppose so. Yes." Stephen's eyes were focused far beyond the shop walls, and Tom noticed. There was silence for a moment, during which Tom fancied he read his friend and benefactor's thoughts.

"So, when do you hit him with the big question?"

"The what?"

"Do we play games, here?" Tom's eyes seemed to dance.

"What in hell are you talking about?"

"All right: You come out of th' woods with the man's daughter, with both your faces lit up like candles, and you been goin' ''round hummin' to yourself for three days, not hearin' a word I say to you. Now, you gonna be a man and ask Papa for the girl's hand, or not?"

"That obvious?"

"Maybe not to a blind man."

"Well, it's more complicated than that, Tom."

"Always is. And I'll just wager one of the complications is real tall, and doesn't smile much."

"Now, you're wrong, there. She's a...a friend, I guess you'd say. To both of us. The books, remember? She's glad you've learned to read. Got some good ideas about things. I really don't know how that one feels about me.

Come to think of it, I really don't know how the other one does, either. But I know she's going to reject Butler."

"Think so? Buck her pa?"

"Told me."

"Way he talked just now, she hasn't yet. He's still high on you."

"And that'll make a difference?"

"Stephen, people ain't blind. Parents c'n tell. If Abby's all lit up like you been, an' I'd wager she is, at least her ma will know why. An' then when she dumps Butler, it won't take a general to figure you're th' reason. Who else is there 'round here? Young, dumb farmers' sons? God knows, you about as ugly as me, but you the best around, my friend." He chuckled.

"What I wanta know is, where'd you learn so much about women? And life, and all? You're not that much older'n me."

"Keep quiet an' watch: That's how you stay out of trouble, how you learn."

~ * ~

Next day the two rode the five miles to the Compton farm for the trade heifer and bull. There was a small, fenced plot for them near the creek now, and it was past time.

"Well, they're still alive, Annie," Isaac called to his daughter as the men rode up to the hayfield. She and Bobby were forking the hay onto a stack around a post while their father raked it with a broad, hickory-tined rake. "Close to dinner time. ''Light down."

"We'll lend a hand. Clouds buildin'. How's everybody?"

"Doin' good. You been gone a spell, we hear. Work out all right?"

"Did, finally. Got a big houseful of furniture to build for down at Scottsville, some pieces for Richmond, things here and there. Have to go to work now, but I get to set my own schedule."

"That's good. Y'get much ground cleared, Tom?"

"Little. Aim to keep on. Figure to feed the stock at first, trade for hay and grain. Like you said, Mist' Isaac, th' place is all hill." He forked great mounds of sweet hay as Anna stood back to catch her breath. She stood taller than he.

"Any fish in this river, Bobby?" Stephen asked the boy.

"Some. Holes startin' to wash in with gravel. Pa says it's because folks cuttin' th' trees ''long th' bank, lettin' th' dirt wash. Still some deep places where we c'n catch us some."

"Buck Mountain Creek that way too, but some good catfish down deep." He pulled hay toward a pile, where Tom pinned it with the pitchfork. "You make this rake, Isaac? It's a fine one: hickory."

"Did. Pulls a lotta hay, but it'll work you. Clouds pilin', all right. Lemme take that fork, Bobby."

"And how've you been, Miss Anna?" Stephen asked her, when he was near enough. The others had worked away from them.

"Well, Mr. Davis. We missed you. I've enjoyed my sewing cabinet. I love just running my fingers over it."

"Good. The wood likes that."

"That's a nice thing to say. Yes, it's as if you give wood a second life, with what you do with it."

"And you give it a third, with your handling it."

"My, how poetic. Did you enjoy your travels?"

"Mostly hawking my wares to surly people, eating cold, bad food at a smoky fire, getting rained on. Not a holiday."

"I'm sorry."

"Gather that in a pile over thar," Isaac called. "I'll bring th' wagon. We'll jist have time t'move it."

"I did find out Tom was sold out by one or more of his late master's kin. He'd thought he might go back there."

"Oh. I'm glad he didn't. Listen, Stephen, you can tell my family about Tom. They like him. They'll understand."

"Thanks, Annie, but that's up to Tom."

They forked the three quick wagonloads of remaining hay onto the stack, interweaving it so it would shed water, then drove and rode for the farmhouse, getting the first heavy drops of the summer rain. They all ran onto the porch, laughing, even Anna. *Damn, she's pretty when she's happy, Stephen thought. Am I what keeps her from smiling? Tom'll have something to say about that, now.*

"Come in here," Sadie Compton called. "Welcome, Stephen, Tom.

You've been gone too long. Lord, Stephen, I'm the envy of every house-wife on this river, my fine furniture. You could probably trade some more."

"What I really need is some of this good cleared bottom land rolled up and spread out over on my place. But mine'll make a little graze, when it's cleared."

"Problem we got is, what t''do with all those good logs," Tom put in. "Hate just to burn ''em."

"Yes, an' ever'body's got too many trees," Isaac observed. "Guess yer doin' right, clearin' jist as y'need th' wood, but it'll sure take a while."

"Well, it doesn't pay to be impatient," Stephen said. "Oh, Miss An-nie, I got a book to loan, you might like. Hope it didn't get wet." He ran out to his saddlebags, then back. "It's John Calvin. Found it in Alexan-dria, upstate. He has a lot to say about reformed theology. You were Pres-byterian, weren't you, Miss Sadie?"

"Yes, indeed. And Stephen, Reverend Carson, who raised me, is set on starting a church here. He's right old, but he's asked Annie to help. Plans to train somebody hereabouts to fill in when he can't get here: it's near twenty miles. Be hard on him, but he wants to do it."

"Well, that's fine. My folks are Presbyterian, down in Goochland. Afraid I've strayed though, with the war and all. Killing people ties clos-er with the Old Testament than with the turning the other cheek Jesus taught."

"War's hard to justify," Tom said quietly, "till the other side comes onto your place, burnin' and killin'."

"Way I feel about it," Isaac agreed.

"Thank you, Stephen," Annie smiled at him." I've heard Calvin has an interesting insight into original sin."

"At least it's a lot easier for me to take than the one most preachers push. I'd like to hear what you think of it. Predestination, too."

"Maybe you oughta be th' preacher, Stephen," Bobby suggested.

"Not me, boy. I'm a sour old soldier, about half mad at the world. Tom's the only one who can put up with me, and that just barely." He caught a twitch at the corners of Anna's mouth, and her eyes were merry. *All right, maybe I've not been whatever the problem is.*

~ * ~

The young stock bawled at being separated from the herd, but followed their lead ropes the miles along the twisting road. And eventually quieted in their new home in each other's company.

The dog had begun marking his territory with a will, and the smell should help keep predators away at night, the men reasoned, and the calves would be secure at night in a new, tightly closed shed they'd built. There were still panthers and wolves around. The land between them and the Compton holdings was all mountain wilderness between the creek and Lynch River.

After supper the men stretched out in the fading light, still damp from the drizzle that hadn't let up. Both of them had been warmed by the welcome and acceptance at the Compton home.

"Well?" Stephen eventually asked, cutting his eyes sideways.

"Well?...Oh, that's right: no games. You got yourself a situation, my man. Miss Annie's a deep one. And I never seen so much pride in a woman. For a long, tall thing like her, not that fine to look at, she's one independent gal. Ever'body'd expect her to tumble easy for the first decent man would have her, an' that's just what she's not about to do. No, the man for Miss Annie Compton is gonna get all of her, or nothin' at all. And he's got to be one helluva man."

"She's a friend. I like her as a friend."

"Maybe. But I doubt it."

"How'd you compare her and Abby?" Stephen watched his friend's face for the reply.

"Now that's a challenge. Let's see..." He pondered the question for some time, eyes closed. "All right: to use as few words as possible, Annie's what Abby'd like to be, if she could."

"What? That's the most outrageous observation ever uttered! All right, then...And *you* are a misguided, misled, deluded, prematurely-aged, half-baked philosopher, and blind, to boot!"

"Hey, you asked. Yeah, and that bit of deep—and I might add, free—philosophy may just be moren' you deserve. Way I see it, only thing for you to do, Mr. Romeo, is saddle up an' ride outta th' country, ''fore you get burned."

Eleven

Abigail Thomas rode up to the shop the next day. Stephen hadn't seen her since that kiss they'd shared.

"I'm goin' down to feed the stock," Tom announced, and left them.

"I told him."

"Butler? Or your pa?"

"Butler. Papa's in Charlottesville. I'll tell him tonight. Mama knows something's happened, Stephen. I've told her nothing, but I catch her watching me. I plan to tell them I don't know what I want, except that I know I don't want Rawlins Butler, and will not consider him."

"I'm glad that weight's off you, Abby. I know how you've felt the duty to your father."

"Yes, and it was silly. We live in an enlightened age. Arranged marriages are history, Stephen. I know Papa wants the security of a plantation for me, but he can't want it at the expense of a loveless life for me. He and Mama love me…I know they do, and they won't force me."

Stephen saw the glow in her Tom had seen, that her mother had seen. All right: She might not know it, but his hand was about to be forced. Or maybe not; maybe it could go on a while, till everything came apart.

"So, then. We're friends, you and I. What exactly does that mean?"

"Mean? Why, we can tell each other...how we feel, share things. Isn't that what being a friend is?"

"How about that kiss, up the creek? Was that a kiss between friends?"

"Oh! I'm...not sure I know about that. I've been trying..." She reddened.

"And am I to listen to you tell me about a new man you've met, and you, about a new girl I may like? I'm afraid this may be a bit more complicated than we figured, Abby."

"I...I hadn't thought about it that way."

"And I guarantee your parents will ask you immediately who it is you like instead of Butler. Don't ask me how I know this, but I do. They just won't believe you when you say you haven't declared your heart."

Her eyes held confusion, then irritation.

"Stephen, why...why are you saying all this to me?"

"Not to anger you. I just think there may be more to it."

"Than being friends? And my heart? How do you know the state of my heart, Stephen? No, I don't want you to anger me, and I don't believe you meant to. But I fear you may be a little afraid to let anyone too close to you.

"Listen, Stephen, I said I need a friend, and I do. And I have enough insight to know you need one, too. Can't we just let it go at that?" She looked into his eyes. "No, I guess we can't quite do that, can we? Let's say, let it go at that for now. How's that?"

"I can accept that. For now. But I have one other thing to say to you, Abby Thomas."

"What's that?"

"You are one hell of a woman." He kissed her on the forehead, squeezed her hand at the door. And watching her riding away down the woods road, he knew he'd won her.

~ * ~

"Now, don't start." Tom and the dog had returned from the little pasture the moment Abby was out of sight.

"Hey, I'm mute." He held up his hands. Stephen couldn't help smile at the word: right out of a book.

"She told him. Butler. Be hell to pay." Stephen bent to his work.

~ * ~

It had to happen, Stephen reflected, sooner or later. He was gone from the shop with the dog, so there was no way Tom could pretend the book he was holding and reading as he worked the bellows was anything but what it was. Squire Thomas came through the door suddenly, in some agitation, and stopped short, seeing him.

"Where's...What the devil's that you've got, boy?"

"Oh...I...It's..." No explanation would come to Tom's startled mind. He stood, dazed, his mouth open.

"You're reading that book! Now, where the devil did you get that? Who taught you to read? Where's Stephen?" The questions were quick, sharp, demanding. "Answer me, boy!" The planter took a menacing step forward.

Tom closed the book, laid it on a bench. He was calm, now.

"The book is on loan from the Comptons, sir. Yes, I can read. Mr. Davis will be back from tending the stock any minute. He can answer any other questions you have. Shall I fetch him for you, sir?"

Thomas stood, unsure. He'd never been addressed like this by a black in his life.

"Oh, never mind. I'll find him myself!" And he stormed out.

He found Stephen halfway back from the little pasture.

"What the hell are you doing, Davis, teaching that slave of yours to read? Don't you know that's against the law? In every colony—state—in the country?"

"Did he tell you I taught him?" Stephen appeared calm, which confused the planter.

"Did he...Well, no, I guess he didn't. Who did, then?"

"I could tell you his former master did, sir, the same man who taught him proper English, but that'd be a lie. I did teach him. I don't lie. Not to you, not to anybody. Now let me ask you a question: Is it the legal issue you object to, or the principle of the thing, a black man reading?"

"Why, the legal issue, of course. The law is the law. There are sound reasons for that law. And I have no respect for a lawbreaker..."

Stephen held up a hand.

"Then no law has been broken, Mr. Thomas. Let's sit here, on this log, since I have no chair out in these woods, while I explain."

"I prefer to stand."

"As you wish." He eyed the planter with a level gaze. "Tom Logan is a free man. I freed him shortly after I acquired him. Recorded, dated, in the Albemarle courthouse by your friend George Henley, attorney. I've taught a free man to read, sir, and that is no crime. The man has an uncommonly good mind and has learned valuable skills. Reading is one of them."

"I...You freed him?"

"I did, sir."

"Well, then...I suppose...I must concede that point. But that is not what I came to see you about. It...Well, it took me aback, you can imagine, seeing that boy, airily reading a book, working the bellows, like any white man..."

"Like any man, sir. But you said you had other concerns."

"And I do." He drew himself up. "I suspect, sir, that you have interfered in affairs that are patently none of your business, and have meddled in a situation affecting my family's welfare."

"I'm afraid you'll have to explain that one to me, sir."

"I mean, specifically, that my daughter has rejected a qualified suitor for no good reason, and I strongly suspect you have influenced her."

"And there, sir, you do me great injury. As a man of honor, I have never paid court to your daughter, made any advances to her, advised her, or interfered with her in any way. May I ask what in God's name you base your accusations on?" Stephen had been striding up and down. He faced the planter now. And if there were social differences between them, it was hardly evident: This was man-to-man, and the squire knew it absolutely.

"No...no facts, I suppose I must admit. But see here: I questioned my daughter closely, because I simply could not believe she'd reject Rawlins Butler out of hand, unless she'd been otherwise attracted. Now, ask yourself: Who else is there in this area? Only one self-reliant, skilled, ambitious man, in a community of backwoodsmen. And every time I mentioned your name, she blushed like a schoolgirl. Now what does that tell you, sir?"

"God only knows, Mr. Thomas. I have no idea what goes on in the mind or fancy of any woman alive, and if you'll admit it, neither do you. They have us there, bless them. But on my honor, I've never initiated any contact with your daughter. Nor have I rudely rejected her visits. All I've ever done was win a shooting match against Butler, which, you will recall, he challenged me to."

"Well, yes, he did that. Cost me eight pounds, too."

"Listen, sir. I know you want the security of a marriage of means for your daughter. I'd want the same for her if she were my own. I will certainly admit she is a lovely girl, and if I had any decent prospects, I would not rest in a suit for her hand, myself. I am honest in owning to that admission. But I am aware of reality, Mr. Thomas. I have the highest respect for you and Mrs. Thomas, and for Miss Abigail herself. I would not—will not—dishonor that respect with any untoward action, now or ever."

"You will not attempt to see her?"

"I have never attempted to see her, sir. And I am certain you are well aware of that." He held the planter's eye. The man's outrage faded.

"By God, I believe you, Stephen. It just seemed so right, her and Butler. That fine place, the social position..."

"If you'll pardon the impertinence, sir, I don't think you, of all people, would ever want to realize some time in the future, that you'd caused a treasure like Abigail to become some man's ornament."

"You don't think...Was that what I almost did?"

"I don't know. You might ask her. I've the idea she loves her father very much, and wants him to know her heart. Her deep heart. From what little I see, there seems a great depth to that young lady. Let her know she means more to you than mere concern for her financial security."

"Stephen, Stephen. I've wronged you, I fear." The older man put a hand on the younger's shoulder. "Forgive a father's misplaced concern."

"No need to ask, sir. If our positions had been reversed, I'd probably have come with a shotgun. But she will choose someday. And he may not be to your liking. May God guide you then, sir."

~ * ~

"Well, the fat's in the fire, ain't it, Stephen? Old man about dropped his teeth, me with that book."

"Yes an' no, Tom. Was onto me hard about that. I coulda spun him something about your learning to read before, but it didn't feel right. He was mad about the other thing, and I'm afraid I owned up. And, of course, he'd hit me with the law thing. So I told him how you're nobody's slave, and I reckon I shouldn't have. That was for you to decide."

"I guess. But I'm tired of it, too. Bein' free doesn't count for much if nobody knows it. Like havin' the cards an' not bein' able to play ''em."

"Well, there're folks like the Comptons and Ike Collins are uncomfortable with the slave/master thing, anyway. And, of course, me."

"Now you, I worry about. I know it bothers you, pretendin', when folks are around."

"So, what now?"

"Well, I reckon th' squire'll tell it around. Some, anyway. An' we can let it out a little, here'n there, see how it fits." He considered this for a moment. "Oh, how'd you come outta the other bit?"

"Well, of course you know what that was about, wise man. I just told him the truth…that I'd never courted his daughter, never cut Butler out, never compromised her."

"Have to tell him you never would?"

"I guess I did. Listen, Tom, she made it clear she doesn't know how she feels about me, though I'd like to think otherwise. Figure to let time pass. If she wants it to happen between us, she'll find a way, even if we have to leave the country. But the squire's been good to me here, and I'll not slip around on him."

"Got more grit than most men."

"And man, does it cost me. You have no idea, Tom."

It cost Stephen every night in his cabin, where he couldn't keep the soft lips and yielding body of the girl out of his mind. More than once he'd stumbled out the door, down the steep bank to the icy spring branch, heedless of snakes, and plunged in to get the remembered feel of her off him. That mouth, those breasts, the arms about him, the fingers...

"All right! Enough!" Torture a man, a pretty woman would. Friends. Just friends. And now he didn't even get to see her. Well, that'd change. The old man wasn't as hard as he'd always thought he was. If she really decided she wanted him, he'd give in. And if that were the case, he wouldn't keep her away, meantime; he wasn't that mean. *But damn, I do want that woman. Do want her.*

~ * ~

There were other dances, other barbecues, picnics. The new church opened in a log building on the river the men put up in a day of heavy hewing, lifting, notching, nailing, pegging, laughter and good food. Stephen and Tom went to this and as many others of these events as their work allowed. They danced with the girls, worked with the men, visited, talked. Gradually, the community came to know Tom as a free black. He was always respectful, always with Stephen, a part of things.

"But I don't fool myself," he said. "If you weren't here, I wouldn't be welcome anywhere. Sure, they like my knives, my tools an' such, but live amongst ''em on my own? No, sir."

Stephen saw Abby, and Annie too, now and then. The girls were friends, at least outwardly…had known each other for years. Both were friendly enough to him, but both a little standoffish too, he fancied. When Abby had made no effort to come see him, he knew her father had told her of his pledge to stay away, and she was honoring that.

Now what in hell have I done to myself? Scared her with that fire-and-gunpowder talk first of all, and now she believes the hands-off promise I made her pa. Me and my big mouth.

As for Annie, he saw her on visits to the Compton farm, and at the new church, where she taught the children and he went some Sundays, with Tom.

"I see our secret's no longer a secret," she'd said, at the church log-raising.

"That's right. Tom sort of got tired being free without really being free. I hope the folks take it well."

"Some will. As long as he's with you, they all will." He hoped that would be true, but just then he wanted this conversation to continue.

"How did you like Calvin?"

"He's so positive. I'm not sure some of his basic arguments are that well-founded, but he has a lot of sound things to say."

"I'll want to study him closer. Theology is such an inexact science. Not at all like mathematics."

And so on. Stephen got the idea Annie was sparring with him, never letting him into her mind. *Well: her business.* It wasn't her he dreamed of holding, loving. And now he'd about cut himself off from the girl he really wanted. *Damn.*

~ * ~

It was market day in Charlottesville, and Stephen needed supplies. He'd shipped his furniture to Richmond, and some to Scottsville with freighters, riding along with them to ensure safe arrival. Now, before going home, he wanted to stock up on food staples, leather, gunpowder. He wandered the stalls of the vendors under the trees in the bright fall air.

"Hello, Stephen." The voice brought him around. She was alone, in a pretty dress with a shawl. His eyes took her in hungrily.

"I've missed you, Abby. You don't know how much."

"Let's walk. Mama's visiting friends, but I had to get out into the air. How've you been?"

"Lonely. When I promised your father I wouldn't see you, I hoped we could still manage something."

"We could have. But Stephen...Stephen, after that kiss, I'm afraid of us. You said that about gunpowder..."

"I wish it'd been a lie."

"I know what you mean now, what you said about being just friends. I want that, but you and I..."

"We couldn't—shouldn't—stop there."

"Yes...No. It just seemed safer, to stay away. And no, it hasn't been easy for me, either."

"Is that what you want? To stay away?"

"I don't know what I want. Do you?"

"I certainly do. I want Abigail Thomas."

"Oh, Stephen—don't..."

"Tell me, Abby, if I were to come see your father properly, declare my intentions, what could I hope for from you? Really?"

"Are you going to do that?" Her eyes were wide.

"I'm having a hard time living without you. I think I must resolve this, one way or the other. If you'll allow me a proper courtship, I'll defy any odds to win you. There: Declared."

"Oh, Stephen. I don't know what to say. I..."

"Look at me, Abby. No, don't look away. Don't put it off. Tell me now what I'm to do. You know what's in my heart; I must know what's in yours. When I held you that time, kissed you, the world changed. I can't go back, and I don't believe you can, either. That gave you the resolve to break off with a man you didn't love. To be true to your deep heart. Now you must follow it."

His voice had dropped to a whisper. They were standing under a great, old tree off the busy court square, away from the people. Her liquid eyes looked into his, as if for an answer, a guide, the way. Then they closed, and her lips parted, trembled.

He took her gently in his arms, her body, her lips at once yielding, seeking, responding. Bronze leaves drifted upon them.

~ * ~

In Philadelphia, a group of seminary students were well into their final year of studies. Though the institution had been forced to operate on a limited scale during the war, by now things were mostly back to normal. And like students everywhere, these soon-to-be men of God were the mixture of dedicated scholars, medium achievers, and those who weren't quite sure this should be their life's work after all.

The capital city boasted perhaps more than its share of attractive young ladies, just waiting to be squired about, and for the most part, those young men saw no reason to exclude female companionship from their lives, now or in their future places of employment. They weren't monks, after all.

A notable example of the well-rounded seminary senior class was one Dwight Millington, of a prominent Philadelphia family, whose parents had urged him to study, not go off and fight for Independence. And a safe profession, they argued, given the unsettled character of the new country, would be the ministry.

Dwight did not disagree. Among his classmates, he often declared that he was "a lover, not a fighter." He was disarmingly handsome, and as life often treats such genetic specimens, things had come easily to him. And sometimes he found it difficult to focus on this life of service he'd agreed to. There was just too much to delight his senses in the offerings of the capital for a man with the world almost literally at his feet.

Dwight wasn't shallow, he kept telling himself. He fully intended to follow this profession with dedication, perhaps even to some outpost where the people were unlettered, in dire need of religious guidance. He could make a profound difference in their lives, he was sure, more so than if he took an established city church, which his connections could surely arrange.

But he was a youth of appetites, which his parents had seen early on. That was another reason they'd urged him to follow a respectable course, above the frivolities so many young men were prone to. Yes, wherever he responded to the call, they were certain their son would be a serious man of God. Just not too far away, his mother had hoped. Some place with civilization, educated people, but not too filled with diversions. Until he could find himself a respectable wife, establish himself as a leading fixture in whichever part of this new world he chose.

Now, out with some of his classmates for a harmless mug of ale and an escape from the rigors of study, Dwight Millington began to feel the familiar urge to rebel. While his companions joked and laughed, he pondered the path to security and the measure of fame his parents wanted for him.

That's not serving God, just following another minister in an established urban church. I want something different, a real challenge. Maybe some frontier village, or just a farming community. Wouldn't pay much, but money's not the object, here. And I'd certainly be my own man in a situation like that, not so much watched over, directed, restricted.

Oh, but I wouldn't want there to be no social life at all. No, not ugly girls without all their teeth, people who never wash, speak in words of one syllable. But Jesus taught and healed among the poor, the homeless, the outcasts; I can do that too.

But I'll also want a wife someday, so tying myself down to a backwoods church and community may not be the answer, either. Possibly I could find a place, if one exists, with a needy congregation plus eligible young ladies. That'll mean a prosperous locality, since culture, education come with money.

So this young man, who'd kept company with more than his share of attractive girls in the capital and enjoyed a good time as well as the next youth, pondered his future. And fantasized about the ideal church, be it a new one among the savage Indians, or one consisting of secure families with that necessary culture.

And yes, charming daughters.

Twelve

He'd been in the big parlor before, but not under these circumstances. He'd never been anywhere under these circumstances.

"I think we'd better wait in here," Gertrude Thomas had said. "Hezekiah will be here shortly. Abby's out riding." She sent the housekeeper for tea. "And frankly, I welcome a few minutes to talk with you myself. We've never had more than a few words between us, Stephen. I regret that."

"So do I, ma'am."

"Yes. Well, to get right to it, my husband told me that you and he agreed you would not press a...a relationship with Abby. Is that correct?"

"Correct."

"Why did you agree to that?"

"Why? He asked me to. I respect your husband a great deal."

"Do you love my daughter, sir?"

"Yes, I do. I have loved her for a long time."

"And yet you stood by while that ass Butler paid court to her all that time, when any man of insight could see she didn't love him. Ah, here's tea. Thank you, Bessie. I'll serve; you may go." The servant withdrew.

"And when she rejected him, any fool could see you were her choice. Didn't you know that? Are you blind?"

"Well, ma'am, right now I am feeling pretty blind." He spread his hands. "The truth is, I came here two years ago with nothing: a hard, bitter soldier, and the squire gave me the chance I needed. Just seeing Abby changed my mind about going West, but I knew I'd never deserve her..."

"Deserve her? You mean be able to buy her?" The woman's face was a hard mask.

"No, of course not. I..."

"That's really what you meant, though…have land, a business, financial security?"

"Well, yes, in essence."

"So what's the difference? Listen, Stephen, a woman doesn't want a man who's buying her, or who needs half a lifetime to build an empire before he comes for her. And she damn sure doesn't want one so hamstrung on his honor he won't fight for her. My daughter needs a real man. Someone who'll love her, protect her, make her feel like a woman.

"Now, you've done just fine in two years. And you'd have done it anywhere. I'm not worried about your being able to put food on the table. I want to know if you're man enough for my girl. If you are, you've got my blessing. If you're not, I don't ever want to hear your name again. Do we understand each other?" Her hands were on her hips, her eyes blazing. Stephen felt intimidated by this forceful woman, but he also found he admired her greatly.

"I think we do. And thank you."

"Good." She softened, reached out to touch him. "Ah, here comes the squire, and Abby's with him."

Stephen felt the battle was essentially over by then. More so when Abby breezed in, took his hand and kissed him on the cheek. He caught a quick smile from her mother.

"Well, Stephen," said the planter, looking from one to the other of the three, "Abby's been fairly bubbling over all the way back from the mill, and here you are. Why do I detect a conspiracy? Has anything been going on I wouldn't approve of?"

"Nothing outside our agreement, sir. But I find that both your daughter and I have come independently to the conclusion that we'd like your permission to become engaged."

"Oh, you would? Well, now. Abby?"

"Absolutely, Papa."

"Gertrude? I assume you've had the opportunity to put this young man on the rack?"

"I have."

"Then what the hell do I have to say about it? I mismanaged the pairing I had in mind, and it hurts to admit it."

"Papa, you're a dear," and she kissed him.

"Oh, but I've a question or two. How'd you two manage to...work this out between you? Stephen had me believing he'd keep his word, and..."

"Oh, Papa. We literally bumped into each other market day, while Mama was at the Henleys'."

"It was the right time at the right place, sir. I don't think draft horses could have pulled us away from each other."

"So. And now, Stephen, second question: Where do you propose to live? Not in that dollhouse?"

"No, sir. The hilltop just across from the shop, over the pond, back a way. It's just over the line between us, on your side, but it'd be a fine site. I can have a sound house up by spring, if I can buy a few acres with it. The men in the community will be glad to help with a raising."

"I'd planned to clear on up from there, toward the mountain. That'd make pasture, but it's mostly too rocky to plow. I suppose we could spare some acreage, eh, Gertrude?"

"Oh, for God's sake, Hezekiah, of course. You don't even know how much land you have."

"Oh, yes I do. To the square foot."

~ * ~

News of the engagement for the planned spring wedding spread through the Buck Mountain community, and up and down Lynch River. A date for the house-raising was set for early December, before snow time. Stephen and Tom hewed beams as their shop work allowed, and set foundation stones.

Abby had designed a traditional two-story Virginia farmhouse, with entry stair hall flanked by parlor and dining room, with a separate kitchen off the dining end to the rear. Later this could be joined, for pantry below and bedrooms above. The ceilings were to be high for summer coolness, and each room would have a fireplace.

Annie Compton took the news of Stephen's impending marriage with the impassiveness usual with her, showing neither remorse nor joy. Isaac and Bobby would help with the raising, and yes, she would go along with the other women, to cut pegs, make food and visit. Bobby was now as tall as she, and was taking his place alongside his father in the fields and elsewhere.

Young Web Collins had married his Lucy, and lived in a cabin the community had helped him build upslope from his grandfather. He'd be present also, with Ike, Abner Cocke, the overseer Ed Byers and many others. Stephen found he had more friends than he'd thought.

He had politely but firmly declined the offer of the Thomas field hands for this work.

"I'm not criticizing your owning your people, Mr. Thomas, but we plan to hire our help. And I want to begin that way."

"Independent as a hog on ice," the squire grumbled to his wife. "Surely he'll not object to Abby's maid Molly going with her."

"We've already settled that, Hezekiah. We're making a gift of Molly to Abby, as we'd always planned. Then she'll free her, and pay her. Her decision."

"Two independent hogs." He threw up his hands.

~ * ~

Raising day came, cloudy but dry. Wagons and riders began arriving at daylight, and Stephen and Ike began assigning the work. The long oak sills were carried by many hands and went onto the foundation stones, and the sill ends were lap-jointed and pegged in. Joist-spacing was laid out, and men began cutting the mortises, while others cut the ends of oak logs square and shaped tenons. As each pair of matching mortises was ready, the log joist was rolled into place, dropped into them, one after another. Then a level line was marked, and men with foot adzes hewed the top surfaces flat for the flooring.

As this progressed and others arrived, Stephen and the other experienced men laid out the bents on blocks in a cleared level space. Each bent consisted of two major posts two stories tall with mortised and pegged cross girts at first- and second-story ceiling levels, a pair of principal rafters, and the angled knee braces that kept them rigid. These massive bents would be raised by the hands of all the adults later in the day, spaced along the sills, joined by wall plates, roof purlins and more knee bracing.

There was a lot to a timber-frame structure. Much hewing of beams still needed doing, and teams of horses were skidding logs out of the forest, as men felled trees where there would later be fields.

Seasoned oak and locust blocks had been split weeks before and kept dry for pegs. Auger holes bored in scrap wood served as size guides for cutting the pegs, which were in constant demand. No metal, nails or bolts would go into the frame: its pegs would secure it. Women and some older children with hatchets and large, heavy knives split and shaped these, leaving corners along their lengths to dig into the round holes to keep them tight.

A steady line of boys brought water from the spring branch for the thirsty men and the women at the cookfires. Most of the food had been prepared ahead, but there would be hot stews from the bubbling kettles, soups, bread from the Dutch ovens.

Abby was in the thick of it, shaving pegs, greeting the women, hugging children. She sought out Annie Compton, took her hands.

"Thank you for coming, Annie. And thank you for being our friend."

The tall girl silently looked her sometime rival in the eyes for a brief moment, then hugged her warmly.

"You needed a friend, Abby. Both of you did. I'm glad for you." No one could have told what was in her heart, just then.

By midafternoon, the first bent was positioned to raise. Temporary blocks secured the lower ends of the posts against slipping as men and women with ropes stood back and pulled, and another group lifted. Then yet more came with push poles as the ropes tightened and the great shape rose. Trailing ropes were siezed by the original lifters, who held back as the big bent reached plumb. The posts and knee braces were bumped into their mortises, each with a shuddering thump. Auger holes were bored, the braces set, pegs driven, then the ropes released. A cheer went up.

"Who'll put up th' pine sprig?" went out the challenge.

"I'll do it. Lemme do it!" yelled little Sam Compton. A ladder was set, and up he scampered, with a small pine bough, to tie to the topmost peak of the frame.

"Awful high, Pa," Sadie worried.

"He's a squirrel, Ma. Tall house though, fer shore."

The other bents followed, and as the light began to fade, men hurried to peg in the plates and enough of the purlins to hold the bents solid. The last bent went up, its plates pegged, in the early December twilight. Another cheer sounded.

Brush was thrown on the fires for light, as more food was passed. Stephen and Abby got around to everyone, thanking each, praising for work well done, laughing. The squire produced a jug of whiskey, then another, which went around freely.

Tom Logan had worked as hard as anyone, never still, hewing, shaping, lifting, mortising. Now he sat back from a fire, a mug of hot cider in one hand, yeast bread and ham in the other, as the neighbors began to leave.

"How you doin', Tom?" Ike Collins greeted, on the way to his wagon. Others waved, greeted.

"Doin' jis' fine right now, Mist' Ike, long's I don't hafta move." He nodded, put down his mug, waved.

"Goodbye, Tom." It was Annie Compton, on her way to the family wagon, with someone's sleeping child in her arms. He stood.

"Miss Annie. You're so very kind to come. It couldn'a been easy."

"You know me too well, Tom. You see into me. No one else does."

"Maybe." A moment of silence. "Do you think I'd be welcome at th' church? By myself?"

"I'm certain you would. Please come. I don't expect Stephen and Abby." She turned away. "I wish them well."

"She'll try, Miss Annie. She'll try."

"Yes, she will. Goodbye, Tom."

~ * ~

The winter had not been especially hard, but the man was suffering from cabin fever, out here in this wilderness. He'd had his main house built, importing expensive labor from out East, and it was comfortable, with the fireplaces kept blazing by his house help. But the days dragged, even with overseeing the maintenance and building, the readying of equipment, the woodworking, land-clearing when the weather permitted.

The man was not a reader, so a stock of books wouldn't have relieved the tedium. Essentially a man of action, he chafed at the forced inactivity. Be better when more settlers populate the area, create some social life, at least.

But these mountains seemed to swallow up his newly-cleared plantation in steep green-forested slopes, rushing streams with their rich bottomland, the whole, limitless fastness of it all.

Well, it would be time soon for another trip back East, which he'd make, even if the river fords were swollen. And if he had to wait a few days for a snowstorm to abate, he could do that. One thing this life afforded him was discretionary time, freedom. He could choose what he'd do on any given day or week, without any constraints but the weather. And he could yes, wait that out any way he chose.

So, back to Caroline County in a few weeks, and the comparative civilization of the planter society there. The taverns on the way were wretched, but with generous payment, he could always secure decent quarters and palatable food. Never been picky about what he ate, anyway.

He'd thought before about getting himself a wife, someone to share in this adventure of the new land. But the marriages of his acquaintances didn't seem that blissful, really. Take that doctor he knew: very attractive young widow he'd married, and one would think the man would be delighted with his situation. But they seemed distant rather than intimate, and the woman was seemingly more of an accessory than a partner.

No, business was what consumed him and his associates, and while a woman could be a companion, one just wouldn't be worth the bother, he'd concluded. And he hadn't the patience for children, with their endless pestering, dirty little hands and runny noses. The challenge of taming the new country was far more enticing, and with his income secure, he could enjoy this life to the full without the complications of tedious relationships.

Now, got to plan this trip out, make sure the overseer keeps a tight watch on th'hands. Sure don't want another one runnin' off like that worthless Tom, on back. Likely got himself killed by a bear, fool thinking he could manage with nothin'. But hell, he didn't cost me anything.

~ * ~

With the orders for furniture, the house-building had gone slowly through the winter. With the remaining purlins up, close-spaced for the chestnut shakes, the structure had needed no decking, although this was an uncommon building method. It meant more mortising, but no sawn lumber.

And the inside walls and ceilings would be of split lath and plaster, sealing out the weather.

The new crosscut saw Stephen and Tom had spent many hours making had been an exercise in fine smithing. They'd begun with a long, medium-carbon content bar shipped from Richmond, which they systematically hammered flat. This meant many heats in the forge, much pounding with sledgehammers, to reduce the two-inch-thick steel toward its eventual flatness. Then there were many more heats, and the use of the flatter, that tool that did just what its name implied, its even bottom laid on the heated anvil steel and struck with a heavy hammer.

Finally the inevitable rough places were ground smooth on the grindstone, a delicate process. Then both surfaces were sanded, with the leather and sand kept perfectly flat on blocks of wood. The teeth were cut out using the hot cut, a chisel with a wooden handle out sideways to keep the smith's hand away from the heat. Then the teeth were set, alternating ones bent slightly to right and left, and sharpened.

Most crosscut saws had identical teeth, but Stephen and his father had observed the advantage of spaced rakers between them that did not cut, but dragged the sawdust out of the wood for more efficient sawing. They hadn't invented this design, but used it extensively.

This treasured saw was used to cut the chestnut blocks for the shakes, and the men rived these soon after the raising. They took turns at the L-shaped froe, and making the roof nails, an endless forging normally reserved for apprentices. Any house, except for a log cabin, required a huge quantity of these.

"Think we should get us one, Tom?"

"An apprentice? Could, I guess. But reckon he'd take orders from me? If he was white?"

"Have to. Or should he be black? I don't care, but we'd have to buy him, then free him. Economics."

"Like me, if I ever want a wife. We oughta think about it, I guess. But you know, Stephen, on that I don't want a dumb wife. And where am I gonna get an educated one around here?"

"Now you lost me. How'd we get onto wives?"

"Oh, I been thinkin', you an' Abby gettin' together an' all, about me, too. Natural. Where am I going? What to?"

"Well, you know you got a home and a business here, people who like you, long's you're breathing."

"And I appreciate it. Lord knows I do. Wouldn't be alive if it wasn't for you. Wouldn't have a skill. Wouldn't have anybody to give advice to, try to keep from doin' stupid things." He grinned.

"You're lonely. You like Molly?"

"No, I don't like Molly. An' don't pair me up like livestock, Stephen."

"Whoa! Only a suggestion. Just thinking that she's free, is all. But you made your point."

"And no offense taken. It's just that...secure as I am here, if I decided to set up shop in Charlottesville, say, or Scottsville, or Richmond, or in the Valley, I'd not only starve, I'd prob'ly get knocked in th' head, stolen again, and this time not get away. I like it here, don't misunderstand, but I really got no choices, do I?"

"Well, maybe not, really. I always thought we'd just be partners. You take the cabin, whatever part of the trade you want, keep the money you make and so'll I. Seems fair. We've helped each other, and nobody's counting."

"Hey, we're like brothers. You're the only white man I could say that to. I won't ever forget that. I guess I am just lonely. But not Molly." His eyes brightened. "Maybe we should get a girl apprentice, teach her stuff."

"Ooh. Abby'd never stand for that!"

"Joke. I'll ask Abby who I might've missed, among the girls. Maybe."

Thirteen

The traveler rode up to the shop on a gray day of thawing rain, cloaked so that it was hard to tell if he were tall, thin, heavy, or just many-layered. He tied his horse and opened the door, stamping the slush from his boots.

"Mr. Davis?" he inquired. Stephen was at the shaving horse, Tom at the forge, shaping a chisel. At sight of the visitor, he froze. The man's face permitted a thin smile at sight of Tom.

"Yes, what can I do for you?"

"Well, you can start, by givin' me back my slave, there. Hello, Tom." And the man drew a pistol from his coat and aimed it at Stephen.

"Whoa, now. Just who in hell are you, mister?"

"Name's Hayes. This boy ran off from my place year or two ago. Would never have found him, but a friend 'n Caroline said you were there, askin' questions. Didn't take much to figure a connection." The man's eyes were small, greedy. He looked from Stephen to Tom, with the confidence a man with a gun always feels. Tom stood rigid, quiet, the hammer and tongs still in his hands.

"Well, Hayes, I know for a fact you stole this man, a free man, with th' help of your friend Doc Weston. Weston witnessed John Logan's freeing him. Now, while you can, you better put that gun away and walk out of here. Your bluff didn't work."

"Oh, but it did. No record of any free Tom Logan in Caroline County. None. Now, you just chain this boy's wrists, Mr. Davis, an' I'll take him along where he belongs. Slaves worth a lot, I expect you know, an' looks like he's learned some, too. Obliged to you for that. But then you've got his work for free, too."

"Last time, Hayes." Stephen leveled his eyes at the intruder, while mentally searching for a weapon. "Recorded in the courthouse here that Tom's a free man. Now, out! While you can still move." His voice was low, deadly.

"Oh, I c'n challenge that. Prior ownership. Had t'do that b'fore. Wastin' time, here. Git movin', Davis!" He waved the pistol.

"One thing more, then: You have one shot. Whichever one of us you get, you might kill, or you might not. But the *other* one of us is for dead sure going to kill you. Not good odds. One of us will rip your guts out, leave you for the crows to eat your eyes, Hayes. Pick your man. And say, is your powder even dry? Awfully wet, out." Stephen had moved his hand a slow few inches to the heavy hickory club on his work bench, used for riving shakes. Hayes licked his lips, looked from one to the other. Davis was the greater danger, but would he risk his life for a black? But then, Tom Logan hated him. Surely Davis wouldn't kill him over a...He swung the pistol toward Tom, wavered.

Stephen hurled the club. Hayes saw the movement, jerked the gun, fired. Tom lunged. The roar and flash thundered in the room as the club struck him in the stomach. In that instant, Tom was on him with the heavy hammer swinging to smash into his skull. He went down, slack, and Tom spun toward his friend. Stephen was on the floor.

"Oh, God, man! Where you hit? Here, lemme see."

The throw had turned Stephen, so he was shoulder-on when Hayes fired, and twisting away. The ball had plowed across his back, bloody but not deep.

"Hurts like hell. Burns, mostly. Not deep, is it?"

"No, not deep. Oh, man, you had me scared, there. Bleedin' a lot. Get you up to th' house."

"No, wait a minute. We've got us a problem, here. We just killed a man."

"I just killed a man. White man, too."

"No, that's not it. He was trying to kill me. That part's all right. But everybody'll wanta know why was he trying to kill me. That part's gonna be harder. Oh, damn, this hurts."

"Oh, man. Yes. Oh, man…"

"All right: I've got it. Get that second jug of whiskey, what's left of it, from the raising. Need it for my back, anyway. All right: Man came in here, drunk. Tried to rob us. Pulled a gun. Shot me. Doesn't matter who killed him. I could have, with the hammer."

"Possible. I sure hit him hard."

"Man, you did, all right. Guess I could've though, even shot. Off-balance, fell over something. Anyway, slosh whiskey on him, pour some in him. Not too much. We'll get the squire to send for the constable, do it up legally…Man, does this hurt!"

While Tom cleaned and bound his wound with cloth they kept for rubbing furniture, Stephen had another thought.

"It'd be best, Tom, if you hadn't even been here."

"Been thinkin' that, but it leaves you hangin'."

"You could've said that another way. No, he shot me; that's clear to anybody. Why couldn't you have heard the shot from up at the cabin, run down and found us?"

"Sounds reasonable to me, but if any of it ever got to a courtroom, from what my master told me, some lawyer'd say you went after him with th' hammer an' he was defendin' himself."

"Oh, you got a devious mind. If they ever train black lawyers, you oughta be one. Ouch! That hurts."

Tom had poured whiskey on the wound, then helped Stephen up to the cabin, where he convinced him to lie on his stomach on the bed. He then went back down to the shop. He was worried about the robbery story, Hayes being a planter, however dishonest. There were only a few gold coins on the body, but he found a few more in his saddlebags.

He was pondering the next step, the next necessary act to make this scene fit their story, when Abby Thomas rode up from the creek ford. *Worst time in th' world for her to be here.*

"Hello, Tom. Whose horse is that?" Her face was shiny in the drizzle, eying the tethered mount.

"Now, I got to tell you this a little at a time, Miss Abby. First, come up to th' house with me. Stephen's up there."

"Up at the…What's wrong? Something's wrong, Tom!" She'd picked up on the tension in the air, in his voice.

"Yes, but Stephen's all right. I'll let him tell you. You go on ''head. And, Miss Abby, he's been hurt, but he's not bad. Go, now." She raced her mare up the twisting path, heedless of the drop to the branch below.

At the cabin, she fairly flung herself off the horse and onto the porch. Throwing the door open, she caught sight of Stephen, lying on the bed, bandaged tight around his back and chest. Blood stained the bandage. The odor of whiskey was strong.

"Stephen! What?" She ran to him, eyes wide.

"It's all right, Abby. Just a scratch. Tom's got me bound up like a cheese, but I'm not hurt badly. Some drunken man came into the shop, must've thought I was somebody else. Started yelling at me; drew a pistol. I hit him with a hammer just as he fired, and the ball cut across my back. Not deep at all."

"Oh, my God! He could've killed you! Oh, I'm so grateful you're alive...What happened to him?"

"Abby, I must've hit him hard. He's dead."

"Oh!" She put a hand to her mouth as the reality sank in. "Oh, but I'm glad. He shot you!"

"He did, and I'm still trying to figure why. Tom heard the shot and ran down, found us. Used whiskey on the wound. Burned like hell, I can tell you, but should heal. He's had a lot of practice patching up soldiers."

"Oh, my poor Stephen. And you never saw this man before? Just came in with a gun and...?"

"Stumbled in, actually. I think he was lost or something. Couldn't understand him, but I couldn't make him put the gun down, either. Something crazy was in his mind, I guess. Last thing I wanted was to kill a man over nothing."

Tom came in the door, after a polite knock.

"Man didn't have any papers on him, Stephen. No tellin' who he was, or from where. Not much in his saddlebags."

"So. Just passing through, you think? Why anyone would come here...I was just telling Abby, he must've mistaken me for somebody else, Tom."

"Could be. Sure a bad whiskey smell to'im. Somebody may have seen him—talked to him—on th' way here. Might've told somebody somethin' that'd say who he was, anyway." This was an idea Tom had wanted to get to Stephen. Hayes had known exactly where he was going, and the name of the man he was looking for.

"Maybe. Abby, we must tell your father about this; have him get word to the constable in Charlottesville. Tom, I'd leave everything where it is for now; let the law take over."

"Take my mare, Tom; I'm staying with Stephen. Tell Papa what's happened. He can send someone to town. Should we have a doctor?"

"No, no, Abby. Tom's done me up tight. If I don't bend, I'll be all right. Bled well. With you to nurse me, I'll recover. Promise."

"Reckon I'll leave you two then, but I dunno—no chaperone." Tom smiled broadly, lightening the mood.

"Get going, Tom; I'm immobile, remember?"

After his grinning friend had left, Abby stroked Stephen's brow.

"You can't move?" She was all concern, her luminous eyes wide, the touch of her cool fingers on his skin soft. In spite of the pain, he began to feel a delicious, dangerous sensation.

"Did I say that? I meant I can *hardly* move."

~ * ~

The lawman was there by dark. He surveyed the scene, smelled the dead man's whiskey-sodden clothes, sniffed his pistol. The squire was with him.

"Y'say th' hired man found ''em, Mr. Thomas? Where was he?"

"Up at the cabin, Josh. Stephen's there now. Ball cut him across the back. He can tell you how it happened."

"And y'know Stephen Davis well, do you? Vouch for him?"

"Of course. Solid man. He's to marry my daughter."

At the cabin, Stephen told the constable only that a strange man had stumbled into the shop waving a pistol, yelling wildly.

"I tried to talk reason to him, but he was drunk, or maybe crazy. Had to've thought I was somebody else. Wouldn't put the gun down. Got my hands on the hammer."

"Not much d'fense ''ginst a loaded pistol."

"It was all I had."

"Wal, Squire, I'll haul th' body in on his hoss. Git him buried. See if somebody shows up, if ennybody ever does. Decent hoss; warn't poor. Had some money in his saddlebags. Drunk, yes. Crazy, prob'ly. If this wuz on th' road to ennywhere, I c'd figger it, but t'ain't. Strange." He went out, shaking his head.

"You'd better come on home, Abby," her father told her. "Tom's got Stephen well taken care of."

"Thanks, sir. She's smothering me with care."

"And you've loved every minute of it. Hasn't he, Tom?"

"Enjoyin' his ill health I'd say, Miss Abby. I'll go help th' constable load that man."

~ * ~

The wound took awhile to heal, and Stephen chafed at the enforced delay in building. He sent for Web Collins.

"Web, I got myself shot. Would you think about working for me awhile? I can do some, but not much."

"Heard ''bout that. Glad y'got th' feller. An' work? I'd shore think about it, Stephen."

"Would you do it?"

"Might. I cain't do that fancy furniture work, though."

"No, mostly on the house. Need to get it ready."

"Whyn't y'git th' squire's hands on it? Hear he offered."

"Stubborn, proud and stupid. Thought you might understand that."

"Reckon I do. Who'd I be takin' orders from, you er Tom?"

"It matter?"

"No. Hell, that man's a deal smarter'n' me. Just wanted to know. Be here in th' mornin'."

He was, and with Stephen directing, the work went ahead. Window sashes were being built of the old-growth pine, and glass had been ordered from Richmond. A quantity of clapboarding had been sawn on the squire's mill, and siding began. Stephen put Web to splitting laths from the pine, thousands of four-foot splits for the plaster interior walls. And every lath would need three nails.

"Tell you what, Stephen," the squire proposed, "you're stubborn, but here's an idea: A smith's apprentice would be free labor, correct?"

"That's right, in return for learning the craft."

"For the time specified. Say seven years. Then he goes away, trained. Now, I've a daughter in this operation, and she's impatient. I'll give you a young boy off the place, and you can own him or free him, as you wish. He'd be just a field hand to me, but you can probably make a craftsman out of him, against all reason. Anyway, that would help get things along, if he makes nothing but nails. What do you say?"

"You, sir, drive a hard bargain. Thanks. I'm not sure I can ever repay your generosity."

"Grandchildren will be fine, Stephen, fine."

~ * ~

A plasterer was engaged from Charlottesville, lime was bought, sand sifted from the creek. Stephen was able to glaze the windows himself, with the standard 8x10-inch panes. Tom had done most of the joinery, but Web soon learned some of this close work, too.

"Those two are my windas, Miss Abby. Ever' time you look outta them, to th' west, y'll be lookin' outta Web windas," he said proudly.

"They're fine, Web. Now, you take this little blanket on to Lucy…I know the baby's due soon."

"Why, thankee, ma'am. Yes'm, baby's due enny time. Her ma's with her, an' Annie Compton comes, too."

"Good. Tell her I'll be by. And when that baby comes, Web, I don't want to see you over here. Stephen can do without you for a few days. Lucy'll need you home."

"Yes, ma'am. Stephen's gittin' ''round better."

"He is, but he'll try to do too much."

The new apprentice, Willie, rarely spoke, but his eyes took in everything. He was quick to learn the basics: how to lay the forge fire, heat and hammer scrap pieces of iron into nail rod. How to taper, cut and head the nails themselves. He'd continue to live at the plantation, Stephen having no place to house him, and that was satisfactory. And with the steady supply of nails, the lathing went up quickly.

Flooring was another matter. The edge-grain heart pine had seasoned a little over the winter, but there was not enough for the entire house. Stephen fretted.

"We're only two people," Abby reminded him. "We'll just leave the other rooms till the wood's ready."

"I wanted it all done for you."

"And you know what I overheard an old hand of ours say once? 'People in hell want ice water, too.' We're not planning any balls or parties soon. We'll have plenty time. For everything." She gave him an arch smile, which he knew was a promise. Which in turn made him more impatient.

"I'm just reminded you're marrying a poor man."

"You're not poor…you've got me."

"Shameless. Kiss me."

"Mm. That's made a ridge on your back. Hurt?"

"Itches. Your fingers feel good."

"You feel good. Proper young ladies aren't supposed to say such things, are they?"

"I love you, Abby."

"Good, ''cause you're stuck with me."

Fourteen

In due time, Constable Joshua Stokes was visited by two men of standing. One was a Dr. Horace Weston, of Caroline County. The other was Rawlins Butler, of Swift Run.

"And what might I do fer you gentlemen?" he asked, after they'd entered his small office in the courthouse in Charlottesville.

"We're here on serious business, Constable," the doctor began. "An associate of mine, a Mr. Jacob Hayes, disappeared in February on his way to his plantation west of the Valley. Now, I know for certain he planned to call on a man named Davis, Stephen Davis, a furniture maker out from here. My friend Mr. Butler here knows the man. And he tells me this Davis killed a man at his place at the time Mr. Hayes vanished. The connection is too obvious, sir."

"I see. An' this Hayes was...you said a ''sociate?"

"In business, yes. He, Mr. Butler and I had certain trade interests in common."

"All right. Well, I kin tell you this much, Dr. Weston: A man come into Stephen Davis' workshop, drawed down on him with a pistol, shot him, didn't kill him. Davis got th' feller with a hammer, killed *him*. Now, might be that'uz yer man Hayes, all right. Clear case of self-d'fense, though. Feller wuz drunk, an' maybe crazy, way Davis told it."

"Jacob Hayes was not the least bit crazy, Constable."

"Mebbe not. But drunk he shore wuz. Smelled like a still."

"Nonetheless, I strongly suspect foul play. And Mr. Butler feels that way, also."

"Any reason fer that? Either of you?"

"Mr. Butler knows this Davis, and tells me he is not of good character..."

"Hah! Beat yer time with Squire Thomas' daughter, that's whar that come from. No sir, Doctor, afraid this county thinks a lot of young Davis. Don't reckon that about foul play'll stick ''round here."

"Then there's the matter of the money," the doctor continued, as if he hadn't heard Stokes. "Mr. Butler informs me Mr. Hayes appeared to have been robbed."

"Don't reckon so. He had some gold on him, few more coins in his saddlebags. No robbin' to it."

"Oh, but he was carrying a chest with quite a large sum when he left Caroline County. Something happened to that money, and we're quite certain this Davis is responsible."

"Y'seem awful sure. But y'said early on yer friend was headin' fer Davis' place. Y'know what fer?"

"That is another thing: He had reason to believe Davis had aided a runaway slave belonging to him. And Mr. Butler tells me the man has such a slave."

"Free black man. Y'oughta know that, Mr. Butler. Ever'body aroun' does. Tom Logan."

"Ah, but that's the very slave, sir. He came off my own plantation. I sold him to Mr. Hayes when he went west to his new place."

Butler had remained silent throughout this exchange. He eyed the constable now, something like triumph on his face.

"Wal," Josh Stokes admitted, after a long pause, "'pears they ain't much to parts of what yer sayin', Doctor, but mebbe, all together, it might add up to somethin'. Part about th' money don't figger, though. If th' man'uz robbed, wouldn't of been any money on him, an' there wuz."

"I can't explain that, Constable. Mr. Butler here understood there was no money on Hayes."

"Wrong, that. It wuz there. I counted it m'self. ''Bout what a man'd carry on him, travelin'.''"

Butler spoke then, determined to pursue the issue.

"The black man, Logan, though, Constable? It seems clear Davis stole the man. Or at least aided in his escape."

"Now, Mr. Butler, I don't aim to offend you, but y'got to understand, anybody hereabouts is apt to take anything you say agin' Stephen Davis with a grain of salt. Y'ain't exactly happy with th' man to begin with."

"If you're saying I'm making false accusations, Constable..." Butler drew himself up. The lawman waved a hand.

"Now, don't git all riled. But both of you should know, this Tom Logan was freed, legal, an' th' record's in th' courthouse here. Made it my business to know that, there bein' so few free blacks around. Now, jist where th' man come from is somethin' else agin, an' mebbe that needs lookin' into some. But that business ''bout a lot of money, that don't wash."

"Constable," Weston spoke crisply, "we can cut through all this conjecture. We believe Mr. Hayes confronted Davis, and that Davis attacked him. It seems evident that Mr. Hayes fired in self-defense. We want Davis charged with murder, to put it directly. He should be arrested immediately."

The constable fixed this self-important doctor with a cold eye. *Pushy feller. I'm th' one decides whether to arrest a man or not.*

"Self-defense, huh? Guess y'don't know Stephen Davis was shot in th' back, Doctor. In the back!"

Confusion registered on both the other men's faces as this fact sank in. Butler had heard of the shooting, but not the details. Weston shot him a questioning glance, but then recovered and returned to the attack.

"Nevertheless, sir, a great deal of money is missing, a slave has been stolen, and our associate is dead. I'm charging this Davis. I will swear out a warrant. It will be up to a court of law to decide the case, but I insist that he be apprehended and jailed." The smug look had returned to Butler's face.

"Wal, we'll look into it, then. But you should know, there's some right powerful folks'll vouch fer young Davis."

"That should not subvert justice, Constable. And Mr. Hayes had powerful friends, too, which are also ours."

"Seems so. Wal, like I said, I'll look into it. Oh, any next-of-kin, yer Mr. Hayes?"

"None. He lived alone."

"Then his horse an' what money there was will be d'sposed of by th' court. If th' d'ceased even wuz yer friend, that is."

"Isn't that obvious?"

"Not to me, it ain't. You got some provin' t'do, Doctor. An' Butler here, he's got too big ''n axe to grind in all this, far's I'm concerned. But I'll see what I c'n find out. Do m'job, all right."

~ * ~

Damn nuisance, this, Stokes fumed, riding the miles past Nixville. *But those men'll keep on. Money must be in it somehow, all right. Butler wouldn't go this far just out of spite. But th' doc said th' three was in business together, some way. If there was money, it'd pay to know how much an' where it come from. Hmm. Man goin' West carryin' money? Wrong way. Where'd he spend it out in th' mountains? Don't make sense. Wal, Stephen'll mebbe shed some light here. Wouldn't hurt to have th' squire in it, too; he wuz there, close as ennybody.*

No, I b'lieve I'll jist go see Stephen first. No need gittin' Squire Thomas worked up over this if ain't nothin' to it. Boy don't need th' trouble of his girl's kin on him neither, right now. All come out soon enough, but go quiet, fer now...

It happened Tom Logan and the apprentice Willie were away at the plantation forge with Ike Collins when the lawman rode up to the shop. He could see men at work on the new house up on the hill, but rapped on the shop door first.

"Come in," Stephen called from his work bench. Stokes entered to find him planing a door. Tools were about, and the smell of wood. Shavings covered the floor.

"Well, Constable Stokes. Come over by the fire. Bit cool out."

"Is. How's th' back? Healin'?"

"Stiff, still. I can do some, like this, but heavy stuff I have to have a hand with. What can I help you with, Mr. Stokes?"

"Wal, Stephen, there's a little trouble over that crazy man come after you here. Seems Rawlins Butler's hooked up some way with a doctor feller f'm over Caroline County, an' they been t'see me ''bout ''nother man wuz in with ''em, they think might be th' feller y'had to kill."

"That right? Did they say who he was?" *Weston, and Butler's in with him. Have to go carefully here…*

"Name of Hayes. S'posed t'of been headin' west to his place on be-yond th' Valley."

"All right. They have any idea why he came here? Sure not on the way most folks would travel from Caroline."

"Gits a might sticky, right there. S'posed t'of been carryin' a lotta money on him, but that don't add right. Y'know, there wuz some on him, but not much. Anyway, yes, this Doc Weston says Hayes told him he wuz comin' here. Somethin' about Hayes having' a slave run off, thought you was in that some way. Butler'd told th' doc ''bout yer Tom, and I reckon this Hayes figgered a connection."

"That's a little thin."

"Thought so m'self. Easy to clear up though, if y'got anything on pa-per says you owned Tom legal."

"I've the bill of sale from his former owner, up at the house."

"That'll do it, then. I know you recorded freein' him at th' courthouse. But this doctor, he figgered you jumped this Hayes, an' he shot you, self-de-fense. Didn't know you wuz hit in th' back.

"Seemed t'me like he'n Butler'd got all this up ''tween ''em. Now, ever'body knows Butler'd spite you in a minute, over losin' Abby. An' that don't signify, not to me. But this doctor, he's keen to nail you, seems like, an' that's got me wonderin' why. Money's th' easy reason, but don't ''pear to've been enny. Doc figgers you got it though, an' he's swore out a warrant on you."

"He has? Don't like that."

"No, an' it ain't jist fer robbery. Murder too, though I c'n tell you that won't stand, no way."

"Well. So I'm supposed to have robbed this crazy drunk who came after me with a gun? Actually, Josh, I could use some money. I'm having to trade everybody in this end of the county to get my house built."

"Knew that. Butler prob'ly told th' doc ''bout th' house an' all. Looks t'me like they cooked it all up on you. Cain't figger why, though. I wouldn't think Butler'd be all that spiteful."

"Wouldn't have thought so. But damn, you said this Weston swore out a warrant? That's bad, with my being all set to get married."

"Butler was almost grinnin' ''bout that. Hate to have this mess you all up, Stephen, but I gotta do m'job, too."

"You have to put me in jail, Josh?"

"Aw, no. But I'll hafta git th' squire to stand fer you. I'se hopin' to keep him outta this till I could talk to you. Put you in a bad light with Abby's family an' all."

"That shouldn't matter, Josh. It'll be plain to him there's nothing to all this but a lot of wind. But you know, I'm like you—what's got this doctor after me? Oh, I should tell you, I met the man back last year, when I was out trying to sell my furniture. Over in Caroline County. His wife liked my samples, but he wasn't buying."

"That right? Y'say ennything to rile him up?"

"Hardly talked to him that much. But he did know where to find me. I told everybody. I'll warrant he told this Hayes, if that's who it was."

"Wal, with th' man dead an' all, an' if there was money, an' it missin', looks like it'll end up in court. Be trouble fer you, I know. An', Stephen, bein's I'm th' law here, I cain't give you no slack, no moren' enny other man. If th' squire'll stand good fer you, ain't no need to arrest you, but looks like I gotta follow this all up. My job."

"I understand that, Josh, and I thank you for letting me know first. We can go up to the squire's now. Let me tell Web and the plasterer up at the house where I'll be."

"That Ike's Web? Married little Lucy Green?"

"Is. Got a baby boy, now. Web's learning woodworking. Good hand. Helping the plasterer now. Jones, from town."

"I know Bobby Jones. Do you a good job. Stephen, I'm sorry as hell this's come up. Be hard on Abby. When's th' weddin'?"

"Supposed to be next month. Say, how long does it take usually, to get a thing like this into court?"

"D'pends on how heavy th' docket is. Right now, things is mostly quiet, ''cept fer th' usual fights, land squabbles. Could be in a week er two, way that Doc Weston wants to push it."

"And Rawlins Butler would like to see it break up our wedding, I know. Sore loser, that man."

"Is. Ever'body knows you outshot him too, that time. Prideful feller."

Squire Thomas took the news almost calmly, dismissing Butler's involvement with a gesture of irritation.

"Narrow man. Thank God Abby wouldn't have him. But this doctor... Did he say where this alleged money came from, Josh? That seems to be the issue here."

"No, and I never asked him. Like to know that; been thinkin'. Th' whole robb'ry thing don't add up, but if there was money, where'd it go to? That's where th' doc an' Butler can come down on Stephen hard. If there was money."

"Well, Stephen, if you'd taken money, which of course you didn't, you surely wouldn't have had to scratch and trade to build your house. It's a testament to his character, Josh, that so many people have helped Stephen."

"Is, and nobody's even thinkin' you got anybody's money, Stephen. But let's figger: Either there wasn't no money in th' first place, an' th' doc an' Butler jist cooked that up to nail you..."

"Awfully thin that, Josh," the planter put in. "I doubt even Butler would take his loss of Abby that far."

"No, don't figger so. Or, there was money, say from th' doc an' Butler, an' mebbe some others, an' this Hayes took it, stashed it for hisself. Could've been that kinda feller, way he acted."

"Now, that's an idea, Josh," Stephen agreed. "He didn't come into my place quiet, like a reasonable man. Had his gun out, right off."

"An' it seems that part fits some, him with th' idee you had his runaway slave. Wrong man, but he was ''parently all het up, an' drunk to boot. I seen that, m'self."

"Well, the fat's in the fire anyway, Josh, with this doctor bringing charges. I'm sorry, Stephen; this'll get in the way of the wedding, unless we can clear it up first. When would it get into court, Josh?"

"Soon, sir, but if you c'n come down to the courthouse an' talk to th' jedge, it'll shorely help things along."

Abby and her mother returned at that moment from a visit to Lucy Collins and Web's grandmother, to learn the news.

"Ridiculous," Gertrude Thomas snorted. "Hezekiah, you go right down and work this out with George Henley. See if he can get it dismissed: No evidence. Or if it must go through some court ritual, he can get it over with quickly."

"Oh, Stephen," Abby was outraged, "You get shot by a madman, and they want to arrest you! Mr. Stokes, what kind of a system is this?"

"Crazy sometimes, Miss Abby. But this doctor's got'n axe to grind, and ''course Butler's got his nose outta joint over you'n Stephen. Me'n th' squire and George can mebbe git th' jedge to dismiss it. Like you said, Miz Thomas, ain't no real ev'dence, just circ'mstance."

"I'll go, then," the planter declared. "Certainly I'll bond you, Stephen, if it's even necessary. And don't you fret, Abby. It's probably no more than Rawlins Butler's pique. Sore loser. We won't let it spoil the wedding." He kissed his daughter on the forehead, went for his coat and hat.

~ * ~

"That about the money is what bothers me, Tom," Stephen told his friend later. "It'd be the reason they're after me. Josh told them I'd been shot in the back, so the murder thing is all hollow. And with my bill of sale for you, Josh says we're clear, there. So it's the money."

"And what money was it? I'd say Hayes was low-life ''nuff for any shady dealin', and looks like there's more to Butler's part in this than just spitin' you. An' we know Doc Weston's another lowlife an' a liar. No tellin' where they got the money, any moren' what happened to it."

"Josh thinks Hayes maybe stole it, hid it out from the others, cutting them out, maybe planned to put the blame on me."

"Now that figures. But we'll never know where. Doc thinks you got it, but a lotta folks can swear you're poor as a church mouse, way you're havin' to scratch out a livin'. And nobody would've left any money on Hayes, if he was robbed."

"Well, this's a mess, with the wedding set and all, but no help for it."

Stephen had worried that his accusers might dig deeper into the matter of Tom's status. Weston could identify him, and would surely use that claim to discredit Stephen in the eyes of judge or jury. He sat at his table, took out quill pen and paper, and wrote to his friend Ned Drake.

~ * ~

Judge Amos Edgerton declined to dismiss the case at the insistence of Horace Weston. Given the seriousness of the murder charge, he wanted to hear all the evidence, even knowing Constable Stokes' account. A trial date was set, to hear that and the charges of robbery and of aiding and teaching a runaway slave, if not stealing him outright.

"The fact is," Weston had argued, "that Mr. Hayes left Caroline County with a large sum of money which was not recovered. And the defendant acknowledges killing a man certain to have been him, no matter the circumstances, and no one else had access to the money. And as to the slave, I can and will identify him."

No argument Squire Thomas could mount would sway the judge, so trial was set for two weeks hence, in mid-May. The judge did allow Stephen his freedom, in the custody of Hezekiah Thomas.

"We'll just postpone the wedding, Stephen," Abby consoled him. "If Rawlins Butler thinks he can somehow disrupt our plans, he's wrong."

"Maybe he's counting on your rejecting me as an outlaw, Abby." It was said only partly in jest.

"Nonsense. He's deluded. First of all, you're not an outlaw. And if you were, I'd still marry you, mask and all."

"You're sweet."

Fifteen

The traveler rode up the creek road one bright warm day, eyeing the bottomland fields appreciatively. The farms were generally small, fields climbing the first slopes up from the creek. The mountains loomed blue beyond the one lone, pyramidal one he rode toward. Not broad plantation land like at home, but fresher, newer. He liked it.

At length, following directions, just past that peak he turned his horse off the road onto a farm track to the right that led along a field hugging a rise to his left. He could see a tall house in the distance upcreek, outbuildings. The way led to a narrowing of the field, then there was a ford into woods on his right.

The shop came into view, with the new house on its height beyond and to the left, across a dammed stream. The sound of hammering came from the house, and the waterwheel turned slowly. Peaceful scene, he reflected, as he dismounted at the workshop.

He rapped at the door, and a black man opened it, a question on his face.

"Hello, Tom," Ned Drake greeted. "Stephen around?"

"You know me? I don't believe—"

"Of course I know you, Tom, and don't you ever forget it. I'm Ned Drake. Ah, here comes the man, now. And who's that vision with him? Omigod, I'm in love!"

Stephen and Abby were walking the path down from the new house, hand-in-hand, not seeing Ned's horse or him, at first. Then he whooped a greeting and, startled, they looked up. He'd swept off his tricorner hat and the sun caught his red hair.

"Ned!" Stephen ran to his friend, caught him in a bear-hug, lifted him off the ground. "Damn, it's good to see you. This's Abby, my intended. And Abby, this wild man is Ned Drake, the Redcoats' worst nightmare."

"Ma'am," Ned was all polished manners, bowing low over her hand, never taking his eyes off hers. "Stephen, just so you know in advance, I intend to steal this lady from you, best friend or no." He was still holding her hand. "Miss Abby, there is not an honorable bone in my body, so beware." His grin lighted the bright day even more.

"I can't believe that, Mr. Drake. Stephen tells numerous tales of your valor, your bravery, and yes, your honor."

"Ah, I'm betrayed. Well, well, Stephen, look at what you have here: first-rate shop, fine house up there, and I know you've a snug cabin somewhere. And this lovely lady...Oh, and how's my man Tom doing? Didn't get the chance to talk to him before I spotted you. Have you made a craftsman out of him yet? Because if you have, I want him back." The grin, again.

"He's a fine craftsman, Ned. Let's go on in. He's learned fine steel work; better than I am, and you know I'm good."

"No shame. Miss Abby, how this hermit ever captivated you will be forever a mystery. But I must know: Have you a twin sister, perhaps? Any sister? A widowed mother, even?"

"None of the above, sir," she laughed. "Besides, Stephen has told me there is, or was, a certain red-haired lady in your life..."

"Odd, I don't recall one." Turning to his friend, "Could that have been in Trenton, Stephen? In the war? Maybe at Guilford? So long ago...Ah, Tom. Glad to hear you're doing well. We miss you at the old place. Show me some of your work. I should never have let you go."

Ned was a whirlwind, hardly stopping for breath as he toured the workshop, then the new house. Partly because of the delayed wedding date, the final flooring, now seasoned in the dry heat of the shop loft, was going in, with Web and young Willie at work. Some new furniture was already in place. The maid Molly, a small, bright girl, was cleaning up after the workmen.

After Abby had ridden away, with an invitation to them for supper the next day, Ned faced his friend.

"All right now, Lieutenant, we gotta get some things straight here. You're in trouble, as I understand it, for knocking some crazy in the head who was in the act of shootin' you. I need details."

The three men sat on the cabin porch and Stephen told Ned what had happened. All of it. It took a while, and Tom brought cold cider from the spring.

"Well, now!" Ned whistled, after Stephen had finished, "There's somethin' eatin' at that doctor. May be money…usually is. Now I'm no genius you know, but I'd lay odds, from what you've told me, that there was money, and it wasn't legal. Maybe th' doc kept it, and he's covering his arse by saying Hayes had it. Or maybe Hayes had it and was holdin' out on them.

"Looks to me like this Butler's just along for spite, though he could be in on something, too. Say he's got a big place near here? How'd you reckon he financed that? I can tell you, it's not cheap, a plantation. Most men inherit a place. You know how hard it is to build from scratch, Stephen."

"I do. But that about Weston keeping whatever money there might have been: He wouldn't have to pin it on me. He could've kept quiet, said he gave it to Hayes. I'd say Hayes must've had that money, and now the rest of them want it. Badly."

"Seems so. Say, what'll become of th' plantation Hayes had out West? You said it was big, Tom, lotta slaves, equipment, barns."

"That's right. Hayes didn't have family. Guess th' court, whichever's nearest, would…what, Stephen? Auction it all off?"

"Probably. But I'd lay you odds our Doc Weston ends up with it. He weaseled his way into the Logan place, widow and all. Seems to have been close with Hayes."

"And while we're wonderin'," Ned mused, "how'd Hayes pay for that big place? The land's easy; still a lot available out there, I hear. But what, Tom, thirty field hands? Wagons, barns, tools. And a good house?"

"We ll, he stole some of us. But yes, a good, big house, and he brought in carpenters from up in Maryland to build that. He did spend money, now."

"All right. Now, Stephen, Tom, let's just say for argument's sake, th' doc, Hayes, and Butler too, were in on some crooked dealings somewhere.

Probably others, too. Now, what better way to hide money than in a plantation operation? I can tell you there's many a man goes broke, bad year or two, without enough cash to keep goin'.'"

"But that's bothered me, Ned. Josh Stokes, too. What would Hayes be doing, taking money West? Where'd he spend it?"

"That's just what I was sayin', my friend: on land, slaves, houses, equipment. Doesn't matter how far in the woods you go, money's still money. Say there's others in this hypothetical group. Say they've maybe stolen a lot of money, or even got it legally, some other way. Say they send it out by Hayes to have him find places for them all. Out beyond law, beyond pryin' neighbors. They move West, get respectable, live like kings, no matter whether they make their places pay or not."

"That's a lot of speculation, but maybe possible. What about it, Tom? Many new places around where you were? Lot of money being spent?"

"Now, you got to realize we were all head-down, hard at it on Hayes' place. Not much chance t'know what went on outside. But yes, there's always been a sort of grapevine among us folks. We heard things: places goin' in, new owners comin', stuff like that. A few of us even got traded, loaned out some to do work other places. Yes, a lot of money bein' spent. Never thought about where it came from: rich people just always been rich people to th' poor ones."

"All right. Maybe I'm just pokin' here, but I'd wager, Stephen, that Hayes did have a big pile of cash on him, probably illegal, say from several folks, to be enough for Weston to go after like he is. And he got greedy. Stashed it somewhere."

"But they'd find him out, surely," Stephen pointed out. "Go after him."

"Not if he planned to run clear out of th' country. Ohio's out there, even if it is full of Indians. Kentucky. On west, St. Louis. He could just disappear, Stephen, with all that money."

"Maybe. But why stop in here? He'd have bigger fish to fry."

"Well, yes there's that...All right, so let's say he wasn't stealin' the money from his partners. Let's say he had an idea Tom was here. You said Weston's wife had owned up to the doc's dirty work. She could've let something slip. Say he just wanted Tom. Worth a lot, with all the new places openin' up. But either way, they want that money. And they think you, my friend, have it."

"I wish. So, legal or not, they'll try to get it back. And if your idea that it's stolen money is right, they're the kind of men who won't stop at a trial."

"You, my old soldier, are in a lotta danger. They'll figure you're spending their cash on your house, your business. Or that you've stashed it for later. Wouldn't surprise me one bit if you get visitors soon. Uninvited ones."

"That bothers me a lot. Tom, what's your idea about Ned's theory? Tom's usually ahead of me, Ned."

"Chills me. Knowin' the kind of men these are, I'm s'prised they haven't come after you already."

"Well, it'd be safer for them if they could recover the money legally. Too many dead bodies would be hard to explain. But saying Ned's on the right trail here, how would they find the money? Put me in jail, or hang me and they'd never find it."

"That's right," Ned agreed. "Don't see how that'd help them. Maybe offer you some kind of deal…get you off, for the money."

"Don't follow that one. Tom? You're thinking something."

Tom had risen, a light in his eyes. Now he held up a finger.

"Men, we're close to it. I don't know how they'd get the money out of you, Stephen, with the trial thing, but think: What could they do to make you tell ''em where it was?"

"Pull out my fingernails? Cut off my private parts?"

"No. I think you know, Stephen…"

"Oh, my God! *Abby*!"

"If th' rest don't know about her, they will: Butler'll tell ''em. He'll figure to get her for himself, one way or ''nother. Now, time's gone by, and they haven't made any such move. Maybe Ned's right: they'll try somethin' less… drastic, first. Maybe they still aren't sure you took th' money…they may even suspect Hayes himself. But I'm ''fraid, for a lotta cash they'll come after you through Abby. More so with Butler in it."

"I'll kill that bastard."

"Now, wait a minute, Stephen," Ned cautioned. "Defendin' yourself from a crazy man is one thing, but layin' for an influential planter is another. ''Specially since everybody knows you were rivals. Besides, you—we— would have to kill ''em all, and we don't know who they are, how many there are, or where they are."

"Well, I'm not waiting for anybody to make that kind of move, Ned. If you're right, and I've the feeling you are, I want that girl protected. Till we get this thing cleared up." He rose, took his hat, his rifle.

"Yes, you go on to her folks' place. Tell the squire to keep watch. Wouldn't let her ride anywhere alone. Tom an' I'll try to piece it all out more. He thinks good."

Stephen dug his heels into the black gelding's sides in his haste. Abby had left not long before, but this new worry wouldn't wait. He loped the horse across the ford, sending sheets of water, then upcreek and up the drive. He dismounted, knocked.

"Come in, Stephen," Gertrude Thomas welcomed him. "You're in a hurry."

"Yes, ma'am. Abby here?"

"Why, yes. She came from the new house just a while ago; surely you remember that?"

"Of course. Mrs. Thomas, there may be more trouble. Is the squire home?"

"No, he's at the mill. Sit here. Now, what kind of trouble, Stephen? Wait, I'll call Abby."

The two returned. Stephen was so relieved to see his love was safe, he had to suppress a shudder.

"What's wrong, Stephen?" She was all concern.

"Maybe nothing; maybe everything. Ned, Tom, and I've been trying to figure this whole thing with the doctor, all that about money—the whole business—and just why they're after me. And what we've come up with, Ned, mostly, is that there probably was money, likely stolen money, from what we know of at least the doctor and the man Hayes. And those men, and maybe more, think I have it, which of course I don't. But—and this was Tom's idea—if they can't get it one way, they may get rough: try to force me to tell them where it is, which I can't do, but they think I can." He paused for breath.

"I'm not following this, Stephen," Gertrude Thomas said.

"Sorry, I'm going too fast. Tom's afraid, and so am I, those men will try to get to me through Abby. Plain and simple."

"You mean...take her hostage? Surely—"

"Butler's being in it makes it likely, ma'am. He hasn't taken our engagement well. And if Ned's right, if there's stolen money—and we've learned more about them that makes us suspect it—such men could abduct Abby, hold her hostage to get me to lead them to it. And I'm afraid if Rawlins Butler can't have Abby one way, he may try another." He sat back, looking from mother to daughter.

"I said he was an ass. But if he so much as lays a hand..." Gertrude was livid.

"I'd like to shoot him myself. But we need to know more. Such as, when did he move onto that place?"

"Oh, it must have been seven, eight yers ago. Before his wife died. Bought it, then started pouring money into it. Hezekiah and I were surprised he built it up so quickly. Spent a lot of money."

"Anybody know where his money came from?"

"Well, that's not the sort of thing you ask, Stephen. But now I'm wondering. Did he ever mention that, Abby?"

"No, Mama. I just assumed he'd inherited it. Do you think he's in on... some illegal thing, Stephen?"

"We can't be sure. But something's behind this effort to get to me. Ned thought they might get me jailed, then offer some way to get me off if I'd lead them to the money. Or some other scheme I can't imagine. If there's really any money, which they say there is. A lot of it."

"What do you think happened to it?"

"It's possible Hayes hid it, either to keep it all for himself, or maybe he was just nervous, carrying it. He couldn't have known what he'd run into, coming to my place to claim what he thought was his runaway slave."

"So he might have hidden it nearby, just in case things went wrong..." The plantation mistress' mind was working.

"I never thought of that, ma'am. Let's see, he'd have ridden down from the Swift Run pike...probably traveled that way often from Caroline, but wouldn't have known this area...Ah, your father's here, Abby."

Stephen had soon told Hezekiah Thomas his fears for Abby. The man nodded at the logic of it, growing agitated at the telling.

"...And I'm concerned for her safety, sir, more so if they lose in court."

"Which they will. So your friend Drake owned Tom before: that'll settle that, if Weston pushes that angle. And Josh's testimony will disprove their murder charge. That leaves the money, if there was indeed money. And you're surely right…that's what keeps them after you.

"All right. Abby, you must not go anywhere alone. Stephen, can you be with her every time she's away from this house? Oh, silly question."

"I will, sir, armed and watchful."

"But they could shoot you from cover, take her…"

"Wouldn't ever find the money that way, sir, if I knew where it was."

"Oh, right. Well, then. Trial's in a few days. You have a pistol, Stephen?"

"One. Could you loan me another?"

"Take two: You mightn't have time to reload. Oh, damn such men! Any chance this is all wrong, that there's no danger…"

"I won't take that chance, sir, though I hope we're wrong."

"We're not wrong," Gertrude Thomas stated. Stephen had come to appreciate this woman as his ally. And just now, not for the first time, he was doubly glad she wasn't his enemy.

~ * ~

Stephen did a little scouting late that afternoon. A man with a spyglass could watch the Thomas house from either Pig Mountain across the creek, or Greene Mountain up from his own place. From a tree, or from any open place. Butler knew Abby rode often, and he or anyone could follow her from the stables, at a distance.

He crisscrossed the near slope of Pig Mountain stealthily, rifle ready, pistols in his belt, on moccasin feet. The leaves were fully out, so any vantage point would have to be clear. Abby had told him of granite outcroppings high on the hill, so he'd start there.

Game trails led around the slope and up from the creek below. Deer and turkey tracks were thick, but no human footprints. All he needed was one, to tell him: no hunters out this late in the year; everyone busy on his farm.

The light was fading when he retrieved his horse and rode homeward. No sign, but he hadn't been able to cover the whole mountain. Tomorrow he'd search Greene Mountain. That was closer to Swift Run anyway; Butler would come that way. So, scout that rise, then go see Abby. She'd hate being cooped up, this fine weather.

Tom had supper ready, and he and Ned interrupted a chess game when Stephen rode up.

"You been scoutin'? Or courtin'," Ned queried, with that grin. "Or both?"

"Mostly scouting. No sign on the mountain across the creek, but it got dark on me. I plan to search this one on up above early morning. Want to come?"

"Sure do. Only got one pistol, though."

"Got an extra. What's that, Tom? Catfish?"

"Is. Ned an' me hit that deep hole downcreek while you were gone. He's a good fisherman."

"Had to be back in the war, didn't we, Stephen? If we were to eat."

After supper, Stephen queried his old friend on his life and times since the army.

"Well, I'm helpin' run Pa's place. I got unhooked from first one woman, then another. Place is about worn out, I'm afraid, growin' too much tobacco. Came near pulling up stakes, goin' West like you, a dozen times. Cousins helpin' with the crops while I'm gone, so no hurry to go back. Like to see more of this if I can. How'd you find this rocky place?"

"Tell the truth, Ned, I was heading for Kentucky till I stopped at Thomas' mill. Abby rode up, and I was rooted to the spot."

"And it took you two years to win her? Man, you need lessons."

"Well, you know Butler was after her. And seemed like she was sort of teasing for a while."

"And," Tom put in, mischief in his eyes, "there was this other complication. He met another woman..."

"Aha! More like it. So when Miss Abby saw you driftin' off in another direction, she tumbled, right?"

"No, no, ''twasn't that way atall. Other girl's tall, plain till she smiles, and that just too seldom. Serious, bookish. She helped Tom learn to read. So of course he thinks the world of her."

"White woman? 'Course she is. But that serious part, that'd put me off. And Tom, if she's nice, she wouldn't put up with me, anyway. How ''bout you? Got yourself a woman?"

"I wish. Nothin' looks good, around here. Stephen an' Miss Annie, th' tall one, have got me all educated, so now I'm a snob. Hafta go up to Boston or somewhere, find me a wife."

"Oh, that's bad. Long dry spell, then. Stephen, this man's an intellectual. If he likes the tall one, I've got to meet her myself. How's she takin' all this about you and Abby?"

"Oh, she's just a friend, Ned..."

"Don't believe you. How about that, Tom?"

"She's moren' a friend, Ned. But she could see first off Stephen had his eyes full of Abby. And Abby's fine, too, ''long with bein' so pretty."

"Breakin' hearts, Stephen! Shame on you. Now I really want to meet this too-tall Annie. Don't get to meet many real ladies, an' I ain't talkin' ''bout lace and powder. Annie's a farm girl, right?"

"Right," Tom agreed, "an' very much a lady."

"And, after knowin' her, Tom, and don't matter she's white, you're gonna be hard to find another woman for."

"Hey, you two experts on women are ''way ahead of me. I'm going to sleep." Stephen rose, left them.

~ * ~

About that same time, the young minister Dwight Millington left the Compton farm after supper and a pleasant visit with the family. He was the new minister of the little log church on Lynch River and had begun a systematic series of visits to the members. The tall Sunday School teacher had caught his eye from the first, with a certain glow about her that evidenced itself when teaching the children.

The handsome young minister was studious, but not blind to even these country ladies. In the few days since his arrival, he'd noted several likely frontier girls, but only Anna Compton had education. And she'd responded to his own energetic, outgoing personality. He couldn't recall ever seeing a smile like that, so much warmer for its rarity.

Annie Compton. Tall as a tree, but carries it well. Sure of herself, that one. Knows who she is, and doesn't try to be anything else. Well. Like ''em better-looking, but I like her mind. Body's not so bad, either...Now, got to remember what I'm here for. ''Course a man can plan ahead for a wife, settle down and all...

In fact, Dwight Millington had enjoyed the favors of several agreeable young ladies in his native Philadelphia before and during his studies for the ministry. A life of service need not preclude the society of women, he'd concluded, and he'd proceeded to enjoy more than one relationship. Now, here at the end of the world, so to speak, at his first church, pickings would be lean. But Charlottesville wasn't that far, and the Reverend Carson had introduced him to families there, among whom were possibilities. There was that lawyer's daughter, with the rippling blonde hair…

But first things first. A surprising number of people attended the new church, which was after all the only one around. So he'd continue to build the membership. Home visits would bring more, he knew, as well as result in some good eating. Dwight liked good food, along with his pretty girls. Before committing to his chosen field of study, he'd also liked good whiskey, but of course all that was behind him, now. Of course.

~ * ~

Back in the room she shared with young Becky, Anna Compton reflected on the young minister. Really fine-looking man, but that wasn't what counted. Or shouldn't be. But she had to admit, she'd rather be around a handsome man than an ugly one. And who wouldn't? Like Stephen Davis: he'd rather be with Abby Thomas than with her, plain and simple. And though she'd shut the door on that possibility, she still had trouble keeping it shut. All right, Abby had her qualities beyond being beautiful. But she was a spoiled child, really. Never been denied a thing in her pampered life…

Oh, stop it! That's past and done with. Get over it…Abby's just who she is, and she's blinded Stephen, the way she's blinded every young man she's ever met. Maybe not her fault…just doing what a pretty girl's always done. And to her credit, she's not shallow…at least not that shallow…

Dwight Millington. Reverend Dwight Millington. Educated, seems sincere. What a rarity here at the back of beyond. Sort of a mirror image of Abby, in some ways. A man of God, surely. But there's a streak of something there that didn't come from seminary. His hands. As if they wanted to touch you, move all over your body, set you on fire…Now, that's foolish. You're not a schoolgirl, Annie!

She went to sleep, picturing the reverend's hands.

Sixteen

Greene Mountain rose behind Stephen's new house and the Thomas plantation, an elongated height running west toward the Blue Ridge. Stephen guessed that a man would climb the gradual slope at the east end of the ridge, then look for a rock outcropping or sheer drop, to afford a view of the plantation. There were several such spots he knew of, and he and Ned Drake slipped up toward them early. They crossed game trails, winding along benchland, on their way up.

One of these, near the ridgeline, showed horse's hoofprints from the day before. Older tracks also showed. The men moved west, keeping to the undisturbed forest floor alongside the faint trail. After more than a quarter mile, they reached a jumble of granite boulders with a view of the Thomas holdings spread below to the south. A sea of horse and boot tracks showed where a man had tied his mount.

"He'll have climbed up onto one of those big rocks," Ned pointed. "He's been here, watching, say for a week."

Stephen tried to remember where Abby had ridden the past few days. Lately, it'd just been from the plantation to his place and back, as far as he'd known. That would have kept her almost too far from this point for a man to ride and intercept her. But at any time, she could decide to ride in this direction up through the fields. Right toward whoever had waited here. The thought made the hair rise on the back of his neck.

"Way I see it," Ned was saying, "is we can hide near and ambush the fellow—could be along any time—or mosey on back home, and just keep her out of his reach. What do you think?"

"You know what I think, Ned. Somebody's after my woman, and he's not about to get her." His eyes were angry glints.

"Knew you'd want to take some action, but look here, Stephen: Aside from findin' out who he is, which you and I can figure pretty easy, we can't exactly shoot him, just for watching the place. He could come up with all sorts of reasons for being here. Don't believe we could just make him disappear, without gettin' you in more trouble. ''Specially since everybody knows about the bad blood between you."

"Hmm. You're probably right. Well, let's work our way on up above here, wait a bit and see who or what happens. We'll know more than we do now, at least."

They climbed to a high vantage point and settled in to wait. Stephen reflected that this was something they'd learned to do well in the war: wait. And it had often been pointless, often some general's whim, it seemed, or a miscalculation. Sometimes they'd even been forgotten, somewhere up the chain of command, out on some lonely outpost, till some harried aide had missed them. Here, at least, there was to be a purpose to their vigil.

Perhaps they'd have to let the man go, Stephen reflected, although the idea galled him. Could Butler just be a yearning, rejected suitor? No, not likely. He or someone, surely had designs on Abby Thomas. And he and Ned had to learn more. So yes, maybe they'd just hide and watch...

But if the man drew down on them, they'd blast him off the face of the earth.

~ * ~

Near noon, Stephen and Ned conferred. Their man hadn't shown, and the next move was unclear.

"Mightn't come at all, today, Ned. Could be just a coincidence?"

"Maybe so. Been thinking about the whole trial thing. I'd say whoever's coming here is just scoutin', giving the doc and Butler a line on the next part of the plan, if the court thing doesn't work. If I was into somethin' shady, I'd wanta keep it low-key, not carrying off women and gettin' the country in an uproar. But it's pretty clear something's up; man's been here, and I think he'll come again."

"But not today, seems like. I'd like to go on down, see Abby. Hell, I'd like to go on back to work on my house. What do you think?"

"You go on. Believe I'll just wait here a bit more. I've some of Tom's biscuits, and there's that little spring near. This just doesn't look right…too many ifs for me. We need somethin' solid to go on, and a man showin' up here could tell us more. Could be coming from a ways off too, and just not here yet. You said Butler's place was some miles away, so that'd fit."

Stephen left his friend, slipped down between the leafed-out trees toward the plantation fields. He was in dense woods, with no glimpse of the open land ahead. It was obvious that anyone could move within a few feet of the grassy slopes below without being seen. The thought chilled him.

At the plantation house, Abby and her mother had spent the morning sewing, and the girl was clearly in the throes of cabin fever.

"I wanted so to come see you, Stephen, but Mama's practically chained me to the house." She kissed him.

"And a good thing, too," Gertrude Thomas averred. "With crazy men about. Have you eaten, Stephen?"

"Not really. Ned and I've been scouting since early."

"Ah. Any sign?"

"Yes, and no. Someone's been staking out a clear space up on Greene, as late as yesterday, but there's no trace of him today."

"You mean," Abby's eyes were wide, "watching us here?" Her mother left for the kitchen, her mouth a grim line.

"Seems so. Ned's up there now. Wanted to wait longer; see if anyone came. I knew you'd be cooped up here, though."

"I'm going distracted, Stephen. I never liked sewing. But what if you catch a man there? What'll you do?"

"Good question. He could say he's looking for a lost cow or something… no way to prove anything. Unless whoever it is makes a direct threat."

~ * ~

That exact question was in Ned Drake's mind as he watched the man below him. There was a spyglass to his eye, and he was scanning the area around the Thomas plantation house. Moments earlier he'd ridden to the rocks, tied his horse, and slipped to a lookout point below Ned.

He didn't know what Butler, or Weston, looked like. The man downslope was perhaps forty, neatly dressed, good boots. Butler? Or a partner, perhaps? Weston?

Then the man took a small mirror from a pocket, and angled it toward the sun. Ned couldn't see just what he was up to, but reasoned it was a signal to someone. Where? He scanned the plantation fields for a return flash: Nothing.

Then he saw it. High on Pig Mountain beyond the fields, a speck of light, flashing briefly. Long and short intervals, a code of some sort. Then the man put the mirror away, sat and waited. Ned resisted the urge to steal closer and put a pistol ball through the man's head, but pondered other action.

Get between him and his horse; confront him with a cocked gun at his head? Find out what's afoot? Ned was fairly certain he could extract the information from the man, given his powers of persuasion, and perhaps his sharp knife.

But it'd be better perhaps, to catch them in some overt act, he reasoned. Find out who the others were, what this meant, though, at least. Then kill them all, as if they were enemy soldiers, and all this would be over with, clean. Whatever was going on here was bigger than a man—two men—with mirrors. *Still, a bird in the hand...*He began to move, quietly, gun out.

Just then he saw two riders emerge from the distant Thomas stables. He recognized Abby's Shelly, and yes, that had to be her and Stephen, tiny, far below in the light of afternoon.

The man below him leapt up and began signaling with the mirror again. The answering flashes came from the far slope. Long and short flashes: What was the code?

~ * ~

At the plantation, Stephen and Abby rode down the creek meadow toward his place, unaware of the signals passing far above them. They were discussing the new house, and trying to act as if nothing were wrong.

"I want some brick for walkways, Stephen. All the mud from building will get tracked in."

"All right. We can haul some from Charlottesville, I'm sure." He was scanning the fringes of forest as they rode. "Let's lay out what you want, so we can figure how many bricks we'll need." Her eyes followed his, but neither saw anything. It was a fine late spring day, too fine for worrying.

"I'll race you to the ford," she challenged.

"Better not. You'd get so far ahead, I'd worry."

"Oh, yes. Oh, I'll be so glad when all this is finally over, Stephen. Nothing's normal."

"Well, the trial's in two days. That may clear everything up, or it may just push things to a head. Either way, we'll know more."

"What was that?" She pointed suddenly up toward Greene Mountain.

"I didn't see anything."

"A flash of something. Isn't that where you left Ned? Just up there..."

"It is. He wanted to wait. Someone must have come. A flash, you say?"

"Bright, like off shiny metal, or glass."

They watched for several minutes, but the signal was not repeated. Could have been sunlight off a spyglass, maybe. Should he ride up there? No, get himself shot. Ned would be more than able to take care of himself, he knew. And he couldn't—wouldn't—leave Abby.

~ * ~

Ned had weighed the choices, and finally decided to wait and watch. Whatever direct action he took could only bring more trouble for Stephen. The trial was in just two days. *Guess we can hold on till then. We know this man's here, and the other one across. It'll be Abby they want; can't see Stephen's place from here. If she's with us, she's safe. Hate like fried hell to let this weasel go, but I guess I must. Gray mare. Maybe I'll be able to describe him, find out just who it is we have here.*

As Stephen and Abby rode out of sight, the watcher put away his signaling mirror, picked his way among the boulders to his horse. Ned saw the long rifle in a saddle sheath, and guessed there was a pistol under his coat. He watched with regret as the rider moved off the way he'd come.

~ * ~

The Reverend Dwight Millington kept hearing about Squire Thomas' family, especially his beautiful daughter. He also heard she was engaged to a local craftsman, and that there'd been a killing a while earlier. A part of his plan to enlarge his congregation included reaching influential, and yes, wealthy citizens. He'd like to call on the squire, purely as a church outreach of course, but his curiosity was also piqued by the image of Abigail Thomas building in his mind. She was said to be educated, cultured. A friend of Annie Compton's, but that young lady had seemed somewhat lukewarm when asked about this friend.

"I know the family attends the Episcopal church in Charlottesville on occasion," she'd informed him. "But with the distance, that's probably not often. You'll find the gentry hereabouts favor that denomination over the Presbyterians and Congregationalists."

"Indeed. How do you think the squire would respond if I invited them to join us here?"

"Try. Mrs. Thomas is a kindly, but direct woman, and the squire, for all his business-like manner, is quite pleasant. And perhaps Abby and Stephen would come. He's interested in Calvin, and reads a great deal."

"Really? And what's this I hear about a...the trouble at Mr. Davis' place?"

"He was attacked by some strange man, from what I hear, who in the fight was killed. Stephen was wounded. A drunken man, who apparently mistook Stephen's partner, Tom, for a runaway slave of his. Oh, you know Tom...he's been here."

"Ah, yes. The black man. Quite personable. Educated, too."

"Tom's a good friend. An example of what one of his race can accomplish, given encouragement. A fine craftsman."

"Yes, I hear that. Perhaps I'll call on the Thomases, then. Would you care to come along?"

"Oh. I really couldn't, sir. Crops not all laid by yet. I'm quite involved with the running of our farm. But thank you for inviting me."

Annie wasn't sure yet just how she felt about the new minister. He was certainly zealous in his mission of saving the world, and she supposed that was to be expected. He was pleasant to be around, solicitous, polite...and so damned handsome. She couldn't deny a certain satisfaction in being associated with him, even just as church teacher to pastor. She was aware the ladies of the community had noted them as a possible pair, and the thought amused her. So far.

~ * ~

"Way I see it, Stephen, they've set up a way to signal each other. Each man could see a different part of the plantation, an' flash the other if Abby headed his way."

"Sounds right. What'd the man look like?"

"'Bout forty. Good boots, coat. Rode a gray mare, Roman-nosed."

"Not the horse I've seen him on, but could be Butler. Anything stand out about him?"

"Not really. Brown hair, medium height, weight. What's Butler usually ride, Abby?"

"Sorrel gelding usually, but he may well have a gray mare, too. He has quite a stable."

Tom had been listening while he sharpened tools, his eyes beyond his work. Now he spoke his thoughts.

"I'm guessing there's a bunch of ''em, Stephen, not just th' doc and Butler. The money's the key: What kind of a swindle do they have, and how big is it? Take more'n' two respectable citizens to pile up as much as it seems they're after. If what Ned's thinkin' is true, there's probably a gang of ''em somewhere, an' they can call in all the help they need."

"Hmm," Ned mused. "I liked it better when there were only two. But I'll wager you're right, Tom. Honey draws flies, and if the honey's here someplace, they'll be swarming."

"Well, from what we've learned and are guessing," Stephen held up one finger, "they may not act till after the trial." Another finger. "And I'd guess they're snooping around likely hiding places now, but they're probably as much in the dark as we are." Third finger. "So they want me to lead them to the money, and my gamble is they won't do anything drastic till they have to."

"Don't count on it." Ned shook his head. "But if we're on guard, we should be able to head anything off. I wanted to wipe that fellow off that rock so much, Abby. Spying on you..."

"That's what our hands call spooky, Ned, and it gives me the shivers."

~ * ~

Doctor Weston, accompanied by his wife Constance, set out in his carriage for Charlottesville. The good weather was holding, so he reasoned he'd arrive early for the trial. The prosecutor, Samuel Eddins, Esquire, would join them there. Samuel Eddins was not your average upstanding frontier lawyer. In fact, he was a member of Weston's organization. The man knew George Henley, Davis' lawyer, and had shown no concern in facing him.

"Paper lawyer, sir. Deeds, wills. No courtroom skills. We can pin this Davis with enough that he'll be inside for a spell, doubt it not."

Weston was convinced the craftsman had killed Hayes for the money, but a doubt nagged at him. Hayes had shown an unpredictable streak, and that much money would tempt him, even knowing there'd be more. And it was just possible he'd hidden the box before confronting Davis.

Which he should never have done. One slave wasn't worth endangering a chest of gold, and certainly not the entire operation. But yes, Hayes had angered easily, and from what Butler had said, this Davis was not a man to provoke. *Well, we'll see about that: the law can be a powerful ally, when we need it.*

"Not to complain, Horace," his wife said, "but I still fail to see what help I can be in court." She hadn't wanted to come at all. Indeed, Constance had been cooler toward him, he fancied, for months now. Trip would do her good. Mr. Jefferson's influence in Albemarle County meant there were cultured drawing rooms and learned people to visit. And of course his beautiful Constance was, outwardly at least, the perfect wife to have on one's arm.

"All you'll be required to do, my dear, is corroborate my identity of Hayes' runaway. I fancy this Davis will have some cohort testify to some fiction, and it could degenerate into my word against his. The man's a murderer, and this is one more way to see that justice is done."

"But you know very well that Tom..."

"Now, none of that. However the man disappeared, Hayes had legal ownership papers. But that's beside the point. Davis helped him escape, or stole him, taught him to read—in short, he's broken the law. That sort of thing endangers all of us who own slaves. You know what happens when they rebel, and it's the sort of meddling this Davis has done that causes insurrections. It simply cannot be tolerated. And I cannot forget that he killed one of my closest friends."

"Oh, of course you're right. I suppose John's teaching Tom proper speech was the first misstep."

"Clearly. My cousin, God rest him, had too soft a heart."

Constance had not confronted her husband directly with her certainty that he was involved in Tom's abduction. There was absolutely nothing she could do about it now, though the injustice of it burned in her. She'd never liked Hayes from the first. But a woman's duty was to her husband, and without his firm hand, that chaos following John's death would have left her even more stricken. Creditors, lawyers, the plantation to run. He'd seemed the perfect harbor. Had seemed...She bit her knuckles and looked out the open carriage curtains at the fair day. At least he didn't force himself on her. Her life could be much worse. She supposed.

~ * ~

Rawlins Butler wasn't quite sure how he felt about the alternate plan, to abduct Abby Thomas. On the one hand, the thought of getting her away from Stephen Davis sent a surge of anticipation through him. But she'd never accept him either, under those circumstances. So of course Weston was right: blacken the man with one or more convictions, and the upright Thomases would abandon him. Just his being accused should have started the process. Forget that innocent until proven guilty principle: Enough of English law lingered in people's minds for there to be doubt, just from the charges. And once they had him locked up... Then he, Butler, the steady devoted planter, would be the girl's obvious choice, even if it took time.

He'd weighed this reckless idea early on, of just snatching the girl and racing West with her, to a remote place out of the reach of the law. Plenty places out there...Hayes had done his work well, locating them. In time she might come around. But he couldn't drag his children along on such a flight. Carrie was ten, Edward seven. Couldn't take them into raw country, let them become savages. And give up his plantation. And of course a rebellious stepmother would poison them against him.

No, better Weston's way. And whatever course they followed, they must never endanger the organization. It was water-tight, a seamless entre into planter society and limitless wealth. And no one got hurt very much, the way it was run. Weston and those above him were geniuses, no doubt of it. A lot of little losses to equal their one big gain…the very soul of simplicity.

If only Davis hadn't taken that money. They'd get it back, of course, but now questions would nag them. *Damn the man. But Weston's right again: kill him now and we may never find the money. Too much money to lose…*

Seventeen

The courthouse was one of the few brick structures in Charlottesville. Thomas Jefferson had practiced law there, and might again on his return from France. The court was a bastion of civilization in the new country, the ruling power among scattered, self-willed settlers.

Judge Amos Edgerton ruled, in his powdered wig and robes, with an austerity and finality widely respected. On court days he arrived in his Philadelphia carriage attended by not one, but two nervous clerks and even his tricorn-hatted coachman possessed more dignity than the average frontier lawyer. Even this man ordered the other slaves about with the absolute certainty that he was chosen of the mighty, and was to be obeyed.

After a few minor matters, settled conclusively by his honor Judge Edgerton, Stephen's case came up. George Henley had not requested a jury, feeling Weston's case was ridiculous—flimsy at best. Now, seeing a number of Stephen's friends and supporters on the benches, he realized that a jury would probably have been friendly. *Well, too late for that.*

After hearing the charges against the accused, and Stephen's pleading, the judge rapped his gavel for silence.

"The defendant has heard the accusations, and has entered pleas of innocent. We shall hear evidence first on the most serious charge of murder. Mr. Eddins, you may proceed with your opening statement."

"Thank you, Your Honor. We shall prove that the defendant did willfully and maliciously attack one Jacob Hayes, late of Caroline County and the western districts of Virginia, without provocation, with intent to rob the deceased, and did viciously strike him with a hammer, causing his death." The lawyer sat, amid hostile murmurings from the crowd. The judge rapped for quiet.

"Thank you, sir. Mr. Henley?"

"Yes, Your Honor. We shall prove that the defendant acted to preserve his life, after being confronted by the deceased, Mr. Hayes, who in a drunken state, did willfully enter defendant's place of work and drew a pistol, threatening him. That said defendant caused the demise of his attacker is not denied, but we shall prove he acted in self-defense."

There it was, Tom thought, the case for and against his friend, the man he owed his life to, who hadn't killed the man at all. *Better if you hadn't even been here…* And now Stephen was on trial for his life. He'd seemed so sure the self-defense story would hold…Tom remembered the sickening crunch of Hayes' head under the hammer, his own rage…raw, unleashed in destroying his enemy. And now Stephen…A Bible verse came: "Greater love hath no man, than to lay down his life for his friend." No, he couldn't let Stephen do this. He'd stand, ask to set the record straight, confess…

But he could not move. In this crowd of white people who might seem tolerant, even friendly, he could not make himself rise, could not do what was right. Sweat poured off him, but no one noticed. As always, no one took note of a black man in pain. He was invisible, until someone needed him. And yes, as a confessed killer he'd be shown no mercy by those same whites…

"I see," the judge was saying. "Does the prosecution have witnesses?"

"To the deed itself, we do not, Your Honor, but we shall present testimony showing compelling motive and opportunity."

"Very well, proceed, Mr. Eddins."

"Call Doctor Horace Weston to the stand."

The distinguished doctor rose from beside his wife, and Stephen noted the color in her face. She was prettier than he remembered, but she seemed agitated. Well, so was Abby, whose hand he reached and took, to be rewarded with a nervous smile. He looked about the crowded room, and saw Isaac

Compton and his family. Annie returned his nod with a visible sigh and a pained look, meant as sympathy, he guessed.

Ned Drake had not focused on Constance Weston until this moment. And his eyes stayed riveted on that face. In it he read more than the story of a young widow married to an older man. He saw a troubled woman, lovely, vulnerable. And lonely.

And Ned Drake was suddenly in love.

"Are you acquainted with the defendant, Dr. Weston?" Samuel Eddins asked, indicating Stephen.

"I met him briefly, over a year ago. He called at our home in Caroline County, purportedly seeking my late cousin, John."

"I see. And did you have cause to be concerned, at that visit?"

"I did. He asked about a slave the deceased, Mr. Hayes, had bought from our plantation. I wondered at the time how he could have known of this slave."

"And did he tell you?"

"He said he'd served under John, who was a colonel, and knew the slave, John's body servant."

"What caused you to doubt..."

"Objection, Your Honor." George Henley had risen. "The defendant is on trial for murder. This has no relevance."

"It would seem so. Does this line of questioning have a point, Mr. Eddins?"

"Directly, Your Honor. Goes to motive."

"I'll allow it. But do make your case."

"Of course. What caused you to doubt the defendant's assertion, Dr. Weston?"

"The subsequent information that the defendant never served under my cousin. The rolls are clear and on record."

"Ah. And what was your conclusion?"

"That he knew of Mr. Hayes' slave because he had aided in his escaping from him."

"Objection! No relevance. Please, Your Honor."

"Objection sustained. Mr. Eddins, the defendant has been charged with such a count, but is not on trial at this time for other than the crime of murder."

"Yes, Your Honor. Dr. Weston, why is it your contention that the defendant killed Mr. Hayes?"

"Mr. Hayes was carrying a large amount in gold in a chest, entrusted to him by my business associates and myself, with which to purchase and equip plantations in western Virginia."

"And what became of that money?"

"We contend that the defendant took it, after killing Mr. Hayes." A murmur ran through the crowd.

"And on what do you base that contention?"

"My associate, Mr. Rawlins Butler, informs me that Davis, the defendant, has purchased fine horses, land, and has built a substantial house, hiring numerous workmen. Not what a poor furniture-maker could afford."

"Certainly. Now, sir, why do you suppose the deceased, Mr. Hayes, a substantial planter and citizen, went to the defendant's place of work?"

"Objection! Calls for speculation."

"I believe I'll allow it, Counselor. Denied."

"Why, to recover his stolen slave, of course."

"I see. No further questions, Your Honor, but I reserve the right to recall this witness."

"Granted. Your witness, Mr. Henley."

The lawyer rose, to the background voices of Stephen's neighbors and friends. The judge wielded his gavel. Squire Thomas' face was red with suppressed anger, Abby's, anxious. Tom Logan was still, with a fixed stare straight ahead.

"Dr. Weston, first of all, did the defendant state that he served in the war under your cousin, Colonel John Logan, or with him?"

"I...I'm quite certain he said under him."

"In fact, sir, Mr. Davis served under General Daniel Morgan, with General Greene's forces, in North Carolina, near the close of the conflict. But the command to which he was attached was called to Yorktown to strengthen General Washington's forces at the siege. There, during those weeks, wouldn't you agree that it is entirely likely that Lieutenant Davis met Colonel Logan, and his servant?"

"I doubt it. John was a senior officer, and Davis a mere enlisted man."

"But a lieutenant, and a valued sharpshooter, sir. But we can learn from him later of this acquaintance. Now, sir, you state that the deceased visited my client to recover his "stolen slave." Did you know that Mr. Davis' partner is, and was, a free Negro, and no one's slave?"

"He may have used some chicanery to free him, but that's Jacob Hayes' slave, Tom." The doctor pointed to an impassive Tom Logan.

"No chicanery, sir, since I handled the man's emancipation myself, quite legally. But we shall get to that, too. Now, sir, you contend that the deceased was carrying a...chest, I believe you testified, of gold?"

"Yes, with a large sum."

"Heavy?"

"Indeed it was."

"How likely would it be, sir, for a man to arrive at a potentially hostile place, confront an unknown adversary, with a heavy chest of gold…?"

"Objection! Calls for speculation on the part of the witness." Samuel Eddins pounced.

"Sustained. But that is a point, Counselor. Would you care to rephrase the question?"

"Thank you, Your Honor. Do you contend, sir, that Mr. Hayes carried the gold when he confronted Mr. Davis?"

"I do. That's obviously the motive for the murder."

"Did you know that the deceased shot the defendant?"

"In defending himself, yes."

"You contend that Mr. Hayes defended himself with a loaded pistol against a blacksmith's hammer?"

"I do."

"No further questions, but request right of recall."

"Granted. Next witness, Mr. Eddins."

"Call Constable Joshua Stokes."

After he was sworn in, the lawman settled into his chair, eyeing the prosecutor. *Take moren' you to rattle me, boy. You may be th' prosecutor, but I seen you work b'fore, an' you got nothin' to go on here.*

"Constable Stokes, did you respond to a summons to the defendant's place of work on the eighteenth of February, 1784?"

"I did."

"And what did you find?"

"Th' d'ceased, with his head bashed in, on th' floor of th' shop."

"And was the defendant present?"

"He was up in his house, all bandaged up."

"How do you know he was shot? Did you see the wound yourself?"

"I seen th' bloody bandages on him."

"But not the alleged wound itself. So in fact, you do not know for certain the defendant was actually shot at all, do you?"

"Oh, fer th' love of..."

"Do you? Please answer the question, sir."

"Did I pull th' bloody bandages offen' Stephen an' break open th' wound? No sir, I did not. An' neither would anybody with any sense."

"So in fact, you have no proof the defendant was shot at all, do you? Did you find a chest of gold, sir?"

"No, I did not. Can you prove there was a chest of gold, lawyer?"

"Move to strike the witness' question, Your Honor. If it please the court, please direct the witness to limit his outbursts to answering the questions put to him."

"Granted. Constable, I'm sure some of this will be cleared up as we go along. Proceed, Mr. Eddins."

"No further questions for this witness, Your Honor."

George Henley rose, walked deliberately toward the witness box. He'd lay this to rest right now…

"Constable Stokes, the prosecution has attempted to discredit the defendant's having been shot. You are certain he was. Can you tell us where he was shot?"

"Yes, sir. In th' back."

"In the back." The lawyer turned to the packed room, watching this disclosure sink in. Faces registered concern, shock. People leaned forward, eyes glinted, mouths were set. Good. He turned back to Stokes. "Is it your experience as an officer of the law, sir, that an attacker, as the defendant has been accused of being, would attack a man *back-first*?"

There was a roar of laughter from the onlookers, shattering the tension in the room. Even the judge smiled. Ned Drake rolled his eyes. Tom Logan felt the knot in his stomach start to dissolve.

"Never seen that, no." The constable shook his head, himself suppressing a grin.

"Now if it please the court, Your Honor, since the prosecution has raised the question, I request your indulgence in clearing up the matter of whether the defendant was in fact, shot. No further questions here."

"Granted. Let's get this settled."

"Mr. Davis, would you come forward, please?"

Stephen rose, stepped to the bench.

"Would you remove your shirt, sir, for Judge Edgerton? Show him the scar?"

Stephen did so. The ridged, angry scar ran across his back, clearly visible. The judge nodded. The crowd caught its breath.

"Now, Your Honor," Henley continued, "Mr. Davis was tended by his partner, Tom Logan, and by his fianceé, Miss Abigail Thomas. Both can testify, if necessary."

"Under the circumstances, that would be a waste of the court's time. Have you additional evidence, Mr. Eddins?"

"Yes, sir. If it please the court, call the defendant as witness."

Stephen took the oath.

"Did you take a chest of gold from the deceased?"

"Objection! This is a murder trial, Your Honor."

"Goes to motive, Your Honor."

"I suppose I'll allow it. Please answer, sir."

"I did not. I know of no gold."

"What did the deceased say to you, before you killed him?"

"He burst into my shop, waving a gun, obviously drunk..."

"Yes, yes. But what did he say?"

"Not clear. Something about a slave that'd run off. I think he mistook Tom here..."

"We're not interested in what you think, sir. So Mr. Hayes came for his slave, his property?"

"He seemed to think so, yes."

"And how did you come to have his property, his slave?"

"Objection! Irrelevant."

"Sustained. Have you no further questions pertinent to this matter, Counselor?"

"Your Honor, I'm trying to show the hostility that led to this defendant's attacking the deceased."

"Back-first. It won't wash, Counselor. Are you done?"

"I…" Eddins looked to Weston, as if for directions. None were forthcoming. "I suppose I am," he replied lamely.

"Good. Defendant is hereby acquitted of the charge of murder." He rapped his gavel. Tom Logan closed his eyes, breathed audibly. Abby was radiant; the squire nodding, smiling. "Now we'll proceed to the next accusation: teaching a slave to read. Defendant has pleaded innocent. You may present your case, Mr. Prosecutor."

"Yes, we'll prove the defendant broke the law by teaching a slave, one Tom, to read. Since you are already on the stand, Mr. Davis, I'll proceed, if it please the court."

"Proceed, then." The judge looked at George Henley, who nodded.

"Did you teach that man," pointing to Tom, "to read?"

"I did."

"When?"

"Right after I freed him. Two years ago."

"I see. And what right had you to free him?"

"Objection! Witness has disposed of the relevant issue."

"Sustained. That's a separate charge, sir."

"All right, then. Can you prove this Tom was a free man when you taught him?"

"Yes. As my attorney has stated earlier, he handled the transaction. Then I borrowed books for the purpose, from Squire Hezekiah Thomas and from Miss Anna Compton. Miss Compton is a teacher, sir. She knew of Tom's freedom at the time."

"I see. No further questions." Eddins held his palms upward.

"No questions, Your Honor," from Henley.

"Any summation?" Both lawyers shook their heads.

"Acquitted. Now to the charge of aiding and abetting an escaped slave…"

Tom Logan was visibly unemotional. Seeing Constance Weston had unnerved him however, since she could and would certainly identify him as her former slave. And he knew she couldn't testify against her husband, even if she wanted to...Or was that the law, here? He wasn't sure. He tried to recall her attitude toward him on the plantation. There'd been so little time, really. John Logan had married late, and was off to war only a few months later. The young wife had had little time with her husband, much less in his servant's company.

It would be Weston's word against Ned Drake's, then. And Ned's was a lie. Well, Stephen's word weighed here too, but so would Constance Weston's…

Samuel Eddins was conferring quietly with Weston. They'd lost two of three, but both felt secure in convicting Stephen of this charge. Now their concern was just how severe a penalty the judge would impose.

Rawlins Butler sat with arms crossed. He was not the man Ned Drake had seen. A small smile played around his mouth. This could still work out: With the prosecutor's help, they could get to Davis in jail, and he'd give up the money. Oh yes, after they got through with him, he'd give up the money. He thought of the burly jailer Weston had paid. And Abby Thomas would surely distance herself from Davis when he was convicted.

And it really didn't matter whether she did or not. Once the gold was recovered, he, Rawlins Butler, would see to it that his rival met with an accident. Perhaps a hunting accident. *You may be the better marksman, Davis, but I can hit you from so far off no one can ever tie me to the deed.* His smile broadened.

"We shall prove, Your Honor, that the defendant did aid and abet the escape of a slave, one Tom, formerly the lawful property of Jacob Hayes, deceased. That he had no legal right to free said slave, and is subject to punishment under the laws of this commonwealth."

Tom was perhaps the only one in the room who noted the omission of his last name. Property. He was just property to almost everyone here.

"Very well. Mr. Henley?"

"To the contrary, Your Honor. We shall prove my client's ownership of said slave, now a free man by my client's hand, with my assistance."

"Proceed, Mr. Eddins."

"Let me remind you that you are still under oath, Mr. Davis. Now, will you please tell the court by what authority you freed the slave in question?"

"I was his lawful owner. I had that right." The lie had never bothered Stephen, and it didn't now.

"Did you? And how did you come to own this slave?"

"In settlement of a debt owed me by his former owner, one Mr. Ned Drake, of Suffolk."

"And had you any ownership paper?"

"I did. A bill of sale, duly witnessed."

"And can this Mr. Drake testify to this...settlement?"

"He can. He's here in this courtroom."

"I see. And what was the nature of the debt you say you were owed?"

"That is for Mr. Drake to answer, if it please the court. It was a delicate matter, and I prefer that he tell it."

Eddins' eyebrows went up. Stephen shifted nervously. The lawyer turned to the judge.

"Your Honor, would you please direct the witness to answer?"

"Well, Counselor, since Mr. Drake is present, why don't you call him to the stand and ask him? Seems a reasonable course."

"Then I shall. No further questions."

"Your Honor..."

"Yes, Mr. Henley?"

"I enter into evidence this copy of a bill of sale for the ex-slave in question. And with it, this copy of the emancipation document, prepared by myself, with appropriate witnesses."

The judge perused the papers.

"So entered. Oh, Mr. Eddins, you'll want to see these."

"Not necessary, Your Honor. We maintain they are fraudulent."

"That's a serious allegation, sir, against another member of the bar."

"No offense intended toward Mr. Henley. I meant the bill of sale."

"Very well. Any questions for the defendant, Mr. Henley?"

"None, Your Honor."

"You may step down. Call your next witness, Prosecutor."

"Call Mr. Ned Drake."

Ned had watched Constance Weston closely and continually. As his name was called and he rose, she looked directly at him. He inclined his head a fraction, and his blue eyes were intent, his slight smile meant for her only. She held his gaze, and her chin came up slightly, her lips parting.

Eddins began his examination with the air of one who knew this witness would lie, and he meant to catch him up.

"Now, Mr. Drake, the defendant claims you transferred ownership of the slave in question, that man there, to him. Please tell the court how you happened to own him."

"Surely, Counselor. Tom grew up on our plantation. He is the son of our Mattie and Joshua. He was my childhood companion, and became my personal servant. I taught him proper English."

"Did you? Yet you claim you gave such a valued slave in settlement of a debt?"

"A very large debt, yes."

"And what was this large debt?"

"Objection! The nature of the debt is immaterial."

"I believe I'd like to hear this, Counselor," the judge demurred. "Denied. Please answer, sir."

"Very simply, sir, I owed Stephen Davis my life."

"In what way?" Eddins could hardly suppress a sneer.

"It's a little involved, I'm afraid, but I'll tell it: It was at the battle of Cowpens. General Morgan had placed the militia out front, and fearing they'd break and run before the British cavalry charge, he asked only one volley from them, after which they were indeed to run for cover. We regulars were entrenched just out of sight under a rise, to receive the cavalry under Tarleton. You must understand, we wanted Tarleton badly, sir…the butcher, the firebrand…"

"Yes, yes. Go on."

"Well, it went according to plan, and we poured our first volley into the British as they crested the rise, right in our faces." Ned noted the rapt expressions of his hearers. "But somehow I'd lost my paper powder packets. I grabbed a powder horn from a fallen comrade, Jedediah Hamlin was his name, from Staunton. Got hit right off—dead. So I reloaded, and hung the horn on my belt. Brits thick, by then, all over us. I got off another shot, but a stray ball clipped the powder horn clean off my belt, and suddenly, a handful of us were alone in a crossfire. I turned and bent to snatch up the horn, and a Brit ball got me. I went down, and another Redcoat came at me with the bayonet. I couldn't move, with the pain; just watched him come." Here Ned paused, closed his eyes, as if reliving the terrible moment. The spectators leaned forward, hardly breathing.

"I knew I was about to die.

"But Stephen Davis, also out of ammunition, had grabbed a saber from a dead officer, and just as the Brit lunged, Stephen swung that saber in both hands. Took the Redcoat's head off his shoulders, neat. He collapsed, spouting blood, and the bayonet went into the ground not an inch from me. I still couldn't move, but Stephen stood over me, shouting, daring the Brits, swinging that saber like the wrath of *God*!"

Ned composed himself.

"We killed nine out of ten of Tarleton's men, but didn't get him, more's the pity. Stephen carried me to the rear as the British force came apart.

"He saved my life, sir. I resolved to repay him, and eventually hit on the idea of giving him my Tom."

Stephen had kept a straight face throughout this oration. He'd known Ned would elaborate outrageously on the facts, and he had. He scanned the faces in the courtroom: To a person, they believed the story. Squire Thomas was transfixed at this narration of part of his hero Morgan's finest campaign. Constance Weston's hands gripped each other, and her eyes were riveted on Ned, whose own face was all freckled earnestness.

"A moving story, sir. But do you maintain that this man"—indicating Tom—"is the slave you owned? And remember, you are under oath."

"I do indeed. We grew up together."

He's good, Tom thought. *A cool liar. But there's Weston, and Miss Constance. I'm going to be sold back into slavery again. Wish I could just run out of here to anywhere. No, white faces all around: Turn mean in a flash. Stick it out. Boys tryin' hard for me, but Weston's a big man...*

"You seem to have recovered from your wound, sir. Where were you hit?"

"That's a little embarrassing, sir. In the cheek."

"The cheek? I see no scar."

"The right cheek." Ned made a motion. "Couldn't sit down for a month."

A roar of laughter broke out, infecting even Judge Edgerton. Ned's brow glistened in embarrassment, but Stephen knew he was controlling that incredible grin. It was hard for him too, to keep from howling in mirth.

"No further questions." Eddins sat, stony-faced.

"No questions, Your Honor," George Henley said.

"Very well. And my condolences, Mr. Drake," the judge chuckled. "Call your next witness, Prosecutor."

"Call Dr. Horace Weston."

The doctor's mouth was set. He'd end this sideshow, and in short order. Make a mockery of the justice system, would they? Make fools of him and his associates? He'd put them in their places. He was sworn in again, since this was a separate charge, and technically a separate trial.

"Dr. Weston, you've heard the last witness testify that man there was his property, which he deeded to the defendant in payment of a debt. Do you recognize him?"

"I do, indeed. That's Tom, my deceased cousin John's slave, later sold legally to Jacob Hayes."

"Are you certain, sir? Many people have said they can't tell one black face from another."

"I'm certain. But you needn't take my word alone for it. My wife is present. She knew Tom well."

"Ah. So the word of an eminent physician, planter and gentleman can be buttressed by that of a great lady. Thank you, sir. Would you say then, that the defendant and his colorful associate have cooked up this story about the slave's true ownership?"

"I would. They're liars and criminals."

"Nothing further."

George Henley rose slowly. *Here's a hostile witness, bent on convicting my client by any means possible. And by inference, attacking me too as an accessory. Hadn't counted on the wife's being here. Looks unhappy. Well...*

"Dr. Weston, what is your interest in prosecuting the defendant on the charge of aiding a runaway slave?"

"Why, to see justice done, sir. We can't have such flagrant abuse of the law. That slave is valuable property."

"And you contend that the defendant in effect stole the slave from his rightful owner, do you not?"

"Certainly. That should be obvious."

"Should be, the slave's being, as you said, valuable property. Why then, in your learned opinion, would Mr. Davis, newly the owner of this valuable property, and against all economic reason, set him free?"

"Objection! Calls for speculation."

"I believe I'll allow it. Denied. Please answer, sir."

"Well, I...I don't know," Weston sputtered. "Perhaps he's crazy, as well as a blatant liar."

"As a medical man, Doctor, would you say the defendant has acted like a crazy man here today?"

"Oh, dammit, man, how should I know? The man's guilty, and deserves punishment!" Weston had clearly lost control.

"I'll decide guilt here," the judge interposed icily.

"Nothing further, Your Honor."

Samuel Eddins was radiant. He permitted himself a smile as he called Constance Weston to the witness stand. Her eyes were wide on Ned Drake's as she rose. She was sworn in.

"Now, Mrs. Weston, would you please clear up the identity of that black man, there. He was purportedly of your household, your late husband's body servant. Do you recognize him?"

Tom's heart sank. George Henley felt his case slipping away. Stephen Davis was certain his lie was about to get him jailed, at least. Abby held her breath. Rawlins Butler smirked.

Constance Weston looked intently at Tom Logan, then for an instant at her husband, and her face changed. Then her luminous eyes turned to Ned Drake, and stayed there. No one could have told what was going on in her mind in that long moment that seemed to cause breaths to stop. She decided. She spoke:

"I never saw that man before in my life."

~ * ~

Horace Weston was furious.

"You brainless *fool*!" he shouted at his wife outside the courthouse. "Do you realize what you've *done*?"

"I know what you did. You sold a free man into slavery. John's trusted servant, who saved his life. That's inhuman, disgusting, and I couldn't let you do it again, and convict another man..."

"You meddlesome *bitch*! You have no idea what you've destroyed, with your—"

"I think that's quite enough, Weston," Ned Drake's voice was a drawl, but it cut through the man's rantings like a knife. Beside him stood Stephen Davis and Tom Logan.

Weston glared at the men, then his eyes darted about in sudden realization. Eddins was still inside, Butler nowhere to be seen. Not an ally anywhere, with those three arrayed against him.

"We're not through with you, Davis," he gritted. "Constance, you come with me," snatching his wife's arm.

"I will not! I'll starve first, you sadistic..." Her color was high, her eyes blazing defiance.

"Get in the carriage!" he snarled.

"I believe the lady has made herself clear," from Ned as he took her arm. Weston hesitated, then spat out:

"Stay, then! But from this moment, you have no home, no possessions. You're a homeless, nameless castaway!" And he drew himself up, glared at his opponents as if daring them to intervene further. He turned disdainfully, stepped up into his carriage, which lurched away.

Constance saw, suddenly, her true situation: She was indeed abandoned, cast out, penniless. She had just cut all ties to any security she had, albeit to a man she had come to despise. Her rage melted inside her as the enormity of her action permeated her being, shrinking her.

Then she felt a hand on her other arm. She turned to find Abby Thomas there, and with her was her formidable mother.

"Come with us, my dear," Gertrude Thomas said gently.

Eighteen

The shop building had been ransacked. So had the cabin. And doors were left open in the new house, showing it had been searched, too. If there had been gold, the intruders would surely have found it. Stephen stood, surveying his strewn belongings and the blatant violation, the invasion of his life, pierced him. Blinding rage mounted inside him.

"This won't be the worst," his friend Ned warned. "Now they'll make a serious move. They've tried the court thing, and this lets us know they won't stop."

"Do we go after them now?" Stephen's hands were flexing, wanting something, someone to grip, tear, pound.

"Be hard to justify. No proof. Helluva system: Man's out to get you, but you've gotta wait for him to strike before you can protect yourself. Simpler when they wore red coats."

Tom began picking up clothes from the cabin floor. His mind was working. *Time to get this all taken care of. It's on my account all this is happening. I owe these men…*

"My concern is for Abby, Ned," Stephen pointed out, forcing himself back from pure anger. "I think we have to eliminate that threat, no matter what. And Constance is in danger, too. Weston's probably trying to figure how much she's heard of what he's up to. If I read the man right, he won't risk her talking."

"I'll gladly blow that bastard to pieces, Stephen. And if you're right, he'll hit her quick, if she knows anything. Spunky woman, but she's not safe, even at Thomas' plantation."

~ * ~

The note was from Tom: 'Back in a few days. You watch out here.' Stephen's old horse was gone, and the rifle Tom now owned. When he hadn't come back to the shop, Stephen had assumed he was at the cabin or the new house. Now it was dark, and they didn't even know when he'd left.

"He's gone after Doc Weston," Stephen declared.

"And by himself. That's dangerous as hell. Should I go after him?"

"If he'd wanted either of us along, he would've asked. Feels like this is his job to do."

"Somebody'll steal that man. He'll hafta travel at night, hole up daytimes." Both of them could envision losing their friend.

"So we wouldn't be able to find him, anyway. No, Ned, I guess this has to be Tom's fight, this part of it. And he's traveled before, with a lot less."

~ * ~

Stephen stopped in at the plantation smithy on his way to the Thomas house next day. Ike was glad to see him, having heard from his employer of the acquittal.

"Glad yer on th' outside, Stephen."

"Yes. Well, I never figured for sure just what that was all about, Ike. Except that they think I know where there's a lot of money, and they want it."

"Reckon what they was gonna do? All right: git you in jail, but what then? Don't make enny sense."

"Hard to make out...Hell, they could have ambushed me out here and done better finding any money—if there'd been any—but maybe they knew it'd be after the fight. Hard to tell what's in a man's mind. You hear that about Doc Weston's wife?"

"Did. Reckon she ''bout got you off, that part. Gonna be hard on her though, way th' squire told it."

"I have a feeling my friend Ned's going to figure in that part, Ike. And I'm afraid we need a little help, here. Now, somebody's trashed my cabin and shop too, looking for that money. Probably several of them, and I fear for Abby. Mrs. Weston, too.”

“Y’need a few guns, then.”

“We do. This thing appears to be bigger than I thought.”

“Wal. Yep, you c’n count on me an’ Web, fer shore. An’ Abner at th’ mill, too. Thinks a heap of you, he does. Few more. Want I should go on up to th’ big house with you now?”

“Yes, come along. The squire will be glad to know we’ve got the manpower.”

~ * ~

Tom Logan forced himself to control the rising anger, the need for haste. Wouldn’t do to get himself caught. Not now of all times, when this job needed doing. No, he’d go as slow as necessary, keep hidden in daylight, go as far as he could at night. He knew some of the roads, but they didn’t all go the right direction. Never mind; he’d get there.

He carried the rifle and pistol he’d traded for, and two knives, with a blanket, some provisions and grain for the horse. Felt a little like back in the war, when he and John Logan had moved with the troops, everything they had with them in the saddle.

After several nights, he finally struck the turnpike north from Richmond. Now he could travel quickly. He pulled his cloak about him, muffling his face against the spring night damp. No one could tell, in the dark, whether he was black or white, under his tricorn hat. And if he spoke, his words wouldn’t give him away: no one would ever expect a black man to use proper English.

~ * ~

Squire Thomas shut down the smithy, the woodworking shop, and the mill, and with Stephen, set up a rotating guard around the plantation. Plowing and planting would continue as well as they could, but the volunteers, with Ned and Stephen, were armed and watchful.

“Ike, I’ll send some help over to plow your fields. Yours, too, Web, and Abner. I value your help here, and I’ll not see you put behind because of us.”

“Thankee, sir,” Ike said. “Man’s got to give aid when he can. Seems a feller’s bound to work for whatever he gits, then fight to keep it. This here’s th’ fightin’ part, I reckon.”

Not for the first time, Stephen Davis felt a surge of affection for his friends and their help. Raising a house was one thing, but taking up arms, putting their lives in danger, was beyond the call of neighboring. He vowed to repay each man, somehow.

"I fear for you, Stephen," the squire cautioned. "With men of the stripe of Weston and Hayes, they may burn you out. I'd say stay with us, but you'll want to protect your place."

"Thanks, sir. I suppose no place is safe with a marksman like Butler around. He could hit me from anywhere, but he knows that wouldn't get him the money. And I don't want to sit here waiting for them to act. Ned and I'll devise some plan, now that you're protected here."

Abby clung to him as he was leaving. Constance Weston gave Ned her hand.

"Thank you, Mr. Drake, for supporting me. I needed to believe I would have friends before I could break from my...from Dr. Weston." Her eyes were large. Ned bowed over her hand.

"An honor, ma'am. You are truly among friends here." And he was certain she knew there was more than friendship in her future.

The two men rode downcreek, planning. Both had their guns out, scanning the trees.

"You were right, Stephen: We've got to go after them. If we don't, if we just sit and wait, it'll be like paintin' targets on ourselves."

"I'm for it, but where do we start? And how many are there, and where do we find them?

"Only one way comes to mind. Now, Tom's either gonna kill Weston, or get himself killed. But he's just one of them. There's Butler, and who knows who else? How many of their other men searched this place? And whoever the rest are, they'll keep after that money."

"So they didn't get me into jail, and we still don't know what good that would have done them. We've got Abby protected. What's your way?"

"Lead ''em to it." He shrugged, raised an eyebrow. Stephen knew he couldn't have heard that right.

"You've finally gone the rest of the way crazy, Ned. That woman dumbed you down? You know—"

"No, now. I know you don't know where it is, but we've got to make them think you're going after it. That'll get ''em moving."

"Get me killed."

"Not till they have the gold, remember. Butler's the only one wants you dead, and I'll wager he wants the money more."

"So you think I ought to go out right in the open, with that target painted on my chest, do you?"

"Just to flush ''em, like you said. See here, Stephen, they're never gonna leave you alone. You and Abby will never be safe. And eventually, they'll kill you just out of meanness, even without the money."

"Not a pleasant thought, that. So what, then? You'll follow, pick ''em off just before they can get me?"

"What I'd planned. Maybe need some help there. From what you say, Butler'd be the one to give us trouble."

"Good shot, all right. But he wasn't the man you saw, and probably not the other one, with the mirrors. So with that many, if they come after me in force, we'll need firepower."

"Will. Wish Tom would hurry back, but he'll be slow, nights and all. Who do you trust, who's not guarding the plantation?"

"Hate to ask anyone. Isaac Compton would come in a flash, but...No, he's plowing. And..."

"And, what?"

"Well, the tall girl, Annie. We were...she was...but no, wouldn't want to involve a woman in something like this..."

"Oh. No, y'don't wanta stir that up again. You really are a heart-break-er, Stevie. But, seeing Abby, I can understand."

"How can we handle it, just the two of us?"

"Well, take it one step at a time: They're watching; you know that. So, if you ride off, or slip off into the woods or down the road alone, they'll figure you're on the way to the gold. I'd say maybe the two men who were signaling were the ones trashed the place. One searches, the other keeps watch. So, say one or both these two follow you. I'm guessing Weston is back home for now. And Butler? Don't know. But let's say they're not here, this soon. There are probably a lot of others, but I doubt if they're close.

Whatever it is they do—robbery, mercantile theft, whatever—they're busy at it, wherever it's done."

"We can handle any one or two men, Ned. They could send for reinforcements, but that'd take time. I'd say go ahead now and let's get the lot of them moving."

"Now? It's late in the day."

"That's right, it is. All right, say tomorrow morning. I'll slip off, maybe with a shovel, as soon as it's light enough that they can see me."

"Where's a good, quiet place?"

"Up the hollow, there." They were at the workshop, and Stephen remembered the glade among the big trees up the spring branch. Nobody went there, except him and Abby.

"Off from where we went up to th' mountain?"

"Yes, little place springs come in. Far enough up away from here they won't have found it."

"All right. Say I ease on up early, before light. Then you go, and I'll be set for whoever follows you."

"Sounds good. But if there are two, take the one aiming at me first. And come to think of it, one will likely hold back, cover the other. That's how I'd do it."

"Yes, and he'd get away when I got the first one. Or they may just shoot you from cover when they figure you've led them to the gold." Ned wasn't grinning.

"Risky. Let's try to think of something better."

~ * ~

Tom Logan had reached the Weston plantation by another dawn. He knew the land well here, and hid deep in the woods, well back from the place. Dark…need dark for this work. He knew the way into the house, through the root cellar. The lift-latch to the house would slip with his keen knife blade, and he'd be in. Then…then he'd kill. Before they could kill his friend, he must strike. Dark business, indeed.

Get some rest, first. He stretched out in the dense cover, hand on his pistol, and slept.

~ * ~

Dwight Millington entered the plantation house, mindful of its quiet elegance. Money here, and taste. The butler led him into the parlor, where two women waited. One was certainly Gertrude Thomas. The other was the loveliest girl he'd ever seen. He couldn't quite stifle a sharp intake of breath at the sight. *Dear God, this is her, Abigail Thomas.*

"Reverend Millington, so nice to see you," the mother greeted. "I'm Gertrude, and this is Abby. The squire will return shortly…he's on one of his tours of the property."

"Thank you for allowing me to call, Mrs. Thomas." He bowed low. "A pleasure, Miss Abigail. I've wanted to call on your family before this, but with the details of the new pastorate, time has flown. But, if I may say so, meeting the two of you is certainly worth the wait."

"Welcome, Mr. Millington," Abby acknowledged his bow. She reflected that this was perhaps the handsomest man she recalled ever seeing. That high forehead, straight nose, intense gray eyes. The polished Philadelphia manners. A fleeting, unworthy thought: that he shouldn't be wasting his life as a man of the cloth...

After pleasant talk about the church, its members and other subjects, Squire Thomas joined them. Urged to stay to supper, the minister acquiesced, and a delightful evening ensued. Abigail Thomas was exquisite: Why hadn't he come here before she...No, that was the sort of thing he'd have to learn to control better. But what a bird of paradise, compared to dear Anna's plain, brown plumage. Despite his pledge of discipline, Dwight knew he must find out as much as he could about her intended. If there were any way, any way at all...

~ * ~

Rawlins Butler watched the house from a safe distance. There was still a slice of moon, and lamplight inside. He made out the two men guarding the place. One was the old smith, and a younger man he didn't know. He'd watched them take up positions at dusk, the old man hidden in a hedge at the front, and the other behind the wellbox at the rear of the house.

He watched the young minister take his leave among good-natured farewells. *Slick-looking one. He'd have been competition too, if the timing were different. Well, too late, preacher. Wouldn't matter after this was over with, anyway.*

He shifted his position to ease stiff muscles. Patience now. This was like hunting: wait for the right time, no matter how long. Maybe it wouldn't even be tonight, but his chance would come.

Her window was dark, but he knew it was unlocked. He knew because he'd seen to it the bolt was broken, the day they were all at the trial. It hadn't been the work of but a moment, while the peddler kept the house servants busy, for the woman to slip inside. The woman was the smartest of the lot, and the least suspect.

His ladder was light but strong, and he knew he could get it to the wall without being seen by the guards.

And he knew that because the guards wouldn't be there when it was time for him to move. He'd considered slipping up on them to cut their throats, but that could misfire if one managed to cry out. No, there'd be a diversion, visible to the guards but not to those inside. And Miss Abigail Thomas would be gagged, bound, over his shoulder and down the ladder before the guards returned.

The prospect thrilled him, like the approach of a fine buck to within range. They'd tried it the other way; now it was time for direct action. Davis would give up the gold for the girl. They were sure of it.

Only he wouldn't get the girl. She'd be far away before daylight, and farther still before they got to Davis. Then...then it would be pleasant if she grew accustomed to him, eventually accepted him. But he knew now that wouldn't happen. That didn't matter anyway...once she was in his hands, beyond the law, whether she accepted him willingly or not.

And with the gold finally in their possession, Abby would simply stay disappeared. Then Stephen Davis would die. It was the only way to keep a good thing intact. With so much at stake, one girl—even this one—just wasn't worth it. And Davis: a gnat. If he hadn't taken the gold, he might have lived to enjoy the girl...although that thought still angered Butler. *Common foot-soldier...*

A candle showed in Abby's room. He could see her shadow inside, moving about. At last. He rose, moved silently back to where the other man waited with the horses.

~ * ~

Tom slipped through shadows to the cellar door, so quietly not even a dog sensed his presence. He felt the old lock, the one he knew so well. If he pushed it just so...then twisted...It was open. His knife blade in the crack between the jamb and the stop: pry the stop just a fraction. Now, blade through: lift the latch. The tiniest squeak as the door opened.

Smells of onions and spices filled the darkness. He placed one foot carefully ahead of the other, avoiding kegs, boxes. The steps, now: third one would creak a little...step past it. Door to the house main floor. Latch string not there, of course. Knife to the jamb crack again...lift.

Down a hall a light glowed under a closed door. He stole toward it, knife out front, hand on his pistol. He listened for voices.

None.

He'd seen the lawyer Eddins ride away before dark, watched as the activities of the day subsided, seen the servants leave, one by one. The upper rooms had been dark: only the one light remained, and it was in this room. Faint woodsmoke smell from a dying fire.

He tensed, touched the knob. It turned silently. Good, the butler was keeping it oiled. Sweat stood out on his forehead. He drew in a deep breath, let it out silently. Then he moved.

Horace Weston felt a rush of air, and a heavy tread. He looked up at the muffled face of the man bearing down on him. An unborn cry became a gurgle as the knife flashed across his throat. The man jumped back, avoiding the blood. The doctor clutched at his throat, eyes bulging, then fell to the floor.

Tom wouldn't allow himself a reaction. Not yet. He scanned the room. Papers. Deeds, warrants. A sheet..."Bill of Divorcement," with scrawled additions in the margins. Good, it hadn't been recorded yet. He took it, read it, threw it into the fire. Then he remembered his master's hiding place. Not a safe really, but a sliding panel in the wainscoting. He pressed it, slid it open. Inside was a locked chest. *The key: be in a drawer somewhere. Desk, drum table...yes, a brass key, that fits.*

Gold. A chest full of gold. A new shipment, waiting for its next relay... Take it. No, blood money. But leave it and the others, whoever they were, would find it. Weston would be replaced...The evil would go on. Hide it? Who did it rightfully belong to? Probably a lot of people, all over. No way to get it back to them...Blood money, no doubt. His thoughts tumbled in his mind; he willed them toward focus.

In the end, he took it, closed the panel. Then he eased out, closed the doors, made his way to the cellar.

The air smelled like new earth as he re-locked the outer door, slipped like a shadow around the dark side of the house. His senses were on high alert as he entered the woods, moved toward his horse.

He was a murderer. Was he a thief, too? Time to think that through later.

He would travel far tonight.

~ * ~

Rawlins Butler saw the candle go out in Abby's window. Just a half hour now. The man with the horses would leave them tied, work his way down to the stables. In half an hour he would strike a small fire of straw, within easy sight of the two guards. As soon as they went to investigate, Butler would move.

He passed the time imagining Abby drifting off to sleep. *Lovely girl. Too bad Davis had to spoil it between us. I could be in that bed, now: show her what a real man is like. Damn commoner...Well, that's all past, now. You won't win, Davis. She'll never be my wife, but she won't be yours, either. Fortunes of war, you might say, and you are the one who started this one...*

Finally, a flame from the stables, and just the shadow of the man as he hurried away. Smoke drifted. The old smith stood, looked about, motioned to the other guard. Together they moved off quickly toward the fire.

Butler gripped the ladder, walked purposefully toward the sleeping house. *Small fire: shouldn't awaken anyone in the house.* He placed the ladder against the wall, steadied it, and climbed. High excitement ran through him as every rung brought him closer to the sleeping girl inside. He could almost feel her in his arms, that divine shape he'd hungered for these many months.

The window slid up silently. He paused, tried to make out the shapes of furniture inside. This was the moon-shadow side of the house and nothing was clear. He stepped into the room. A familiar fragrance hung in the air.

Hers.

The canopied bed came into focus. He moved toward it, his feet silent on the braided rug. He took a cloth from his pocket, held it ready to stifle an outcry. He listened for any sound from elsewhere within the house. All was quiet. He parted the bed curtains, his blood pounding, a singing in his ears.

The bed was empty.

Wait, this is her room. The candle had been lit...Then faintly, the sound of distant voices from the stables: the two guards.

She's not here! Where...? Out, then, quickly. Quickly!

He was on the ladder again, the window closed. Down, then take the ladder, run.

Great drops of sweat fell from his face as he joined the other man at the horses, the ladder gripped in his hands.

"What happened? Where's..."

"Not now," he snapped. "Take this ladder. Ride!"

Nineteen

Ned Drake slipped from the cabin early, with a long rifle and two pistols. A hush lay over the little hollow, with the music of the small stream the only sound. He followed a path for some distance along the high ground through laurels and beech trees, till it dropped down along the spring branch. Well ahead was the glade Stephen had described, crowded with huge trees and mossy boulders, just visible in the rising light. A small open space appeared, with a bench of soil above the water. He scraped the leaves and twigs away here, making it appear to be freshly-dug soil. Then he moved beyond, and settled behind a huge poplar tree to wait.

Back at the cabin, Stephen ate by the fire, waiting for full light. Then with the sun up, he put on a buckskin jacket to conceal his two pistols, took his rifle. Outside, he reached into his small toolshed for a shovel. He tied the dog, looked quickly around, and moved off upstream. Apprehension prickled his skin, as he imagined eyes on him, eyes sighting a rifle.

He looked over his shoulder often, because his followers, if any, would expect that. Once he thought he caught movement far behind, but the woods were heavy. *Could be an animal. Let's see, they'll skirt the house, stay away from the dog, close in behind me farther up this way. If there are two of them, they'll be on each side, probably high for better visibility. Have to move in, though, to see much, with all this growth.*

Ned Drake watched his friend come up the stream. *Looks just like a man with something to hide. Or dig up, in this case. Now, I've got to make sure nobody shoots him before we can get him—or them.*

That thought was in Stephen's mind, too. He moved to the scuffed place and drove his shovel into the ground, leaving it handle-upright. Then he quickly climbed the right slope and doubled back, well away from the stream. He knew these woods well, and kept moving quietly until he was halfway back toward his cabin. Then he slipped down to the stream and turned up it again.

Just ahead was a sandy bar in the lee of a big stone outcropping. He could see his own tracks across it, but no others. Ned would have avoided the sand, and so had any followers. Perhaps they had been higher up, then. There was another bar further up, about where the woods thickened. They should have come down there, if indeed they even existed.

He moved stealthily, scrutinizing every tree trunk, boulder, laurel bush. Nothing yet. The other sandy stretch was just ahead. He kept his eyes beyond as he moved, alert for any outline, any movement.

A second set of tracks marked the sand. Water was still seeping into the depressions, angled from the right slope.

All right, that's one. And he's headed right toward the shovel. But where's his partner? Not behind me, I hope. No, he couldn't watch the other's back unless he was close. Up on one of these slopes, then. This one came from the right, so I'll climb left. Not far, now.

Ned watched the man come. Same man he'd seen on the mountain that day. Rifle at the ready, scanning, moving cautiously. Ned searched the slopes beyond from behind his tree. First man would see the shovel and either wait for some activity, or signal his backup before moving in. Stephen would hold back, pick up the second man…

Stephen could see his first stalker as he came into sight of the shovel, well ahead. The man stopped, then turned his head back, to the left. Following his eyes, Stephen finally made out a shape crouching above, blending with the deep shadows. From here he couldn't tell, but he didn't think he'd ever seen either man before.

The first man motioned his partner down, then moved stealthily forward. *Man with a gun always feels safe. Bad flaw.* He eased into position, leveled his rifle. So did the backup man, clear now in Stephen's sights.

Just then, Ned Drake showed himself for an instant, then just as quickly, disappeared again. The first stalker fired, an instant too late, taking bark off the big poplar. The backup man swung his rifle, and Stephen shot his right leg from under him. The man screamed, the rifle flying. The first man snatched a pistol, but Ned's rifle boomed, and he fell, shot through the heart.

Stephen was upon the wounded man, kicking his rifle away, grabbing a pistol he was trying to draw. Blood spurted from the artery in his leg. He stopped screaming, clutched his leg, in shock. Stephen slapped the man repeatedly.

"You have about ten seconds to live," he told him. "Who'er the others in this with you?"

"I..." The man's eyes were bulging. Stephen held the two pistols on him, cocked them both. The eyes focused on the muzzles of the guns.

"*Who?*" It was a roar.

"Butler! Doctor...from over Caroline..."

"Who else?" The pistols moved to his face.

"Lawyer, from...Eddins. Don't shoot!" The eyes went wide.

"That all?"

"Butler's got a man...Dinkins...up on th' pike, flat of th' mountain...part-way up. Albert...Dinkins. All I know...Hayes dead..."

"But there are more?"

"Maybe. Doc gets...th' money...East, somewheres..."

"You men were going to shoot me from cover." A cold accusation.

"Jist...jist follerin' orders…Orders, like in th' war. You…were in th' war..." the man's eyes went from Stephen to Ned Drake, towering over him. Then, seemingly in an instant, they clouded, went blank. His grip on his leg loosened, and with a shudder, he died.

"Lost a lotta blood quick, Stephen. Pale's a sheet. Who was he?"

"Don't know. One of them. How about the other man?"

"Same one I saw before. Prob'ly from East, one of the doc's fellows, I'd say. So, seems Butler, this Dinkins, Eddins and Doc are what's left. Unless Tom's got to the doctor."

"I'll wager he has. He feels he owes me—us. I'd say the good doctor's hours are numbered."

"Well. Let's bury these two somewhere. Save a lot of questions. Then we can go after Butler."

~ * ~

At the plantation house, Ike Collins told Squire Thomas about the fire.

"Small straw fire, but close t'th' stables. Me'n Web run down thar, but warn't nobody ''round. Now, that fire didn't start by itse'f, Squire."

"Certainly not. Sounds like a diversion to me. Did the dogs go after anything?"

"Nossir. They milled ''round with us, was all. Nothin' else happened till th'' other men come on, middle of th' night."

"And you saw nothing strange here at the house?"

Abby had listened to this exchange. There was only one reason anyone would want to divert the guards from the house.

"Come with me, Papa," she drew him aside. "Now, who would profit from getting the guards away?"

"Someone who wanted into the house."

"Double-bolted. And I was thinking of that last night, and went to check on my window bolt. It was broken."

They had climbed the stairs to her room. She showed him the latch, which looked as if it had been pried loose.

"My God," her father breathed, "Someone could have climbed up here." He looked about the room.

"So I slept in the far guest room, Papa, with the door bolted. And I barricaded this door from outside." She was on her knees. "Look at this." She held up a grass stem from the rug.

"Why didn't you say something?"

"It seemed a silly fear, till I heard about the fire. I didn't want to alarm you. But I've been on edge ever since we figured that those men might try to get to Stephen through me. Now it looks like they tried." Her level eyes were on her father's.

"Those scoundrels! They'd have used a ladder. May have left some sign. Our own house not safe! Oh, child, you've your wits about you." He held her to him. "But who could have broken the lock? How did someone get in here? Who..."

"I asked Cook. She said a peddler was here when we were at court. They all went out to see what he had. She said there had been a woman with him. Maybe she got inside somehow. But who would know which was my room? Only Rawlins Butler. No one else could have told them."

They were outside now, the dew beginning to burn off. But there was clearly a path where no dew clung, where someone had come to the wall. Abby knelt.

"Here, Papa. See these two depressions? Ladder." She looked up. "And up there, just under my window, see those scuff marks?"

"Scoundrels!" He was casting about, looking off toward a copse of trees. "There'll be tracks there, Abby. A second man would have started the fire, lured the guards. Then..."

"Yes. Then, if I'd been in my bed..."

"Oh, my daughter!"

"But Papa, it wouldn't have been easy." Her eyes were hard. "I had a loaded pistol with me."

~ * ~

It was noon when the two men returned to the cabin, Ned surveying blistered hands.

"Gentleman planter's not s'posed to work that hard, Stephen. Where's the field hands when you need ''em?"

"Got some salve here, somewhere. Abby's mother's always worrying about me, playing doctor."

"What I need is sweet Miss Constance to tend me in my hour of need. Damsel in distress—we can comfort one another."

"You've got two blisters and you're whining. That'd have earned you a tongue-lashing in the army."

"This ain't the army, me bucko. That was war; this is love."

"She's married, remember?"

"Not for long. Doc divorces her, she's mine. Little like rescuing the maiden from the dragon, y'know?"

"Maybe. And come to think of it, I'd say Miss Constance is probably a widow by now anyway."

"Oh, yes: Tom the Avenger. You know, that's one helluva man. I have to remind myself he's black."

"Why should you? We've both seen a sight of meaner specimens who were white, and right recently."

"Have. Tom makes me question the whole slave system."

"Finally. They can all be taught, Ned."

"Maybe not all."

"All. Did you know Abby's teaching Molly?"

"Hell you say. Clever wench, Molly. Shame Tom's not drawn to her."

Ned rode to the plantation, ostensibly to report to the Squire on their activities of the morning, but more of course, to bask in Constance Weston's care and concern. Stephen wanted to be close to home in case Tom returned. He could easily be wounded, if he returned at all.

~ * ~

Rawlins Butler was worried. The two men watching Davis hadn't reported in. He'd let Dinkins return to his place on the pike while he planned another way to abduct Abby Thomas. *Wouldn't do to try the same thing again. Any fool would recognize the fire as a diversion. It worked, but that damn girl...*

And where were his men? *Maybe following Davis.* Drake had ridden to the plantation alone just minutes earlier, but what about Davis? Maybe leading the men to the gold right then. Maybe. This could still turn out well, if they got it. Leave Abby alone, then. But kill Davis, if the men didn't. He would stalk them now, after that trashing of his place. And well, with Davis gone, who knew? Things could still work out with his former intended.

*We can find another Hayes. Weston is smart; he'll have any gaps filled quickly enough. I just wish I knew...*He stood, paced, trained his spyglass on the plantation house again, far below. He wasn't sure what his next move would be, but perhaps some opportunity would present itself, possibly even Abby's riding out alone, as she often did.

~ * ~

Tom had not traveled as far the night before as he'd wanted. But once on the road, without the added weight of the chest, he'd made better time. By dawn he'd reached a place up a brush-choked streambed where he felt secure. He hid the horse and himself well off the road, then before dropping off to sleep, replayed in his mind the killing—murder—in detail. *Yes, I'm a murderer now. Killed him before he could defend himself. And I guess I'm a thief, too.* He focused on the hiding place where he'd left the chest of gold. *Maybe some good could come of it, some way, sometime…*

The urge to ride North had been strong: just leave this country where a black man would never be free. Go North, find a city he could live in as a craftsman. Philadelphia, New York, Boston.

Long way. And what, when he arrived? If he arrived at all. Would anyone honor his freedom papers? Or simply take them, and him, to enslave him again. And could he even reach such a city?

Besides, Stephen and Ned are my friends. If a black man can have real white friends…Now, stop that! Stephen saved my life, risked himself to free me. Taught me…No, he's a true friend. Ned's got slaves, or his father has. But he waded right in for me. And, I'll have to admit it…with them I can be a lot freer than I could otherwise.

But when will that change? Will it ever, with the way they look at us, treat us? Be many years I'm afraid, generations even. Oh, maybe my grandchildren…Would be nice to find a wife, have some children. Teach them what I've learned. About all any man can do for his children…

Twenty

"I want to see Stephen." Abby was firm. Ned's story made her realize how close she'd come to losing him, again. "You can ride with me, Ned. I'll be safe with you." The brown eyes were pleading. "Papa, please, say I can go to him."

For her part, Constance Weston had listened raptly to the story of the ambush, and Ned Drake's stature rose in her eyes. Her own future was so cloudy...Did she even have a home? A livelihood? Anywhere to go, beyond these kind people? There were only distant relatives...she recognized Ned's appearance as Providential, and she also knew by now, how tenuous life for a woman alone could be, in this place and time.

Speaking out for Tom, and these people, had been the right thing to do, but it could well have burned her bridges. She would never—could never—go back to Horace, but what next? One day at a time, that was as far as she could look. But now she knew Ned Drake would definitely be a part of each of those days.

~ * ~

Rawlins Butler couldn't believe his good fortune. There was Abby, riding with the Drake fellow, across the open fields toward Davis' place. Without hesitation, he scrambled from among the rocks, freed his horse and rode quickly down between the trees to the hidden trail he knew well, down the slope of Greene Mountain.

All right…let them get far enough from the plantation so she won't turn back. Davis was likely gone anyway, or he'd have heard from the men watching him. He could shoot Drake from the woods' edge and ride Abby down, cut her off. She'd be fast, but he'd have a precious start in the confusion when Drake fell. He remembered the place they'd had the shooting match…lower end of the long creek field.

I know my spot…

~ * ~

Stephen was chafing at his work. Web had gone home for sleep after his guard duty, and the work of stair railings should have been engrossing. But he kept thinking of Abby. And Tom. And the whole business of missing money and dead men, and what to do next. Butler had to go; that was certain. Then the lawyer Eddins, which would be harder. And Dinkins. Dinkins, whoever he was, sparked a nagging question in his mind, one that wouldn't quite come into focus. Hell, he didn't even know the man…*Flat of the mountain, on the pike…*

He set the work aside, paced the shop. No clear answers. Then he caught up his rifle and went outside into the spring day. He, Ned and the squire needed to plan. He turned back, wrote Tom a note, and saddled his horse.

~ * ~

Rawlins Butler waited, hidden in trees as the riders approached. He and his horse were breathing hard from the tree-dodging ride. Let them pass, fire, then mount and cut Abby off from a return up the field. If necessary, he could reload and shoot her horse from under her. No way to lose, now. It'd be shooting Drake in the back…hardly sporting, but this was war…

They were abreast. He held his horse's nose to keep him quiet, mindful of Drake's scanning the trees. He was behind a giant oak, but with a clear line of fire, once they were downfield. Drake kept turning in his saddle, and Butler held his breath. A long, tension-filled moment.

Now. He released the horse's nose, braced the rifle against the tree in one fluid, practiced move, aimed quickly.

The horse snorted. Drake spun around just as Butler squeezed the trigger. The rider pitched forward. Abby stared in horror as the echo came back from the treeline beyond. She was frozen for what seemed minutes, her hand over her mouth.

Butler leaped onto his horse, spurred him out to the right to head the girl off. She saw him, hesitated a fatal second deciding which way to run, then dug her heels into her mare's flanks. By then, Butler was at full speed, closing. He reached her where the field narrowed toward Stephen's place, with good ground still ahead.

She swerved her mount to elude him, but he'd anticipated that, hauled his horse close, reached out. He clutched her around the waist, wrenched her off her horse. She screamed, flailed. He braked his own mount before turning him toward the road. The girl tore at him, but in his triumph, it was as if he were made of steel.

Invincible, by God! I'm invincible, woman, and I've got you now! He was aware of her scent, and in his triumph, realized fleetingly that she was completely powerless now, completely his, to possess without limit.

Stephen Davis had emerged from the woods downcreek just too late to see his friend shot off his horse. What he saw was Butler racing his horse toward Abby, and Ned down. Too far to reach them. He threw himself off his horse into a crouch, drawing his rifle to his shoulder. But Butler had her in that instant, checking his horse, eyeing the way to the road. Stephen could see a pistol in his belt.

Abby's arms were flailing as she beat at her captor with her fists. As Stephen sighted, all the minute details of this incredibly difficult shot crowded his mind: her moving arms, the split-instant pause between the horse's stopping and his turning, the almost nonexistent breeze. In the same flash of time, he realized he could not let the man go, try to follow. He'd hold Abby at gunpoint, and might well kill her. And of course he'd kill her eventually, anyway.

Butler started the horse's turn to the right. He held the thrashing girl in his right arm: his side, then part of his back would be toward Stephen. In a lightning flash, every instinctive calculation clicked into place. He was the sharpshooter, the marksman, a killing machine. His finger tightened...

*What the hell! I can't risk this shot! She's...*A shudder ran through him, and his eyes blurred.

In that instant, Abby Thomas jerked Butler's pistol from his belt. He grabbed for it, but she'd cocked it, and jammed it at him and pulled the trigger as he twisted her wrist. Flash. Roar, smoke. He stiffened, blood gushing onto the horse, onto the girl, then pitched off the horse.

The instant Butler was free of Abby, Stephen squeezed the trigger, leading him in his fall. But the chance of hitting the girl was too great; he shifted the rifle as he fired. And he knew it was not a good shot.

The horse had lunged ahead at Butler's spurring, and the man's foot had caught Abby as he fell. She was unseated, in mid-air. She flung the gun aside, arched, clutched the horse's neck, her lithe body like a cat's, twisting to maintain balance. Even in that charged second, Stephen marveled at her skill with the horse. With an arm around his neck, she brought his head down, stopped him, came down on both her feet.

Stephen was in the saddle, speeding toward them. No time to reload, but he aimed to ride Butler down if he were still alive. Almost certainly he had a second pistol, and the man was still somehow writhing, twisting on the ground.

With only a few feet to go, Butler raised himself, sighting the second gun. Stephen crouched, hauled his horse sideways, ducked, as the pistol discharged in a bloom of fire.

He didn't feel anything. The horse didn't falter. He looked, and saw the gun flying from Butler's hand, his body lurching.

Smoke rolled from Ned Drake's rifle up the field, and the sound echoed from both hills.

Abby crouched, her eyes wide in horror at the blood on her hands. Stephen leaped off his horse, reached her, clutched her to him. Her body was rigid, then she was shaking, gasping for breath. She fixed vacant eyes on his face, pushed at his chest with her bloody hands, drew away from him.

Shock. She's in shock. He pulled her back to him, but she twisted away, fell to her knees, sobbing. He picked her up, still resisting, and carried her to where Ned lay, clutching his side. Stephen set Abby down, held her there with one hand.

"How bad is it?"

"In the muscle. Not deep. Hurts like hell. What's wrong with Abby?"

At sight of Ned, blood all over him, the girl had convulsed, her eyes rolling up in her head, and passed out.

"Shock, I guess. She shot Butler, came off that horse like an acrobat, then came apart. Thanks for that shot…you saved my life."

"B'lieve I owed you that one. This morning didn't count."

~ * ~

They'd carried Abby to the plantation house, still unconscious. Her mother tended her. Ned lay, the side wound tightly bandaged after a liberal clensing with whiskey, on the bed in a guest room. Constance Weston had cleaned the wound and then applied one of Gertrude Thomas' salves. She never left his side. Stephen hovered at Abby's bedside, answering the mother's questions. Squire Thomas strode up and down, occasionally smacking his fist into his hand. His lined face was grim, rage running through him like a tide.

When Abby regained consciousness, her eyes were haunted. Stephen tried to talk to her.

"No. Not now…Just let me…The blood. The killing…I shot a man…shot Rawlins…This killing has to stop, Stephen."

"You didn't kill anyone, Abby. But he'd have killed me, and you too, eventually." He kept his voice calm, soothing.

"I…guess I know that, but…I just don't want to think about it, just yet."

"Let's let her rest, Stephen," her mother advised. "It's been a shock."

She closed the door behind them. Stephen felt completely helpless. Gertrude Thomas gave his arm a squeeze.

~ * ~

Eventually, after arranging for Butler's body to be transported, and sending word to Joshua Stokes, the squire got down to the matter at hand.

"Stephen, you say that fellow told you the lawyer Eddins was involved, along with the doctor. Those two will be hard to eliminate."

"Yes, and a man named Dinkins, up on the pike. He didn't know any others. Said Weston received the money from East somewhere. Probably a syndicate of some kind, organized, taking a toll of money stolen from all over."

"So Weston's the key figure. Eddins would see that all the legal details were in order, like the places Hayes was buying and outfitting." He turned to Constance. "Mrs. Weston, do you recall anything of the doctor's business that could help us, here?"

"Not really, sir. He had many visitors, and always conferred with them in private. He seldom traveled, since the war. He no longer tended the ill."

"Well, madam, it appears your husband has been the brains behind a rather extensive operation. Begging your pardon, but you must have suspected something, to break away as you did." The planter's inquiry was not unkind, and he placed a fatherly hand on her arm.

"I was so terribly unhappy, sir. Seen in perspective, Horace's actions were all so...I felt so used, looking back on it all. And I've never been able to escape a feeling that he might have had something to do with...with John's death."

"Indeed?"

"He was so much better. In Horace's care, of course. Then...then one morning..." She turned away, remembering.

"Oh, you poor dear girl," Gertrude Thomas soothed. "You were so very brave, to walk away..."

"I...sensed that you—you all—were not accidental, Mrs. Thomas. I'd prayed for help, of any kind. Then when I realized Horace was, for whatever reason, falsely accusing Mr. Davis here, and trying to enslave a free man again...suddenly I just could not stay with him. Not another moment." She turned tearful eyes on Ned Drake, who took her hand gently.

Stephen, despite the gravity of the situation, almost rolled his eyes at his friend's smooth opportunism. *A veritable scoundrel, but so fine a scoundrel, and so fine a friend. And of course there'll be more vintage Drake...* There was.

"I have not been a religious man, Miss Constance, but I see God's hand in this," Ned said, his eyes intently on hers.

Stephen drew the squire aside. Mrs. Thomas discreetly withdrew, also.

~ * ~

"The man Dinkins is a key, here," Stephen was telling his listeners, including the squire. "He's been in on searching for the money. Now I'd wager Hayes stopped at his place up on the pike before he came here. Perhaps for directions or overnight. It would be normal to check in with members of the band. We don't know this man, but he'd have heard of you, sir, and maybe me too, no farther than we are. So Hayes must have had the gold when he left Dinkins to come here. And somewhere on the way, he surely hid it, to pick up afterwards..."

"Or this Dinkins could have the gold, himself," Ned interposed.

"Possible. But too much effort's gone into getting it back. I'd wager, if Dinkins had taken the money, he'd have run completely out of the country, disappeared. I would guess the men in this ring have long arms."

"Unless this Dinkins is shrewder than the average criminal," the squire mused. "Certainly we never suspected Butler, and the doctor and Eddins don't fit the stereotype at all, Stephen. Dinkins could actually have the gold, and just be pretending to the others you have it."

"Well, yes, Dinkins is an unknown quantity. But I'll find out what he knows. Eddins will, as you said, sir, be harder."

"I've a notion Judge Edgerton will be interested in that man, to the extent that he'll be, shall we say, neutralized at least. I'll have a talk with Amos next court day, if not sooner."

"Ah, then it's down to this Dinkins—"

"You're not going alone." A flat statement from Ned.

"Well, I..."

"Definitely not," the squire declared. "Get Josh Stokes. Or...Tom? What of Tom, now?"

"All I know is his note said he'd be back in a few days, sir."

"Oh, yes. And also, we mustn't forget, Dr. Weston's still out there."

"I've the conviction that Tom may have acted, sir, on that matter. I'll not be surprised if the good doctor is but a memory, even now."

"Stephen, in any other circumstances, I'd be shocked at that disclosure. Now, I trust you're correct. We could be nearing the end of this ordeal."

"I'm about ready for it to be over too," Ned agreed.

~ * ~

Abigail Thomas kept seeing the blood gushing from Rawlins Butler's side, spilling warm on her hands. She'd shut out the horror of it when she had to, to come safely down off that plunging, rearing horse, but it kept coming back. And Stephen and Ned had just that morning killed two more men, as if there were nothing to it. And in that secret, lovely place...And those weeks ago, that man at the shop: her betrothed had bashed his head in—all right, it was self-defense—as his way of dealing with the situation. How much longer would this go on? How many more killings? Murders? *No, of course they weren't murders. But—*

Whatever happened to the peaceful life she used to have here? Peace: it'd been shattered. Inexplicably, her mind turned to the young minister, Dwight Millington. A man of peace, that one, surely. Not the hard, killing machine Stephen seemed, just then. It was not a fair comparison, but one that persisted.

Back in his cabin, Stephen was assailed by misgivings. The dying man hadn't known the extent of the operation, or wouldn't tell him. And even with Weston gone, the lawyer Eddins could surely send more men. This Dinkins... Was he a minor figure, or perhaps one of the top men? He had to find out. Dinkins was close; he'd know soon that three more of their men were dead. Did he have the authority to send reinforcements? Or would he just disappear when he learned the syndicate was undone?

Late. I'll decide in the morning. Big day: three dead men who wanted to kill me. And Abby, really hit hard by it all. Guess I'd forgotten how normal folks react to killing human beings. But she'll get past it. Has a lot of her mother's grit.

It'll be a day or so before the news gets around. I guess, if Weston—and Eddins—are still around, I'm not safe. Or, if Tom's taken care of Weston, and the judge can possibly—what was it, neutralize?—Eddins, then Dinkins is my only real worry. Far as I can know...

It wasn't like Stephen to oversleep, but it was bright daylight when the dog's barking awakened him. He peered out his window, over the muzzle of his rifle. Then the dog ran, wagging his tail.

Tom Logan rode into view. The last few miles, where everyone knew him, he'd been able to travel in daylight. He dismounted, leaned his rifle against the porch.

"You reckon a wore-out travelin' man could get a bite to eat around here, mister?" he grinned.

~ * ~

"It doesn't feel good, Stephen. I'm a murderer, plain and simple. Man needed to die, in th' worst kind of way, many times over. But it wasn't like he could defend himself—had a gun on me—just a cold killin'. Not like Hayes…he was tryin' to kill us."

"I know, Tom. You never get past that, if you're human. Abby's having a hard time dealing with what she had to do. But you must believe, if you'd given Weston an instant, he'd have yelled for help, and you'd have hanged. And, don't doubt such a man had a loaded gun close at hand. Thank God you didn't give him a chance."

"I tell myself that, and yes, there was a pistol in his desk drawer. I'm just not a killer, Stephen. A weakness, with what's happened. I forget sometimes: only th' strong survive."

"That's right. And you've eliminated the key man in this…this syndicate, or whatever it is. And we all thank you. Squire Thomas believes Judge Edgerton can take care of the lawyer Eddins, and that leaves just one man we know of. Name's Dinkins, if the man I killed had it right."

"There's a Dinkins up on the pike the Comptons know. Has a rough little tavern, up partway where the mountain flattens out. Hasn't been there long."

"Could be the man, all right. In with Butler. I was about to go pay him a visit, but the folks are telling me I must have help."

"Prob'ly wise. And he might come after you, with others. Maybe ought to get to him before he hears what's happened."

"I was thinking that. Tomorrow. You game?"

"Try goin' without me."

~ * ~

The young minister was busy writing his next sermon when the news of the violence came. Isaac Compton stopped by the church, and Annie was with him on the wagon.

"Rough times, Reverend," Isaac said. "Bunch of ''em come after Stephen Davis, an' he had to be right harsh with ''em. Strange part was Rawlins Butler, respected planter hereabouts. Shot th' man was protectin' Abby Thomas, an' tried to carry her off."

"No!" The young man was visibly shaken. "Had this to do with that trial in town, Mr. Compton?"

"Seems so. S'posed to've been a lot of money lost, an' th' bunch figgered Stephen had it."

"I heard he was acquitted on all charges. I've not met him yet, but he does not sound like a man to trifle with."

"Fer shore. An' Abby fought this Butler, grabbed his gun and wounded him. Takin' it hard though, Ike's wife said. Not used to killin'.'"

"Certainly not. Killing is seldom the answer." Images of that lovely girl, no doubt horrified at the carnage. "Perhaps I should call on them."

"Mebbe so. Be glad when this's over with. Stephen's worked hard to get set up, an' this business has ''bout put a chock in it."

Annie had noted the dismay on Millington's face at word of the attempted abduction of Abby Thomas, and at her distress. *So this young man too, was under the girl's spell. Well, to be expected. Only you're too late, Reverend.*

After they left, the minister tore up his notes and began again. This violence would be on the minds of his congregation Sunday, and it was a good place to get in some points for the Lord. But his mind kept straying to Abigail Thomas. Perhaps she was in need of some gentle counseling, in her agitated state. That, of course, was part of a minister's job, after all.

~ * ~

Stephen was able to get a little work done on his house, after a brief visit to Abby at the plantation. She was better, but her eyes drifted off while they were talking. He noticed her twisting her hands, and remembered the blood on them. He tried to console her, assure her it was almost over.

"Will it ever be over, Stephen? Really over? How many more men will ride up, with wild notions, to stalk us? I'm just so sick of it. Butler shooting Ned. His coming after me...His blood on me..."

"Try not to think about it, Abby. It'll pass. It has to pass." But her body was rigid when he tried to hold her. The demons had not left her yet.

It was not much of a success, that visit. Gertrude Thomas had taken him aside, out of Abby's hearing.

"She's not that tough, Stephen. Butler was a bastard, but he was a person she knew well, not a faceless enemy, and she had to shoot him. She did it, and had to do it, but it's all hit her, now it's over with. She'll need some time to put it into perspective, see it all as the necessary action it became." She squeezed his hand assuringly.

By late afternoon, after Tom had slept, he joined him at the new house. They put the stair railings in place, talking, planning.

"Two possibilities," Stephen pointed out: "Either Hayes had the money when he left Dinkins, and hid it on the way here, or Dinkins has had it all along, just pretending to go along with the idea I'd taken it."

"Hmm. That lasts's not likely."

"Why not? He could be that sharp."

"Could be. But eventually, since you didn't know where the money was, they couldn't get it out of you. Then they'd have gone after Dinkins. Tight operation like this, they'd make it mighty hard on a defector. No, I believe Hayes hid the chest."

"Oh, good thinking. But where? Not around Dinkins' place, or he'd have found it. Hayes didn't know the road well to our shop. Didn't confide in any of their people, that's for certain."

"Let's keep an eye out then, when we ride up. All leafed out, we won't be able to see what he could in Feb'uary, but we could get lucky."

~ * ~

"It's just sort of overwhelmed me, Reverend. Part of me knows I, we— must protect ourselves…justifiable force. But I keep seeing the details so clearly: the blood, the..." Abby covered her face, shaking again.

He resisted the impulse to put a consoling hand on her shoulder. Her mother held her, rocking her gently.

"It's harder on her than any of us imagined, sir. We've done what we must here, but it's taken its toll."

"I can certainly see that. But there is a place of quiet rest, Miss Abigail. Don't try to fight this alone. Jesus is the Prince of Peace…He'll take your burden, if you'll let Him. We're never given more than we can handle, but too often it seems that way. Having your faith to support you will be the differ-ence, I can assure you. It would be so much harder if that weren't the case."

She quieted, began to listen. Dwight Millington had a soft voice when he needed it, reassuring, enveloping her, penetrating this scary, unfamiliar state she'd been in. Gertrude Thomas, who'd been on the point of terminating the visit, saw the young man's calming effect, and allowed him to stay. Grad-ually, he drew Abby out, getting her to talk of other things: horses, the crops, the workings of the mill and the many other industries of the plantation.

He'd had some experience dealing with the grief of others, and he put all his skill into diverting this girl from the things that haunted her. The underlying message was that life was still here to be lived, and that she must not dwell on the stark events that had obsessed her.

He's good for her, the plantation mistress observed. *I guess Stephen's still just too deep into what he has to do, to reach her. She probably sees him as a little ruthless, just now. I'm glad he is, if that's what's necessary, but my little girl isn't as hard as I am. I guess I'm glad she isn't, come to that. Physically strong, wiry rider, tomboy, but so very vulnerable...*

So, in effect, Abby found herself pouring her heart out to this pleasant stranger, whose only motivation surely was to help her. He was a minister, after all, a dedicated man of God. She realized she'd spent very little time in church recently, and felt some guilt. She'd have to talk to Stephen about that.

Twenty-one

They were riding north, to strike Swift Run and on to the base of the mountain where it joined the pike from Richmond on west. The road ran past the Norton farm, across the Lynch River, then the stream coming out of Bacon Hollow. Further up, they reached Swift Run itself, where the roads crossed. Downstream several miles was Butler's plantation; ahead the junction with the Richmond pike near Stanardsville. To the left, up the creek, was the way to the flat, partway up the Blue Ridge. So far, no likely hiding places for the gold had appeared.

"You know, Tom, Hayes could have come directly down from Stanardsville. Miles shorter that way. Maybe he didn't contact Dinkins at all."

"Been thinkin' about that. Makes more sense than going away up the mountain, then back down Swift Run: two sides of th' triangle instead of one. And he'd have taken th' creek road on th' way back for sure, seems like."

"But that'd mean he hid the gold somewhere between here and home, Tom, so he could pick it up without going back."

"And it's pretty built-up. Better hidin' places up the Run, if I remember what Isaac Compton told me. And, he'd have hidden th' chest soon after leavin' the pike. Heavy, all that gold." Tom knew just how heavy. He hadn't told Stephen about the second chest. Not sure why, but he hadn't. Yet. He would of course, but just now, seemed the fewer complications the better.

And then he got a flash of insight: if he were somehow caught and say, tortured to tell the other chest's whereabouts, that'd fit with their enemies' tactics. And perhaps that was their plan if they'd managed to get Stephen locked away in jail. Surely Weston's money could buy a way to beat him into a confession while in there. Or so they might have believed. That could have been their first plan, before Abby. Stephen was speaking:

"So he'd have to come back the way he went, to get the gold. So one way's as good as the other, then."

"All right. I'd say, let's go this way, just in case there's an obvious hidin' place, then up the pike to Dinkins' place, then back down the Run. Longer of course, but we'll cover both roads that way."

"Glad I got you along, Tom. Need somebody to do the heavy thinking."

He slapped his friend on the back.

The road gave up no secrets, however, and they struck the pike a half hour later. Westward it climbed the first slope of the Blue Ridge, with the piedmont spreading out below, then clear on to Richmond and beyond. It was a fine late spring day, with cottony clouds drifting high. The switchback road climbed easily, and they reached the level stretch before noon. Soon the road up Swift Run joined from the left, and there were several farms here along the creek.

Dinkins' tavern was a small log cabin, one story with a sleeping loft. The immediate aspect was one of the rough, bare necessities for travelers: the better accommodations were in Stanardsville, to the east. Tom stayed out of sight as Stephen rode up to the structure.

The woman at the fireplace crane was middle-age, tired.

"Have dinner in a half hour," she straightened, pushing a strand of straw-colored hair from her eyes. But he saw that those eyes were hard, searching. "Y'come up from Richmond?"

"That way. Mr. Dinkins around?" Stephen tried to sound casual.

"Down to th' barn. Help's off t'day. Yer horse need feed? His brother's around here, some'ers."

"No. Just came up from Stanardsville this mornin'. Just be a minute." He thanked her, turned and left, slipped back to Tom.

"Now, I'll get him behind the barn. You keep an eye out: got a brother somewhere around. Shouldn't take me long." He led his horse down toward the barn, which was situated on a shelf of land over the creek.

The man looked up from mending harness, and recognition showed instantly. Stephen had seen him somewhere, too...Dinkins backed away, eyes casting about. Stephen stepped behind the barn and drew his pistol.

"Where do I know you from, Dinkins?"

"Ain't never seen you b'fore."

"Not good enough." He cocked the pistol, shoved it into the man's face. "Now where?" The eyes widened in fear.

"Reckon t'was at..at th' trial. In Charlottesville. I'se thar."

"Ah. With Weston, and Butler and Eddins. Now I won't waste time, Dinkins. A dying man told me you were in on this organization Weston headed. All of you thought I had money—a lot of money—a man named Hayes was carrying West. I don't, but maybe you do. First, did Hayes come here?"

"I dunno no Hayes." The man's face was sullen now.

"I'll give you two seconds to live, Dinkins. Answer me!" He pushed the gun barrel into the man's forehead, and his eyes said he meant it.

"All right! Don't shoot! Hayes was here. Had th' gold with him. Wanted t'know whar you was. Didn't know, but I tol' him how to git to Squire Thomas. Said he knowed you was close. Took th' gold with him."

"That's better. Now, what was your part in this...operation?"

"Mister, I jist run m'place, here. They stop in, pay me. I do some work fer Butler. I don't know nuthin' moren' that. They run gold West, all I know. Hayes, he come th'u mebbe twicet a year. I didn' even know th' doc an' Eddins, till th' trial..."

"Why'd you go?"

"Butler said to. Said I needed to know who you was...'case you was let off..." The man licked his lips nervously.

"He say why?"

"Wal, they all figgered you had th' gold...th' stuff Hayes was carryin'. Figgered to git it outen you, some way. I dunno no more'n' that. Honest I don't..." He was pleading. Stephen felt as if he were kicking a sick dog.

A bad taste was in his mouth. He remembered Abby's revulsion at all the killing…

"Maybe you don't. But listen here: Weston is dead. Butler is dead. Two more men who followed me are dead. Eddins is under arrest. And if I ever even see you again, Dinkins, I'll kill you. You got that? I'll kill you on sight." That he meant every word of this too, was ice-clear in Stephen's deadly voice.

He left the shaking man, motioned for Tom to follow, and the two rode off down the Swift Run road.

"He hasn't got the gold," Stephen said. "Not sharp at all. Says he was just hired help, and I guess maybe he was."

"You're letting him go, then."

"Hell, I couldn't just kill him outright. Told him all the others are dead. That should put enough of a scare in him. Don't believe we'll see him again."

"Hope not. But doesn't seem they'd have a weak link like that in their chain…"

"Maybe you're right. Hardscrabble place, though. Hard to imagine he was in on anything big."

Stephen tried to put himself into Hayes' shoes: He'd have left the tavern early, carrying the heavy chest. Looking for a place on an unfamiliar road to hide it…

This road had forded the creek twice the first half mile, but there were no caves or rock overhangs that would have been likely spots.

"You know, Stephen, I've gotta bad feelin' about that fellow back there. Now he knows the others are dead, he might be the kind who'll either figure you do have th' gold, or he'll keep looking for it for himself, maybe along here."

"Told him I'd kill him if I ever saw him again. I'm sure I scared him."

"Maybe. But he'll think you did that just to keep him away from the gold."

"I suppose so. You're saying I should have just killed him?"

"I guess I'm sayin' he's still around, and he knows too much. He's a loose end. You'll hafta keep looking over your shoulder."

"Hmm. I guess you're right. But I just didn't have the stomach for an outright killing. Not like he was...Now I sound like you, with Weston."

"I know. Nasty business, this stayin' alive. But what I'm wondering now is, how long's it gonna take that fellow to come searchin', or to come after you? And surely with help?"

Stephen felt the hair on the back of his neck rise, as he often had during the war. Dinkins could be right behind them...

"Maybe not long at all. Maybe now," as he looked back up the empty, deeply-shaded road they'd come down.

"My thought, exactly. If he's even half smart, he'll let us lead him to it. You wanta keep looking, go for the gold, or get on away from here?"

"Well, you're right. He won't stop, with all that money at stake. If he gets it, he has no one to fear from the syndicate, now. Strong motivation. Maybe we should go on back, finish him now. Unless we can think of something else."

They were stopped at a turning of the road, where the water in the run had cut into it. Wagon drivers had tumbled big granite boulders down from the slope on their left and across to fill and divert the creek bed and hold the road. Up in the woods was just a glimpse of a sheer rock face, from which the stones must have broken loose long ago. It was the first possibility they'd seen since leaving the pike. It would also have been the first Hayes would have seen...

"I'm going up there, Tom. I'll wager there's a pocket or crevice somewhere there. Why don't you watch out for us?"

"Will. And you watch for snakes. I'll lead th' horses on down a ways and wait. You take your time and watch, too. If he does come, we'll have him between us." Or them, Tom thought, almost certain Dinkins would bring backup.

Stephen climbed up into the heavy growth above. The face didn't appear to be large, maybe six feet high. But with the big stones jumbled below, there could be a space somewhere. There was a seep here, and moss covered the stones. *Cold back when Hayes came, probably ice here then.*

The rock face ran to the right, and the stones were dry there. The brush was leafed out, making a screen. He peered out, up the road again: Nothing.

Then he worked his way across at the foot of the face. No cave. And the face tapered into the slope just ahead.

Well. Work down again, then. Can't see the road from here. That Dinkins...He could be sharper than he seems...Now, what's this?

A tall slab of stone sloped up, leaned against a boulder. *Could be a space under there. He knew he needed to check the road first...Keep quiet, though, nobody'll know I'm up here. Just have a quick look under, first. Tom is watching...*

At that moment, a hidden Tom was watching as a man moved stealthily on toward their tethered horses. Tom slipped out, his knife drawn.

~ * ~

There was a space under the leaning slab. Stephen could see daylight through it, from the other side. *This could be it...*

Heart pounding in anticipation, Stephen laid his rifle aside, crouched, looked inside. Old leaves had blown in. He reached in warily, pulled them apart. Could be a skunk den, or a bear. Snakes...

The chest was there. Right where Hayes had hidden it. He hauled it out. *Heavy. No wonder: full of gold. Locked, of course. Did Hayes have a key on him, when...? Don't remember. Has to be it, though.* He rocked back on his heels, a grin spreading.

All this trouble, this violence, killing, made an evil kind of sense now. But this find also meant it was over, finally. A curse to be moved on from, to allow them all to get on with their lives, forget all about it as the months, years passed, be able to have lives again. He thought of his betrothed, and how this would surely clear her head, heal her. The thought made him warm inside.

"Jis' you hold real still now, Davis," Albert Dinkins spoke over the muzzle of his rifle. "Toss that pistol over here. Y'made more noise than a buncha Redcoats stumblin' ''round up here. And lookit whatcha done found fer me. Damn'f you didn't." He looked the chest over. "Now, y'got th' key?"

"Dinkins, I didn't even know there was a chest of gold till you men came after me."

"Mebbe so. Why else kill old Hayes, though?" A pause. "Why *did* y'do it?"

"Like I said at the trial, he came in, drunk, gun out, hollering..."

"Naw, Hayes warn't drunk. Left my place cold sober. Said y'stole his slave. Not much t'kill a man fer though, damn field hand. Cain't figger it. But, don't much matter now, ennyways.

"Oh, you ast me whut my part wuz in th' operation? Wal, I'll jist tell you, since it don't signify now. Y'see, I'se in th' army, same's you. They taught us t'kill, y'know? Kill ever' damn Redcoat we seen. Wal, man gits good at a thaing, folks notices. Now, I didn't git me no promotion er nothin', but Doc, I come to his notice when he was patchin' up th' boys, y'know? An' well, he puts it to me ''bout whut I'se gonna do after th' war...''

Stephen was gauging the distance to his rifle. Too far. Where was Tom? Why hadn't Dinkins seen that the horses were gone? Had he even seen Tom back at the tavern? His horse? This man wanted to talk, to brag. Let him. Buy some time...

"...Cut a long story short, I become their hired gun, y'might say. If a feller got t'holdin' out, stealin', I'se th' one went after him. Sometimes hadda use m'head, which I'm good at, jist so you know: use m'wife t'git ''em distracted. Allus got our man, too. Ever' time...Wal, ever' time but one...''

"That right? How'd that happen?" Keep him talking. Tom would come, hear them talking, move up.

"'Twas thar at th' end of th' war: Yorktown. Doc, he'd tol' me this colonel, don't ''member his name now, but he was gittin' 'spicious 'bout whut Doc an' his boys was doin'. Had t'go, this off'cer did. Wal, I'd 'bout had m'fill of bein' ordered 'roun' by off'cers, ennyways, see, so I jis' made sure that ol' boy got hisself hit, accidental-like. Didn' know it then, but 'twas actual Doc's cuzzin. That Doc, he was a cold one, now...

"But y'said he's daid. Don't matter none I reckon, now. Never paid me much, ennyways. 'Nuff fer that ole tavern, is all. Workin' me'n th' ole woman half t'death, that place...This much money, I kin git me ennything I want, even 'nother woman! Now, ain't that a sight?" The man laughed, pleased at the prospect. Then he sobered.

"Only thaing is, you got t've had help, if whut y'say ''bout th' others is true. I know th' squire; he had men aroun' his place. Seen 'em when Butler'n me was after his girl t'other night. But y'said Doc's daid, an' Eddins 'rested. Now, I need t'know jist who I gotta watch out fer, all this gold an' all. Reckon I'll leave th' country, but like t'know who's apt to come fer me. Gold 'uz ours, but seems like you got more fingers in th' pie. Now, I know y'got that Drake feller..."

"Ned Drake got shot two days ago. Butler shot him."

"Don't say? No wonder y'was some testy, back t'my place. Wal, that's one gone. An' th' squire: know 'bout him. Ain't worried none 'bout that lawman in Charlottesville: Dumb-ass. Oh, an' yer black boy. Reckon my brother's got him 'fore now. Sent him on ahead to draw down on him. Be here in a minnit, I reckon. Figger t'stuff both yer carcases some'ers. Hole thar should jist 'bout do it.

"Y'know, we figgered you fer a hard case, Davis. I was shore y'd shoot me back t'my place, but y'didn't. Bad mistake. Figgered you'da learnt better, in th' war. Y'got a feller cornered, y'don't let 'im go. Little like gittin' a snake pinned down: let loose an' he'll bitecha. Oh, better move over now, slow, away from that rifle."

Stephen had sat back on the slope during this long oration, trying to ease closer to his rifle, his mind running, trying for a way out. He hadn't found one. He shifted, away from the long gun.

"You could just take the gold and go, Dinkins. I didn't know about it before, and I could forget, easily."

"Now, you wasn't list'nin', Davis. I jist this minnit said: y'got a snake down, y'don't let him up, er y'll git bit. Trouble'th you is, y'don't learn. Like, y'don't jedge a feller jist by th' way he looks. Back at my place, you figgered I'd scare, 'cause I'se a pore ole ragged country boy, not much sense. But who's gotcha now, an' got yer jigaboo, too? Like they say, y'cain't jedge a book..."

"By its cover." Tom Logan finished, a cocked pistol shoved into Dinkins's back. "Take his gun, Stephen."

"Oh, damn. That bumblin' brother of mine, he jist done whut I said not to, din't he? Figgered he c'd take enny dumb-ass slave, an' now..."

Stephen had risen, stepped aside out of the rifle's field of fire, to reach for it. Dinkins handed it over, turning slightly from the muzzle in his back.

"Whut'd y'do, boy, cut his throat? Didn't hear nuthin'. Better hope y'din't cut m'brother's throat now. Be real upset if'n y'done that. Go hard on yuh. Slave killin' a white man...this country don't like that sorta thaing atall."

The man seemed relaxed, almost cheerful. Odd, Stephen thought. Doesn't realize what's coming. Deluded…

"Y'talk too damn much, Albert!" a woman's voice cut through the air. Stephen spun aside, bringing the rifle around.

"Where'n hell y'been, woman? Shoot ''em!" He lunged away from Tom's gun, snatching out Stephen's pistol he'd taken from him. Stephen just glimpsed the woman's head and shoulders and her rifle as he kept dodging. *Let a snake loose…*

He fired from the hip as Tom's pistol boomed. The woman's rifle spouted flame, but it had jerked skyward when his ball took her. Dinkins crumpled, and Tom grabbed the pistol. Stephen climbed to the woman.

"Stupid, stupid, both of ''em…" she was muttering, blood pouring from her upper chest. "Hadna been fer me, they'd…both be…" She convulsed, lay still. No pulse.

"Why didn't she just shoot?" Tom asked, shaking his head.

"Had to let him know she was here, I guess, so he'd have a chance. He had just the one gun. And I'm thinking she was probably the brains behind Dinkins…like she said, he wasn't too bright. Had to brag about all he'd done."

"What'd he done?"

"Gunman for the syndicate, the way he told it, but I find that a little hard to believe. And by the way, he shot John Logan too, for Doc Weston. Seems the colonel had suspicions about Weston's operations. But I'd not be surprised if this woman weren't the real killer. Never know now."

Twenty-two

Stephen and Tom had debated what to do with the three dead bodies, eventually deciding to bury them deep in the woods.

"Maybe not the thing to do, Tom, but it'll be simpler. Far as anybody knows, they just picked up and left the tavern, guns, horses and all. Now, there'll be a lot of questions, even this way, but not as many as if we hunted up the law on this. If it's all right with you, we can tell it that Dinkins had left the country, maybe after learning that the organization had come apart."

"What do we do with th' gold?"

"Well, we found it, and I'd as soon tell the truth about that. Give it to Josh Stokes, let him try to find out where it belongs. I'd say Judge Edgerton will know what's best there."

"Sounds right. You gonna tell Abby? About our killin' the Dinkins bunch?"

"Well, now. Probably not, just yet. She's so broken up about Butler and the other two Ned and I killed, seems it'd be best to keep quiet about that."

"Maybe. Hard way to start out a marriage, though, keepin' secrets."

"Don't see that burdening her with that knowledge would help, state she's in right now."

"Like I said, maybe. But back to the Dinkinses. What do we do with their horses?"

"Been thinking about that. Guess we'll just turn ''em loose. They'll wander back up to the tavern, eventually. There'll be questions about that too, though. You got any other ideas?"

"Not good ones. I agree with you about not tellin'. Be only our word that it happened the way it did. But I'd say, slip back to the tavern with their horses, get shovels, if we're gonna do this job. And I guess, even if it complicates th' mystery, these horses bein' there, it'd be best. If it was me comin' to th' tavern, I'd say it looked like they just left, like you said. That way, it'll look like they left on other horses, maybe to make it harder for anybody to track them."

"Hmm. Well, I can't do any better than that. Let's do it."

~ * ~

It was nearing dark when they finished, and they rode in the fading light, taking turns carrying the chest. The miles fell away, and they reached the Norton farm late. But lamps and candles lighted the house, and several wagons and riding horses were drawn up before it, tied.

"Think something could be wrong here?" Stephen asked.

"No tellin'. Let's leave th' chest here behind this stone wall and go see."

It turned out that several families had gathered for an impromptu dinner and hymn-singing at the Nortons', and some were just leaving. Stephen and Tom were invited in, offered food, which they gratefully accepted. Anna and the Compton family were there. She, along with others, expressed sympathy about the recent violence.

"I'm sorry, Stephen, that all this had to happen, right in the middle of your and Abby's plans. We heard she wasn't well..." Her eyes asked the question.

"Thanks, Annie. I'm afraid Abby wasn't ready for anything like Butler's abducting her, and certainly not for her having to try to kill him, the way it happened. She handled it well, until it was all over. His blood got on her, then she saw my friend Ned all bloody, and it sent her into shock, I guess."

"I'm so sorry. It's probably un-Christian of me, but Butler needed killing. We also heard he was one of several men in some sort of...illegal venture..."

"I told 'em that, Stephen," Ike Collins volunteered. "But it uz more'n' that, Miss Annie. They aimed to kidnap Abby to git Stephen to tell 'em whar that gold wuz. But y'know she'da never come back alive, if Butler'd got her."

"Poor Abby. I was going to call on her, but Reverend Millington went yesterday instead. You just missed him here."

"Sorry. Haven't met the man yet. Tom says he's a powerful preacher. I'm glad the church is doing well. How're you managing with the children?"

"They're a joy, really. We have a mid-week Bible study, along with the Sunday School classes." Her face softened at thought of the children, and Stephen thought she might actually smile. He remembered her smile, and found he'd missed it.

"Guess I'll have to start coming to church with Tom, now that things have quieted down. Or at least I hope they've quieted down. I've had a little much of men wanting to kill me."

"Do come, and bring Abby, certainly." Then her face darkened. "But, Stephen, there's really only one way to deal with rabid people trying to kill...Oh, I shouldn't say that...Forget I said that." Her knuckles were to her mouth. Stephen looked at her intently. This woman wouldn't be shocked at a little blood on her hands.

"Way I see it," Isaac Compton put in, "if a snake's after a man, he's gotta kill it, 'fore it bites him." Stephen noted the snake reference, again. *Yes, Dinkins and the others: snakes.*

"And yes, it may seem un-Christian on the surface, Miss Annie," Tom said, "But I can't see letting a killer go on killin'. Not only is removin' him a favor to society, but it'll keep him from destroyin' himself more."

"That's deep, Tom," Stephen responded. "I like that reasoning." His eyes were still on Annie.

"I'm afraid I believe we must purge the rotten apples from among us," she said. "That probably means I have a long way to go in my faith journey."

After they took their leave and retrieved the chest, Stephen couldn't help continuing the comparison between his betrothed and Annie Compton. But then he shook off that train of thought. Abby'd get over this...just the shock. Something Tom had said months before kept coming back to him, though: *Annie is what Abby would like to be if she could. Well, that was just Tom's opinion.*

"Y'know, Stephen, that Annie's quite a woman. Wouldn't doubt but the new preacher'd be the man for her."

"Well, good. I've always liked that girl a lot. Be glad to see her find a man worthy of her."

~ * ~

Constable Joshua Stokes heard the story, without the Dinkins part.

"Well, seems there was a lot more to all this than we figured, Stephen. Damn 'f I know what to do with all this money, though. Guess Judge Edgerton will know. No tellin' who it b'longed to before.

"One thing puzzles me. Got word that Doc Weston, up in Caroline, had got hisself killed. House locked, but his throat cut. Now, folks seen lawyer Eddins leavin' 'fore dark that day, an' mebbe he's th' one. Judge had me arrest Eddins, said he'd got word th' lawyer was part of all this. Could be they had a kinda fallin' out? Ennyway, looks bad for him, bein' th' last to see th' doc alive an' all. Bloody damn business.

"But seems like most of ''em's out of th' picture now. Prob'ly never hear from that Dinkins feller th' squire mentioned; reckon he's clean out of th' country by now. I sure hope there ain't no more to it, anyways. Y'need to git on with yer life, you'n Abby. Set th' date, yit?"

"We sort of put it off, Josh, when all this started. She's had a hard time with the Butler thing—almost killed him, you know—so I'd say we won't rush the wedding."

"Reckon not. Well, I 'preciate yer bringin' this money in, though it'll prob'ly be a headache, tryin' to git it whar it belongs. You're an honest man, Stephen. Mebbe oughta run fer somethin' in politics."

"Sounds like a sure way to get past being honest, Josh."

~ * ~

Abby was getting over her bad experience, but she often seemed distracted when Stephen talked with her. He was patient, not bringing up wedding plans yet. Oddly, she seemed almost disinterested in the finishing details of the house, and he could find little to engage her.

"I guess she just needs time," her mother told him. For her part, Gertrude Thomas was concerned about her daughter, but was also somewhat impatient with her. This was life on the frontier, after all, and a girl had to accept some harsh realities. But yes, they had sheltered their youngest child, and yes, she had gone through a traumatic experience. Not really fair to Stephen, though, this drawing in on herself. Only the new minister seemed able to console her.

Stephen finally met the man, after Tom had persuaded him to accompany him to the church that Sunday. His sermon centered around the Old Testament "eye for an eye" philosophy, as counter to Jesus' teaching of turning the other cheek. Millington would fix his own eye on each member of the congregation as he preached, and the young man seemed almost accusatory when his gaze met Stephen's.

Stephen was certain his own troubles had prompted this sermon. *Well, I suppose my methods do run counter to the Gospel, Reverend. Maybe Tom and I'll study the Good Book, try to find some answers.*

Afterward, Tom introduced Stephen to the minister, whose eye, however, had not softened toward him.

"I heard of your unfortunate experiences, Mr. Davis. I can't say I agree with your actions, but then I wasn't there. No judgment intended."

"I'm not sure what else I could have done, Reverend, when in the sights of the enemies' guns."

"Of course not. And of course you're most welcome here, sir. I'd hoped Miss Thomas would come too, but I realize she's not herself yet. Please give her my concerned regards."

Annie Compton was surrounded by children, and her beatific smile was almost constant. She hugged them, sent them to their parents, one by one. *Give me something to smile about.*

"Hello, Stephen, Tom. What did you think of our minister?"

"I get the impression he disapproves of me, Annie."

"Really? In what way?" She seemed genuinely surprised.

"I think I was the object of his sermon. What'd you think, Tom?"

"Seemed he did go outta his way to focus on Stephen, Miss Annie. But I reckon folks attach a little stigma to a man who's had troubles, even if he's not at fault. Sort of a 'blame th' victim' mindset."

"Oh, I hope you're wrong. Of course I didn't hear the sermon, with my class going on at the same time. But he did mention some Old Testament bloodletting earlier, and I got the impression he was working it into his message. But tell me, how is Abby? I must go see her."

"She's improving, slowly. Yes, you'd be good for her, Annie. I think she needs someone she can talk to, besides me and her folks. And unfortunately, she's not talking that much to me, really."

"Oh, I'm sorry to hear that. I hope that's not more of what Tom just said about blaming the victim."

"I don't know what it's all about, Annie. I'm afraid she's seeing me as a sort of grim avenger, all at once."

"I don't think this is violating a confidence, but Reverend Millington says she just seems overwhelmed by all the killing, no matter the circumstances. Now, I know Abby's not that shallow. Surely she expected you to defend yourself, and her." *And she'd have thought you a coward if you hadn't.*

"Mystery to me. But do go visit her, if you can. I'd value your assessment, as I value your friendship." She could see he was serious, and she felt some of his pain. Without a word, she took his hand, squeezed it, eyes on his. Then she turned, joined her family at their wagon.

~ * ~

Gertrude Thomas welcomed Abby's visitor with a warm hug.

"Annie. So good of you to come. My daughter's having a hard time getting over her...experiences."

"I can imagine so. We can't know how we'd react until something like that actually happens. Is she in bed?"

"No, she's up, but hasn't gone out at all. Not like her to be off her horse. Just mopes all day, and has bad dreams. The minister's been helpful, when he's come."

"I'm glad for that. He seems a sensitive and dedicated man." Annie didn't add that Millington was also obviously smitten with Abby, another man's betrothed. He'd just transparently mentioned her entirely too often.

She was in her room, gazing absently out the window. Annie rapped on the open door. Her friend turned, rose.

"Annie. Hello, it's good to see you. Oh, and you've brought flowers. Thanks." She took the tall girl's hands. "I'm afraid I'm not doing too well, here. Everyone tells me our troubles are over, but I can't seem to get things out of my head. Here, sit with me. Bessie will put the lilies in water."

"I heard a little about how it's been for you, from Ike, and from Stephen. He came to church with Tom."

"He said he would, but I haven't talked with him since. I couldn't muster the energy to go. I don't know what's wrong with me, Annie, but I'm afraid I'm not being very nice to Stephen. And I know nothing's his fault, but...I...well, he's just become so...I don't know how to put it. It's as if I'm almost afraid of him..."

"Surely not. Afraid of Stephen? How could that possibly be, Abby? You're perfect for each other."

"I believe that. And when he told me months ago, about what he did in the war, killing all those soldiers who were trying to kill our men, it... well, it seemed almost like something out of Greek mythology...he was a romantic hero."

"And what's happened to change that?"

"It's just that...Oh, Annie, people just seem to get killed around Stephen. Whatever started it, it just keeps on. I'm afraid of what might happen, later. Will something else come up, and will he have to kill again? I feel as if I'll never know when the next person around him—us—will die. Or that...one of us will. That sounds crazy, I know it does."

"It's not reasonable, Abby. You know they found the money, turned it over to Josh Stokes. It's all over now, surely."

"I want to believe that. But you know, things Reverend Millington has said, about violence, revenge, killing...all of this has a tinge of evil I can't understand. I don't blame Stephen. We heard that doctor had been killed, over in Caroline County, and we know that couldn't have been Stephen. But the whole thing of Rawlins Butler trying to abduct me—he actually tried to break into this house, Annie, before—and his shooting Ned Drake, and then...I just can't think about it."

She buried her face in her arms and sobbed quietly. Annie could tell the pictures were before her eyes again: the blood, the dying man, partly by her hand. She held the shaking girl, spoke softly to her, stroked her hair as she would a crying child.

"Abby, Abby. There, now. Try to put it out of your head. It's all over with. Evil did come, dear friend, but it's past now. And Stephen did what he had to do, for him, for you, for all of us, really. He is a hero, Abby, your hero. Don't confuse him with the enemy here. He loves you. You know that. I'm sorry things got in the way, but you have to get past this."

Gradually the shaking stopped, the tears subsided. Abby raised her eyes, her streaked face to her friend's.

"I know I must, dear Annie. I know I can't mire myself in...whatever this state is that's snared me. I fear Mama is getting impatient with me, although Papa's been a dear about it. And poor Ned, he's just mystified, like Stephen. They all try to help, even Constance Weston—she's really sweet. But so far, only Dwight—I mean the minister—has been able to draw me out of this...condition."

"He seems quite dedicated, Abby. He's very concerned for you."

"Truly a man of God. You work together at the church, Annie. What do you know of him?"

Now that's an odd question, from a woman engaged to another man. I'd hate to think it, but you're really a little spoiled, Abby. Things have always come easily for you, and now...No, mustn't think that way...

"Oh, just the facts. He may have told you he's from Philadelphia, went to the Institute there. Does not like war, violence, which you'd expect. Very good with the children and the older people in the congregation. Reverend Carson did well to entice him to come to us. I'm quite certain he could have gone to a city somewhere with a large church, wealthy, influential members."

"But what's he like, working with him?" A spark of interest shone in the eyes that had been so dull.

"Pleasant. He asks about people, seems genuinely interested. For instance, learning that I read a lot, he's made a point of getting me into discussions about literature, authors. He's very well read himself."

"I could tell that. You must enjoy working with him."

"I'm really not there that much. Wednesday evenings we have Bible study, but I teach the children during the sermon on Sundays." *So Abby was not immune to the charms of their handsome young cleric. But it was doing her good to talk, question. I'm here to help, and I will. But this is more than a little strange...*"Your mother tells me you haven't been outside, Abby. Nor on horseback. Your Shelly will think you've abandoned her."

"Oh, yes. I must get out. Weather's fine." A pause. "Would you...would you go for a walk with me, Annie? While you're here? I confess I've been a little...afraid...I guess. Even with Mama and Papa near."

"I'd have thought you'd go with Stephen, Abby. He should be your strength, your anchor..."

"But I told you, I've this irrational fear that I can't identify, when he's here..."

"Now, not to be blunt, but that's something you absolutely must get over. After all...Haven't you two set a new date?"

"I...we...No, we haven't. And I just can't face that right now, Annie. Again, I know it's ridiculous, but I'm just not ready yet."

The two stopped for a word with Ned Drake, who'd never met Annie, though he'd seen her in court that time. *Guess I was just too interested in Constance at the time.*

"This is Stephen's comrade from the war, Annie Compton, Ned Drake. And this is Mrs. Weston, who I fear is recently widowed." Constance had risen from Ned's side on the parlor couch. She extended a gracious hand. She was quite pretty, Annie saw, in her black. She knew some of the circumstances of the woman's situation, having seen her at the trial. It was clear here that she and Ned Drake were already close.

"Mr. Drake. Stephen has spoken of you often, and always with great admiration. Mrs. Weston, you are a courageous lady. I'm honored to meet you both."

"The pleasure, as they say, is all mine," Ned responded, looking up at this young lady's considerable height and taking her hand. "You must know Stephen counts you as a great friend." Then he added quickly, "of his and Abby's." His grin covered what he perceived to have been a slip, and it communicated itself to Annie, who smiled in return. The radiance of that smile was not lost on him.

"Thank you, Miss Compton," Constance inclined her head graciously. "I have told the Thomases I believe my meeting them and Mr. Drake was not accidental. There are Providential forces at work, I'm certain."

"I'm convinced of it, ma'am. More than we can recognize."

After telling her mother where they'd be, Abby donned a hat and the two girls walked in the meadow toward the creek. The day was fine, and it occurred to both that being indoors with one's private demons was a waste. Abby said so.

"A day like this out here, and I can't imagine being depressed. Thank you so much for coming to me, Annie. You're a true friend."

That appears to be my lot in life: being a friend. I expect our dear reverend, though he may pine in vain for you, will overlook me, also. As did Stephen Davis, whose blindness I never expected. Well, now I'll never set my cap for a man...I guess I've too much pride. Deadly sin, I know, but one I seem to harbor...

"It is the year's best day. I'm reminded that Reverend Millington says that any day God gives us is wonderful, given the potential, the promise, even through sleet or rain. There's always so much to be thankful for." *Now, how did he get back into the conversation?*

"A godly sentiment, and a humble one. He's so different from the men around here, don't you agree?"

"Certainly, since he's not from around here. I'd say, from my limited experience, that people from large cities would be in general, more...cultured, I guess. Though I've no fondness for cities. And certainly you and your family have never lacked for culture out here."

"I guess not. But I'm quite sure that I'd appear as a rustic country girl among the parlors of Philadelphia. Oh, let's go back by the stables. I must let Shelly know she's not forsaken."

All right, good sign. Perhaps I've been able to draw this poor thing out, after all. And I mustn't judge. I might have gone to pieces too, in the middle of a gunfight, with my former suitor's blood all over me...No, I wouldn't have. But there's something rotten here in Nixville, with her attitude toward Stephen. And I won't allow myself to think it's fascination with our Dwight. I simply will not.

At length, the two returned to the house, and Gertrude Thomas saw right away the change in her daughter. *What a gem Annie Compton was! She'd accomplished more in two hours than all of them, all these days. Even Stephen hadn't been able to reach the girl. Of course, the minister had helped. Hmm, perhaps those two will get together, if he can adjust to Annie's height. That had intimidated most men, so far. Surely this devoted cleric could see past that imagined obstacle to the real woman inside. Annie was such a dear.*

"I know it's too far to come visit me at home just yet, Abby, but do try to come to church with Stephen. It's only halfway, you know. We'd love to have you," she was saying as they neared the high porch. Ned had asked to be moved carefully outside onto a wicker settee, and both Constance and Gertrude were tending him. He smiled appreciatively at the change in Abby. *All right...now maybe she'll be able to get through this better.*

"I shall; I'm sure of it. Oh, Annie, thank you so much for coming. I know you must be swamped in work this time of year. To make time for me... You're so sweet. Give my love to your mother, and Becky. Bobby must be grown, by now. And dear Sam. I'm afraid he's my favorite."

"I will. And you simply must not allow yourself to stay in that room, Abigail Thomas. If I hear of that, I'll threaten you with another visit, and bring my switch." Annie hugged her friend, who hugged her back. Ned Drake pointedly appraised the tall girl, approved mightily, and Gertrude Thomas silently thanked God for her.

"Tell your mother I'm coming to see her," the plantation mistress promised. "And, Annie, I'll bring Abby with me."

Twenty-three

Sunday morning, Stephen, Tom and Abby rode together around Greene Mountain and upriver to the new church. It was a cloudy day, but it didn't smell like rain. Stephen had found Abby more receptive to him, but still reserved. She had been the one to suggest this outing, however, and he had quickly agreed. Any response was better than her secluding herself, as she had since Butler's death.

Tom kept the conversation going, sensing that things were still a little awkward between his friends. He too, had his problems with having killed Weston and the Dinkins brothers, dealing with his nightmares by himself. It was good to draw these two out, smooth things over between them. *Best medicine for the soul's always been to do for others...*

So the trio came to the church clearing in almost normal spirits. The collection of wagons, riding horses, and a few buggies gave the rough log structure, with its attached plank classroom, a festive appearance. Church for these settlers was almost as much a social event as a worship service. Friends hailed the new arrivals, and the Compton family came forward as soon as they'd tethered the horses.

"Welcome, Miss Abby," Isaac greeted. "So, Stephen, y'didn't git run off f'm here after last time, I see. Tom, always glad t'see you. He shook the men's hands, bowed to Abby.

"I'm so glad to see you, Abby," Annie welcomed her. "And Stephen, Tom, I hope you'll all keep coming back." She claimed Abby to take her to see her classroom and the children. Stephen, who'd been told of her almost magical effect on his fianceé, gave a silent thanks for this friend.

Abby rejoined them at the start of the service. Tom sat with the few blacks at the back of the sanctuary. The small choir, without benefit of accompaniment, sang an introit, and Reverend Dwight Millington welcomed his flock.

Stephen was aware of Abby's intent focus on the minister from the moment of his first appearance. He was a good-looking man, he conceded, and he'd already heard his persuasive delivery. Well, he'd been good for Abby, though not as good as Annie Compton. Women needed other women in times of trouble, he'd always heard, and here was proof.

The topic was 'being our brother's keeper,' and the minister branched off from his Scriptural bases into friendship, support, sacrifice for others. Stephen thought of Tom, Ned, and others of his army comrades. There'd been a lot of sacrifice in his life, a lot of being each others' keepers. He felt honored to remember this.

Abby hung on every word.

As was his practice, Millington's eyes rested on each listener in turn. Stephen felt Abby tense next to him as the minister's gaze locked with hers for a long moment. A prick of irritation touched him, but it passed.

The man was good: his references were sound, to Stephen's Presbyterian ear, his Scripture apt, his delivery persuasive. People were supposed to be moved by his sermons. And Abby was. *All right, maybe do her good. Well, can't hurt me, either. Suppose Tom's right: get some religion into our lives. More so if Abby's going that way.*

But he'd like to know more from Annie Compton about this man. If he were smart, he'd match up with that good woman. Maybe a little smooth for a country girl, though...*Nah, she could handle him. Get some cow manure on his boots, do him good.*

After the service, Annie joined them again, noting Abby's rapt expression. So did Stephen. So did Tom. All three were glad to see her more nearly back to normal, but all three were also a little uncomfortably aware of her almost worshipful reaction to the minister. And that man added to it with his warm post-sermon welcome.

"Miss Thomas. So very glad you could come. Welcome back, Mr. Davis, Tom. Miss Compton, I was told your care had restored this lady's spirits, and now I see it for myself. An angel must have been with you."

Abby couldn't keep her eyes off that young man, and complimented him on his sermon twice. Annie Compton caught Tom's attention, and silently rolled her eyes. Stephen stood by, hearing the chatter, feeling like an uninvited guest.

The minister himself broke the awkwardness, moving off to greet others of the congregation. Several of the women came up to Abby, concerned for her recent indisposition. Sadie Compton, Ike Collins' wife, little Lucy Collins and Nell Cocke formed a circle around her, welcoming her. It gave Stephen a moment with Annie.

"Thanks so much, Annie, for getting Abby out of her...whatever it was. She'd never have come today if you hadn't drawn her out. Mrs. Thomas thinks you're a miracle worker."

"I wanted to help. You're both my friends, Stephen." The dark eyes showed nothing, but Annie was thinking Abby had another reason for this visit.

"And we value your friendship; all of us do." Stephen was about to ask something about whether Annie and the minister might have a future together, but realized that was patently none of his business. He ended by lamely thanking her again, squeezing her hand in goodbye, turning back to the group.

The ride home was quiet, with Abby now and then noting something the preacher had said, or Tom's comments on bits of news he'd heard. Soon they lapsed into silence, Stephen's an uncertain one, Abby's withdrawn. Tom eyed those two with a searching appraisal. He turned in at the lane to the shop, while the others rode on to the plantation.

Stephen decided the time didn't seem right to bring up plans. Let more time pass. Abby was better, but she seemed to brighten, then turn inward again.

He visited with Ned and the squire for awhile, but felt out of place.

And while he shouldn't have, he declined Gertrude's invitation to supper as graciously as he could.

Abby seemed relieved.

~ * ~

"Things'er just not right, m'friend," Tom observed. "Your lady's gettin' over her depression, but the two of you act like strangers."

"Don't I know it? Think she's comparing?"

"Sure is, and I'm disappointed in her. Our smooth-tongued preacher's got more on his mind than th' Gospel, I'm afraid, and he's come along at just the wrong time, with Abby all in pieces."

"That'll pass, I'm sure. She's just still shaken up. Glad we didn't tell her—them—about the Dinkins shootout."

"For sure. She finds out about that, she'll likely think you're Satan incarnate. And me, too."

"And you know, like you said, a man shouldn't have to keep a thing like that from his wife. The two should be able to talk anything out, not have it push them apart like a wedge."

"Seems so. ''Twouldn't be right, just now though, to bring that up. We'll have to deal with our own consciences on that'n."

"Justified. Totally. We had to wipe that bunch out, or we'd never have been safe. I've the feeling that woman was the dangerous one. She'd have kept on, done some real harm. We both know that."

"Do. But I got to ask: What're you gonna do about Abby? Clear she's got the eye for th' reverend, and that'll be a burr under your saddle from now on, unless it's cleared up, an' soon."

"Well, I was going to let time pass, let her get over her...depression, you called it. Get back to normal. Let it work itself out. Got to tell you though, seeing her all wrapped up in that fellow's every word, I guess I'm somewhat jealous."

"Two kinds of jealousy. One comes from a feelin' of inadequacy, and that's stupid. Other one's serious, means somebody's doin' you wrong."

"Yes, and maybe a third kind. Grows out of pride, possessiveness."

"Ah, an insight. You're sharper'n I remembered, Stephen."

"Got my moments, I guess." A long pause. "You think I'm maybe being given a look at the real Abigail Thomas before it's too late?"

"Ouch! Don't believe I'll touch that one."

"Well, if I'm able to be objective, I can say she dumped Butler because I looked better to her. And she'll dump me because the preacher looks better. Probably one or two before Butler, too."

"Oh, we are acid, here. You're being harsh. Th' girl is not that shallow. Or maybe I just hope she's not."

"I wonder. She's had everything she wants, all her life. I felt I had to prove up, before I could seriously speak for her. Her mother convinced me that was nonsense, that all I had to do was be a man—the right man—for her. Now, I wonder. I know she's almost afraid of me now: man of violence, killer. Is the preacher just an excuse, Tom? Am I really the villain to her now? Or is it that she's smitten with him? Infatuated? I don't know what to think."

"And we both know, with a woman involved, that we'll never figure it out. But if y'want advice, seems to me there are two ways to go: Let it take its own course till it gets clearer, or force it to a head. Knowin' you, the first one'll take more patience than you've got. But I wouldn't take th' bull by th' horns just yet, either. Girl's still off-balance."

"So maybe a little of both?"

"Maybe, but it won't be fun, an' you'll be hell to be around, mean-time."

~ * ~

The Reverend Dwight Millington pushed his pastoral prerogative to the limit in his calling on Abigail Thomas. While either of them would deny there was any impropriety in his counseling sessions with her, it quickly became clear to the perceptive Gertrude Thomas that her daughter was not acting like a young woman engaged to marry another man.

"Abby, do you know what you're doing to Stephen, with all this time spent with the minister? Don't you recognize how he—and the rest of us—must see this?"

"Mama, there is absolutely nothing improper between Dwight...the minister and me. He's a great comfort, a great help in my getting over the shock of...of the killings." Pain came into the dark eyes.

"Nevertheless, your intended deserves your concern, your attention. Just what do you mean to do about him, Abby?" The voice was both gentle and a bit stern. Gertrude wanted this cleared up.

"Oh, I wish I knew! It's as if he's a totally different person, Mama. He was kind, gentle, understanding, loving. Now he's so...hard, I guess. Violent. A man who's killed, again and again. How will I know when that might happen next time?"

"Now, that's not reasonable and you know it. Stephen didn't ask for any of the trouble that came upon him. A gang of criminals threatened him—and you—and he took care of it, as a real man should."

"I guess you're right. But there had to be another way. Dw...Reverend Millington is a man of peace, completely on the other side of the issue. I'm so comfortable around him, Mama. I know it sounds unfair to Stephen, but I need to work through this, see what it is I really feel. Can't I do that, without hurting Stephen?"

"Maybe you could, if you'd talk it out with him. He can't know what to think of the way you've been behaving. He's a fine man, Abby, and I thought you saw that a long time ago. Don't let your—fascination—with this young minister turn your head from your good sense."

"Oh, I'm not doing that, I'm sure. He is incredibly handsome, but I believe I'm seeing past that, to the man's dedication, his concern. He's a man of God, Mama, and I find I need that just now."

"All I'll say then is that you simply must clear things up with Stephen. That's not something you can put off any longer. Your father and I agree on this, Abby. We recognize that you went through an unnerving experience, but that's behind you now, and it's up to you to go on, whichever way you choose."

"You make it sound so final..."

"Oh, child. We love you very much, and we don't want you to make a serious mistake here. But you must make a choice, if that's what it is, between the man you're betrothed to, and this new person who's come at an awkward time."

~ * ~

Abby thought about this ultimatum, and still didn't know what she should do. She sought out Ned Drake, healing daily from his wound, and just now on his feet.

"Ned, you know Stephen better than anyone. I'm having a hard time getting the way I feel about him back to where it was before...before the violence. I would never have thought I'd react that way…after all, you were the one wounded, and Stephen is alive only because of you. But it shocked me so badly. I haven't been able to see Stephen in the same light, since. What do you think is wrong?"

"Ah, a real dilemma, my dear lady. And I'm going to have to say something to you that you will not want to hear…"

"But I have to hear it. I have to know what to do." It was almost a wail.

Ned saw past this girl's beauty to what he recognized as an untried, really immature child. That his best friend had so fallen in love with her hadn't troubled him before, because he could see much potential in her. But the shock, the blood, the violence had so shaken her, she hadn't been entirely rational these past weeks.

And that preacher hadn't helped, with his oily commiserations. Ned was no stranger to that technique, and he resented it for his friend. He was hesitant to chide her, being so in debt to the family for their care and their harboring Constance Weston. But neither did he want to see Stephen on the rack any longer.

"Well, Miss Abigail, we all recognize and appreciate your recent trouble, but you seem over that. Now you must realize it's time for a clear choice in this, and no one else can do that for you. Stephen thinks the world of you, but you must still feel the same for him or it's just the wrong thing, going ahead with him. I wish I had some words of wisdom from my checkered past and experience, but I don't; this one's up to you. Make the wrong choice now, and you'll be miserable for the rest of your life.

"But do talk this out with Stephen. You've been avoiding doing that, and you must not do so any longer. He's no monster, whatever you've come to think of him. He'll be rational, I know. But there are times when there's no easy way out of a situation, and this appears to be one of those times. I believe any of us who like and admire you both would give you the same advice."

So they all think I'm mistreating Stephen. That I'm selfish, and letting my head be turned by Dwight. I'm not a shallow person. I'm not! People always said I was a tease, but they were wrong. I loved Stephen, really. I just don't know whether I still do in the same way or not.

Time. I need time. But I guess, to be fair, I need time away from them both, to sort it all out. I don't really believe I've let Dwight replace Stephen in my affections; it's just that things aren't the same between us. Maybe I just wanted us to be in love too much, and it wasn't real to begin with.

They're right: I must talk with Stephen. But I'm not ready to go to him yet. I don't know when I'll feel I can ride alone again. But he'll be here. He's always come, and we'll talk. We will...

~ * ~

The house was finished. Ready for the bride and groom. Only Stephen wasn't sure if there'd be a bride. The place was big and hollow, even with the new furniture he'd made inside it. The house hung like a cloud over the pond and shop, a large, reproachful hulk, unfulfilled.

He and Tom worked on furniture, projects in steel, passing the days that seemed necessary before he could clear things up with Abby. It was good to have work for his hands, to keep his mind from its ache over the girl. Several times he tried to visualize her as she'd have been if she weren't so beautiful, if she were plain, to get an idea of what her real qualities were. He couldn't manage that. Abby was who she was, and being plain didn't fit in.

And he compared her, for the hundredth time, with Annie Compton. That girl wasn't beautiful, but she wasn't plain, either. And maybe Tom was right: a lot of woman there, for the right man. He just hadn't been the right man, not with Abigail Thomas there. And it occurred to him that he hadn't exactly treated the tall girl well, with his eyes so full of that same Abby Thomas.

Well, Annie was just a friend. Never been more than that, and that was fine. People could be friends, whether men or women. Tom, Ned, Annie: all friends. *Nothing wrong with that.* But the nagging feeling persisted that Annie Compton would not treat him as Abby was now. No, that woman would choose, and never waver. Why wouldn't that damn preacher see what a gem she was, and get out of his and Abby's life?

You didn't shoot a preacher. Or beat hell out of him, even if he deserved it. You tried to be civilized, above violence, the jealous, animal anger that exploded into blood. You spoke politely, observing the niceties. And as for the girl? You waited, as he was waiting. Then you cleared things up, for better or for worse.

And now maybe it'd been long enough. Things weren't getting any warmer, with the passage of days. Ned was almost well. He and Constance would be leaving soon. George Henley had arranged for the management of her plantation until she could return there, and Ned had definite plans to become master of that place with her. *Good for old Ned.*

But back to the question...*Yes, I've waited long enough. I'll go over tonight, get it over with. If she tries to put it off any longer, I'll take that as a rejection, and to hell with it.* She'd been a big part of his life for almost three years, but he didn't have a woman before he met her, and he could be that way again.

Damn house, sitting up there. Result of a lot of work, neighborly generosity, good times, anticipation. Damn shame if this doesn't work out. Be hard on the Thomases, too…he thought a lot of both of those people. How'd he get along with them, if Abby...?

Why the hell can't the daughter be more like her mother?

Twenty-four

It was with growing agitation that Abigail Thomas viewed the coming confrontation with Stephen. She paced, tried to read, worked outside with her mother among the flowers. Gertrude knew this was to be the night of crisis, and she was concerned for her daughter, but knew she must do this.

"Why don't you ride, Abby? Just down to the blacksmith shop, maybe around the meadow. Stay in sight; nothing's going to happen here. Do you good; settle your nerves."

"Maybe I will. Just for a bit. It is a fine day. Yes, I will. Be back before long. I'll check in with Ike, and the hands in the fields, all right?"

"Of course, dear. And don't worry so: Stephen will understand, no matter how you feel you must handle it."

Maybe, she thought as the stable hand saddled her mare. *Maybe Stephen will be gentle, as I know he can be. He's really quite a man, raising himself from a hired man to a fine craftsman, with the best prospects. Compared to him, Rawlins Butler was a pompous, arrogant boor. But Dwight Millington, now...*

Abby rode around the green meadow, getting into the rhythm of the horse, the day. Don't dwell on anything, now. Just let the day soothe you. Stop in and see dear Ike first.

Or maybe not. I'll ride to the creek. Put my bare feet into the water, the way I've done all my life. No sound like water over stone to take cares away...

She stopped upstream of the bridge, tied the horse to a willow branch. Then she stepped to the water, took off her boots and slipped her feet into it. It had just a hint of chill from the springs up by the mill, but it felt wonderful. *Just let my mind unwind, now. Empty my head, let the afternoon fill me with its peace.*

It was there Dwight Millington saw her, from across on the main road. He hadn't meant to stop this time, realizing he'd spent too much time here for it to be entirely decorous. But the sight of Abby through the barely-moving willows, her auburn hair loose, her bare feet in the tumbling water, her lovely face serene...It would have taken a stronger man than he to resist that vision.

He rode across the bridge, dismounted as she turned at the sound. He didn't take his eyes off hers as he secured the reins and his feet moved him toward her. She rose, returning his gaze, her hand absently brushing her hair back. Her lips were parted, her breathing coming faster.

He reached for her, and the two of them melted together in the screen of the willows. The singing of the water enveloped them as their lips met, their bodies pulsing, the world forgotten.

~ * ~

Stephen rode up past the shops toward the plantation house. It was late afternoon, and Ike had left for home, the field hands back in their quarters. It was a quiet scene, contrasted with the tumult inside him. Looking ahead, he saw the squire on the porch, eyes shaded against the late sun, searching across the meadow. Then, seeing Stephen, he waved, came forward hastily.

"Abby's not back from her ride, Stephen. Gertrude let her go a while back, just around close. Probably down by the creek. Want to go with me for a look?"

"Surely, sir. I'm glad she's riding more." He was scanning the willow fringe at the creek, then the edges of the fields. The squire walked to the stables alongside him, and had his horse saddled.

Stephen told himself there was nothing to worry about now. The entire band of marauders had been disposed of as far as they knew, and Abby could surely ride in her own fields. The two men took opposite routes, around the clearings, to meet again down toward Stephen's land.

As he rode, concern mounted inside him. She wasn't herself entirely, yet...*All right, she's just found a quiet place to think things through. God knows I've been doing just that, too.* It was getting late, though; she should be close. But of course her horse hadn't thrown her. Not that horsewoman.

But his circuit didn't reveal Abby, or her horse. *Then surely her father has found her, other side of the plantation.* He'd go on to the end of the long field, wait.

He'd called her name several times, expecting her to emerge from the woods. Now he waited near where he'd come from his place.

Hezekiah Thomas rode into view, alone. Stephen spurred his black across the field.

"Nothing? No sign?"

"No, and now I'm really worried. You saw nothing either?"

"Didn't. Probably back at your house by now. Let's ride that way first, before we assume anything."

"Good idea. She'll be there, no doubt of it. But Stephen, now that we have a few minutes before you see her, I should tell you this: She's made up her mind to talk things out with you. She's realized she's been acting distant with you, and her mother and I have encouraged her to clear the air. I'm convinced the...trouble is past, and things can go ahead as planned."

"I trust you're right. And I'd decided this was the time, too, for us to be frank about where we stand. I don't intend to be unreasonable, sir, but I've endured about all I can of the uncertainty."

"I can understand that, my boy. She just hasn't been able to see the necessity of what had to be done. Perhaps we've shielded her too much against the realities of life, Stephen. But anyway, I truly believe it's all past, as I said."

Well, good to have Abby's family on my side, at least. But blood's thicker than water, for certain. If it comes down to it, I'm still the outsider here. Well, I've been there before...

As they rode past the empty blacksmith shop, Stephen saw a small page from Ike's account book on a nail. He rode closer, the older man following.

"What's that, Stephen?"

"Don't know. Not like Ike to leave a note up where it'll get blown off. I'll put it away." He dismounted, took the paper.

It wasn't a list. Or a bill. He recognized Abby's handwriting.

"It's from Abby. Here, take a look." Handing the paper up.

"Oh, I don't have my spectacles. Read it for me, will you?"

Stephen took the note back, scanned it, his mind still on the upcoming meeting with the girl.

His face froze.

"Oh, my God! Oh, my God!"

"What? What's it say?"

"It...It says...Oh, my God, sir. She's gone!"

"Gone? What...? What does it say, man?"

"It says...It's to you and to me...It says she's gone, with Dwight Millington. It says she couldn't face me...couldn't disgrace you, and...They're gone, sir. She begs us not to follow them. To Philadelphia, with him..."

"No! Why, I'll have him horsewhipped! I'll...We can catch them. Bring her back...She's not in her right mind..." The squire was turning his horse in circles, starting off, returning, unsure of just what to do next.

Stephen had slumped, in the realization that it was all over. The hope, the rationalizations, the mental compromises. All over. Abby was gone. And in that same moment, he realized that nothing, nothing would be gained by going after her, trying to bring her back, change her...

"No, sir. You may do as you wish…she's your daughter. But it's obvious she's made her choice between Millington and me. I've no desire to pursue her. None at all. I'm afraid it's over, sir. Over and done with. I only hope she can find happiness..."

"That man can't abduct my daughter! See here, don't you want...Can't you see he's duped her, turned her mind? Surely you..."

"No, sir. I believe she's entirely rational. She's had him in her mind for weeks now. I kept denying what I knew to be true. I kept hoping..."

"Gertrude. I must see her, let her know. She'll know what to do…Come up to the house, Stephen. I must..."

"No, sir. You do what you must, but I've...I've accepted the inevitable. He has money, comes from a good family…they'll not be destitute.

"I must go now, sir. Thank you for all your kindness. Tell Ned to stop by before he leaves." He turned his horse and rode away, leaving the squire speechless.

~ * ~

"I'll send men. They'll have gone by his place, surely. There'll be time..." Hezekiah Thomas was striding up and down before his wife, who'd been as shocked as he. Now however, her mind had grasped the situation.

"Don't count on it. They both have good horses, and we won't catch them. Besides, what would you do? Arrest him, drag her home like some criminal? She's a grown woman, Hezekiah. She's made her choice, foolish as it may seem to us."

"Foolish? You're damned right it's foolish. And I can't believe Stephen Davis just turned and rode away...He—"

"He's got a hell of a lot more insight than you do right now, my dear. No, Abby's followed her heart, for better or for worse, and there's not one thing we can do about it. Cage her up here and we'd destroy her. No, she's caught up in the romance of it, along with not being able to face Stephen, and it looks to her like the way out. And who knows? Maybe it is."

She went to him, put her arms around him. He was trembling with rage, disappointment. She spoke to him soothingly, gradually quieting him. Letting their daughter go like this wasn't what either of them wanted, but like Stephen, they must eventually come to accept it.

More so when a letter arrived from Philadelphia a number of days later, full of contrition, but ecstatic at the same time. Their little girl had grown and gone.

~ * ~

Stephen plunged into his work, resigned to a return to his solitary state. At least he had Tom now, whose quiet support and occasional counsel kept him sane. The two worked wood, steel, speaking little, sharing their days.

Ned Drake had produced a buggy from somewhere, and he and Constance Weston stopped by on their way to Caroline County.

"I'm so sorry, Stephen," Constance sympathized. "Both of us felt certain your match with Abby was made in heaven."

"Yes, old man. Connie and I feel a little sheepish having each other, and you left out in the cold."

"I'll survive. Tom and I'll get old and sour together. You let us know when the wedding is, and we'll come. Do us both good to get away."

"We've decided," Constance announced. "It's two weeks from Saturday. We want you there. And Tom, you'll want to come, see everyone. At least some of our people are still there, and they'll be glad to see you."

"I'd like that. Miss Constance, you don't know how happy I am that you an' Ned have found each other. That an' my freedom are the two good things out of all of this, and I do so thank you."

Ned took Stephen aside.

"Only one thing I've got to say to you, old friend."

"Only one? I could use a whole headful of wisdom, right now."

"Only one: You get your stubborn arse over to see Annie Compton before another day goes by." He thumped Stephen on the back, turned, and climbed a little stiffly into the buggy.

"What was that all about?" Tom asked, as the sound of the wheels faded toward the creek ford.

"Just Ned, putting his nose into my business, as usual."

"Thought that was my job. Gangin' up on you."

"Oh? What gems of wisdom do you have to heap on me, now while I'm in no shape to resist?"

"I suspect Ned's already told you."

"I guess he has, at that."

Above them, the empty house mocked him.

~ * ~

At the Compton farm, Annie heard the news from a neighbor of the Thomases. Her hands stopped shelling the peas into the bowl on her lap. She sat stone-still in the chair on the porch, eyes unseeing, while more local talk went on between her mother and the visitor. *Abby's gone. With Dwight Millington. The good reverend. Abby's run off, from Stephen, from her family, from everyone and everything.*

Abby's gone...

Her first reaction was one of joy, tinged with guilt that she should feel that way. Stephen had been her hope, the only man she'd ever considered, but he'd fallen in line with all the men who'd laid eyes on Abigail Thomas. She'd been so disappointed in him, more than slighted. She'd never considered the idea she could be any sort of competition for Abby.

But Stephen wasn't the average untraveled, unlettered country boy, eyes a-goggle at the planter's daughter. Quite the opposite: he'd been through hell in that war, with haunting dreams still, Tom had told her. He was a complex man, deep. But all the more reason he needed a woman who was more than a pretty face, to share with, work alongside, to love.

And yet he'd chosen Abby over her; that was the simple truth, no matter the details. And yes, she'd swallowed it, been friends with them both, done the gracious thing, in spite of her feelings. And come to the realization, finally, that she was never to have that kind of pairing, that joyous courtship and promises to be fulfilled.

She hadn't been angry at not being chosen. No, disappointed said it best. Hurt. Stephen just hadn't turned out to be the man she'd thought he was. She knew now she could never have trusted him with her heart.

And now, what was next? He'd stay away: he had at least that much decency. He wouldn't come crawling to her, asking her to take him—Abby's leavings—after all that had happened. Or would he? She guessed that would be the measure of him: whether he stayed away, aware of his shame and his blindness and his ill-treatment of her (yes, it was that).

And if he did come? Would she welcome him, forgive him, set aside pride again, be gracious? Again? That would require some thinking about. That might well be beyond her capacity, this time…

But I want him.

If he did come, that would clearly mean he wanted her now too, but only as his second choice. And if she hadn't been good enough for him before, how could she accept his condescension to her now? No, this was beginning to resolve into simple humiliation for her, unworthy as that reaction might be.

She prayed that Stephen Davis would not come to see her.

Not yet.

~ * ~

More days went by, during which the entire community learned of Abby's elopement with the minister. Stephen didn't go anywhere, preferring to work in the shop, keep out of sight. He was humiliated, of course, but he really just did not want the endless sympathy, questions, probings he knew would come. Just let it blow over, see what's next. He'd go to Ned's wedding, get that behind him, then figure it from there. Good old Ned. He and Tom were the best friends a man could have.

And both of them think I ought to go see Annie Compton. Make a bigger fool of myself than I already am. But, hell, she's a friend, too...Maybe, after we get back from Caroline County...But what would I say to her? 'Hello, Annie. Now that my woman has run off, would you like to be second-best?' She'd take a stick of firewood to me, and Isaac would shoot me.

No, she'd do worse: she'd be kind and sympathetic. Sweet woman, really. Shame she's white, or Tom...Oh, hell, I'm fantasizing.

Guess I could eat my pride and go ask her to forgive me for being such an ass for the past nearly three years. Problem is, I can't forgive myself for being so blind. Well, I'm sure as hell not perfect, and blindness is a part of that. Pa said a craftsman needn't be an ignoramus, but I'm surely feeling that way. A friend... Not fair to her, though, getting a relationship started, then running off after another girl...and yes, she was more than just a friend, wasn't she?

No. No, it was never more than that: friendship. Why should I feel so rotten here? I never promised Annie, never led her on. Did I? All right, I gave her that sewing cabinet. But then she insisted on trading me those pigs. And yes, we traded books too, talked literature. I let her in on Tom's secret when I probably shouldn't have, but that turned out all right. So, we were friends, and we still should be. Why should Abby's betrayal change that?

Answer is, it shouldn't.

Ned: 'Get on over to see her'. Tom: same thing. They think I must have myself a woman or I'll shrivel up and die or something. Hell, Tom does all right alone. Or I imagine he does. And Ned's never been without a woman, except in the army, and he made up for that every time we came to a town.

But I don't want to lose her friendship. And maybe staying away could do that. I remember the time she said she had to talk her parents into coming to visit us because I hadn't been to see her. Yes, she is one sweet woman...

He saddled the black gelding.

"Goin', huh?" Tom asked, from the shop door. "You know, Sunday's soon. You could just go to church with me, see her there. Reverend Carson's coming out from town."

"Not ready for the whole congregation to poke at me, Tom. Anyway, what makes you think I'm going where you think I'm going?"

"I heard the wheels in your head turnin'."

"Damn intellectual." He rode away.

It would be hard, facing the whole Compton family in his shame, but he knew he had to do it. Either that, or just ride on out of the country, slam the door on everything here. Pretend it was November, '81 again, riding toward Kentucky. No, he wasn't ready to do that just yet. In a few days they'd go on over to Caroline, then maybe he'd take stock, go down whichever road was the likeliest.

He'd slipped a hand mirror into his saddlebag, not sure he'd give it to her. It was a precious piece of silvered glass from Richmond, and he'd carved the cherrywood handle and oval frame with a leafy vine. Seemed sort of cheap, to give her something, now that his first choice was...

Now, dammit, Annie's not—was not—my sweetheart, first or second choice.

But, if it seems like the thing to do...He rode on, thinking.

...But the root of the problem is, I want her for my sweetheart. I do.

He rode over Greene Mountain, past the Morris farm, over the rise, down to the river and up it toward the church. He hadn't wanted to go the other way, past the Thomas plantation. Not just yet. That would be embarrassing as hell, and he'd put it off as long as he could.

The church: Preacher hadn't even left a note, he'd learned. Probably riding hell for leather, he imagined, afraid the squire, or he, was on their trail. Not worth it, in any way. Not to him. Things like that had a way of making a man see the real picture, and the one with Abby and him in it wasn't right. He just hadn't known that at the time. Wanted it too much.

Ah, hell, I hope you both have a good life; I'm through moping and feeling sorry for myself. All I have to do is get past the curiosity, and the jokes at my expense, and I can start over, somewhere. Kentucky, maybe. Or here. Doesn't matter, really. Can't run from things: Face them and get on with it. Is that maturity, maybe? Who the hell knows.

It was late afternoon when he rode up to the Compton farm. Young Sam spotted him first and ran to greet him.

"Hey there, Sam. Folks at home? Man, you're growing like a bad weed."

"Hi, Stephen. Ever'body's here. Been hayin'. Pa won't let me use th' scythe yet, but I cut me a bunch with th' sickle. He said I done good."

"I'm sure of it. Been forever since I been t'see you all, and here you're nearly grown. Folks all well?"

"Are that. C'mon up to th' house. Annie an' Ma'll wantcha to stay to supper, fer shore." The lad skipped on ahead to tell of Stephen's arrival.

And from a window, Annie Compton watched him come.

So, he's here. To see me? Or all of us, as friends. No, it's to see me, I fear. And that means he and I can have no future...

Just that brief, easy exchange with the boy left him feeling better, he found. Good friends, these. Man ought not leave folks as sound as these, go off and hide somewhere.

"Ev'nin', Stephen," Isaac called, coming onto the porch, drying his face with a towel. "'Light down and stay. Been a spell."

"Has. Been meaner than ''n old bear with a sore paw, so I figured to stay hid awhile."

"Reckon so. Well, we're glad t'see you out. Know you'll stay to supper, an' don't even bother sayin' you won't. Say, I've got a jug of fair whiskey out in th' barn. Want a nip?"

"Well, I can't think of a good reason to refuse, Isaac, unless Miss Sadie'll get after us. Don't wanta rile that good woman."

"Oh, she don't mind, long's nobody gits silly 'bout it. Why, it's good cough med'cine. And dern good t'clean a cut." He paused. "Er a hurt place." He managed a grin.

The men walked out to the barn, talking crops and weather. Isaac didn't seem put off by this visit. And it wasn't as if he'd come courting the man's daughter. Or was it? The farmer dug around in hay and came up with an earthenware jug, shook it, and offered it. Stephen sampled it, returned it.

"Good: frog eye bubbles. Whose is it?"

"Zach Marples, on up th' creek. Some of his is real fine, an' some only so-so. This's 'bout in between, I'd say." Gitcha some more now."

"Better not, or your womenfolks won't speak to me. Thanks though, it's smooth."

"Oh, Zach keeps th' best fer hisself, I know, but it'll do. Say, I got me a fine sorrel mare in a trade. Come have a look."

So time passed in talk that was not exactly easy, but not strained either, until the men returned to the house. Sadie Compton came out, and impulsively gave Stephen a hug.

"So glad t'see you, Stephen. Oh, you've let this old man pour whiskey down you, haven't you? Shame on you, Isaac. You know Stephen's not a drinkin' man."

"No, but a touch don't hurt a mite, an' you know it. Y'ain't never seen me drunk, an' y'll never see Stephen drunk, either. No harm done."

"Guess not. Come on in here. Supper's almost ready. Becky's helpin' with th' cooking now, and it's a sight of work off me. Annie! Stephen's come fer supper."

That lady appeared, wiping her hands on her apron, and gave Stephen a somewhat guarded look of acknowledgement. *Damn, it has been a long time.* He reached for her hand, which she let him take, but without enthusiasm. He tried to forestall the awkwardness.

"Annie, it's a joy to see you. I've been right unsociable lately, and I couldn't think of any folks I wanted more to help me break that bad habit."

"I think we can welcome the hermit, Stephen. It's good of you to come." Her words were welcome, but her eyes told him nothing. He thought again that he never knew what was in her mind. But well, so far this hadn't been so hard...

"And Lord, Bobby. It hasn't been that long, and here you are, shooting through the roof. He's a man grown, Isaac. And Becky, you little sweetheart, you're a young lady now. Makes me feel old."

Supper with these people was peppered with crop talk, small talk, inconsequential talk. Annie didn't say much, and while she did not avoid Stephen, he was left with a feeling that much was going on in her mind. With the rest of them, the talk grew easier: no prying, as if they were picking up where they'd left off, before Stephen's self-imposed exile. That part was a good feeling. But he caught each of them stealing quick glances at Annie.

Afterwards, the family sat out on the porch, still talking. Then, seemingly without any design, one by one drifted off, until only Stephen and Annie were left. An occasional mosquito buzzed, but they weren't bad.

"Well, Annie, I'm glad you didn't run me off, although that's what I deserve."

"In what way?" The question was polite, but distant.

"Well, it sort of makes me look cheap, coming to see you only after what I thought I wanted has come apart."

"What you thought you wanted? You don't still want it?"

"Not really. I was even able to wish them happiness, on the way over here. I had to work through a lot to that stage, but I'm there."

"That's good. You were treated badly." Was that sympathy? Or just his imagination?

"Maybe. Or maybe things just had to happen this way, with the end result of opening my eyes." He gave her a direct look.

"I guess I'm glad to hear that, for your sake."

It became clear to Stephen that this visit might be a start, but nothing more. So, a change of subject:

"What's to become of the church now?"

"Reverend Carson is looking for a replacement minister, of course. He plans to come as often as he can, but he's really concentrating on mission work now."

"I see. In the new settlements? Out West?"

"Yes, and that's something I'm in accord with him on. Many are needed."

"You're thinking of going out to the frontier?"

"Possibly. I haven't made any definite plans." Then: "I have a lot to think about." She was neither discouraging nor encouraging him. It looked like it was time for him to leave.

"Well, thanks for having me, Anna. And thank your folks for me." He rose to go.

"Goodbye, Stephen." She gave him her hand, and seemed about to say more, but did not.

As he rode through the dark, Stephen reflected that he couldn't really have expected this girl to welcome him with open arms. He remembered the miller's wife, Nell Cocke's words: "Don't no girl like to be left." Indeed. And he'd left Anna Compton, blinded by the squire's daughter. He also remembered again what Tom had said that time: Anna's what Abby would like to be.

All right then, so he'd lost the one, and now might well have lost the other, too, and it was no one's fault but his own. He'd had a choice, early on, and he'd made it. Wrong choice, and not handled well, so he guessed he was going to have to live with the consequences.

He just wasn't ready to give up yet, though.

Twenty-five

Stephen shaved carefully, put on his best shirt.

"Looks like you're going to church," Tom observed.

"Looks like it. Been too long holed up here. Folks'll pry and poke, but I have to get it over with. You're going, aren't you?"

"Matter of fact, I'm taking Molly."

"Hell you say! When did this happen? You never liked Molly."

"Oh, I've got to know her, workin' around the house-building. She's really pretty sharp. You know, Abby taught her to read."

"Did know that, yes. Well, you old dog, you. She have a horse to ride?"

"That's another thing. I've bought one, from the squire. Figured to ride your old one myself, like always."

"Of course. So you've been slipping off up to the plantation, you sly old man."

"More 'n once. You been so deep in work, mopin' around, I coulda run off to South America an' you wouldn'a missed me."

"Well, that's all past. Got to a point, a few days ago, when I needed to start putting my life back together. I say good for Abby, if the preacher's what she needs. Good for him too, and maybe good luck, with that one."

"Things must've gone well, other night."

"I don't really know, Tom. That's part of why I'm going to church today." Memory of that woman who wouldn't leave his mind moved him forward like a magnet.

The three of them rode over the mountain trail and up the little river toward the clearing. People were arriving, on horseback, in wagons. The girl Molly had been chatting with Tom, but she became quiet now, and her expressive eyes grew large.

"It'll be all right, Molly," Stephen reassured her. "You're with us."

"I know it will, Mist' Stephen. Seems strange though, bein' able just t'go, like this. New feelin'." Her round, dark face held an expression of wonder. Stephen realized how it must have been for Tom at first, too. *The things we take for granted.*

Anna Compton spied them first, almost as if she'd been watching. She greeted them, with that smile that he'd missed so much. *Give me something to smile about.* That hadn't been an idle request, all those months ago...She took charge of Molly immediately, leading her away to show her the classroom, as she had done with Abby. The other settlers welcomed Stephen back, and Tom, who'd become a regular. There were whispered comments out of their hearing, but Stephen ignored them, appearing for all the world as if nothing had happened.

"Isaac, your daughter and Tom are about to convert me, looks like. Big job, though."

"Not so big, Stephen. Lord knows you're almost as big an' ugly as me, but you ain't mean. Hope for you, yet."

"And here's Ike. Hello, old friend. You all right? You too, Mrs. Collins?"

"Well, if 'tain't th' hermit. Been missin' you at th' shop, Stephen. Ever'body has. Th' squire an' missis, too. They're plumb tore up about... thaings."

"Oh, I got myself kicked around a bit there, Ike, but I'm still here. Tough old soldier."

Stephen sat with the other Comptons during the service, but his mind was on Annie. Had her words been sympathy for a friend? Or was it possible she could forgive him, and there might be a promise there? Hard to tell, with that one. Certainly his visit hadn't generated even remotely the forgiveness, the gentle sweetness he felt sure she was capable of. He guessed what happened next would come down to what he really felt for this girl and how hard he wanted to work to win her. She'd once said she knew a part of him...That was quite obviously more than he'd ever know of her.

The Reverend Carson was given to long sermons, and Stephen registered only part of it, with his puzzling over any future he might have with the tall girl. He could remember, in perspective, that she'd given him hints that there could be more there than just friendship, before Abby. But she'd been friends with Abby, too. Was there anything behind that graciousness?

At last, the congregation rose for the final hymn. Stephen had heard little, reasoned out even less. He found he ached. From tension, he guessed.

Outside, he shook the ancient minister's hand, complimented him on the sermon, spoke to several others. Tom and Molly were talking with a group of blacks from surrounding farms. They could go home without him. He took this opportunity to wander toward the classroom.

She looked up from sending the last child on his way, and the smile she wore became a little strained.

"So glad you and Tom brought Molly, Stephen. She needs to know she's among friends, too."

"I'm learning the hard way how valuable friendships are, Annie. Can we talk? Or must you go with your folks?"

"I'm afraid I must go. But of course you're always welcome at my family's house." *Her family's* house…*What exactly does that mean? Well, maybe that's the way to go, then: start over, court her, do it right this time.*

"I shall visit soon. Goodbye, Annie."

Yes, goodbye, Stephen, my friend.

~ * ~

"So how was your day with Molly?" Stephen was home late, but he couldn't say where he'd been. Just riding around most of the day, still puzzling over what course of action he should take, if any.

"We had a good day. She's reading books from th' plantation library, like we did. Dry stuff, but we can talk about it, an' we do. She's all right, really. Little dazed at findin' herself free still, for what that's worth—and it's worth a lot. You look like th' bird that th' cat got. Do I ask what happened?"

"You can. Annie's not giving me anything much in the way of encouragement. I'm hoping we can talk, after we get back from Ned's. About us, about things in general. You know I've never known what was in that girl's mind, Tom, and I still don't. But I like her, like being with her.

"But you know, probably, that I've been mulling over just picking up and going West, starting over out there somewhere. That's not out of the picture."

"Be a damn fool t'do that, Stephen. Ned'll tell you that, too. So will anybody an' everybody you tell that to. Why..."

Stephen held up a hand.

"Tom. Tom. I didn't say I'd give up and run off yet."

"Oh. Oh, well...you knew that girl wouldn't just fall into your arms, Stephen."

~ * ~

The ride to Caroline County was a retracing of Tom's nocturnal route of a few weeks previous. This time he got to see it all in the daylight, and marveled at how he'd been able to pick out the route, with so many intersecting, unnamed roads. They went to this plantation or that, to this mill or blacksmith shop or store, with only a general direction toward anywhere distant. Their route eventually crossed the Richmond pike many miles east of Stanardsville, and continued across creeks and rivers that seemed always to go at the wrong angles.

Tom had ferreted out back roads, taking longer, but had not gotten seriously lost. Now they asked directions often, some of which were accurate, and discovered more shortcuts and fords and bridges off the main roads. The result was their getting to Constance Weston's plantation in just over three days of fairly brisk riding, in plenty of time for the festivities.

Tom was greeted like a long-lost relative by the few remaining Logan servants, and by the others, who had heard of him. Constance was a gracious hostess, more in her element than Stephen had seen her. Ned wore a perpetual grin, going about the business of the plantation with the overseer George Henley had retained, getting things in order.

The place hadn't been required to be a paying operation, with the doctor's other, illicit income, and it was plain there would have to be some strict measures to get it back in shape. Stephen could see that would be a daunting prospect, since Ned was not well off, but it didn't dampen that prospective groom's spirits. Stephen recalled what his friend had said about being an impoverished but genteel planter's son.

"We'll survive, Stephen. I can run a place, even one this threadbare, and I will. Connie and I will have to learn to do without, but she has the grit for it, and hell, I can work as hard as any field hand when I have to." The grin was just a little rueful. But Stephen knew Ned would do whatever was necessary here, old soldier that he was.

He and Tom toured the plantation. Fields had been neglected and allowed to run to sprouts. There was only a small force of farm workers, Horace Weston not having wanted to bother with farming beyond the table necessities. It was clear that some equipment, stock, perhaps even furniture, would have to be sold to raise money to get things running again. They hoped Constance would be up to the challenge.

But the great house was all hospitality, denying the stark fields outside. Ned's family had come, his father a jovial man of great appetite, his mother little and red-headed, one sister tall and plain, the other short, plump and pleasant. Unfortunately, Constance had no close relatives, but she embraced this new family, along with friends from neighboring plantations and farms.

Meals were large and varied, the house staff being excellent. The wine cellar was still well-stocked, and the pantry, though strained, gave adequately. To all appearances, this was to be a lavish event among the gentry. Stephen wondered how many such plantation celebrations were like this: outwardly opulent, but in fact hiding grim ledgers. He began to try to imagine ways he could help his friend.

"Let not your heart be troubled, my comrade. I'll have to hit the parents for a loan to get by for a bit, but we'll make it, as I said." But Stephen recalled his friend's mentioning that the elder Drakes' plantation was worn out, and not that productive. Well, they were going into it with a will, and he had firsthand experience that told him that would prevail, given the right circumstances, and perhaps a hand from God, if so disposed.

"Be a shame for Miss Constance to hafta put aside her ball gowns," Tom mused when he and Stephen were alone. "But I've the feelin' she won't have to. She's a good woman, I owe her, and I've a surprise for them."

"A surprise?" Are you a magician too, Tom?"

"No, but I'm a secretive devil. You come with me now, Stephen. Got a surprise for you, too."

"I'll follow you anywhere I guess, Tom. What's on?"

"You'll see. Gettin' a little frenzied around here. Let's go for ourselves a ride, get out into the air."

"We've been riding. Or didn't you notice? Oh, all right. You've got something going here, and I could use a good surprise."

They took Tom's nighttime route to tangled woods at the edge of the plantation, and he guided them to a remote spot. They dismounted, tied their horses. Stephen shook his head in dismay, but followed his friend into the heavy brush.

"Just here, somewhere. Stump there...Log over there...Here we are." He bent, moved aside bark and leaves, and lifted a heavy, locked chest.

"Now, just what the hell is this? Oh, oh, I think I know..."

"Yep. Got the key here, too. All right, take a look inside now." He unlocked the chest, opened it.

"Oh, my God! Tom, there's a king's ransom, here. More than the other chest, surely."

"Seems like it. I took it from the doc's study. Figured it'd disappear otherwise, with Eddins and the others still out there. Like th' other one, no tellin' who this belonged to originally, an' no way to find out."

"So you're a rich man, Tom, and nobody deserves it more..."

"No, we're rich men, Stephen: you, me, and Ned. Now tell me a better idea." He sat back, not able to keep a grin off his face. "Looks like crime pays, sometimes."

"No crime, doing away with that doctor. And he didn't get to enjoy these last two hauls, either. Well, I'm damned, Tom. You continue to amaze me."

"Fortunes of war, way I see it. We all been through some hell, Stephen, in those long years of war, th' trouble since. People stealing us, tryin' to kill us. Ned broke, after he an' Miss Constance doing for me. Figure it's our turn to be on top now."

They met with Ned later that night, getting him away from the others.

"Got a little weddin' gift, Ned," Tom announced, winking at Stephen. Both of them looked about ready to burst with some news, Ned observed.

Probably some good old boy joke on the bridegroom. Well, he could use a good joke…

Then Tom opened a wooden box and poured gold coins onto a table, watching his friend's eyes. It made a huge pile.

"Where in the hell did you get this, Tom? I thought you and Stephen gave that chest to the authorities..."

"Did. And this's your third of another one I knew would disappear if I let it. No way to find out who it belonged to, so I figure we three split it. Counted it all, and this's your part. Oughta pay for some improvements around here; maybe keep you an' Miss Constance from eatin' nothin' but turnip greens for a while."

"Oh, my God, Tom! You're a lifesaver!" Ned grabbed him in a bearhug, danced around the room with him.

"Hey, leggo me. I can't breathe, Ned."

"Oh, sorry. What a friend you are! I never thought, when Stephen and I cooked up that story...Who says crime doesn't pay?"

"I said that, too. Oh, but I want you to think about somethin', Ned. Not putting any strings at all on th' money, but if you and Miss Constance would consider it, I'd take it as another personal favor if you'd see if you could free your people here. Should be enough here to pay ''em wages for a long time, if you see it that way."

"Well...Now that's a thought. You know, Tom, before I met you, I had the same blind notion most whites have, that blacks can't learn, have to depend on us whites. You proved me wrong. Then Abby's Molly, who hadn't any background at all, learned to read, and has become a bright young lady...Hard as hell to justify keeping slaves after knowing you two. And I know Connie'll feel the same way. Why, it was the idea of Weston getting his hands on you again that made her leave him. I'd say it's a done deed."

"Thanks, Ned. You're the kind of friend nobody could forget. ''Specially that performance in th' courtroom. I don't wanta know how much of that was true."

"And you never will. It'll get better next time I tell it, too. Oh, Stephen tells me you're spending time with Molly. That's pretty fine."

"She's all right. Don't know where it'll go yet, but we're comfortable with each other."

"Well, you let us know if there's to be a wedding. Wouldn't miss it."

Twenty-six

Stephen had been going in circles since leaving Annie Compton. After her cool reception of him, he could not imagine her accepting him anytime soon. But the realization that he'd never known what Abigail Thomas really had in her mind was greater with Annie. Not a good comparison, he knew: The one had been literally spoiled from her birth, while the other had toiled alongside her father and brothers like any field hand. Educating herself. Becoming very much a lady. Nothing shallow about Annie. And as Tom had observed, she had a lot of pride. More than she'd swallow easily, if at all.

But what about him? Even if he eventually won her, would he tire of the tall girl and go off sniffing after the next pretty face he met? He'd surely done it last time, letting Abigail's beauty blind him, like a young boy with his first infatuation. Like Dwight Millington.

And, more important, would Annie be afraid he'd do just that? Again? She didn't have the kind of surface attractiveness that would give her unlimited choices among men. Would she live in dread of his leaving her? Probably the other way around, really. He could only imagine the intensity, the force with which such a woman would deal with a man who'd betray her. *Cut my head off, and I'd deserve it. No, I could never leave a woman like her.*

But I do know I'm too recently away from that thing with Abby. I'm just smart enough to realize that major decisions made when a man—or a wom-

an—is off-balance, trying to get over a bad time, aren't sound. Abby looked good to me, and I know I made her look even better because I wanted her so much. And now Miss Annie looks good, and how much of that is my wanting her? A man's head and his heart don't often agree, it seems.

He spoke of this to Tom, on their ride back home.

"You know, Stephen, you gettin' smarter all the time. Woman like Miss Annie, if she'll have you, you want to be dead sure everything's right before you commit yourself to her, 'cause there won't be any turnin' back. And that's not a one-way proposition: she'll wanta be sure, too. She may not think she has th' options you do; there won't be a whole lot of men out there'll be drawn to her, or more important, come up to her standards. You, on th' other hand, will always find some milkmaid you could talk yourself into likin'."

"Now, Abigail Thomas was hardly some milkmaid."

"About that: What'd she likely have been, without her money and position? Not to put her down, but what'd that pretty face'd won her, without all that?"

"Hmm. You ask hard questions, you know that?"

"Whoever told you this life was easy? It's all hard questions."

"I guess so. And it's harder now, because Annie let me know I can't just slip back into her good graces."

"Did, huh? Smart woman. Let you know a little of what you'd put her through, did she? That's to be expected though, Stephen, even though I know you don't like it. But it also shows me she's a long way from bein' sure of you, yet. An' another thing: It's been easier for you to be objective, her stayin' distant, cool, th' way she can."

"I hadn't thought of that. She's sure made it clear I've got to win her confidence, wouldn't you say?"

"Seems that way. She's not one to play games. Could also be she's written you off you know, knowin' her the way we both do."

"I don't think I like that explanation. I'd been trying to convince myself we were only friends, for a long time, now. And I might have gone on, if I hadn't gotten burned...You have no idea, Tom, the depth to that woman."

"Got my notions. Maybe too smart for you."

"Maybe. How does a girl get that sharp, stuck away on a farm like that?"

"Hide an' watch. What I did. When you're back out of sight against th' wall, you see a lot, learn a lot th' folks out in th' dance will miss."

"So. Best thing for me to do would be to go slow, wouldn't it? Not rush things till I get back on my feet better. See if I really want to court Annie seriously. Which right now I'm fairly certain I do."

"I said you were gettin' smarter. And just what's your rush, Stephen? You've already faced folks, and found they've been pretty decent about you getting' shot down. I'd say, go on up and make peace with th' Thomases, an' live your life for a while, before you do anything rash."

"Guess I've always been impatient. I can take whatever time's necessary for a thing to be right, but I've got to have it happen. Got to see to the end of it." He was quiet for several minutes. "So, to change the subject entirely, tell me, what are your plans, Tom? Now that you're a rich man?"

"Don't have any. I've about given up on goin' to Boston or someplace like that. Folks got their warts around here, but that'd be true anywhere. Want to see how Molly an' I turn out. I've had to get past some pride issues there, I can tell you. Girl grows on you, though. Now, you talk about options: she and I don't have any, even with th' money."

"No, I guess you don't. But sometimes that's not so bad. Picture Abby and the preacher, now. Both always be the object of predator men, and women, always be having to deal with the temptation that each could do better with someone else. Be hard to have much of a relationship, I'd guess."

"Maybe. Hard to put yourself into other folks' shoes, though. I wouldn't be too hard on them. They've made their bed: got to lie in it."

~ * ~

Just what to do with the money didn't trouble Stephen, or Tom, but both decided against any lavish spending. Best to have it for real needs when they arose. As craftsmen, they had no designs on acquiring land or building bigger houses. There were always worthy causes to be supported. Someone would have to help pay a new minister when one could be found, for instance. That was something neither man had contributed to before, beyond a modest Sunday offering. And there were orphans and widows, always.

Stephen had made it a priority to find out about the welfare of Rawlins Butler's children. The plantation was theirs by inheritance, and was being run by a cousin, so it appeared that loose end was being handled as well as could be expected. Just what those children knew of, or thought, of their late father's activities, Stephen didn't know. They did know he hadn't been the planter's killer, but that he had been involved in some way. He assumed they also knew why: the entire region knew of the attempted kidnapping. Or maybe not. He hoped they weren't growing up holding a grudge against him.

There was another consideration, too: Whatever was left of Weston's organization could well know who he was and where to find him. The doctor had certainly been the brains behind it all, but there was the unknown other end of the ring, those men who actually robbed, stole, somehow acquired the money. They'd certainly rebuild the operation around a replacement for Weston. And they'd know someone had taken that second chest of riches. Wouldn't take much speculation to suspect who, probably, although the doctor's killer had never been found. Such men were to be reckoned with, and he'd have to keep his eye out. Seemed a man could never let his guard down in this life.

~ * ~

So the men had come home again, and set about doing what they'd always done here. Tom was in demand for his fine tools and knives, and Stephen had furniture orders to fill. It seemed things could settle back to normal.

But he wanted to see Annie. Get some more progress made with her, if that's what it was. Maybe find out more about where he stood in her estimation, too. Should maybe wait though, like Tom said. Only he wasn't good at waiting. Seemed, looking back, that tactic had usually gotten him into trouble. Or maybe it had worked best, letting knotty situations sort themselves out. Sort of mixed up, he was, now.

But it shouldn't be hard to let some time go by: keep his hands busy, let the summer end, find out for sure and for all just what it was he really wanted, here. Yes, curb any impulses, rash actions, as Tom had counseled. Learn to wait this out, because it was the most important decision he'd ever make in this life, he was sure of that. Best not to make it any more complicated than it already was.

But after a few days he found himself chafing, speculating, agitated to the point that he couldn't get any work done, couldn't find any peace. And almost without realizing what he was doing, he was suddenly riding the miles to the Compton farm. And he was aware of another impatience, to get there quickly, which he hadn't known before. This time he not only had the carved mirror, he meant to give it to her, no matter what. As usual, he'd timed his visit for the end of the day so as not to interrupt the farm work. His anticipation grew with the miles up the placid little river into the westering sun, and he found himself imagining different reactions she might have to his visit, and he planned what he'd say to each.

Isaac saw him first, leading a workhorse from the fields. Stephen waved, led his own horse over. The man was not smiling. Apprehension rose in him. He'd expected things to be the same here, and suddenly that dimension might no longer be the case.

"Everything all right, Isaac? Hope nobody's sick."

"No, nobody down, Stephen, but big changes here, I'm afraid." His eyes were troubled, and seemed to avoid his friend.

"Changes? What's been happening?"

"Well," and the big man put a hand on Stephen's shoulder, looking him in the eye now. "To put it plain, Annie's gone. Left with a wagon train of missionaries, goin' west to Kentucky territory. Had her mind set, and well…" The man's face showed confusion and sadness.

Stephen had trouble taking this in. Annie Compton was gone? Had gone West. Just like that. So that was why she hadn't warmed to him at all…No, it was the other, his having made his choice between the two women, all those months back. And she'd accepted it, in her gracious way, his rejecting her. Friendship wasn't all she'd wanted, then, like he'd kept getting hints. She didn't parade herself like Abby, didn't blind him to what should have been obvious, but she'd wanted him—the two of them together.

Two people and a piece of ground.

And now she's gone. Out of my life. And now I know for certain she's all I want—need—ever needed. I am one blundering, blind fool. Pa's ignoramus: sure goes a lot deeper than being partially educated.

"She did mention that, but I…I thought we could talk it out. Isaac, I was every kind of a fool, going after Abby Thomas when your daughter was everything a man could want. I didn't treat her right, and she's far too much woman to take that. You can't know how sorry I am, and how I know I never deserved Annie. I'd vowed to make it up to her, do whatever it took to get her to forgive me, let me show her how I've finally got the blinders off…" He trailed off in confusion, self-contempt. His eyes strayed to the creekside, the mown fields, the white clouds piling in the west, all the aspects of a peaceful late afternoon, there in spite of the turmoil within him, the tide of self-loathing.

"Now, Stephen, no need to git all down on y'self. Enny man with eyes'd tried to pair up with Abby…"

"No, Isaac, only a blind fool, and I'm that fool, no way around it. And I reckon I'm the one who has to live with it now. Man has to face up to his mistakes, and this one will do me for this life, for certain."

"Aw, now. Come on out to th' barn, an' we'll have us a drink…"

"Better not, or I'll get knee-walking drunk on you. No, I came to try to start over with Annie, try to get her to give me another chance, and now I've let that chance get away from me.

"I'd better be on my way, Isaac. You all have been really good to me. Best friends a man could have. And for me to make Annie feel like she was second choice, that was just too much for that fine a woman to put up with. No, I'd best get along home then, try to keep from doing something crazy."

"Now, you come on up to th' house, Stephen, an' eat with us. Sadie'll whip me if I let you go off…"

"You tell that good woman I'm just not fit to be around, Isaac. I've got to get by myself now, quick as I can. I know you understand." He put a foot into the stirrup, anxious to be away, although realizing the need had nothing to do with his friend, this place.

"Afraid so." Again he put a hand on Stephen's shoulder. "We tried to talk her out of goin', but you prob'ly know Annie well enough to see that wouldn't do."

"Yes. Well, goodbye, my friend. I'll let some time get by, let the pieces settle some, figure what's best to do, then." He mounted, rode quickly away.

Back down the river in the fading light, his mind a whirl, his fists clenching, opening, his eyes beyond the deep green gloom of the trees.

The moving water spoke softly, his horse's hooves struck the dirt road in a rhythm, night closed in like a cloak.

Stephen Davis grieved.

~ * ~

The weaving line of wagons followed the Shenandoah Valley south and west, through the farms established mostly by German settlers down from Pennsylvania. Not that many days now, and the way would lead up over Big Stone Gap and to the west. There, the route would be through mountains and deep valleys so narrow only a shelf of land alongside a rushing creek could support a wagon track. Very much Indian country, still. Kentucky had been their shared hunting region, but now the white settlers were taking up the land, pushing the settlements ever outward.

With every mile, every turning of the wagon wheels, Anna Compton felt the permanence of her leaving home, family, all that was familiar to her.

And of leaving Stephen Davis.

Joining this band of missionaries hadn't exactly been spur of the moment—she'd weighed the option over a period of time—although the finality of it had come suddenly and sharply. But in spite of her misgivings, she was determined to go ahead. If only the regrets would leave her, she could lose herself here, devote her life to this work she'd chosen.

There would be raw settlements in Kentucky, scattered pioneers with no access to education for their children. Or to churches, God's Word. Even small wilderness meeting houses would provide centers for fellowship, sharing, and above all, the worshipping that would give their lives meaning. And she could help, as she had always helped, and that was to be her life.

If only I could get Stephen out of my mind.

~ * ~

The pack horse was loaded with a few tools and supplies for the journey. Stephen looked around in the waning summer light one last time, at nearly three years of his life here. He'd made himself visit the Thomases, who now seemed somehow diminished, in size and standing, since their daughter's leaving. He'd said goodbye to the smith, the miller, the other friends here. In his pocket was a note from the Reverend Carson.

"Hope this is the right choice this time, Tom."

"Believe it is, things bein' like they are. Know just what you're gonna do there?"

"Whatever and everything that's needed, Tom." Two people and a piece of ground: Kentucky ground? "If I lose this time, it'll be after one hell of a fight." He shook his best friend's hand, mounted, turned the horses.

West.

Above the stream, the new house sat, empty now, but soon to hold the blacksmith Tom and Molly Logan, free citizens, with the promise of children, generations to come. As he rode away, Stephen felt somehow the house, built with so many generous hands, could foresee that, and it held a glow.

Meet Charles McRaven

Charles McRaven has been called an 'active historian'. He is a skilled log cabin builder, stonemason, timberframer, blacksmith, and consultant on historic structures, as well as pastor of a small, rural church. Rev. McRaven writes about people who work with their hands, those who are close to the land. He is also a former journalism college professor and newspaper editor. He and his wife Linda, a former *National Geographic* picture editor, live in the woods in central Virginia.

Letter to Our Readers

Enjoy this book?

You can make a difference

As an independent publisher, Wings ePress, Inc. does not have the financial clout of the large New York Publishers. We can't afford large magazine spreads or subway posters to tell people about our quality books.

But we do have something much more effective and powerful than ads. We have a large base of loyal readers.

Honest Reviews help bring the attention of new readers to our books.

If you enjoyed this book, we would appreciate it if you would spend a few minutes posting a review on the site where you purchased this book or on the Wings ePress, Inc. webpages at: https://wingsepress.com/